Praise for David J. Williams's
THE MIRRORED HEAVENS

"A crackling cyberthriller. This is ͡
Sterling. David Williams has hacked into the future."
—Stephen Baxter, author of the Manifold series

"*The Mirrored Heavens* is a 21st-century *Neuromancer* set in a
dark, dystopian future where nothing and no one can be
trusted, the razors who rule cyberspace are predators and prey,
and ordinary human life is cheap. It starts out at full throttle
and accelerates all the way to the end."
—Jack Campbell, author of the Lost Fleet series

"Explodes out the gate like a sonic boom and never stops.
Adrenaline bleeds from Williams's fingers with every word he
hammers into the keyboard. The razors of *The Mirrored
Heavens* would eat cyberpunk's old-guard
hackers and cowboys as a light snack."
—Peter Watts, author of *Blindsight*

"An action-jammed and audacious look at a terrifyingly
plausible future. Highly recommended."
—L. E. Modesitt Jr., author of the Saga of Recluce series

"*The Mirrored Heavens* is a complex view of global politics in
time of crisis. Williams understands that future wars will be
fought as much online as off. It's also rousing adventure with
breathless, nonstop action—Tom Clancy on speed.
And you will NOT be able to guess the ending."
—Nancy Kress, author of the Probability trilogy

THE
MIRRORED
HEAVENS

DAVID J.
WILLIAMS

BANTAM SPECTRA

THE MIRRORED HEAVENS
A Bantam Spectra Book / June 2008

Published by Bantam Dell
A Division of Random House, Inc.
New York, New York

Book design by Carol Malcolm Russo

Library of Congress Cataloging-in-Publication Data
Williams, David J., 1971–
The mirrored heavens / David J. Williams.
p.   cm.
ISBN 978-0-553-38541-0 (trade pbk.)
1. Intelligence officers—United States—Fiction.
2. Terrorism—Fiction.   3. United States—Fiction.   I. Title.

PS3623.I556495M57 2008
813'.6—dc22
2008005917

Printed in the United States of America
Published simultaneously in Canada

www.bantamdell.com

OPM 10 9 8 7 6 5 4 3 2 1

To those who believed

CONTENTS

TEXT OF THE TREATY OF ZURICH

The United States of America and the nations that comprise the Eurasian Coalition, hereinafter referred to as the two contracting powers,

> Proceeding from the premise that war between them would have devastating consequences for all mankind,
> Asserting that a bold posture of political and environmental cooperation is critical at this juncture in history,
> Believing that the exploration and use of outer space should be leveraged exclusively for those activities most likely to further the welfare of humanity,
> Declaring their intention to achieve at the earliest possible date the cessation of the corrosive arms race that drains resources vitally needed elsewhere,
> Have agreed as follows:

Article I:

The two contracting powers obligate themselves to refrain from every act of force, every aggressive action, and every attack against one another.

Article II:

The two contracting powers undertake to establish a Joint Environmental Commission, based in Zurich, whose members shall be charged with proposing worldwide environmental standards for industrial operations; the two contracting powers shall then act jointly to secure the ratification of these standards by all nations.

Article III:

The Joint Environmental Commission will operate in coordination with a Joint Space Commission, based in Zurich, whose members shall be charged with crafting plans to transfer as much industry as feasible to points in orbit and on celestial bodies.

Article IV:

The two contracting powers recognize each other's sovereignty over their respective nets/information architectures and commit to keeping each other informed regarding communication protocols between them.

Article V:

The two contracting powers recognize each other's right to equatorial launch facilities. In this regard, the Eurasian Coalition will continue to maintain the exclusive right to make treaties with nations within the continent of Africa, while the United States will continue to maintain the exclusive right to make treaties with nations within the continent of South America.

Article VI:

The two contracting powers recognize each other's territorial sovereignty over those segments of the geosynchronous orbits above their areas of terrestrial interest. Such sovereignty will include segments of additional adjacent orbits, as determined by the Joint Space Commission.

Article VII:

The two contracting powers confirm the Eurasian Coalition's territorial sovereignty over Lagrangian point L4 and confirm the United States' territorial sovereignty over Lagrangian points L2 and L5. In addition, Lagrangian points L1 and L3 are recognized as neutral, demilitarized sites.

Article VIII:

The United States renounces any exclusive claim to the Moon. The Eurasian Coalition will exercise sovereignty over territory amounting to no less than 25 percent of the Moon's surface and no less than 25 percent of the Moon's resources. Furthermore, both powers commit to a joint control of the Mare Imbrium north of Archimedes Crater. This shall occur within six months of the signing of this treaty.

Article IX:

The two parties to this treaty will establish a Joint Arms Control Commission, based in Zurich, whose members shall be charged with proposing reductions in both strategic and tactical weaponry, subject to ultimate ratification by the governments of the two contracting powers. Such reductions will be made according to the following general principles:

- Withdrawal of all nuclear munitions from outer space
- Demilitarization of the Arctic Ocean
- De-targeting of space-to-ground weaponry
- De-targeting of ground-to-space weaponry

- Registration of all major military bases
- Registration of all submarine sorties from base
- Limitations in total number of hypersonic missile engines
- Limitations in nuclear megatonnage

Article X:

Effective within two months of the signing of this treaty, the two contracting powers undertake to cease the testing of all classes of directed energy weapons.

Article XI:

Upon amendment/ratification, the measures proposed by the Joint Arms Control Commission will be verified by agreed-upon satellite overflight and physical inspections of bases.

Article XII:

In the event of a conflict between the two contracting powers concerning any question, the two parties will adjust this difference or conflict exclusively by friendly exchange of opinion or, if necessary, by an arbitration commission based in either Zurich or Geneva.

Article XIII:

The present treaty will extend for a period of ten years, with the understanding that if neither of the contracting parties announces its abrogation within one year of expiration of this period, it will continue in force automatically for another period of five years.

Article XIV:

The present treaty shall be ratified within the shortest possible time. The exchange of ratification documents is to take place in Zurich. The treaty becomes effective immediately upon signature.

Drawn up in three languages, English, Russian, and Chinese, January 1, 2105.

Signed for the United States:
Alec Morgan, Secretary of State

Cosigned for the Eurasian Coalition by the Slavic Bloc:
V. I. Brusilov, Minister of Foreign Affairs

Cosigned for the Eurasian Coalition by the Republic of China:
Chen Xuesen, People's Minister of State

A.D. 2110

PART I
IMMERSION

I t's time," says a voice.

Thirty klicks above Earth's surface. Thirty minutes after takeoff. A small room within a large jetcraft: Jason Marlowe opens his eyes.

He looks around. No one there.

"Prep for drop," says the voice.

He sits up. Gets up. Goes to the washbasin. Lets water dash itself against metal and skin. He runs his hands along his face. He wonders if something has changed.

"Stop it," says the voice. "Move it."

He turns away. He starts to pull things onto his body: vest, pants, belt. Light boots. Redundant biomonitors around his arms. A knife strapped below his left knee. A pistol below his right. Everything else he's going to be wearing is contained in the hardware standing in this room's corner.

"Suit up," says the voice.

The armor's the standard heavy model. Too standard. It's not even his. Marlowe climbs within, wondering as he does who else has worn it. He wishes they'd shipped his own suit as quickly as they did him.

"Power up," says the voice.

Vibration churns through him as the suit seals. Lights come to life around his face. He turns, feels pneumatic joints dig into him. He stops to adjust them. He calibrates the suit's cameras to ensure 360-degree vision—sets the range-finders, lets numbers chase themselves across the displays, interface with the ones within his head. He walks to the door, slides it open, walks down a corridor. He goes through into another room.

"Load up," says the voice.

But Marlowe doesn't need to listen to know what to do with the ammunition racked upon the walls. Or the fuel pipes that emerge from the ceiling to slot into his armor's tanks. He watches his screens as those tanks fill. He wonders who he's going to demolish this time. They told him while he was asleep. Told him he'll remember when the time comes. It's the same thing every time. He opens one more door. He looks down the corridor beyond, feels the adrenaline hit him in one pure wave.

Another ship, far higher: the Operative's rising into space for the very first time. He can't believe he's never been up here before. Nor can he believe how several hundred tons of metal clank as the winds of atmosphere hit on the ascent. For one crazy moment he thinks it's all over. That all his missions on Earth have led up to this one blaze of glory—one blast of flame to crash back into Atlantic.

But the only thing that's falling is the burnt-out first stage. The massive engines plunge to ten thousand meters—

and then switch on their own engines, turn west, hurtle back to base, and reuse while high above the Operative turns dials, prowls frequencies, listens as the pilots call out telemetry readings, watches as blue of sky becomes black of space. Ocean rolls into the window as the craft rolls onto its orbit. The last remnants of day slide over western Atlantic. Eastern Atlantic is swathed in early evening.

And Africa's given over to pure night. But the maps on the screens within the Operative's eyes show him all that matters anyway. He gazes at the Eurasian fortresses strewn across Sahara—watches across the minutes as their own launch routines crank and the Moon casts shadows on the sand and the immensity of desert at last gives way to Nile. And what's left of the Middle East. The Operative was thirty-eight when it got flash-broiled. He's fifty now. He's starting to wonder how long he's got before he drops below peak condition. How long the enhancers that course through his body can fight encroaching age. Surgery after surgery. Drug after drug. Training that's ever more intense. And then this mission: to infiltrate his own side's off-world forces and terminate irregularities with no little prejudice.

A summons he wishes had come a decade ago. The Operative has fought Jaguar insurgents in Central America. He's iced his own side's defectors as they tried to run the border. He's battled the East's agents in the neutral territories: Europe. Australia. South Africa. Argentina. He's taken out targets all over the world.

But never in space. He doesn't know why. Maybe up until now his handlers optimized him for gravity. Maybe their orbital brethren are territorial. No reason they shouldn't be. Every outfit divides against itself. Bureaucracy builds in the back office while agents work the field solo or in teams. The other member of this particular team is holed up in one of the lunar bases. The Operative is supposed to meet him there.

But first he's got to do one orbit. So that the craft can line up the angles for the translunar burn. The Operative pictures what's left of that craft: the engines, the cargo-modules, the cockpit. He's just aft of that cockpit, in a room where passengers sit. He's the only one that fits that description. He got slotted on here special. He takes in the roof of the world below him. Moonlight glints across receding snowcaps. Memory gleams within the Operative's head. India's on his mind. A nation caught between the Eurasians and the rising oceans, its power crushed and its coastlines swamped. Everybody who could got the hell out.

And the Operative was down there once, caught up in that crunch. Tracking down a scientist on the run from Mumbai who was trying to sell her expertise in the Kuala-Lumpur markets—until the Operative caught up with her, persuaded her to give it up for free. Now she's doing life in a laboratory in New Mexico. A comfortable life, to be sure. Far more so than the Operative's own.

Which right now consists of sitting in a metal room and watching dawn creep across the Pacific toward China's endless cities. Looking at that ocean reminds him of the trance he woke from just before the launch. Those swirls of sea are far more real than the swirling in his head. He remembers the way his handlers prowled his dreams—remembers the bit about SpaceCom and the bit about Lynx and the rendezvous somewhere on the nearside. And that's about it.

Save for one other memory of the time before he boarded. A memory of the launch complex spreading out beneath him as the elevator trundled up sixty stories of rocket. He could see all the way to jungle. He could hear the tanks pressurizing for main-engine start. But that was an hour ago. Ignition's long past. That rocket's gone.

All that's left is spaceship.

• • •

Claire Haskell's coming awake. It doesn't come easy. Her head hurts. The seat in which she sits is shaking. She's in motion. She opens her eyes.

To find herself in the rear of what looks to be a jet-copter. A low ceiling curves above her. The straps of her seat curl over her. The cockpit door is plainly visible from where she sits. It's shut. She feels the same way. She feels there are things she can't recall. It's always like this when she wakes from trance: before awareness folds in, lays bare the residue of dreams. Ostensibly, those dreams look the same as any others. But they give themselves away with telltale signs she knows too well—the green of the old man's eyes, the soft tone of his voice, the particular ambience of a room. It seems there *was* a room. It seems she was there, out upon some sea. But that chamber had no windows. The one in which she sits now does. Each one is covered with a plastic shade. She reaches over to the nearest.

But now the dreams surge in upon her. They remind her who she is. They remind her who's been at her mind again. Those dreams: there was a time when she regarded them as her succor. There was a time when she grew to hate them worse than death. But lately it's been both thrill and revulsion simultaneously—and with such intensity that she's no longer sure she can even tell the difference. And what does it matter? *All primary briefings of agents take place under the trance, get remembered by those agents only in retrospect.* It doesn't matter how she feels about that. Emotions are incidental. Facts aren't—her charge, however difficult, her lot in life for now, is to tend these thoughts that aren't hers, to shelter them and incubate them, and then do whatever they may ask.

And now she's waiting for that moment. But her hands aren't waiting. They grasp the shade. Her fingers fumble with the clasp. She rips aside plastic to reveal window. She blinks. She stares.

And draws back as she realizes what she's looking at.

Marlowe's got two minutes. Lighted arrows show him the way, but he no longer sees them. Disembodied voices goad him on, but he no longer hears them. All he hears is the soundless noise that's building up within him—the silent siren that accompanies the moments that play out before the run...out of that formless dark in which the word goes down, out into the events in which he writes that word across flesh. He races down another corridor. It's getting narrower. Up ahead, a door slides aside. He runs through the opening and down a ramp.

He's in the underbelly. The ceiling's lower here. Technicians step in from left and right. They check his suit's seals. They check the thrusters on his back and wrists and ankles. They make some adjustments to the minigun that's perched on his right shoulder. They wave him onward. Marlowe moves past more ladders, closes in upon one ladder in particular. Blank screens are everywhere. He feels the stare of invisible eyes upon him. He's going straight for the door at his feet. It seems to lead directly into a crawl space—a tiny alcove that he might have missed had the arrows not led him straight here. But it's not an alcove. It's not a crawl space.

It's his ride to ground.

"Get in," says the voice.

But Marlowe's paying no attention. He climbs in, activates magnetic clamps. The door folds in over him, encloses him in darkness. But only for a moment—and then screens snap on inside his skull as his armor's software syncs with that of the craft. Coordinates click into place. System specs parade past him. A vibration passes through him. The locks that hold his craft in place retract. He starts plunging toward the city stretching out below him.

One orbit almost done, and now the Andes rise toward the Operative's ship. They don't get very far. A few more minutes and those peaks are crumpling back into what's left of jungle. The remnants of that green are cut through with great brown and black streaks. Amazonia's seen better days. From up here, the cities are shrouded in smog so thick they look like little more than massive craters. If a meteor plunged into them, it'd be hard to tell the difference.

"And this is on a *good* day."

The voice is coming from the speakers. It's one of the pilots. But it may as well be a million klicks off. The Operative feels it slowly impinge upon his consciousness. He feels so high he feels he was never anything else. He waits for all eternity.

And then he speaks.

"And when it's bad?"

"All you'll see is junkyard."

"Price we pay for cheap launch real estate."

"The only people down there doing any paying are the Latins," says the pilot. "For shortcutting their way into the modern era."

"That's one way to look at it."

"It's hard to understand anything down there without understanding that."

"Didn't realize you flyboys studied history."

"Nothing we don't study," the pilot says languidly. "Nothing but ways of killing time."

"So come on back here and let's have a chat."

A spluttering emerges from the speakers. The Operative assumes it's a laugh. "I don't think so."

"Why not."

"No fraternization with the cargo. Cockpit door remains shut."

"Says who."

"Says the ones who told us to add you to that cargo. As you well know."

"So why are you speaking with me?"

"Because this isn't a social call. I'm just letting you know we've got clearance for the burn to Moon. As soon as we hit Atlantic, we're in the window. Which will take us within a hundred klicks of Elevator."

"No shit?"

"None at all."

"Visible from this window?"

"Eventually. But visible on the screens right now."

"Put it through."

But the thing is, there's no vantage that's advantaged to frame the foremost wonder of the age. There's no such thing as the whole thing. The joint construction of the superpowers: the Elevator is four thousand klicks long. It circles Earth twelve times each day. It stretches from the lower orbits all the way toward the mediums. Any view that takes in the entirety is too removed to register the thickness. Any view that catches that thickness can't hope to catch the length. So now something that looks like a luminescent tendril cuts in on the screen. It rises from the horizon. It vanishes into the heavens.

"So that's it," says the Operative.

"Come on, man. You must have seen it before."

"Only on the vid."

"How's this any different?"

"Because now I'm up here with it. Where do we hit closest proximity?"

"Where Amazon hits Atlantic," replies the pilot.

"Belem-Macapa? That's almost where we launched from."

"Yeah. That window'll give you a great view of the whole town."

"What's it like?"

"I'll give you one guess."

It's like being underwater. The architecture of Belem-Macapa's visible only indistinctly: buildings towering out of the smog, towering back into it. Stacks of lights shimmer through the haze. There's no way to see the ground. There's no way to see the sky. Haskell cycles through the optical enhancements she has at her disposal. All they show her are the other vehicles in her convoy—several other 'copters in the air about her, several crawlers roaring at speed along the skyways and ramps that twist among the buildings. And those are just the ones in sight. A quick glance at her screens reveals the real extent of it: at least forty vehicles in the immediate vicinity, several flanking formations off to either side, and—two klicks up—ships roaming through this city's upper reaches, ready to swoop down at the first sign of any trouble. She wonders if it's all for her. She's tempted to feel flattered. It's the closest she's come to feeling anything all day.

But that's starting to change. She shouldn't be this close to the action. Not physically, at any rate. She's a razor. She's supposed to sit back and work the wires from afar. She's not supposed to be thrust into a live war zone. As if on cue, more things surface within her. More pieces of her purpose. She marvels at the spaces they fill—marvels, too, at all the gaps they still leave. What they reveal has the feel of a plan laid hastily. It has the feel of the same old story: get them before they get us—and turns out that she was the right woman for the moment. She's sick of it. She can't get enough of it. Her pulse is quickening. So is her mind. The city streams past. Her destination looms on the screens ahead.

Stealth pod tumbling from the heights: and within that pod is Marlowe, watching the sun sinking to the west, watching all the readouts, watching as he drops toward Belem-Macapa's sprawl. It's like the swamp to end all swamps: swarms of roving jet-copters are the insects, while the city's highest spires reach out of the murk like reeds. The levels below that waver in the gloom. The levels below that are invisible.

Even to Jason Marlowe. He has the sensors, sure. But he's not using them. He doesn't dare. All he's using are the maps he's been given. He's got the city's simulacrum burned into his brain. He sees the way the city looks beneath its veil. He sees what his pod's descending into—feels the pod jettison, feels his suit's glidewing buffeted by turbulence even as visibility drops toward nil. What's left of the sun dissolves. Marlowe turns his attention to the buildings in his mind, drifts in among them.

The Amazon twists and turns, closing on the ocean. The Operative gazes down at the city that's sliding into view, watches as it swallows the river in smog.

"The epicenter of the latest flare-up," says the pilot. "That's not just environmental meltdown. It's scorched-earth warfare."

"Come again?"

"They're burning their own buildings to blind our satellites."

"Ah," says the Operative.

"The latest round started up ten days ago," says the pilot. "It now extends through half this city's districts. They say the Jaguars view it as a test of strength. They say that if they can force us to withdraw, they'll show the world who really rules this continent."

"They wish," says the Operative.

"You're saying we have all the answers?"

"Nobody has all the answers, flyboy. All I'm saying is that all they're doing is killing their own people."

"Not to mention our soldiers."

"Who are a hell of a lot cheaper than our machines."

"You sure?"

"Look," says the Operative. "Hate to break it to you, but everything you see down there is *collateral*. If the Jaguars torched the whole thing, they'd be doing us a favor."

"And the economy of South America—"

"Would collapse? Already has. Doesn't matter. Only thing that means anything is our control of the equator. Don't you get it, man? The profit margins that gives us in vacuum turn those cities into write-off."

"Maybe it once did," says the pilot. He sounds testy. "Maybe. But not now. You can't write off a whole war."

"Jesus Christ," the Operative mutters. "I thought you said you'd read history? I thought you thought you knew something about the way this world works? What you're looking at isn't a *war*. It's just a fucking *domestic disturbance*. And all we're laying down is just a little police action. Isn't space supposed to give you some perspective?"

"You wouldn't believe what space has shown me," the pilot hisses. "But that doesn't mean that I'm going to see things your way. If what you say is true, why don't we just withdraw from all those cities down there. Abandon them. Seal them off."

"You probably would if you were in charge," says the

Operative. "Problem with you flyboys is that you've got no sense of the subtle touch. You can't seal off a tumor. Can't withdraw from cancer. If we left the cities to the Jaguars, they'd mobilize all urban resources against us. They'd be fanning out through the jungles and the sewers. They'd be assaulting our launch bases in nothing flat."

"If that's true, then why don't we just nuke them?"

"We may yet."

"But why haven't we yet?"

"Because no one's used a nuke since Tel Aviv and Riyadh."

"So?"

"So this is the era of détente. The second cold war ain't that far in the rearview. The last thing anybody needs is for one of the superpowers to start frying populations wholesale. How do you think the East's analysts are going to rate the situation's stability if we start charbroiling the Latins?"

The pilot doesn't reply.

"Exactly," says the Operative. "And while you're at it: don't forget the East has a similar problem in Africa."

"Lagos and Kinshasa."

"And about twenty other cities."

"Didn't they once contribute to our Latin problem?"

"By supporting the insurgents? They may still."

"No kidding?"

"And we may still be returning the favor."

"You're joking."

"You're naïve," says the Operative. "Don't you know what *détente* means?"

"I've heard many definitions."

"So let me give you the one that counts."

"Namely?"

"Same game. New phase."

"That's all?"

"Believe me: that's enough."

• • •

They've reached the perimeter. Haskell watches as her 'copter sweeps past skyscrapers that have been transformed into mammoth firing platforms: whole sections of walls, whole stacks of floors removed to allow scores of gun-emplacements to be situated within those scooped-out innards. Giant metal nets drape here and there, connecting other buildings. The whole area looks like the domain of some monstrous spider. The 'copter starts to weave in among those nets. It's a complicated route. Haskell counts at least three distinct lines of defense, each one containing untold fields of fire.

Though she knows full well the real point of this place isn't defense. It's the reverse. It's the way modern urban warfare gets waged. Establish bases in the city in question, use those sites to launch forays into the concrete wilderness all around. Hedgehogs, some call them. Hell on Earth might be more accurate. Haskell never thought she'd be in the middle of one.

But there's a first time for everything. She feels her stomach lurch. The 'copter's circling. Those circles tighten around one building in particular. The craft floats toward it, touches down on the roof.

The engines die. She hurriedly pulls her breath-mask into place, strapping it onto her chem-suit—just in time as the hatch swings back. Helmets peer inside. But Haskell's already coming out—"Out of my way," she snarls, and they back away quickly.

She leaps lightly to the rooftop, looks around. Two other jet-copters sit alongside hers. Soldiers in powered armor stand at attention. Barbed wire rings the rooftop's perimeter. Buildings protrude out of the murk beyond like fingers jutting up from quicksand. The sky overhead couldn't be more than two hundred meters up. Half-seen lights move through it.

"Get me off this roof," says Haskell.

"Yes, ma'am," replies one of the soldiers. He turns. She follows him toward a single-story structure set atop the center of the roof. As they reach its door, the soldier steps aside, gestures for her to enter. She steps within, finds herself on a metal-grille stairway. The door closes behind her. She hears atmospheric purifiers working as she descends.

At the bottom of the stairway she finds a room. It looks to be some kind of storage chamber. A single door's set within the opposite wall. Two men stand before that door. One's another power-suited soldier. The second isn't. He's wearing civilian chem-clothes. His face is gaunt. His eyes are pale.

"Claire Haskell," he says.

"Yeah?"

"My name's Morat. You can take your breath-mask off now."

"Thanks," she says. But she leaves it on.

"It's clean in here," says Morat.

"It doesn't feel that way," she replies.

"You get used to it," he says.

She stares at him. She pulls her mask off, lets brown hair fall back. He grins at her naked face.

"Welcome to what's left of Brazil."

"Thanks a lot."

"How was your trip?"

"Uneventful."

"So it was good."

"Until I got here, yes."

"A sense of humor," says Morat. "I like that."

She doesn't reply.

"Come with me," he says.

Morat turns, opens the door behind him. He starts to walk down a corridor, stops, turns back toward her.

And beckons.

"Come with me," he repeats.

This time she does. The soldier steps in behind her. She realizes that she can hear his footfall. She really shouldn't. She thought those suits were supposed to be silent. Evidently, this one's not. Or else the pre-zone rush is rendering her all too sensitive . . . because she can hear everything—the slight clank of feet against the floor, the tiny hisses of gas from neck joints, the whirring of cooling motors . . . all of it trailing in her wake down the corridor.

At the end of the corridor's an elevator. Its doors slide open. Morat enters. Haskell follows, turns—looks into helmeted visor. The soldier's stopped at the elevator's threshold. The doors slide shut. The elevator starts to drop. It's just the two of them now.

"Can we talk freely in here?"

"Nothing's ever free," Morat replies, pulling out a pistol. "Particularly not talk. This is cleared terrain in theory. In reality"—he hands her the pistol, hilt first—"you'd better hang on to this." She takes the weapon. He flips open a panel in the wall, pulls a lever. The elevator shudders to a stop.

"Where do you want to begin?" she asks.

"With you."

"There's so much I can't recall."

"And so much you're about to."

Blind man in the city: but Jason Marlowe utilizes the coordinates programmed into his heads-up as he maneuvers his glidewing amidst the buildings of this megalopolis. Occasional thinnings of the mist reveal vast grids of light, stretching out of nothing, dissolving into even less. Marlowe's steering in toward one grid in particular. It swims toward him on the heads-up display, one column protruding past the others. He can't allow himself to drop below its roof. He's got to slow down: he works the flaps, sails down toward it. Suddenly it's filling the screens. He braces himself. And then he's striking that roof at speeds that knock the breath from him—even as he jettisons the glidewing, rolls along the roof, springs to his feet in a semicrouch.

Marlowe looks around at the buildings that tower around him. No one seems to have spotted him. He steps lightly to a trapdoor in the rooftop's corner, wrenches it open. He finds a ladder, disappears within.

The maw of delta-city has now moved to the very center of the window. The Operative stares down at the spires that rise out of the clouds that gather more than two klicks up.

"Penthouse suite," he says.

"The Citadel," replies the pilot.

"The what?"

"*You* don't know what the *Citadel* is?"

"Maybe I'm just testing you."

"Test away, asshole. I'm not afraid of you."

"Maybe you should be."

"Maybe you don't know shit about the biggest hedgehog of them all. Room with a view. They say the Jaguars can't get within a kilometer of the basement."

"A kilometer's a pretty specific number," replies the Operative. "Particularly when it involves classified operations. You're merchant marine. Where are you getting all this from?"

"Information's harder to lock down in space."

"Give me another example."

"How about *you* give *me* an example?"

"Such as?"

"What's your business on the Moon?"

The Operative laughs. "Who says I have business on the Moon?"

"That's where we're supposed to drop you, isn't it?"

"Maybe that's just my transfer point."

"And maybe it's not. Come on, man. We've got three days together."

"So?"

"So indulge me. It's not like I expect you to tell me the *truth*."

"Then what the hell do you expect?" asks the Operative.

"How about a good story?"

"Even if it's a lie?"

"Remember what I said about killing time?"

"I thought you said this wasn't a social call."

"So I'm mixing business with pleasure."

"So put the Elevator back on that screen."

"I never took it off," the pilot says.

"Where is it?"

"Lower right-right."

"Put it at the center."

"Sure thing."

It's the surest thing there is. It's scarcely two hundred klicks distant. It's practically a drive-by. Yet it still requires magnification to make out the workers on its side—still requires magnification to discern how they've jury-rigged whole series of pulleys to haul themselves along it while they lay down the maglev tracks along which the freight will someday flow. The Operative lets his gaze stray down toward the Elevator's extremity at Nadir Station some hundred klicks below. Below that's only atmosphere.

"Am I ever going to get to see it out that window?" he asks.

"You could if the window weren't facing Earth."

"I can see it's facing Earth. What I'm asking is, is that going to change soon."

"Man's in luck. When we prime the burn we'll shift our angle. You should get yourself a good view then."

"Excellent."

"So what's going down on the Moon?"

But the Operative's just noticed something going down on the screens.

"I'm an envoy," says Morat.

"I'd guessed as much," replies Haskell.

"I'm an envoy," he repeats, as though her words compel reiteration. "I report directly to the handlers."

"How direct can it be when you never see them either?"

"As direct as it needs to be for me to give you your final orders. You've been primed across your dreams. You face me in the flesh for activation."

"Tell me what's going on."

"You already know what's going on," he says. "We're getting hammered."

"By the Latins."

"By the Jaguars. The Latins didn't mean shit until the Jags gave them a voice. Five years ago, these cities were virtually pacified. Everything was locked down. Look at them now. The governments we bought and paid for don't dare to go inside. The militias are like iron filings over which a magnet's passing. They're focused like they've never been before."

"Which is why I'm here," says Haskell.

"Which is why you're here." Morat smiles without warmth. "This city is where they're making their latest push. It started ten days back. Now it's as bad as I've ever seen it. I tell you, Claire—we either find a way to break them, or else one of these days it's going to be the other way. And if we're going to win this, it's going to have to be CounterIntelligence Command that gets in there and does it. The other Commands won't. Army's a hollow shell. Space rides high and disdains dirt. Info avoids the human touch. Navy steers clear of anything that isn't ocean. The Praetorians have their hands full safeguarding the Throne. It's going to have to be CICom. It's going to have to be you, Claire."

Silence. For minutes. For hours. Is she tripping on the pre-zone rush? Maybe. A structure's forming in her head, aggregating out of nothing—it spins before her. It's everything they told her while she was sleeping. It's the codes that will allow her to beat what she's about to face. Yet it's as blurry as the mist outside. It needs the trigger words that Morat's about to give her to make it real. Those words don't have to make sense on a conscious level to unearth what's been buried further down. If they do, it's only because Morat is choosing to bind them up in context. But context is optional.

Codes aren't.

"Is this building empty?" she asks. She realizes that Morat has just spoken. That her reverie's all gone down in one moment.

"Of course not," Morat replies. "It's filled with our soldiers."

"If they're our soldiers, why are they wearing Army colors?"

"Because ArmyCom's been divvied up by the rest of the Commands."

"I hadn't heard."

"Shouldn't let yourself get so out of the loop, Claire. Army did, and now it's dead in the water. They're keeping the name, but that's about it. CICom got the franchise for all operations in this city. The Throne's charged Sinclair with cleaning the place up."

"Have these Army units been reconditioned?"

Morat looks at her like she's stupid.

"Where are we in relation to this hedgehog's perimeter?" she asks.

"About two or three streets from the edge. We extended the perimeter to encompass these blocks only yesterday."

"And which floor are we heading to next?"

"The ninety-fifth," he replies. "It's the one we were tipped off to."

"Who tipped us off?"

"An informant. Highly placed in what we believe to be the Jaguars' command structure."

"Is this informant reliable?"

"Reliable enough."

"Enough for this?"

"What are you getting at?"

"That it might be a trap."

"Of course it might be a trap. But if it's not, we could roll them up. It's worth the risk."

"You mean it's worth risking *me*."

"Well," says Morat, "I don't think Sinclair imagines that you'll be sacrificed. He likes you, Claire. He tells the handlers you'll live forever. Even if it *is* a trap—he thinks you'll be the one who'll be able to get out and tell us all about it."

"I can't tell you how good that makes me feel."

"You're getting pretty close to insubordination."

"I'm not interested in your threats," she replies. "Not interested in the old man either. Just tell me what we've got here."

"What we've got here," says Morat evenly, "is a tunnel back in time."

"Excuse me?"

"A tunnel back to the way things used to be." He grins. "A tunnel straight on through to the way they still are."

"Are you on drugs?"

"No," says Morat, "but I know you are. I know you razors. How else do you bear the blast of zone? Can't even say I blame you. But let me tell you this, Claire—what you're about to enter is no ordinary zone. Or rather, it was ordinary once upon a time. Just not now. Not any longer."

"You're talking legacy."

"Of course. This city used to be two. Belem and Macapa: a few decades back, they became one. Right about the time the first world-net got sundered. Right about the time the super-powers were building walls around their nets and calling them zones and the Euros were establishing theirs: this place was preoccupied with concerns that were far more local. She was the platform for the last rush to take down the Amazon. And when the bulk of green was gone, and the strip-mining of the Andes took off—once again, this was the place to be. Now she's ours. Whether we like it or not. She's got twenty million people. And ten million of those live outside the zone."

"You mean they live beyond *our* zone."

"Many of them live beyond any net whatsoever. Many don't. This gateway I'm about to show you—as best as we can tell, it leads to conduits that constituted the center of this city's power grid in the year 2060. It's been buried a long time. We thought it no longer existed. And we might still be right. It might not be active anymore. In fact . . ."

He keeps on talking, but Haskell's scarcely listening. At least not consciously. It hardly matters. What matters is that his words are confirming the glidepath down which her run's going to slot. Visions burn through her brain: images, plans, *recollections*. The wrinkles of the old man's face. The walls of that room. The surface of that sea. She sees once more those sterile corridors. Once again the codes course through her. The operating systems and the software of half a century back crystallize inside her mind. The parameters of the still-functioning nets of yesteryear echo through her head. They burn within her skull, flare behind her eyes; they course straight through her, and all the while that pale gaunt face keeps talking.

"See, Claire," it says. "We're not idiots. We've long sus-pected the Jaguars have a net of their own. That they're not just coordinating between cities by means of couriers. And we've long suspected that net's physical. Our jamming mechanisms are too good for them to use wireless in any but the most tactical of situations. Which means they run that net through wires that lie beyond our maps. But the problem is that what's beyond those maps is also out of our control. As out of control as this city. If there were more of a government here, we could clean them up comprehensively. But outside our own fortresses, law's a product of the street. That leaves a lot of net-fragments remaining for the Jaguars to exploit. We've shut many down. But there are many others. Some of them are linked. Some aren't. Some are just islands. Maybe this one is too. We don't know. We've been looking for a way in from our zone. We've been looking for a way in from any of the fragments we know about. So far we haven't found one. Which doesn't mean there isn't one. As you well know."

"I do," says Haskell, and she does. She knows that when a layperson says *zone*, they think of something monolithic, something sleek and grey and all-encompassing. Something that couldn't be further from the chaos of the truth. A tangle of interfaces, a web of trapdoors, mirrors, dead ends: layer upon layer of construction, some of it fitting evenly, much of it not, so much of it built at cross-purposes, or simply without coordination—as uncoordinated as the traffic that flows through it. All that data skating over all the ice that crusts above a sea of legacy. Rarely does anything go any deeper. Unless you're talking about something that's pretty covert. And you can pursue that covert data if you like, can dig in that sea's own bed through the strata of bygone technology, back through quantum cables, back through fiber optics, back through copper wires, back through what's abandoned—or at least uncharted. As uncharted as the link to an antique power grid might be . . .

"But we found it," says Morat. "On the ninety-fifth floor. X marks the spot. We dug in the place where we were told, and we found it."

"And now you want me to crawl in there."

"And get on the trail of the Jaguars' net. And if you find it—if there really *is* a link between these wires and their lairs—then come back without tipping them off."

"Who I am coordinating with?"

"Me."

"I mean what other razors? What other mechs? I'm assuming this is part of a combined operation?"

"Sure it's a combined operation. But you can leave all that to me, Claire. The word's come down from the old man himself. Both kinds of runners hit this city tonight. The razors work the wires and the mechanics kick in the doors. But the razors *aren't* working the mechs' leashes. Not this time, anyway. The whole thing's too compartmentalized. And your part is crucial. What you're crawling into could be the lair of the Jaguars. Or it could be nothing."

"Or it could be a trap," she repeats.

"Or it could be a trap. But if it's not, we could end this war tonight. *You* could, Claire. We need someone who can get in there without triggering any alarms. Someone who can tell us where to strike. We need your talents, Claire. It'd be worth a lot to your future."

"So would living," she replies. "How secure is this perimeter?"

"As secure as I can make it. This place has been swept. Along with this whole block. It's clean. If they have anything rigged, it'd be inside the zone itself."

"Great. And if I find something?"

"Map out the physical locations of the executive nodes of that network. And then get out."

"In that order?"

"In whatever order you can manage."

"Right," she says. She breathes deeply. She looks around her. "I'm ready to do this."

"Excellent."

"You're acting like I have a choice."

"You always have a choice, Claire."

"Can we get out of this shaft?".

"We can." He turns to the wall panel, adjusts the controls. They start to descend. They gain speed, hissing down through scores of floors. They slow. They halt. The door slides open.

Nothing. There's nothing here. It's as if there never was. Marlowe's making his way down ladders and stairs and through trapdoors and it's as if they've all just been dormant, waiting for his presence. Yet he can feel the presence of the ones he seeks close at hand. The force they have in here probably isn't large enough to set up watch over the whole building. They're probably keeping as low a profile as possible. But sooner or later he's going to reach their perimeters.

Probably sooner. For now he's reached apartments that are inhabited. Open doors give way to living quarters—laundry hung all about tiny chambers, kids squawking, mothers screaming. Marlowe moves through them like a ghost, his suit's camo cranked up as far as it'll go, letting him take on the ambience of wall, of doorway, of ceiling—whatever surface he's in front of at whatever moment. The most trouble he gets is from a dog that won't stop barking. It knows something's up. But Marlowe ignores it, becomes one more thing in that animal's life that'll never reach the lives of the humans who feed it.

He descends through several more such levels. He steps over sleepers, moves past men and women engrossed in card games, drinking, laughing—he reminds himself it's Saturday night, wonders how much it differs from all the other nights that go down in this city. Truth to tell, the cities up north aren't that different. They've just got more money to blow on this kind of thing. Not to mention a better chance of surviving to see tomorrow's parties.

But the lower he gets, the more the ones going on around him fizzle out. Finally he finds himself moving through deserted halls once more. Most of the overhead lighting's gone. And now Marlowe's circuits are humming. His heads-up's giving him the alert: there are sensors in here. There are wavelengths brushing against him like cobwebs. But his suit's camoed in more than just the visible spectrum. It's state-of-the-art.

Now put to the test.

Intervention on the Elevator: the Operative watches through the magnifiers as two patrol ships move in toward the construction area. They're drifting cables—and fixing those cables to the web of scaffolding that encrusts the Elevator's spine. Hatches open. Suits emerge, fire jets, flit in toward the workers clustered along the scaffolding.

"What's going on?" says the Operative.

"Looks like a raid," replies the pilot.

"Any idea why?"

"What do you know about those workers?"

The suits are going to town. They're fanning out through the scaffolding. They're grabbing workers, dragging them out of latticed depths. There seems to be struggling going on in several places. Several workers are being hustled into one of the ships.

"Less than I thought," says the Operative.

"Here's a hint—those guys aren't drawing a salary, friend. They're not in it to win it. They're either soaking up the radiation on that thing or else they're breaking rocks beneath the Mare Imbrium."

"They're convicts."

"And usually political ones. Sentenced to life by definition. Nothing left to lose. Someone was probably doing petty sabotage. Or plotting hopeless escape. Shit, man. This kind of bust happens a lot more often than you'd think."

But someone must be refusing to go out easy. Because now another swarm of suits is billowing from both ships. They latch on to the scaffolding, start getting in there. The Operative shakes his head.

"Look at them go."

"This is getting good."

It's getting even better. Because now the jets of both ships are flaring. Those craft are still tethered. They're turning on their axes. The KE gatlings in their tails are starting to track on something.

"Hello," says the Operative.

"Shit," says the pilot.

Both guns fire simultaneously.

The elevator doors give way to a room that's really a warehouse. It cuts through at least three stories. Catwalks line the walls. Power-suited soldiers stand at intervals along the lower catwalks. Some kind of structure occupies most of the floor—sections of plastic wall partition the space into many sections.

Morat leads the way into the maze. Occasional glimpses through open entryways reveal equipment, crates, dust— sometimes all three and always at least the last. At first Haskell wonders why the partitions haven't been removed. But then she realizes that what's about to happen is for her eyes alone: hers, and maybe Morat's—and now he's leading her into one particular room. It contains a metal rack in which a console sits. Wires protrude from the floor, nest around that console like snakes. Five screens gleam atop it.

"Here we are," says Morat, halting. "We've dug in, hooked up these interfaces. When you jack in, the connection goes live."

Haskell just stares. At the screens. At the console. She walks toward it. She halts in front of it, looks it over. She turns back to Morat.

"I'll watch your flesh," he says.

She says nothing—just turns, adjusts the manual controls. Takes out the implants, connects them. Slots them into her head. The hooks hang heavy in her skull. She sits down on the floor. Crosses her legs. Glances up at Morat.

"The fuck you will," she says as she jacks in.

Marlowe's given up on the stairs. He switches to the elevator shaft. He squirts the components of an acid compound from the finger-cartridges of his glove, lets that acid activate and corrode a hole in the elevator doors. He climbs through into the shaft. The light here is very faint. He loops a tether around a beam, drops down the shaft's length. He sees sensors positioned in its walls. He feels their emissions scrape against him, watches his suit run countermeasures. He wonders whether he's showing up on anybody's scopes.

That's when something emerges from the gloom below. It's the elevator car. It's about twenty-five floors beneath him. It's just gone motionless. Marlowe doesn't know how fast it can move. He only knows that it's time to get out of the shaft.

But before he can do that, the doors to the floor immediately above the elevator car open. He goes very still.

Two figures in light battlesuits leap into the shaft, land on the elevator's roof. They're looking upward. Not as high as Marlowe is. But high enough. Marlowe watches on his heads-up as the spectrums start to get crowded. He realizes that the suits are probing. That they're about to detect him. The stealth part of this run is officially over. He lines up his targets.

No half measures: the KE gatlings triangulate, slice through scaffolding like it's so much matchwood. Shreds of suit and meat spray out in slow motion.

"Shit," says the Operative.

But the pilot says nothing. And now the workers are swarming in among the power-suits where the big guns can't touch them. They're bringing the suits down with sheer numbers. They're grabbing weapons, turning them on their assailants.

"Shit," says the Operative.

But all he hears is silence.

"You still there?"

There's no answer. Now the ships are opening up on everybody in that section of the spine, friend and foe alike. It's a total massacre. One of the ships suddenly explodes—opening up like a tin can packed with gunpowder.

"*Shit*," says the Operative.

It's the same ship into which the prisoners were taken. The Operative wonders what was in those workers. The other ship fires its thrusters, swans away from the scene of the killing.

The scaffolding starts to drip. Starts to melt. Workers just disappear—or at least parts of them do. Those still alive are fleeing. It's not helping. That whole section of the Elevator is being targeted by distant guns. The Operative can't see them. He can't see what they're projecting either. Directed energy is invisible in vacuum. But he can see the precisely calibrated result. The Elevator itself is unscathed. But no one in that construction zone could have survived. The Operative is starting to wish he wasn't so close to whatever's going down.

The screens shut off. Leaving only wall.

And window.

And zone. And somewhere in that zone's the mind's horizon. And somewhere past that horizon's a center that's still unfound. But all you've got right now is day torn apart by night: dark sun rolls overhead, higher in an even darker sky, and the run's on, kicking in around you, churning into your deepest recesses, making them aware of one another for the first time. Rendering inconsequential all that has come before. Dreams, ego, consensus of memories, nexus of consciousness—all these are fictions. The zone is not. You know that. You know how it goes (even though you forget it every time)—past the tipping point, and the only way out is in. The universe: nothing but momentum. The world: vanished in the face of the real one. The run: that which transcends all mundane confusions.

Claire Haskell wouldn't have it any other way.

So she drifts deeper. This place is strange. It's definitely alive. It's definitely zone. And yet it's not. It's so old. It's almost incomprehensible.

Which is why she's unleashing the codes. She's flipping through templates. She's mating them, breeding them. Thousands of generations beget themselves and die. She keeps their genes on file, archives her data-banks with the patterns of their bones. Then she regresses back across the eons, tracing the paths of software ancestry. Logic quotients climb. They climb still farther. They converge in upon each other. They touch. It all shifts into focus.

Ever get the feeling you're being stalked? Here's how it works. Everywhere you look there's nothing. Not a thing: just the hollow sound of your own breathing echoing in the darkness of your mind while you probe the spectrums for evidence of what you suspect but just can't prove. Yet in truth it's probably nothing. Not a thing—just the sensors overreacting again. You cast your beams this way and that. You scan the readouts from every angle. You're coming up short. You're ready to pack it in and get the hell out of this shaft.

And that's the last thought of your entire life.

Marlowe opens up on the two suits at point-blank range, his wrist-guns set for flechette swarm. The armor worn by Marlowe's targets is good. It's nowhere near enough. Marlowe cuts through it like he's wielding a giant buzzsaw. The figures he's facing suddenly aren't figures anymore. Marlowe fires his thrusters, plunges down the shaft toward what's left of them. He lands on the roof of the elevator car. He leaps through the open doors from which the dead men emerged.

He's in another corridor. He moves down it at speed, firing point-blank at the men who are rushing from the doors that line the passage. They've got their weapons out. They scarcely have the chance to use them. The barrels on Marlowe's wrists howl. The minigun mounted atop his right shoulder chatters on automatic spray. Men duck in under his guns, grapple with him. He runs power through his armor's skin, electrocutes them. Nozzles protrude from his helmet, spray forth gas. That gas isn't just toxic. It's also thick. Clouds waft up against Marlowe's visor. He switches to thermal. Most of the heat sources are now writhing on the floor.

But now more suited figures are stepping into view at the corridor's other end. They're opening up on Marlowe—who fires two micromissiles from his hip-launcher in rapid succession. The first screams down the corridor toward the suits. The second's set on a lower yield. It takes down the wall adjacent to him. He steps through that opening, feels the whole place shake as his first projectile slams home. He moves through another doorway, keeping low—almost crawling now. He's not slackening his pace. It's as he expected. Most of these men aren't even Jaguars. They're just militia conscripted into service. They're huddling in the rooms as he passes—some of them firing at him, some of them not daring. But the shots Marlowe's sending out on all sides don't differentiate between those who cower and those who fight. He leaves a trail of bodies behind him.

And then he steps on a mine.

Primitive construction, not showing up on any scanner: looks like people here knew not to go any farther down this particular corridor. Nor is that mine small: walls, floor, and ceiling get torn to shreds as Marlowe's hurled off his feet and twisted sideways, tumbling to the now-exposed level below him. He hits that lower floor with a force that almost knocks him senseless. He's far too full of inhibitors to feel any pain. But his screens have all gone dark. His suit's computer's out. He can't move.

Through a visor caked in dust he can see faces peering down at him. Men start to jump down to where he's sprawled. They're clearly celebrating. One of them leaps onto his chest and starts dancing. Marlowe reaches out with his tongue, hits something that's neither flesh nor tooth. He hears a whirring as his backup systems kick in: men whirl their guns toward him but he's already lifting his arms and firing at point-blank range. Shouts of triumph turn to screams. Marlowe hits his thrusters, blasts back to the upper level as militia units scatter. He rockets down the corridor, sparing scarcely a glance at the screens that show the damage to his armor. Primary systems gone, outer hull compromised . . . he tunes it out, keeps going.

And reaches his target. It's an armored door, set within armored walls. Guns mounted within those walls triangulate upon him. He destroys them—fires his thrusters, reaches the door, slaps a hi-ex charge on it, reverses back down the corridor, detonates the charge. Pieces of debris are still falling as he pivots back toward the remnants of the door.

But whoever's in there isn't going to go out easy. Bullets fly past him, ricochet down the corridor. The bomb-rack on Marlowe's left shoulder spits out grenades—the first into the room's ceiling, the next set for one bounce to allow it to careen deeper into whatever lies within. Immediately subsequent to the first explosion—but still before the second—Marlowe's entering the room at floor level, his rack flinging an incendiary grenade out behind him as he moves quickly along the wall. Several bodies lie about the gutted chamber. Shreds of armor and spent ammo casings are scattered everywhere.

Marlowe has no time to inspect any of it closely. He knows that the flames now licking in his wake will only hold off survivors for a short while. And he still doesn't know how much opposition remains ahead of him. Or whether the senior Jaguar agent he's after is here after all. The whole thing might be a trap. If it is, it's a remarkably elaborate one. He steps over bodies on the floor and through the door opposite.

The Operative's been trying to get the crew to talk to him. But they're no longer up for it. His access to the cameras has been shut off. Along with his access to everything else. The whole world's gone silent. The only frequencies in use now are the ones shrouded in code. And the Operative isn't in on any of the secrets. He's been left to keep his own counsel.

So he does. They're clearly within the vicinity of a live situation. The Operative's hoping that any moment now the ship's engines will slam into action and leave this whole mess behind. But he knows how such situations tend to work. He's keenly aware that those who manage these sorts of crises always respond the same way: quarantine the area in question, shut down the comlinks, contain the scene. Which means that all he can do is sit here until this gets resolved.

And kill time.

He gazes out the window. The city's moving slowly toward its edge. Ocean's creeping in. What's left of the sunlight glistens all along the water save for the space occupied by the massive shadow cast by the city's pall. Somehow, the Operative's totally taken by that shadow—at the way the city lights bleed out through it, at the way other lights shine here and there within it, at the way its black blurs into the greater dark of deeper ocean. He feels himself drifting. He feels his brain going as blank as it did before the launch. He feels that city unfolding through him. He wonders what's going on inside it.

But the next instant, he doesn't have to wonder.

Ancient zone's suddenly crystal clear. Check out those corners coming up everywhere. Check out those doorways where there weren't even walls before. Check it out: Haskell's perspective telescopes outward in all directions. She watches as openings take their place within larger structures.

It's just like Morat said. She's staring backward into time. She's gazing at long-ago wreckage. The map of old Belem clicks into her head, along with all that city's infrastructure—and the lines she's in wind among that infrastructure, just a few wires among so many millions. Somehow these survived. Somehow they weren't dug up. Somehow they got overlooked.

She sees why. They got disconnected, the ends sealed. But there's still data swimming through these lines. An isolated network: and some of the data within looks legit—small-time enterprise trying to eke out existence amidst the urban chaos. But most of it's small-time crime: porn, snuff, drugs—all the flavors of vice licking back and forth in search of download. And there's a lot of download points, too—lot of illicit subscribers, paying for the right to get some kind of net.

This doesn't surprise Haskell. Access to the main zone, the integrated zone—the *American* zone—can't be taken for granted. Not down here. Ninety-nine percent of the population on the northern continent's a part of it, but that number plummets the farther south you get. Meaning that those in the Latin fringes just have to make do. These zone-fragments are illegal. But as long as the Jags aren't involved, no one cares.

But that's the point. That's why she's looking at all the data set in motion by those who pay protection to the local gangs for the use of rogue systems powered by rogue generators that squat in forgotten basements and derelict rooms. That's why she's trying to determine what the larger pattern used to be—intimations of supply lines that once wound inland from the sea...query grids stacked along the floor... even graffiti on the walls: taglines left by bored programmers long since buried far deeper than these wires. She cruises up and down those long-gone roads. She runs up stairways, down ramps, through shafts.

And all the while, she does her best to keep it stealthy. Because she knows her eyes may not be the only ones scanning. She knows that if they're looking, she probably won't know it—that if they see her, she might not even guess. She might not even feel it coming either—just one bolt from the black to smack her dream-body senseless, send her meat-body flopping on the floor of the warehouse that's so far away that she can barely remember what it was like. But that's the nature of the recon. That's the nature of this probe.

Which now detects something. Two things, actually. Anomalies. Each of them concealing the other. She can't see one without seeing both. And they're in different places. It's a neat trick. But she's trickier. She strips away all the history, rips out all the nonessential. She tunes out every last fragment of peripheral traffic, regards what's left.

These anomalies aren't data. They're doors. They're white where all else is black. They're stars in the land of void. They're lava in the land of ice. They're different. She takes the readings, confirms them, locks in the references. She approaches those gateways. Reaches them. Looks through.

And watches as zone-shard shifts from universe to foreground.

This is no isolated fragment. She's looking at the Jaguar net. There's no doubt now. The contours of it show at least some of the codes her own side has captured in the past. It shows her others she's never seen. Not to mention an expanse she never would have dreamt of. In one direction she can see something that leaps away from the city, tunneling under jungle and through mountains, all the way to what must be Lima, where it opens up to still more networks. In another direction's Sao-Rio. She imagines those conduits: old telephone lines, cables, comlinks run beneath the floor of jungle before it all came crashing down. She can see that the place she's been crawling in is a nexus. That the Jaguars have been using it to link their operations elsewhere with their operations in this city. She traces those links in turn and can see all the data now. The structure's clear enough: patchwork quilt of legacy, and this place is just one thread. Belem-Macapa is just one piece. Just one limb in a stitched-together body.

So where the fuck's the brain?

Because once she's mapped that, she can get out. Back to Sinclair's people. Back to the ones who put her in here. *She* gets the maps. *They* work out the vectors. And then they wipe out the Jags in one clean sweep.

Something catches her eye. New data seems to be flowing. Haskell focuses on a series of lines that carry particularly heavy traffic. Each line winds through buildings. Each terminates in what looks to be a dead end. But something's crouching at each of those ends. Something that seems to be winding up through incremental stages of activation.

Even as she takes this in, she's noticing the same thing going down in other cities. Sao-Rio. Greater Caracas. Japura. In each city, it's the same: communications back and forth. Things being queried. Things responding . . . but what does it mean? Is this a pattern she's just now seeing? Is something changing? Is this the key to it all? Was this happening already? She can't figure it out.

For just another moment, she lets it clarify. During which time those nodes keep brightening. To the point where she realizes it's not just her focus getting better. It's not just her read on this place improving. These changes are real. They're making her current position far too dangerous. The Jaguars could be on to her. She's got to beat a retreat. She's got enough to go on. She starts to withdraw.

But they move first.

Marlowe looks around. The chamber he's in is perhaps twenty meters by another fifteen. At least one level has been cut away above it to accommodate its vaulting ceiling. Yet in all this space, it's the center of the room that really gets Marlowe's attention.

Because that's where the missiles are.

Five of them. All of them protruding from a cylinder-shaped launcher that sits upon a dais. Each is about three meters long, with the green cat-skull of the Jaguars painted upon its nose cone. All around lie consoles, electronic equipment, bundles of wire. Marlowe creeps in toward the launcher. Smoke from the flames behind him is beginning to waft into the room. But he pays it no heed. He reaches that center structure and leaps forward, vaulting over it, holding his arms and guns perfectly level.

Two meters in front of where Marlowe's just landed, a man sits cross-legged, calmly gazing up at him. The man's skin is darker than that of any of the guerrillas Marlowe has encountered thus far. Greyish-black hair falls down around his shoulders. He regards Marlowe with a strange mixture of interest and indifference. His eyes are as black as his hair must once have been.

"Yanqui." The voice is low. It sounds almost amused. "You were too fast for us. We thought we would have had more warning. We failed to prepare for just one man."

The Jaguar's stalling for time is transparent. But Marlowe needs information. This is almost certainly the man he's charged with bringing back—but the missiles have changed the nature of the mission automatically. The man opens his mouth to speak again, but Marlowe cuts him off: "Where'd you get the missiles?"

"Missiles?" The man rises to his feet. He smiles. Marlowe's wrists flex upon the edge of trigger. "I see no missiles. All I see are the teeth of the Great Cat."

"The jaguar?"

"You defile its name even as you speak it, Yanqui. Just as you defile our land. Do you not recognize these weapons? When the gate to their cage is lifted, they will go faster than the wind, and they have more cunning than do mere men."

"You're saying that these missiles are hypersonic?" Marlowe doesn't dare turn and inspect the engines to confirm the claim. "Tell me where you got them, or I am going to kill you."

"Shoot me if you like, then, Yanqui—" Accepting the invitation, Marlowe lowers his left arm and switches to regular ammo, blowing the man's right kneecap into splinters. Blood and flesh spray through the air. The man goes down—and then rolls over and looks up at Marlowe. Blood's pouring from his shattered leg. He's still smiling. And still speaking as calmly as before.

"My soul has already gone to join my ancestors, Jason Marlowe. But I left my body behind to tell you that the Jaguar of all our souls is even now among us. Ready to purge this land of all who oppress us. Ready to lick clean your bones. Are you listening now, Yanqui?"

"How do you know who I am?" says Jason Marlowe, and thrusts one of his guns into the man's smiling face. "So help me God, man, you'd better tell me what you're saying."

"But I'm saying nothing you can understand." Spittle flicks onto the barrel of Marlowe's weapon. "Except for the fact that your people are about to be dealt retribution in full. As for how I know your name—Paynal, He Who Walks Upon the Wind and Carries Their Decrees, has imparted much to me. He has informed me that They have decided that if you can pass Their servant's test of quickness, then you are worthy to play your part in the final drama."

"If you keep talking, the next bullet's going straight through your teeth." Marlowe knows he shouldn't even bother to make the threat. He knows that he should kill this man right now. But he also knows that he won't. Now he's wondering if he'll be able to shoot him at all. Somehow this crippled man bleeding on the floor has gained the upper hand.

As if sensing his advantage, the man laughs. "The test of quickness, Yanqui. In your language they call it 'beating the bullet,' do they not? But no matter—you've already failed it, as you sit here prattling with me. For behold, my spirit-guardians have crossed the threshold and are here to join us—and in mere seconds so will my mortal sentinels." As the man speaks, Marlowe suddenly senses a presence moving up behind him, creeping in between the blind spots of his sensors. He can even *see* it—some kind of cat that seems to almost glide around the base of the missile platform, its tensing muscles rippling as it prepares to strike—

Whirling, Marlowe confronts only air—and then instinct saves his life, for instead of drawing up dumbfounded, he keeps moving, diving as his adversary's knife (replete with powered saw-edges to shear through even heavy armor) flies through the space where his head had been a moment before. Dive seamlessly switches to somersault, leaving him on the floor, firing backward over his head, riddling the man with bullets. The whole action has taken less than two seconds. Whoever he was, this man is now dead.

His comrades, however, are clearly still alive. Marlowe can hear shouts drawing closer—the blaze-battling operation reclaiming this piece of the building. Marlowe leaps to his feet, turns his attention to rigging a hi-ex charge onto the missiles   and discovers that the situation is even worse than he'd thought. Not only are the missiles hypersonic, but so are the payloads: each nose cone contains ten tactical warheads, each one fixed to its own hypersonic motor and capable of acting as an autonomous missile anytime after firing. How many more such missiles might there be in this city, sitting inside a continental defense perimeter that encompasses three-fifths of the U.S. launch infrastructure, each base crouched within its own defenses—defenses that would be hard-pressed to withstand an assault with this kind of weapon from this kind of range ... the implications keep on stacking up in Marlowe's mind, and each is but one pulse in the staccato blast of signals that he's sending out toward the jet-copters and zeppelins overhead, toward the satellites an instant beyond—but none of them can hear him: Marlowe's signals are bouncing back upon him. The room's walls must be lined with something—anything to prevent those outside from probing to discover its contents.

Then two men race into the room. Marlowe scarcely looks up to shoot them down. His bomb-rack tosses more grenades through the doorway through which they've come. Then he sets the missile controls to manual, starts the ignition sequence. He starts racing forward, extends the fins on his armor. He sees the walls in front of him begin to slide away, just as he'd hoped they would. Fragments of cityscape glimmer through the heaped mountains of the chem-smoke. He hears thunder roar to life behind him—feels himself seized by his thrusters, hurled forward, out into the city.

He watches the 'scraper falling away behind him, sees a sudden flash blossom behind him as his charge detonates. None of that explosion's nuclear. The charge was set to destroy those warheads. But the blast must have touched off a Jaguar ammunition cache: because now the walls around the floor where he just was rupture, blast outward, tumble downward even as the whole building totters—and then collapses. It comes down like a house of cards, debris flying up in great chunks as it disappears into the murk below—and Marlowe refuses to think about the innocents he's just killed, because there might have been still more missiles in that building, and what in God's name does *innocent* mean down here anyway?—what did it ever mean?—so he's just blasting on upward, searing right past other buildings, broadcasting the specs, the situation—everything—to anyone who'll listen.

This time everyone hears. But no one has time to do a thing about it.

• • •

Like rain falling in reverse: the Operative watches through widened eyes as thousands of missiles rise out of the gloom that swathes Belem-Macapa. The def-grids swing into action: satellites start raining countermeasures down upon those weapons—and upon the city beneath. The Operative winds his vision up and down the scale of magnification, takes in a blaze of lights, takes in the clouds of missiles climbing up the gravity well. Many are winking out of existence. Many are arcing back toward the Earth. Many just keep climbing. The Operative stares transfixed as they move toward him. He can't see if they're going to plunge down upon the planet or try to make it all the way to vacuum.

But what he can see is that the city from which they launched is writhing under the def-grids' barrage. If it was burning before, it's positively incandescent now. The glow shining through the smoke is visible from space. The Operative can see it without amplification.

Until a shutter slides across the window. The Operative tries to disconnect it. Nothing doing. He curses—and stops cursing as he feels the ship start to rumble. The attitudinal jets are firing. The Antares is turning on its axis. He braces himself for the burn that will send the ship hurtling toward the Moon and as far away from this mess as possible. He waits for it. But the seconds keep on ticking by.

It's all happening around Haskell. But not in the way she expected. Suddenly the Jaguar net's diminished: nearly all the terminal nodes vanish. Information flows behind in their wakes—shows the trail of exhaust that's splattering over the naked faces of the instruments that sit in the physical world, shows Haskell ghost-images of things

fast receding, swimming out into the sky that can't even begin to match the one she's in. She stares.

She gets it.

Even as they almost get her. They spot her for real. She
doesn't know how. Maybe it was some random check. Maybe
it was their sudden shift to full war footing. Maybe they've
been stalking her the whole time. It doesn't matter. What
matters is the long, scaled tongue that suddenly flicks toward
her from out of the inky depths. She dodges. It misses. She retracts. It comes after her. She takes evasive action, takes herself in among all that data, does her best to blend in. All she
needs is a moment. But it needs far less than that to nail her. It
sails in toward her. She sees it as it really is: a grinning cat-
skull that's nothing but jaws enclosing her. She scatters herself into pieces, confuses it for a moment. But not nearly long
enough. It looms before her eyes. She meets its eyes.

But suddenly it's reeling. It flails. She flails with it. What
else can she do? This net is under attack. It's being pummeled.
It's cauterizing whole sections of itself in the name of survival. Whole portions of existence are getting sheared off. The
links to all those cities disappear. They're gone. The lines
through which she's racing are buckling. Yet all the while
the scattered fragments of her body are converging upon the
light. She sees it now: the square that denotes transition. The
door to salvation. The way out. She sails toward it. And still
that tongue follows her. It reaches for her heart. It winds
about her leg. She dissolves that leg. She raises her arms. She
shouts.

And jacks out.

Smoke is streaming in front of her eyes. Sparks are coming off the cluster of screens. The room's shaking—just as
she's being shaken by Morat. He pulls the jacks straight off
her. Pieces of her skin go with them. She blinks. She bleeds.
She looks at him. He looks at her. Smoke pours between them.

"We have to leave right now," he says quietly.

"No shit," she says.

That's when soldiers on thrusters land amidst them, haul them out of the room without a ceiling, over the maze that's not a maze, back out into the warehouse. Back out to the elevator. The room's on fire. Smoke's pouring down the catwalks. Noise is everywhere. The soldiers cluster around them.

Morat turns to one. "Lieutenant—what's the status outside?"

"They're attacking in strength all along the perimeter, sir."

"How close are they to this building?"

"Sir, we think they're inside, sir."

"You *think* so?"

"We've lost contact with everybody beneath level forty."

Morat shoves Haskell forward, sending her stumbling toward the lieutenant.

"Take the razor," he says. "Save the razor. Take her up the shaft right now. Do it yourself. What's left of your platoon can get in there and be the shields. I don't care who gets hit. I don't care who dies. Just *save the fucking razor*. Get her out of here. Assume this hedgehog's getting overrun. Assume we're fucked. *Do you understand me?*"

"Yes, sir," replies the lieutenant. "What about you?"

"Leave one squad with me. We'll dismantle this equipment and follow you."

"Sir: if they're inside the building, you won't make it."

"Don't tell me what I will or won't make," says Morat. "Just go."

They're going. And Haskell knows why he's staying. To gather the equipment—or make sure it's properly destroyed. So he won't have to tell Matthew Sinclair that he let the Jaguars root through everything CICom knows about their net. The soldiers are blasting the elevator doors down, adding to the smoke inside the room. They don't take Morat's instructions literally, though. The lieutenant's got the most guns. So he hands her to one of the sergeants. Soldiers scramble into the elevator, ignite their thrusters. Some go up the shaft, some go down. The elevator car's well below them. They rain explosives down upon it, send it crashing down for good. The sergeant grabs Haskell with both arms—"Sorry about this, ma'am," she says, and steps forward, leaps. Haskell feels the heat of the jets on her face. She's being hauled upward. Floors whiz past. Cables streak by. All of it's wreathed in flame and shadow. Haskell feels the distance between her and sky narrowing.

Something slams against her. She hears an explosion. She hears a scream. She feels something wet hit her face. She feels her escort's grip loosening. She tumbles from that dead grasp. She starts to fall down the shaft.

Something grabs her. "Got ya"—and she's pressed into his arms: "for fuck's sake protect her head," someone shouts, and someone else is screaming that the Jags are in the shaft, and she finds herself thinking it must have been a trap after all. But she's just clinging on to this arm, on to both arms, and her face is pressed up against the side of the soldier's visor, and through it she can see distorted eyes peering intently past her at what's reflected in that same visor: the ceiling shooting down toward her like she's in a needle and it's the plunger—and then the soldiers open fire and blast it away and they all blast straight through onto the roof.

Which is a shambles. As is everything beyond it. Buildings are burning, collapsing. Beams from heaven stab here and there, shimmer in the fog. The thunder of detonations rolls across the city. Belem-Macapa's entered a new stage of its agony. The soldiers on the roof are firing in all directions. Haskell's escorts shove her through a jet-copter's open hatch. They're screaming at the pilot to gun it. He needs no such urging: the 'copter rises. Haskell's being strapped in by its gunner. She's about to pull on her breath-mask: but now the doors slide shut and the craft switches over to its own recycled air as its motors switch into overdrive. She's watching the rooftop fall away. Everything turns to cloud.

Suddenly there's another explosion, and way too close—the rumbling of the engines shreds away into a high-pitched whining. The 'copter staggers. For a moment, it continues on its course.

But only for a moment.

"What the fuck's happening?" yells the gunner.

"We're going to crash," the pilot says matter-of-factly.

The gunner's lost it. He's screaming. But Haskell's saying nothing. She's just lying back as the craft plummets downward. The plummet's not total. The pilot's still got some kind of control. But only just. They churn through smog. Buildings whip by. She hears the gunner praying. She hears the pilot cursing. He's working the controls with more than just his hands—twisting his whole body this way and that, as though he could pull the craft out of its descent through sheer muscle. But to no avail. They scream in above a rooftop, just miss a pylon. She catches a glimpse of water. She catches a glimpse of ships. She thinks she must be dreaming. She braces herself.

They hit.

Marlowe can't do anything but keep moving. His camos are turned up to the full. He's stealing through the city like a wraith. He's staying indoors whenever he can—hurtling down corridors, rising up shafts. He leaves his thrusters offline whenever he's outside. He doesn't want to make himself any more of a target than he already is. All he wants to do is get out of here.

Which is going to be tough. He's glad his suit still has atmosphere despite the battering it's taken. Because oxygen's become a major factor. As has heat. The temperature's at least twenty degrees warmer than when he made his entrance. It's not hard to understand why. The flames off to the south are as tall as the buildings around which they lick. Their light brings a new kind of shadow to this dark. He's intent on getting as far away from it as possible.

Nor is he the only one with that idea. The mob's afoot at every level of the town. They're swarming over the skyways, doing their utmost to escape. Marlowe's trying to take the road less traveled. He's trying to avoid the stampede.

Not to mention the fighting. Which is everywhere. Machines swarm like insects. The local militias are giving everything they've got. Before tonight, most of them would never have dared to take on the United States directly. Now they've got the inspiration. Or maybe just the insanity. And wherever the Americans aren't in range, old scores are being settled. Local rivalries are being carried through to culmination. Artillery's going to work from the rooftops, even as those rooftops get sheared off. Vehicles are exchanging fire with one another as they move along those bridges. Hi-ex is going off like it's going out of style. The further out of control this gets the more Marlowe recalls being told how smooth it was all going to be. He can see the faces of his handlers all too clearly— those honeyed words, those knowing smiles. It's all he can do to stop himself from smiling now.

But he restrains himself.

The Operative is having difficulty keeping himself in check. He's cut off, with no way to tell what's going on outside. There may still be trouble on the Elevator. There's definitely still trouble going on below. He envisions all strategic reserves being rushed into the Latin cities: troops dropping down from orbit, buildings getting smashed, whole blocks laid to waste.

But all that's only retaliation. It can't turn back the clock. Nor can it tell him what's going on. Is there a connection between the mutiny on the Elevator and the missiles from the city? Could some of those missiles have been aimed at the Elevator? The Operative doesn't know. Nor does he know the extent to which he's already caught up in it. He'd love to just ride this one out. He'd be happy to just slip right on by. He doubts that's going to happen.

So now he's thinking furiously. The Elevator. The Earth. This ship: in theory, crew of two. But in practice, God only knows how many they've got in that cockpit. And if they end up turning out to be hostile, that's not the only place they might be. Adjacent to his feet are hatches leading to the cargo-modules. There's a lot of volume that way. The Operative pictures all those chambers. He pictures all that cargo. He thinks of how easy it would be to hide in there. . . .

With an effort, he draws himself back from his own mind's edge. There's a reason they sent him. It may be the reason he's in this right now. He can't make any assumptions. Least of all about the nature of the mission. Missions have a way of changing. They also have a way of only revealing their true nature once they've started. Besides—if there really *is* any trouble on this ship, he knows what to do. He won't even have to think. However many of them there are: he'll make them wish they never heard the word *airlock*. In truth he's starting to feel that way already. He's starting to wonder why he's waiting. After all, those bastards in the cockpit have cut him off, deprived him of his data. He's in dire need of more. He can think of exactly one way to get it.

Haskell becomes aware that something's wrong. She's cold. She's wet. She doesn't know where she is. All she knows is she's tilting on her side. There's a noise coming from somewhere. A voice.

"Ma'am. Can you hear me, ma'am?"

"I can," she mumbles.

"You've got to wake up."

"Why?"

It all comes back in one awful rush. They've crashed. This is aftermath. She opens her eyes. She's still strapped into the cabin of the jet-copter. It's mostly dark. It's leaning toward one side at a nasty angle. It's half-filled with water. The gunner's lying in that water, body contorted at unnatural angles. The upside-down face of the pilot is peering into her own. He's leaning down from the hatch that's now become the ceiling.

"Where are we?"

"We're in the drink," he says. "And you'll be in your grave if you don't take those straps off and climb up here. Can you do it?"

"I don't know," she replies.

"Try."

So she does. She undoes the straps. She hauls herself up them to where the man's hands are waiting. She ignores those hands—instead grasps the edge of the hatch. Everything hurts. But it seems like it's all still functional. She pulls herself up onto the top of the stricken jet-copter. She crouches there, takes in the river. The water's lit up by the flames licking from buildings on either side of shore. A mirror image of those flames looms within the water, torn through with ships. Cranes tower over Haskell's head. Tracers and lasers whip through the smog. It looks like a total free-for-all.

"This isn't good," she says.

"No," he says. "It really isn't."

"Is your gunner dead?"

"He isn't the only one."

She looks at him. He seems very young. He doesn't seem scared. He crouches there with her.

"You're beautiful," he murmurs.

"We're not going to die," she replies.

She pulls on her breath-mask. There's a whining in the air

close at hand. The pilot looks at her in surprise. His eyes cease to focus—he tumbles off the 'copter and into the water. Haskell throws herself back inside the craft as more bullets strike its hull. She hangs from the door's edge, her feet dangling in the water that's flooding the craft. She pulls her head up through the doorway.

To find herself gazing at figures on the far shore. They're sweeping her position with fire. They're cramming themselves into ships that line the docks—ships that now float out into the water, start their motors. Shots smash in around Haskell. Shouts carry across the water. The words that shouting contains aren't coherent. They don't need to be. Haskell's never heard such venom. She's beaming out the emergency evac codes. She's praying. She's getting no response from either. She resolves to do the only logical thing before they get their hands on her. She takes out the pistol Morat gave her, checks it over. She starts counting off the final seconds.

M arlowe's picking up steam. He's out of the worst trouble spots. He's got his thrusters going. He's more than halfway through the city. He's going straight on through till he gets out into country. It's a simple plan. It doesn't need to get complex. Nothing's touching him. Nothing's seeing him. He's got it made.

It's then he gets the call.

"Marlowe," says the voice.

"Yeah."

"We need you to take a little detour."

"Yeah?"

"We've got an asset down near you."

"So?"

"So we need it picked up."

"This suit's taken a beating. You've got no one else who can do it?"

"If we did, I wouldn't be calling. We're coming apart at the seams, Marlowe. We've got a grade-A disaster on our hands."

"Which I'm almost clear of."

"And you'll get clear again. You're hell on wheels, Marlowe. You've got to make all speed. Over and out."

Even as the last words are reaching Marlowe's ears, coordinates flare before him. They show city. They show river. They show the point where he needs to be. They show his own position—now rapidly changing direction.

L isten," says the Operative.

The one word hangs in the chamber with him. His is the only voice that's sounding. He's the only one who definitely hears it. He doesn't let that stop him.

"I know you're watching. I know you're listening. I'm not on your manifest. But here I am anyway."

There's no reply. The Operative regards the door to the cockpit. It's heavy. It's sealed. He unstraps himself. He floats away from the window and pulls himself toward that door.

"You were told to take me aboard and run me to the rock. You were told to ask no questions while you did it. Not like you need to. You know all that matters already."

He reaches the door. He runs his hand along its edges. They're absolutely airtight. In the event of hull breach, ships go modular. The Operative lets his fingers slide down its metal grooves. He smiles. He keeps on talking.

"You were hoping you weren't going to get any closer to me. You were hoping not to breathe the air that I'm inhaling. So was I. No reason I'd want to make this complicated."

He stops the movement of his fingers, pulls his hand away from the door. He holds on to the walls on either side. He turns his body slowly in the zero-G. He looks directly into one of the cameras. The smile broadens on his face.

"But now it's very simple. You're going to open this door or I'm going to open it for you. Might not be much of a door left by that point. Might not be much left of my patience. But it's up to you. Long as you make up your minds right now. I'm going to count to three."

He's at two when the door slides open.

Marlowe's one klick out. He's got his thrusters flaming. He's got his full fins extended. He's burning in between the burning buildings. He cuts in above the river. He races just above its waters, rounds the bend beyond which his target lies. He opens fire.

The target's in a downed 'copter floating in the middle of this channel of the Amazon. Hydrofoils are closing in upon it. But Marlowe's not shooting at the ships. He's taking aim at the cranes that tower above them with his micromissiles, letting explosives strike home at points precisely calibrated. He watches the cranes start to topple.

Most of the militia never see it coming. They're smacked dead amidships by metal. They're knocked in pieces beneath the water. Those who aren't hit are taking hi-ex from Marlowe's second barrage. Detonations roll along the river. Heavy guns on the shore open fire. But he's accelerating in toward them, using the last of his micros to nail the buildings that loom above them. Debris buries the guns and all who man them.

Marlowe changes course once more, streaks in above

tangled metal and shattered ships. He cuts in toward the craft that's the cause of all the commotion. He alights upon it. Looks down.

Bullets smash into his helmet, bounce off. He leaps down to his assailant.

"I'm on your side," he says. "I'm CICom."

"Says who."

"Says my codes," he replies. He beams them to her.

Her contours show her for a woman. Her breath-mask prevents him from seeing her face. Which is fine by him. Faces are currency. No sense in giving them up for free. And yet there's something about this woman that grips him immediately. Maybe it's because she just tried to kill him. Maybe it's because she's still got that razorwire dangling from her head.

"Hold on to me," he says.

She doesn't want to. He can see that. But she does it anyway: steps toward him, embraces him, clasps her arms around his back, looks out over his left shoulder.

"I'm blocking your shoulder rack," she says.

"I'm shutting it down," he says. "Careful of the main motors."

"This isn't going to work," she replies. "You're going to be dodging left and right up there and you're going to shake me off."

"You're right," he says. "Get down."

She does. A hatch opens on one of his arms. He starts pulling something out.

"A tether," she says.

"Yeah," he says. "But I figure this is a better use for it than going up a wall. Get back up here."

She does, grabs the tether from him, starts lashing it about the two of them. He starts tying knots. A few loops and it's done.

"Is that too tight?" he asks.

"Not for what we're about to do," she says. She reaches down, pulls out her boot knife, slices off the excess tether.

"You ready?"

"Can you see?"

"Absolutely," he replies.

And reignites his suit's engines.

Face impassive, the Operative pulls himself through the doorway and into the cockpit. Two men sit within its cramped confines. One wears a cap. The other doesn't. On all sides are clustered all manner of instrument banks. Narrow windows cut through those banks. Space flickers in those windows.

"So here he is," says the man with the cap. Beneath his headpiece sits a pair of bushy eyebrows connected by a scar. The contours of his nose and cheekbones are angled in a way that makes his default expression a sardonic one.

"Yes," says the Operative.

"The man himself," says the hatless man, whose head is shaved clean like that of the Operative. This man's older. He looks at the Operative like he's gazing at a talking horse.

"I'm Riley," he says. He gestures at his colleague. "He's Maschler."

"You're the one I was speaking with," says the Operative.

"That's right," says Riley.

"You're the one who cut me off," says the Operative.

"Started you up too," says Riley. "Let's not forget that."

"We're the ones who hauled you from the bottom of the well," says Maschler. "We're the ones who broke your surly bonds. Without us you'd still be eating dirt. Surely that counts for something?"

"Oh," says the Operative, "it does."

They look at him. They're hanging on his every word. They don't want him to see that. But to him it's clear how on edge they are. He's never felt more relaxed.

"It's the reason I knocked," he adds.

"Ah," says Riley.

"And now you're going to tell me what's going on."

"Who says we know?" says Maschler.

"You know a hell of lot more than I do." The faintest edge is starting to creep into the Operative's voice. "You're in the cockpit of an Antares. You're hauling a few hundred tons of cargo. Your communications are supposed to be continual throughout the initial ramp. You've got cameras pointed in every direction. You've cut me off from the outside world because you thought I might be involved with what's going down. And I am. But only in the same way you are. So help me out here, gentlemen. Because it's the only way I can help you."

"You can't help," says Riley. "I wish you could."

"What's going on out there has nothing to do with us," says Maschler.

"It does now," replies the Operative softly.

"We just want to run our freight," says Riley. "We never looked for trouble."

"We should have shut off those cameras," says Maschler.

"It's okay," says the Operative. His voice is soothing. "It'll be okay."

Maschler and Riley look at each other. "You tell him," says Maschler.

"No you," says Riley.

"You start," says Maschler.

And Riley does.

• • •

 The journey upriver. Once you start along that winding road you don't stop. You just keep on rushing toward that distant source.

"You've set the water on fire."

"Like I had a choice."

He didn't want to. But there was too much floating hardware chasing them. So Marlowe's hit downstream with jets of flame. The fact that there's more pollution than water in that river means it's burning merrily. Now the only thing they have to outrace is fire. Smoke is wafting everywhere. The temperature's starting to rise.

"How you feeling?"

"Warm."

"But still breathing."

"I'll let you know when that starts to be an issue."

Marlowe figures that will be soon. The tolerance of a breath-mask is far lower than a suit's. The people out there must be dying in the thousands. And that's just in this district. He doesn't even want to think about the rest of it. The rising that the Jaguars had sought to bring about is finally underway. The city's final demise has finally begun. The canopy of smoke is growing ever thicker. The topography's getting ever more complex. The river keeps on forking—into channels that diverge, converge, intersect with one another. But Marlowe steers his way through them with the confidence of one who's got nothing save the latest maps.

"Complicated," says the razor.

"It's Amazon," he replies.

Roof closes in above this channel of the river. The smoke in here's too dense for anyone lacking masks to breathe. But through that smoke they can see the combat all around them. Looks like this is the day of reckoning among the river-pirates. Shantytowns along the shore are in the throes of combustion. The combatants spare scarcely a shot for the

ones now streaking past them and back into the open.
Though open's a relative concept. The smoke's almost thicker
than it was within that enclosure. The heat is overwhelming.
Marlowe's temperature readouts are climbing inexorably.

"We're not going to make it," he says.

"I know."

Not that it's not obvious now. The fires sweeping the
buildings on both shores are merging, covering the river
ahead. They're blocking the way forward. There's nothing but
smoke and flame in front of them. Oxygen's being sucked up
to heaven, taking God knows how many souls with it.

"One choice," he says.

"Right," she replies.

They streak upward.

Somewhere in that sky two men regard a third.
They're not accustomed to having their cargo
crash their party. They're not down with the notion
of taking orders from their freight. They're used to being
firmly in control.

They're making a rapid adjustment all the same.

"We don't know the whole story," says Riley.

"We don't know what the hell's going on," says Maschler.
"No one's told us a goddamn thing. We've been cut off."

"We only know what we can see."

"That's all I want," says the Operative.

"The missiles."

"Yes," replies the Operative.

"They weren't just from Belem-Macapa."

"They came from all the Latin cities."

"The damage is near total."

"Damage where?" says the Operative.

"They wiped out Cabo Norte."

"And three other major bases."

"Must have been quite a sight," says the Operative.

"But that was only half of them," says Riley.

"The other half were pointed upward," says Maschler.

"Pointed where?" asks the Operative.

Maschler and Riley look at one another. They look back at the Operative.

"Pointed *where?*" he demands.

"At the Elevator."

"And did they hit?"

"Of course not."

"They were climbing the whole way. They were sitting ducks."

"But they were just the first wave."

"The first wave," repeats the Operative.

"Yes," says Riley.

"And the second?"

"Was fired by the neutral satellites," says Riley.

"Seventeen of them," adds Maschler.

"All in close proximity to the Elevator."

"They unleashed space-to-spacers."

"At point-blank range."

"But the def-grids rallied."

"They turned those weapons into powder."

"They did the same to the satellites."

"Sure wish you guys had let me catch this live," says the Operative.

"What else could we do?" says Maschler. "This way, we have no records of it. We never have to admit we saw it."

"You and a hundred thousand other people," laughs the Operative. "Earth-to-spacers try to nail the Elevator? Space-to-spacers rigged on neutral satellites try to finish the job? Are you kidding me? It's not like this is going to be much of a fucking secret."

But he knows he's wrong even as he speaks the words.

Secrets aren't a function of who knows them. They're a function of who doesn't. The sky's been classified for fifty years now. Civilians can neither write nor film what it contains. Those who wear uniforms have more leeway. But they know when to be discreet.

Especially when they're seeing things they've never imagined seeing.

"Besides," says Maschler, "we didn't know what your role in all this was."

"My role," replies the Operative. One eyebrow arches.

"You could be a plant."

"You could be a sleeper."

"A sleeper for who," says the Operative.

"For the Jaguars," says Maschler.

"This is much bigger than the Jaguars," objects Riley.

"This is the devil's night," says Maschler.

"Because of those missiles," says the Operative.

"Never mind those missiles."

"The missiles don't matter."

"Then what does?" says the Operative.

"This," says Riley.

He hits a switch. The lights in the cockpit fade. The stars intensify. Riley gestures at the left-hand window—points toward a strand of luminescence strung among the stars.

"That's the Elevator," he says.

"Yeah," says the Operative.

"Listen to me. She's got forty main motors. One every hundred klicks. She's firing them all on full-retro. She's been doing that for the last five minutes. At the rate she's going, her lowest point is going to hit atmosphere in five more."

Maschler's hands play over the keyboards. One of the display screens lights up. A complicated pattern floats atop it. Green lights drift toward a larger strand of blue.

"That's the space around this section of the Elevator," he says. "At least a hundred ships are moving in from all directions. A lot of those ships are ours. But we think some of them belong to the East. It looks to be a coordinated operation."

"Is this going on at other levels of the Elevator?" asks the Operative.

"Yes," says Riley.

"And no one's signaled to you what's going on," says the Operative.

"What the hell would they signal?" asks Riley.

"What else is there to say?" asks Maschler.

"The Elevator's been jacked."

"We're forfeit."

"But at least," says the Operative, "you had the good sense to tell me all about it."

They have the good sense to speed up as they climb. They roar out of smoke that's drifting up from city-cellars. They roar into smoke that's drifting down from the city's middle layers. They race through patches of smog even thicker than that smoke.

"How are we doing?" the razor asks.

"I can't tell."

"Makes two of us."

Wind tears against them. It's all Marlowe can do to keep control. Particularly given how much damage his suit's sustained. He adjusts his main jets, compensates with steering thrusts from his wrists and ankles, adjusts again.

"You strapped in okay?" he says.

"I'll let you know as soon as I'm not."

Buildings tower above them. They rise past more fires. They start to draw fire of their own. Lasers flare past. Bullets hum by. Marlowe starts to take evasive action.

"This is getting tight."

"Militia hotbeds," says Marlowe.

"So why are we going through them?"

"Because they've got to peter out eventually."

"What makes you so sure?"

"Because we've almost reached the Citadel."

From whose confines the U.S. props up one part of the fiction that's called Brazil. Toward whose shelter Marlowe and his passenger are now racing. But now Marlowe's picking up something on his screens. Something that he's less than happy to see.

To put it mildly.

"Pursuit," he says.

"How far back?"

"Couple klicks."

And closing. Suited Jaguars: there are several of them. Rising from the depths of city. Spread out in a wide formation. He can see their suits' jets flaring. He can see rocket-propelled grenades streaking from their arms. He veers off at an angle, starts to weave in amidst the buildings.

"Full-strength strike squad," he says.

"They must have tracked me," says the razor.

"They must have tracked *me*," says Marlowe.

"Sounds like we've both given them reasons to hate us."

"God I hope so."

"We need more speed."

Marlowe's trying. He's pouring it on. But he has to keep taking evasive action to avoid getting hit by the warring militias. He has to keep dodging. Which means he can't go hell for leather on the straight. Which means they're being overhauled.

Quickly too.

"Feed me your data," says the razor.

"Why?"

"So I can help you help us."

"Fine."

If there's something she can pull, he's all for it. He sends her his armor's signals. He senses her somehow reversing those signals. Suddenly she's tapping into his comps. She's right inside his head.

"What the fuck!" He almost loses control, finds his gyros steadied by a mind that's not his own.

"I feel so close to you," she replies. Her voice is emanating from in between his ears. It sounds amused.

"Who asked you?" he says.

"You," she replies.

"What are you doing?"

"Using your brains," she replies. "Or rather, your suit's."

And she is. She's commanding that processing power while Marlowe sends them flying over farther upward. Her mind is meshed with his. And both minds can see that now the Jaguars are getting out on their flanks. Classic pincer movement. In a few more moments they're going to close the noose.

"One chance," says Marlowe.

"Agreed," she says.

They move together in the moment.

Three men in a room that's no ordinary room. Lights of controls play upon their faces. Lights of space play upon their minds. These three men know they should never have met. They know they shouldn't be here. They know they should be well past the edifice that lurks outside.

But there it is in the window anyway.

"What do you think we should do?" asks Riley.

"Who says we have to do anything?" replies the Operative.

"Because that's a military operation going on out there," says Maschler. "Because we're right in its vicinity."

"Precisely why we're doing nothing that'll call attention to ourselves," says the Operative.

"But it's not like they can't see us," protests Maschler.

"Exactly. We're just one more piece of freight."

"If we wait ten more minutes, we'll leave the window," says Riley.

"We'll have to make our way around the planet again," adds Maschler.

"I don't think you understand," says the Operative. "Break for the Moon now, and those ships will break you into pieces."

"Are you sure?" says Riley.

"How do you know?" says Maschler.

"It's what I'd do," says the Operative simply.

"But we have to do *something*," says Maschler.

There's a flash in the window. All three men shift, pivot— do whatever they have to do to turn in the zero-G toward it. They see the problem immediately. Something's just exploded nearby. The screens show beams of light stabbing forth from the Elevator. Another ship detonates even as they watch. The telescoping cameras take it all in—take in ships maneuvering across space, taking evasive action, doing whatever they have to do to render themselves more difficult to hit. From points elsewhere, directed energy lashes back at the Elevator. The cannonade stops.

The maneuvering continues.

"Yeah," says the Operative. "I guess staying here's a little problematic."

"That's what we've been telling you," says Riley.

"Current orbit's not going to get us out of here quick enough," says the Operative, as though Riley hadn't spoken.

"Who the *fuck* is on that thing?" says Maschler.

"Shall I hit the gas?" asks Riley.

"You'll do nothing of the kind," says the Operative.

"What do you mean?" says Riley.

"What the hell are you on?" asks Maschler.

"All sorts of things," says the Operative evenly. "But what I said a moment ago still applies. Start this bitch up, and our boys will finish you forever."

"Then what the fuck are you suggesting we do?"

"*We're* going to do nothing," says the Operative. They look at him. Maschler starts to splutter protest. The Operative holds up a hand to silence him.

"But as for me," he adds, "I'm going to make a call."

The mech changes course while Haskell starts raising hell with the suits of the strike squad. She slots herself in along now-familiar code-routes. She starts running interference on the pursuers' comlinks. And while she does, she and the mech are veering toward a building that's been subjected to heavy shelling. They streak through a hole in the building's side and into shattered halls. They burn through corridors, take down doors. They brake, turn, charge on up into elevator shafts, climbing as fast as his motors will let them. Haskell clings tight. She feels minds out there writhing, feels walls surging past her. They brake to a halt in front of more doors, smash them down, break out of the shaft—hurtle down more corridors, find another opening, race back out into the city.

Catching the flank of the strike squad unprepared. Two suits, both within a quarter-klick: the mech's firing out along a broad front. He blasts one with armor-piercing rounds from his wrist-guns. He shreds the other's helmet with his mini-gun. He flies on past the tumbling bodies, pours on the speed. And while he does so, Haskell's putting pressure on the rest.

"How's it looking?"

"Fucked two more of their suits," she says. "The rest have disabled their links."

"But they're still intact."

"That would be a safe assumption."

Or at least the working one. They keep on burning upward. They figure they've bought themselves a few more seconds. And they're pretty much within the Citadel's outer perimeter now, moving in between the lesser hedgehogs. They should be safe.

Only they clearly aren't. There are still militia all around. And disconcertingly little combat. In fact, most of the militia don't even really seem to be fighting. They just seem to be moving. In the exact same direction that Haskell and the mech are going. They're driving their vehicles along the ramped skyways. They're flying their 'copters at full tilt. Haskell and the mech are weaving in and out of the really dense areas, using the smoke to provide all the cover it's worth.

But now the space around them is beginning to broaden and the smoke up ahead's clearing. The sky itself is coming into view.

So is the Citadel.

"Oh Jesus," says Haskell.

"Doesn't matter," replies the mech. "We're not stopping."

They streak in toward it.

The Elevator's center is more than two thousand klicks above the Earth. Which means it orbits at a slower rate than do ships at the level of the Antares. Now that it's got all its brakes on maximum, that delta's increased even further. It's moving out of the cockpit window, falling behind.

But as far as the Operative is concerned, it's still way too close for comfort.

"Don't bother calling," says Maschler. "Communications are fucked."

"When did you lose them?" asks the Operative.

"We never did," says Riley.

"Stop talking riddles," snaps the Operative.

Maschler shrugs. "All we've got is mission control on automatic feed. It's not like we're in touch with anything that's up for conversation. All we've got is just updates every minute confirming our position."

"And the order to stand by for translunar injection," says Riley.

"But no order to initiate the burn," says Maschler.

"We've tried to raise the emergency channels," adds Riley. "They're not responding. No one is. We've asked for clarification of the situation. We've received nothing."

"Let me try," says the Operative. "Key in whatever codes you need to give me access."

He couldn't pick up shit earlier. But that was when he was back in the bowels of the ship. Now he can pipe directly into the ship's own lines. He can commandeer the main comlinks. He can raise Earth directly.

So he does. Wireless signals dart out from within his skull, words wrapped within codes that vector through the ship's mainframe before streaking out into vacuum. The Operative plays with the frequencies, fine-tunes the direction of the dishes on the hull.

Somewhere on the planet something hears him.

"Get off this line," says a voice. It echoes in the Operative's head: a growl shot through with static. The weight of atmosphere hangs heavy on the words.

"I'm using the channel I've been instructed to use in case of contingency," replies the Operative. He chooses his words carefully. His lips aren't moving. Neural implants are doing all the work. "I'm following my orders. You can see my position."

"I can," says the voice. "What do you want?"

"I want confirmation of this ship's original flight plan to be relayed to its pilots."

"We can't do that," says the voice.

"Why not?" says the Operative.

"Because it's out of our hands. You've got a real knack for timing, Carson. The place is in lockdown up there. You're smack-dab in the middle of the largest joint U.S.-Eurasian operation ever conducted."

"So the East really is involved."

"What did you expect? The Elevator's joint property, isn't it?"

"What's happened to it?" asks the Operative.

"Hostiles have seized it," says the voice.

"No kidding," says the Operative dryly. He pauses. Then: "Who are we talking about here?"

"That," says the voice, "is the question that I'm going to have to cut you off to get back to."

"So it's not the Jaguars," says the Operative.

"Whoever it is is coordinating with them," says the voice. "That's the operating assumption. But we're having a hard time believing they're the ones who've managed to get aboard that thing. We recommend you hold tight for now. If the situation deteriorates, take whatever measures you have to in order to preserve the mission. But as long as the situation's stable, stay put."

"You've got a funny definition of the word *stable*," says the Operative.

But the presence in his head has disappeared. The voice is gone. The Operative's eyes refocus on the cockpit. He takes in the faces of Maschler and Riley.

"You okay?" says Maschler.

"Sure," says the Operative.

"Did you get through?"

"Sure," says the Operative.

"And?"

"And nothing."

"Nothing," says Maschler.

"Nothing?" asks Riley.

"You get used to it," says the Operative.

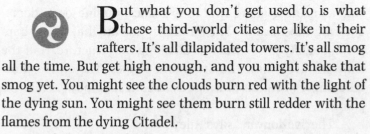 But what you don't get used to is what these third-world cities are like in their rafters. It's all dilapidated towers. It's all smog all the time. But get high enough, and you might shake that smog yet. You might see the clouds burn red with the light of the dying sun. You might see them burn still redder with the flames from the dying Citadel.

"Fuck," says Marlowe.

Half of the Citadel's towers are no longer visible. Its ramps hang askew in air. All too many of its platforms are shattered.

"So much for refuge," says the razor.

Yet as they rise past it, long sticks of light stab down from somewhere far overhead, shoot past them, and strike the complex below. Explosions flash out into the gathering dark. Towers topple into the murk that laps around them.

"Those are our guns."

"Yes," says Marlowe.

"We're killing our own side."

"Our own side's already been killed. That place has been taken."

"So keep on climbing."

He accelerates. They leave the Citadel behind, rush upward toward sky and sanctuary.

. . .

The Elevator's barely visible from the window anymore. But the cameras make up for everything the window lacks. The Elevator's lowermost point is starting to glow. It's hitting atmosphere. Far above, swarms of ships are closing.

"How long before we leave the launch window?" asks the Operative.

"Eleven minutes," says Riley.

The first ship touches. The telescoping lenses show powersuits clustering along that ship's sides, pulling open doors, entering the Elevator. The cameras indicate that this is happening at fifty-klick intervals all along the structure. Half the ships involved show the Stars and Stripes. The others show different sets of stars. Marines from both superpowers: they're going in.

"They've done it," says Riley.

"They're there," says Maschler.

"Prime the engines," says the Operative.

"I thought you said we weren't going anywhere," says Riley.

"Never say never," replies the Operative.

Besides: priming isn't the same as firing. The one enables the other. It doesn't compel it. So now Maschler and Riley are swinging into action. They're cycling fuel through the tanks, readying the trajectory, prepping everything they can. It gets their minds off the waiting.

But not for long.

"Who are they facing in there?" says Riley.

"Have they issued demands?" says Maschler.

"Now what would make you think I'd know a thing like that," replies the Operative.

"Well," says Riley, "do you?"

"I'd be guessing," says the Operative.

"Well," says Maschler, "what's your guess?"

"My guess," says the Operative, "is that there's only one demand."

Maschler and Riley look at him.

"Eat shit," he says.

Suddenly the cockpit lights up as though someone's stuck a blowtorch right outside it. The cameras show nothing save flash. The screens go haywire. Half of them show critical malfunctions. The other half are blank.

"We've got a problem," says Riley calmly.

"The Elevator's gone," says the Operative. "Give me heavy blast."

"Got it," says Maschler. He's back in his seat, wrestling with the controls. So is Riley. Who looks up with consternation on his face.

"Circuitry's been fried," he says.

"EMP," says the Operative.

"EMP," confirms Riley. "We've been swamped with fission."

"Fission," mutters Maschler.

"Shut up," snarls the Operative. "Switch to redundant systems."

"They'd be burned too," says Maschler.

"Better pray that's not so," says the Operative.

"Surely it's safer if we just hold course," says Maschler. "The blast's already hit us."

"He's right," says Riley. "The radiation's already soaked us. It's already done whatever damage it can. So what the fuck does it matter if we move now?"

"You're failing to take into account one thing," says the Operative.

He gestures at the window, at the space where the Elevator was. At the space where more explosions are appearing. Explosions of ships out there: ships getting struck by something that's getting nearer.

"*Debris*," he whispers.

• • •

Twilight's shredded by an overwhelming light. It blossoms through the eastern heavens. It's turning what's overhead into nothing save red. It's turning the mech's screens into nothing save static.

"Fuck," he says.

"What are we *in?*" yells Haskell.

What they're in is armor that just got fucked. It's sliding back down toward the city. The mech is fighting with the controls. So's Haskell.

"Allow me," she says.

"Have it your way," he replies.

Her way's tough. The EMP penetrated the damaged armor in several places. Nine-tenths of its circuits have been knocked out. Haskell's throwing together a network out of what's left. She's improvising. She's firing thrusters. She's clinging to the suit. She's not stopping its fall.

Just altering its direction.

"The Citadel," says the mech.

"Only chance," says Haskell.

"It's swarming with militia," he says.

"Who were being shelled by our space-to-grounders."

Meaning that maybe that militia isn't crowding the topmost floors. Though what the story is with those space-to-grounders now is anybody's guess. Because the sky itself is burning.

"Keep your eyes on the ground," yells Haskell. "I'm going to give this suit back to you in a second."

She's not kidding. Though when she says *ground* she's taking licenses. She's swooping in toward one of the Citadel's topmost ramps. She veers at it, hits the brakes—smacks straight into its surface. The suit skids, sprawls. Haskell reaches for her boot knife, slices through the tether that's holding her in place. She pulls herself to her feet.

The mech doesn't.

"Give me back control," he says.

"There's no control to give," she replies.

"Great," he says.

He hits the manual release and the armor comes open at the back like corn being shucked. He pulls himself out, pulls a breath-mask from a compartment as he does so, yanks it over his face. He gets to his feet.

And stares upward.

"Jesus fucking Christ," he says.

"He's not here," says Haskell.

But maybe He's coming. A line of silver is stitching across the sky. Liquid light running up and down the heavens: it's making mockery of darkness. It's breaking into pieces before their eyes.

"The Elevator," breathes Haskell.

"Must be," says the mech. "Get down."

Shots are whizzing above their heads. They're kissing ramp. They're crawling along it. They reach the door to the tower that it abuts and scramble inside. Bullets whine around them.

"Don't stop," says the mech.

Nor do they. They race up a stairwell. It's littered with bodies in and out of armor. Some of those bodies are still smoking. The mech gets in front of Haskell. They keep on climbing stairs.

They reach the topmost floor. The room's heaped with consoles and chairs and bodies. The air's still thick with the fumes from the firefight that went down here scant minutes ago. Through the windows they can see remnants of the Citadel still protruding above the clouds. One window's missing altogether—along with part of the wall around it. The whole scene shines with unearthly light.

"Stay away from the windows," says the mech.

"To the roof."

Haskell pulls open one last door, sprints up one last set of stairs. These are narrower. They end at a trapdoor on the ceiling. She pulls it open. The sky that's revealed isn't really sky anymore. It's just something twisting through all manners of colors.

"Now what?" says the mech. He's still standing at the bottom of the staircase, trying to cover the control room and trapdoor simultaneously.

"Now we get help," says Haskell.

"Can you raise anyone?"

"I can't even signal."

The EMP pulse fucked her head almost as much as his armor. Half her thoughts have faded into blur. Half her eyescreens are gone. She can still function. But her zone capability is gone.

"So how are you going to get us out of here?"

"Let me get back to you on that," she replies.

"Fuck," says Maschler.

"No luck on the redundants," says Riley.

"Reboot," says the Operative.

"Already tried that," says Maschler.

"So do it again."

They shut the whole thing down, slot new batteries in, start it back up again. The batteries work. The screens flare back to life. But there's no life in them. They're spewing gibberish.

"Fuck," says Riley.

"Maybe all that shit's going to miss," says Maschler.

"Care to stake your life on it?" asks the Operative.

"What would you have us do?" asks Riley.

"I'd have you start the engines," says the Operative.

"Thanks," says Maschler.

"Let me clarify," says the Operative. "You've already lined us up. We don't need to steer. All we need to do is fire the burners."

"Huh," says Riley.

"So?" asks Maschler.

"So how do I get to the motors?"

"Go outside," says Riley.

"Great," says the Operative. "Let's go."

"All of us?" asks Riley.

"You and I will suffice."

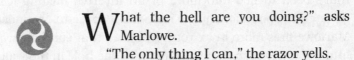 "What the hell are you doing?" asks Marlowe.

"The only thing I can," the razor yells.

She's firing tracer rounds through the trapdoor, letting them go at rapid intervals to flare across the sky.

"Morse code," she says.

"They're probably a little busy up there," says Marlowe. He goes from body to body, taking various devices: several grenades and a phosphorus charge that someone apparently was about to detonate to prevent this room from falling into Jaguar hands. Marlowe hooks his newfound possessions onto his belt. He hears a noise outside, looks up.

Just in time to see something roar past the window.

He screams at the razor to stop firing. She does. They hear something land on the roof.

"They must have come up from the basement," Marlowe shouts.

"We've got no armor," whispers the razor.

Marlowe looks around the control room. The suit he glimpsed outside had light armor: not a match for what he was wearing earlier but far superior to what he's got now. Marlowe steps back into the jumble of debris and bodies on the floor, kicks a shattered suit aside, grabs the assault-cannon that suit's still clutching, rushes back up the staircase. He's shouting at the razor to get out of his way. He rushes out onto the roof, starts firing at the suited Jaguar who's just alighted upon it: and who now gets drilled through the visor by hi-ex armor-piercing rounds from Marlowe's weapon. The Jaguar goes down, smoke pouring from his helmet. Marlowe hears suit thrusters below the level of the roof: he hears the razor scream. He races to the edge of the roof, leaps.

For a moment he's plunging. As he does he catches a glimpse of another suit, hovering in front of a nearby tower that's been turned into more of an inverted melting icicle through the pounding of the now-silent space-to-grounders. Marlowe fires more hi-ex rounds, blows that suit backward into the tower even as he plunges past the hole in the wall of the control room—and sticks his feet out, finds purchase, twists into the control room itself. His head just misses torn metal. The Jaguar who's just entered the control room through that hole is advancing on the staircase where the razor's ensconced. Marlowe opens up: the suit whirls, burning—and then exploding as its motors ignite. Marlowe fires several more rounds for good measure, steps past what's left of that suit.

And hits the floor. Because every window's being shattered. The room's filling up with fire. Marlowe crawls along the floor to the staircase, steps into its shelter. The razor's standing there, her gaze flicking between the sky and a still-intact computer monitor set into the wall.

"Bought us maybe thirty seconds," he tells her.

But the woman doesn't answer save to gesture at the sky. Marlowe glances at it—sees some kind of signal light flashing up there. "They're responding," the razor says.

"What are they saying?"

"They're not sending ships."

"Then we're fucked."

"Not quite," she says. She starts to explain but stops as the room beneath comes under heavy fire. A barrage of explosive shells starts tearing away what's left of those walls. The stairway they're in shakes. It keeps on shaking.

And stops. The firing cuts out.

"What the fuck," mutters Marlowe.

"Beats me."

But then they hear it from somewhere down below. It's some kind of distant rumbling. Some kind of far-flung echo. It seems to be coming from within this building rather than outside. It's not just one thing either. It's many things. It's the same thing. It's many voices.

Shouting.

"The militia."

"The suits are whistling up the dogs." Marlowe eyes the stairs.

"We've got to move."

"Where?" Marlowe leans into the doorway, hurls frag grenades across the room and down that stairwell. But when the explosions die away, the shouting's still there.

Only louder.

"How long do you think we have?" asks the razor.

"Maybe about another thirty seconds," replies Marlowe. "How long do we need?"

They hear something else through the shouting. Something's scraping along the roof, closing on the trapdoor. It's dropping through.

A tether.

"Grab it," says Marlowe.

She does. And as he follows suit, he primes the phosphorus charge, tosses it at the foot of the stairs. The tether's going taut. They're being hauled at a run up what's left of the stair-way. They lift their feet, loop their legs around the tether. They soar through the trapdoor, leave the roof behind.

And rise into the burning heavens.

 Riley and the Operative make their way back through the chamber in which the latter rode out the initial climb. They trail cable out behind them.

"Careful," says Riley.

But the Operative says nothing. It's noticeably colder back here. The light from the glowsticks they've triggered plays fit-fully upon the walls.

"Look familiar?" asks Riley.

"Not anymore," says the Operative.

Riley shrugs. He moves to the door that leads to the cargo. He works the manual, slides the door open. The two men float like undersea divers into the bay. Which—since it's nearly full—is really just a narrow passage.

"What's in here anyway?" asks the Operative.

"Seed," replies Riley.

"Plant or animal?"

"I think it's both."

"I hope it's shielded."

"Do you think that radiation's killed us?"

"It will if we don't start this fucker soon."

"I'm not talking about our machines. I'm talking about our bodies."

"Oh," says the Operative, "those. Who knows? These ships are hardened against background. But a nuke in close proximity—that's something else again. My guess, we should be okay. But"—he gestures at the cargo around him—"I hope you weren't planning on having kids."

"Never planned on anything," mutters Riley.

They reach the door at the rear of the compartment. The Operative opens it. The room thus revealed is mere airlock. The Operative climbs in. He opens a locker, starts putting on a spacesuit, slotting equipment onto that suit while Riley slots the cord he's been trailing through the airlock door's cable-grooves. He locks them into place, hands the terminus to the Operative. The Operative inspects his helmet. He stares at Riley.

"One rule," he says. "When I knock on that door, you open it. Got it?"

"Got it," says Riley tonelessly.

"Then *begin*."

He lowers his helmet—seals it as Riley seals the door. He turns to the next door: even thicker than the previous one. He unlocks the seals, winches the hatch open.

And stares straight out into planet.

It fills the view, a massive sphere half in shadow. The Operative crawls out toward it: edges through the airlock, deploys magnetic clamps, moves out onto the strait. He feels like an insect scurrying into infinity. He watches infinity spread before him, scattered through with stars. And the occasional explosion: flaring, dying away. They're the casualties. They're getting closer. The Operative keeps on crawling. The hull's curve is sharpening. The planet's curving away.

Finally the engines are silhouetted before him. The Operative doesn't break pace. He clambers out into a wilderness of pipes and wires. He's as careful with the cable he's trailing as he is with his own suit: ensuring that nothing snags as he makes his way past the main turbines, out onto the side of one of the engine nozzles. He reaches the nozzle's edge, climbs inside.

Metal closes about him. Space outside gets cut off. He worms his way deeper. It gets narrow fast. He crawls through into the reaction chamber. It's just big enough for him to fit within. He crouches for a moment in the enclosed space—and then shoves the cable's end into a vent, fixes it in place. The cable now stretches all the way back to one of the cockpit batteries. The Operative envisions Maschler's hand hovering over that battery. Waiting for the signal . . .

But it hasn't come yet. The Operative retraces his footsteps feetfirst. He wriggles out of the reaction chamber—wriggles back into the engine bell. He reaches that nozzle's edge, climbs back out upon its exterior side. He begins climbing back up the engine block, retracing the cable's trail.

But he stops when he gets near the turbines. He starts opening the maintenance hatches that lead to the turbine gears. Normally the gears would be powered by the fuel they themselves power through those pipes and into the reaction chamber. But in order to set that fuel in motion they need pressure supplied by the peroxide, whose tanks are arranged in such intricate geometries down near the Operative's feet. He uses the tools in his suit's glove to unscrew safety after safety. He sees more flares bursting from the corner of his eye. He feels time closing on him like a vise. He flicks off the last safety, reaches beyond that safety, and releases one last switch.

Peroxide bubbles through a tube beneath his hand. The turbines start up. The Operative feels them churn. He pictures fuel and oxidizer being drawn into the reaction chamber. He pictures that chamber filling up. He yanks the cable hard.

And holds on.

Light blasts from somewhere behind him. Something slams straight through his suit and brain and just keeps going. Vibration washes over him in waves. He knows the hammer in his skull for concussion. He knows the wetness in his ears for blood. He feels the acceleration full against him. He pulls himself up along the turbine and hauls himself over the fuel tanks. He feels heat—even as he leaves the engine behind and gets out on the hull once again. But the warmth's quickly vanishing. The temperature's dropping.

Steadily. His suit's clearly holed somewhere. Maybe he snagged it. Maybe it's just burning through. Regardless, he's starting to get short of breath. He's starting to see stars for real now. The ship rumbles against him. It's all he can do to hold on. He knows his time's down to single seconds.

So he cheats. His hand goes to his boot knife. His knife goes to the air tank on his back, stabs in, rips along it. Air shoots out. The Operative positions himself: lets go of the cable, lets himself slide back along the hull. He feels air shoving him. He feels air being sucked from him: he takes one last breath, reaches out to the door, grasps the hatch, holds on while his vision starts flashing. Dissipating air's momentum tries to haul him onward. He jettisons the tank, pulls himself in, slams the hatch behind him, seals it. Black and red press in upon his vision. He strikes his hand against the inner door.

It opens. Riley's face is staring into his own—now unmediated by visor as the Operative hauls his helmet off and gulps in air. Riley looks at him, says something.

"Save your breath," says the Operative. "I can't hear a fucking thing."

Together, they make their way back toward the cockpit.

Together they rise into the skies. The Citadel drops away beneath them. The tether to which they're clinging is retracting rapidly. The city starts to spread out beneath them. There's no electricity left in it now, only flame. Smoke billows from countless fires. The lights in the sky shimmer on those rising clouds.

"Here they come," says the mech.

The militia are swarming onto the roof. Four suits are

flashing past them—rising toward the two who cling to the tether. But as the suits pass the tower, there's a flash: the top of the structure is blown apart by the charge the mech rigged there. White-hot phosphorus flings itself everywhere. Bodies fly. Two of the suits get taken out.

But two remain. They climb. They're opening fire. Haskell and the mech do the only thing they can: let go, drop along that tether, grab it again. Shots rip past them. It's a trick that only works once. There's nowhere left to go. They fire desperately at the closing suits.

Which suddenly get riddled. Hails of bullets rain down from long range, dissect the suits almost simultaneously. Chunks tumble back into the city below.

"About time," says the mech.

But Haskell doesn't answer. She's just staring at the thing that's spreading out across the sky. It's like nothing she's ever seen.

"The roof's caving in," she says.

She's not kidding. Gigantic streaks of orange and white are sliding across the sky, glowing ever brighter as they drip in toward the horizon. They're what's left of the Elevator. They're what happens when something big meets atmosphere. She can't tell where this mother of all meteor strikes is going to hit. She only knows that it's going to change the world forever when it does. It looks like it's coming right down on her head. She's guessing the real impact will be somewhere to the east. But that's almost worse. The tidal waves set in motion will put both sides of the Atlantic beneath the water. It will be the kind of event that only satellites witness. Only the damned will see much more than that.

Suddenly the sky above them goes white. It's like the Earth has been thrust up against a supernova. Final nightfall's ripped apart by false dawn. The superpowers have combined to destroy their joint creation. The def-grids on both sides have unleashed. Warheads are striking home from stations elsewhere on the planet. Directed energy's blasting down from space. Crossfire becomes annihilation. There'll be nothing left to hit the ocean. EMP drenches them anew.

"I'm blind," Haskell says.

"Me too."

But not permanently. And eventually their sight fades back in. To reveal a city that's now a distant fire and a sky that's still a long way from black.

And this tether hanging in between.

"Where are we going?" says Haskell.

"The only kind of craft that's guaranteed to still be up here after all that EMP."

"A zeppelin."

"Exactly. I passed several on the way down."

"Then you kicked off in style."

"And you?"

"I think they briefed me off the coast and shipped me in."

"What do you remember before that?"

"You."

And the mech starts to say something, stops. Opens his mouth again.

"What do you mean?" he asks.

"I just mean you're familiar."

"How would you know?"

Because she saw his moves under pressure. Because she was inside his head. Because the whole time she's been fighting for her life she's been fighting the realization that the man she's with is more than a stranger. She wants to tell him all this. She wants to tell him that he's the living ghost of memory. But she's not sure.

And she needs to be.

"Because I've seen you before."

"This has been tough," says the mech. "You need some rest."

"But first I need your name."

"My real one?"

"No," she sneers, "just one of the ones you've discarded."

"You're asking me to break regulations."

"Is that so bad?"

"It is if I comply."

"Did regulations stop the sky from tumbling? Did regulations save that city from dying?"

"They might yet see us through this mess."

"They're what *caused* this mess," she says. "They're the root of the fucking problem."

"Heads up," he says.

A shape is looming out of the night above them. It's hundreds of meters in length. It blots out the stars. It blots out afterglow. It's hauling in the remainder of the tether.

"We're here," he says.

Rough hands grab them, haul them inside a room on one level of a much larger gondola. Haskell and the mech watch while the soldiers who've just pulled them in pull in the remainder of the tether. They stare at each other while a burning city floats through the dark several klicks below.

"You're Jason Marlowe," says Haskell.

"And you are?"

"Who do you think?"

She removes her mask with one hand, brushes brown hair back with the other. He stares at freckles and sweat—pulls off his own mask to reveal black hair and a bloody nose.

"Hello," says Haskell.

"Fuck's sake," he says—and steps forward to embrace her. But she just steps away, leans back against the window.

"I *knew* it was you," she says.

"They didn't tell me."

"Didn't tell me either."

"Guess they've got other things on their mind right now."

There's a pause. Soldiers continue to move around them,

closing the trapdoor through which they've just come, storing away the tether. One of them turns to Marlowe and Haskell.

"You're both wanted in the medbay," he says.

"In a minute," says Marlowe.

"Now," the man replies. "We need you out of this room so we can lock it down."

"You've got it wrong," says Marlowe. "It's the reverse."

The man stares at him.

"We need *you* out," adds Marlowe.

"Don't take it personally," says Haskell.

The man stares for another moment, comes to a quick decision. He snaps orders to the rest of the soldiers. They stop what they're doing, exit the room in haste. Haskell and Marlowe hear them muttering among themselves. The words *razor* and *mech* feature prominently in the conversation. The door shuts behind them.

"As direct as ever," says Haskell.

"Some things never change," replies Marlowe.

"We've got maybe five minutes before they send someone down."

"They can send away," says Marlowe. "I doubt anyone on this ship outranks us. And I'm willing to bet none of the handlers are anywhere near *this*."

He gestures at the window. She gazes at the colors rippling across the heavens, at the fires burning down below. Powered craft are starting to move through the skies once more, their lights flickering here and there amidst the dark. She takes it all in, glances back at him.

"So what is it you wanted to say?" she asks.

"I'm still trying to figure that out."

She looks at him. There's a long pause.

"Look," he says, "I just wanted to be able to say *something*. I hadn't expected this."

"Well," she says, "sorry to surprise you."

"I'm rolling with it."

"Are you?"

"Trying to."

"You and me both."

"They'll bring the wall back down between us," he says. "We'll be debriefed, tossed back into the mix. We didn't see each other in ten years of runs—"

"Which was deliberate."

"I know," he says. "That's what I'm saying. We're only here right now because of pure chance."

"They're going to think we're trying to sneak away like we used to." She tries for a mischievous smile but just ends up looking as tired as she feels.

"We should get you to the medbay."

"Me?" She laughs. "You're the one wiping blood off your face."

"Small price," he says. He smiles sadly. "You know, I'd like to see you before another ten years have passed."

"You will," she says, though she's not sure if she believes that. "They owe me after this. I'll see you again. Or at least be in contact."

"In contact," he says.

"In contact," she repeats. "At least. It's the least the old man can do. He almost got me killed tonight." She looks at Marlowe. "Thank you, by the way."

He waves that aside. "You shouldn't be so hard on Sinclair. I hear he hears of nothing but your exploits. You're CI's rising star."

She forces herself to smile: nods, mumbles something.

"What was that?" he asks.

"I said, I'm feeling faint. Let's get to that medbay. See that?" She gestures at a light approaching out the window. "Probably a 'copter to offload us."

"And then they'll send us on our separate ways."

"They already did. Here we are again. It's just a matter of waiting."

He stares at her.

"*Everything* is, Jason."

"Not for them." He points past the approaching ship at a night that continues to flare colors. The city's conflagration continues apace. Faint dots are aircraft swarming over it in renewed fury. Explosions and tracers are flying into the air. They're kilometers below, barely visible. But it's clear enough that the fighting's still going on. That the dying's continuing.

"They're already there," he says.

The Operative and Riley arrive back in the cockpit to find Maschler still sitting in his chair. He's staring out the window, holding what looks to be a small telescope up to his eye. He glances around.

"Congratulations," he says.

"He's deaf," says Riley.

"But he can read lips," says the Operative.

"You didn't tell me that," says Riley.

"You didn't ask," says the Operative. "And I wasn't exactly in the mood for talking. Besides, I don't need to read shit to know that the first thing you're going to say when I emerge from a live rocket engine with blood dripping from my ears is *jesus man are you okay*. Maschler: any sense as to how far off the ramp we are?"

"Hard to say with this kind of crap at my disposal," says Maschler, setting aside his instrument to float in front of him. "But it doesn't look so bad right now. We're only off by a few degrees."

"That'll grow," says Riley.

"So what?" says the Operative. "The point is that we're a

hell of a lot less likely to get impaled by anything now. We launched within the window, brothers. That'll be enough until we get rescued."

"Rescued," repeats Riley.

"Rescued?" asks Maschler.

"What the hell else are we going to do?" says the Operative testily. "I'll admit I find the thought distasteful. But I'm fresh out of ideas. It's not like we can land. It's not like we can dock with anything. In fact, it's not like we can do shit except cruise through space until we either hit something or the engine conks out for good. We're flying deadweight, gentlemen. Besides, a med scan wouldn't be such a bad idea right now anyway. I'm sure we all could use it."

"He's right," says Riley.

"Of course I'm right," says the Operative. "It's over."

"Good," says Maschler.

"But what *was* it," asks Riley.

"How about if we agree to call it the end of the beginning?" asks the Operative.

"You mean there's more?" Maschler asks.

"I would assume so," replies the Operative.

"So what happens next?" says Riley.

"If I knew that, I'd be giving orders instead of carrying them out," says the Operative. "But with any luck, yours won't be more than a bit part. Just keep your head down and keep on hauling freight, okay? That should suffice to see you through. Doesn't matter what's going down or who comes out on top: they're going to have a need for people like you."

"I'll take that as a compliment," says Riley.

"You should," says the Operative. "That's how I intended it. Survivability's the ultimate praise. You guys should be fine from here."

"And what about you?" says Maschler.

"What about me," says the Operative.

"What's this all mean for you?" asks Riley.

"I'm still figuring that one out," says the Operative. "But for now, the same as you. We get picked up, we get checked out, we get a new rig, we head on toward our destination."

Riley starts to laugh.

"What's so funny?" says the Operative.

"What's not?" he replies. "I'd forgotten all about that fucking rock. Strange, eh?"

"Strange indeed," agrees the Operative. "How about we get some brakes before we get there?"

But Riley just keeps laughing.

PART II
INCURSION

Of course," says Matthew Sinclair, "the whole thing's a joke."

He looks at Marlowe and Haskell. They look at the face upon that screen: the face of the man who heads up CounterIntelligence Command. They wonder what the hell he means. It's been two days since the Elevator was blown from its orbit. Two days since the greatest man-made object became the greatest piece of wreckage. Tens of thousands are dead. Fission has ruptured the atmosphere so badly that the sky's still glowing.

For the life of them neither Marlowe nor Haskell can see what's so funny.

"This manifesto," says Matthew Sinclair. "It's a joke. They know it. And they know we know it too."

"Then why did they write it?" asks Marlowe.

"Because," says Sinclair, "they wanted people to talk about it."

Looks like they got their wish. People can't shut up. Information's traffic flows like light and quenches like water.

It's never the same thing twice. When you think you've caught it in your hands, it's already changed forever. But here's the thing about information.

It can't compete with rumor.

"Wiping out the Elevator would have accomplished that," says Haskell.

"Right," says Sinclair, "but this way they lay claim to an *identity*."

Some identity. Some name. *Autumn Rain:* do those words contain the keys to the mind that's set all this in motion? Does this manifesto lay out their real agenda? It hints at utter madness. It suggests the outlines of something all too sane.

"Yet the population of this country hasn't read it," says Marlowe.

"Not officially," says Haskell.

"Exactly," says Sinclair. "Keep in mind, too, that *what's* said is a lot less important than the fact that *something's* being said."

"Meaning?"

"Meaning this document's words don't matter. Not in the slightest."

"I don't know," says Haskell. "Those words might sound pretty inspiring to someone who's looking for a reason to hate the government."

"Not inspiring," says Sinclair, "insipid. Read it again. 'For too long have those you call leaders mortgaged your future'? 'All of history has waited for this moment'? It's one big joke. On us. Claims of nomenclature notwithstanding. It means nothing. Nothing at all. Which isn't to say there aren't meanings hidden within it. Invert comedy, you get tragedy. We've got both now. So we're looking at it from every angle. We're parsing every phrase."

He goes back and forth, thinks Haskell. She looks at the face projected on that screen and wonders at the contradictions it utters, contains. She looks at that face, struggles to contain herself. She feels her heart overflowing: looking at that man right now, beard sharpened to a fine point, shaved skull extruding metal, metal walls behind him.

Just like she always dreamt him.

"But we haven't succeeded in finding anything yet," says Marlowe.

"Ever the practical one, Jason," says Sinclair. "No. We haven't. We've deployed specialists to calibrate the minds behind these words. They can't tell us anything. They can't even tell us if it was written by human or machine. They're useless."

Haskell shakes her head. "Then why are we talking about it?"

"Because," says Sinclair, "it's not their minds I'm interested in right now. It's yours. The Rain?—they're out there somewhere. Assuredly. But you're right here."

"And where are you?" says Marlowe.

"Exactly where you see me," replies Sinclair.

"On that screen," says Haskell.

"Yes, Claire," says Sinclair. "On this screen. But right here with you all the same. For the first time among so many times, you're not recollecting me in the trance. You gaze upon me in the moment. We've got no time for anything else."

"How can we be sure you're really Matthew Sinclair?" asks Marlowe.

"How can you ever?" says Sinclair. "I like you, Jason. I like your verve and butchery. But I also like Claire. She's so different from my others. Truth to tell, I can't decide which of you I like more. That's why I've brought you here."

"To find out?" asks Haskell.

"If you like," says Sinclair. He seems amused. "You sit and watch me on this screen. You think I pull your strings. It's an easy illusion to subscribe to. But what you must understand is that you're the ones who hold the power. Because you're the ones who go out into the world."

"To be tested," says Marlowe.

"To be sure," says Sinclair. "And these times test us as never before. Jason: Claire will be your razor. She'll pull *your* strings. Claire: when you first met Jason, he was just starting out. Now he's one of our best mechs. You're going to have to work to keep up with him. I think the two of you are going to like working together. But even if you don't, you're going to have to act like you do if you want to survive where you're going."

"And where *are* we going?"

"To stop the Rain, of course," says Sinclair.

"And we really know *nothing* about them?" asks Haskell.

"Of course we know something about them," says Sinclair. "We know that they got onto the biggest thing our species ever built and turned it into junk."

"Right," says Haskell. "Thanks."

"You don't understand," says Sinclair. "They didn't just destroy the Elevator. They got *on* it. They got *into* its core stations. And they didn't want us to know they'd done that."

"How do we know that?" asks Marlowe.

"Surely your minds are sharper than this. The Rain was clearly hoping to use proxies to do their work. And to destroy the Elevator at a distance rather than reveal to us just how thoroughly they'd penetrated its security. They gave the Jaguars hypersonics. Ground-to-grounders that knocked out almost ten percent of our equatorial launch architecture. And yet those were a mere diversion from the ground-to-spacers those Jaguars were firing simultaneously. They almost got the Elevator."

"But they didn't," says Haskell.

"What makes you so sure the Jaguars and the Rain aren't one and the same?" says Marlowe.

"Please," says Sinclair. "The Jaguars are formidable. Both of you did well to face them. But don't let your emotional involvement distract you from the fact that they've never manifested spacefaring capabilities. We don't even think they have the expertise to build hypersonics on their own. So we're pretty sure that someone gave them those weapons. Someone who also rigged seventeen neutral satellites with space-to-spacers. Think of it—someone infiltrated the ground-to-space supply networks of two of the Euro combines. Someone sent up rockets instead of spare parts. Someone configured robots to rig those rockets. Someone did all that right under our noses."

"And it didn't work," says Haskell. "Which forced them to play their ace."

"Indeed," says Sinclair. "As hard as it was to rig the neutrals—as difficult a feat as that might seem—getting onto the Elevator was even harder. And getting fission devices into its control centers should have been impossible. Which is why they didn't want us to see that they could do that."

"What makes you say they themselves were *on* it?" asks Marlowe. "Maybe they just hacked it."

"Right," says Sinclair. "Now you're asking the right questions. Let's break down the events: 18:20 local time—the Jags unleash hell on heaven and earth; 18:22—rogue space-to-spacers rigged on the satellites of the Lvov and Wessex Combines bracket vacuum. But nothing touches our behemoth. The def-grids of its escorts take down everything that even comes close. Now. What happens then?"

"It blows up," says Marlowe.

"Fourteen minutes later," says Haskell.

"Without warning."

"From the inside."

"True enough," says Sinclair. "True up to a point. That much you know. Now let me tell you what you don't. The official record says that nothing happened on the Elevator before the blasts that finished it. But that's not quite accurate.

T-minus twenty minutes: we get a tip from some of the workers coming off shift that some of the workers who've just gone on shift aren't really workers. We move in on one squad in particular. We start busting people. One of our ships gets taken out. We take out everyone in sight. T-minus sixteen minutes: the Jaguars open up. T-minus fourteen: the rigged neutrals follow suit. T-minus thirteen: the Bridge goes offline, along with its entire garrison. Offline as in not responding to anything whatsoever. T-minus twelve: all the Elevator's engines fire in reverse on full throttle. The thing starts slowing down. Not gently either. Hundreds of construction workers start getting knocked into space. Pieces of construction start flying off too. SpaceCom marines scramble from nearby orbital platforms. The Elevator's starting to drag atmosphere. Nadir Station's starting to get warm. But structural integrity's still intact. Zenith Station is still reporting in. They're seeing nothing. They're evacuating. Marines from east and west are closing in. A DE cannon rigged just aft of the Bridge opens up on them, gets some of them, gets itself blasted into powder. The marines get in there. They land. They enter the Bridge. And then—nothing but white light."

There's a pause. The screen flickers.

"No one told us that," says Haskell.

"That wasn't in the news," says Marlowe.

"Of course it wasn't," says Sinclair. "It's embarrassing."

"They seized control of the Elevator before they destroyed it?" Haskell shakes her head. "How can we hide a thing like that?"

"We can't," says Sinclair. "It's not like people don't know. Just not everywhere. It was reported on neutral vid, sure. So now it's more fuel to feed the rumors over here. I'm sure it's the same in Moscow and Beijing. . . ." His voice trails off.

"Why did they wait so long to detonate the Elevator once they had the Bridge?" says Marlowe.

"It's simple," says Sinclair. He pauses, glances again at

something offscreen. "They were toying with us. That's the only conclusion that kind of sequence points to. Once they knew that they had to reveal that they'd been able to get fission devices aboard, they postponed destruction as long as possible. Drawing more of our forces into the blast radius. Winding us up. Making us feel it."

"They really got nukes in by infiltrating the *work teams?*"

"Call it one option among many. Look at it this way: the thing was four thousand klicks long. Three main docking stations—Zenith, Nadir, and the Bridge—and ten minor ones. Cargo shuttles coming in around the clock. Thousands of workers—far too many, in retrospect—with most of them from the joint-control area in the Imbrium. Plus more than a hundred dedicated wireless conduits. But in the end, there were only two ways on. Whether they employed physical mechanisms or simply deployed a particularly adroit hack, there were only two ways to go about it."

"Us," says Haskell.

"Or the East," says Marlowe.

"Exactly," says Sinclair, beaming suddenly as though at a favored pupil. "Exactly. They either infiltrated us, or they infiltrated the East. Which brings us back full circle. The president and the Eurasian leadership have agreed to establish a joint tribunal. Joint investigation, cooperation in the face of the common threat, all the right words. All the right phrases. But it's all nonsense from the word go, and everyone in the know knows it. Neither superpower will open to the other. Each suspects the other. The president has told me—"

"You've spoken with him?" asks Haskell.

"Of course I haven't *spoken* with him," snaps Sinclair. "And don't interrupt me. I don't mind it when you're in the trance. You can't help yourself then. You can now. And try to keep your wits about you. Standard precautions preclude direct two-way dialogue with the Throne for all but a few of his Praetorians. What in God's name would make you think we'd dilute such precautions now? Now: the Throne has *informed* me that he's deeply concerned that the Coalition is either behind this, or else will use this as an excuse to reverse the détente that sits at the heart of all his policies. But he also worries that the Rain may be the device of some faction within our own midst. Worst case is that such a faction is itself the tool of Coalition hardliners bent on war. Absolute worst case is that they've penetrated the president's own security network."

"They might have penetrated the *Praetorians?*" asks Haskell.

"We can't rule it out," replies Sinclair.

"How are the other Commands taking all this?" says Marlowe.

"They're afraid," says Sinclair. "As they should be. As we all should be. All of us—we've let the Throne down. Heads are rolling right now. And they're going to keep on rolling. There's a glitch in the system, and no one knows where it is. But everyone knows this: if the Rain got into the Elevator, there may be very little that's beyond their reach."

"Do we have evidence of them reaching?" says Haskell.

"I'm sure we do," says Sinclair. "Probably right under our noses. We just haven't recognized it yet. It's not like we're not trying. We've been tearing up the Latin cities street by street. At our request, the Euro Magnates have frozen the assets of the Lvov and Wessex Combines, and have allowed the joint tribunal to deploy investigators across the Earth-Moon system to audit the assets of those combines. I say 'allowed,' but we were only going to ask once. Though I can tell you right now that angle of inquiry isn't going to reveal a thing. There's only cutoff conduits and burnt-out trails down those routes. Whoever the Rain are, they're not leaving clues that obvious. And as for the Elevator—well, there's not much evidence left there, is there?"

Neither Marlowe nor Haskell replies.

"But, to your point," continues Sinclair, "the biggest question isn't what the Rain have done so far. It's what they're going to do next."

"Sure," says Haskell, "but what do *we* do next?"

"Hit the Moon. Stop them."

"The Moon?"

"The equations stipulate a convergence of circumstantial evidence and current vulnerability," says Sinclair. "We know they got inside the Imbrium mining contingents. That may or may not have been their main way in. But it's one of the only things we have to go on. The main risk is that's two days in transit when you won't be fully leveraged. Jason won't be able to do a run on anything, and Claire, your hacks will be at a disadvantage due to the distance to either Earth or Moon. But we have to take that risk. The Moon's essential. Half our fleet is in its vicinity. If anything goes down there on the scale of the Elevator, we would be profoundly discomfited."

"When do we leave?" asks Marlowe.

"As soon as I stop talking."

"I mean, when do we leave the planet?" asks Marlowe.

"As soon as we can launch you," says Sinclair.

"From where?"

"Houston. We're prepping a booster even now. It's ours—crewed by CICom personnel. But it flies the merchant marine colors. We'll slot you right into the freight routes. You'll go to ground in the lunar cities. You'll rendezvous with other assets. And then you'll start the hunt in earnest."

"And the plan of operations?" asks Marlowe.

"What else do we *know*?" says Haskell.

But Sinclair just holds up one hand.

"All in good time, my children. All in good time. You'll get the second phase of the briefing when you arrive at Houston. And the third when you reach the Moon itself. Staggered updates to ensure that we keep pace with events. All I can say right now is that we have to throw the dice. The tension between East and West is rising even as the hunt for Rain intensifies. All our agents are going into the field. All the training you've received, all the runs you've done—all of it's just been preparation for these times. Trust each other. Trust no one else. Trust me when I say that Autumn Rain represents a threat without precedent. They will strike again. I guarantee it. Unless you stop them. Unless you hit the Moon and stop them."

The screen goes blank.

As specialization became the order of the day—as seekers of truth drilled ever deeper into the unknown, creating ever more minute taxonomies of knowledge, branching out along ever more arcane classifications...inevitably, the most significant discoveries in science lay more and more in the blurring fault lines among disciplines. The mapping out of the subconscious can be considered just such a development. As can the attempt to manipulate it through the nervous system. Yet even by the early stages of the twenty-second century, the pincer movements converging across mental and physical realms had yet to link up completely.

Which means that it's not entirely unsafe for the Operative to dream.

Which hardly makes it safe. So if the Operative dreams, he doesn't know it—insofar as he has them, his nighttime reveries have been deliberately situated at the fringes of his cognition. Thus he lies sleeping after his arrival, in a room deep within Agrippa Station, on the Moon's nearside equator. Only to suddenly come alert in a single instant:

Wake. Wake in a chamber. What chamber? This chamber. Darkness surrounds you, and walls surround the darkness. Surround the instant. But cannot isolate the question: why have you woken? Why are you lunging forward? Reflex: the Operative's thoughts trail his actions by a long chalk; he's moving at a speed that belies the low gravity, pivoting out of the bed, careening into the man who's entered his room, pinning him back against the wall panel with a heavy thud.

For a moment all is still.

The Operative is the first to speak: "Well?" His lips might be parting. His teeth definitely aren't.

"Carson," the man says, "it's Lynx. Don't you recognize me?"

"Christ." The Operative releases his grip. He half-pivots, takes a step or three backward, and triggers a glow-light, though his eyes don't really need it. Still: the man thus revealed wears a SpaceCom uniform. His skin's ebony. His hair's dyed silver. A thick pair of opticals perches on the bridge of an aquiline nose. The ears aren't small. The mouth hung between them is grinning.

"It's nice to see you too, Carson," says Stefan Lynx.

Brain and muscles and reflexes keep open channels within the Operative. He stares at Lynx.

"How did you get through the door?"

"Who says I used the door?"

The Operative glances around with his peripheral vision. Notices that one panel of the wall is tilting ever so slightly askew.

"Shit."

"Is right."

"Christ, you're taking a risk. Is this room wired for sound?"

"You bet," replies Lynx, "and all the wires lead back to me."

"So we can talk."

"That's what we're doing, isn't it?"

"Sure," says the Operative, "that's what we're doing. What do you want to talk about?"

"I want to talk about your trip, Carson. How was it?"

"You know damn well how it was," says the Operative. "It was a little too eventful."

"Eventful?" Lynx's laugh sounds like a cat being strangled. "That's one way of putting it. Another's *luckless*. So much for standard transits. That was supposed to be the easy part. Your dice had better up their fortune quick if we're going to get much further, Carson."

"They already have," says the Operative. "I got out of it, didn't I?"

"Sure," says Lynx. "You got out of it. Albeit not without a dip in your white blood cell count. I should imagine things got pretty tight in that metal tin. I hear you even called planetside."

"Yeah," says the Operative. "They were real helpful."

"Of course they were," says Lynx. "Your sarcasm notwithstanding. Sometimes the best form of help we can receive is to learn that we're going to get none. But the little dustup you got dealt into at least let me dispense with my envy, Carson. You were supposed to travel in style. You were supposed to get the shortest route possible. Unlike mine. I had three layovers before I'd even got past the geo."

"I presume that's called covering your trail."

"Yeah," says Lynx, "it's also called economics. But you're special, Carson. Even with the complications, you got to hitch a fast ride."

"So?"

"So someone down there likes you."

"I doubt like has anything to do with it."

"You're damn right it doesn't," says Lynx. "You're at Agrippa now. Deep in SpaceCom territory. So let's get started."

"With what?"

"With the *mission*, Carson."

"Go on."

"It's changed."

"How?"

"How would you guess?"

"Something to do with Autumn Rain?"

"Got it in one, Carson," says Lynx. "Got it in one. The Elevator's got this whole place buzzing."

"Who the fuck are we dealing with, Lynx?"

"That," says Lynx, "is the question that's got me crawling Agrippa's tunnels like a goddamn sewer rat."

"You're hacked into the SpaceCom systems?"

"I am," says Lynx. "I've been doing my bit. Fair and square, Carson. Now it's time to talk about you."

"No," says the Operative, "it's time to talk about what you've found."

"Same difference," says Lynx. "Same difference. You wouldn't believe what's in Agrippa's comps, Carson. I've been poring over it. It's been pouring over me. It's good. It's fascinating. But it's useless. So far."

"No trace," says the Operative.

"Not yet," says Lynx. "But now that you're here, we're going to get on the board. We're hunting big game now. We're going to find these fuckers, Carson. And then we're going to tear their fucking hearts out."

"You think the Rain's on the Moon?"

"We know they infiltrated the Imbrium miners on the Elevator. But here's the thing, Carson: what you and I think doesn't matter. What matters is what the Throne thinks. Last night I received word from the boys downstairs. Real-time, Carson. So they could vector us onto the new player."

"And SpaceCom?"

"The original mission still stands. Turning the Com upside down and shaking out the change is still part of the objective. But we're also going to leverage them in our search for Rain."

"What the hell does that mean?"

"It means that one vector of this mission is finding out what Com intelligence knows. Finding out what they're finding out. Finding out what they're not."

"And do we have an actual plan of operations?"

"We have an *initial* plan," says Lynx.

"Which is?"

"Your getting moving."

"Where to?"

"The south pole."

"The where?"

"You heard me."

"What the fuck is down there?"

"Sarmax."

"*Sarmax?*"

"How's your hearing, Carson? They told me that might be an issue after your adventures up the asshole of that rocket."

"I fucking heard you. What the hell's he doing at the south pole?"

"That's where he retired."

"Sarmax *retired?*"

"Come on, Carson. Don't tell me you didn't know that."

"I knew he left active service. But no one retires altogether."

"Not officially," says Lynx. "But think about it, Carson. The reflexes only go so far. And the conditioning's only useful through a certain threshold. Comes a point when knowing that you'll have your own little beanpatch can work wonders for one's motivation. Beanpatches, Carson. You live long enough, you might even get one yourself."

"I doubt I'd want it."

"Why?"

"Because I'd guess that retirement has a catch."

"Namely?"

"Well," says the Operative, "take Sarmax. I'm guessing that you're about to tell me to go down there and kill him."

Lynx laughs again. It's even worse this time around. "Hardly, Carson. Hardly. You've got it all wrong. You're going to go down there and break into his base of operations. You're going to cut through his defenses. You're going to ransack his files. You're going to rape his comps. You're going to find out everything he knows. And *then* you're going to kill him."

"Why?"

"Because he's been careless."

"Do we have evidence?"

"Of course."

"And?"

"And what?"

"That's it?"

"Got a problem with that?"

"Maybe I do."

"Because so far the boys downstairs have had no problem with you, Carson. They had no problem at all with you sitting in the sleep and mumbling on about how eager you were to get up here and rendezvous with me and do whatever the fuck I said. Of course, it never occurred to them that once you got upstairs you might start to get second thoughts about the whole thing."

"I'm not getting second thoughts, Lynx. I'm just trying to understand this."

"So let me clarify it. You off Sarmax and tell us what he was up to before he bit it."

"And he's hiding out down south?"

"He's not exactly hiding."

"Meaning?"

"Meaning he got more than just a beanpatch when he retired. Or rather, he may have gotten just the beans, but he's parlayed them into a lot more. He runs a holding company that spans a number of enterprises. Most of them involving extraction of water from the south pole icefields."

"Sounds profitable."

"It is."

"And where's the man himself?"

"Shackleton. That's where he's got his HQ. It's quite the fortress."

"How do we crack it?"

"It's complicated," says Lynx.

"So?"

"Way too complicated to get into here," says Lynx. "Time to go, Carson." He beams data directly into the Operative's skull. "It'll download automatically on the train. Give you all the operational details. Every last one."

"No kidding?"

"No kidding. We need to pick up the pace. I've maneuvered it so that the Com technician I'm passing you off as has been assigned to Shackleton. There's a lev leaving in forty minutes. From equator to antipodes in one straight shot."

"And what about you, Lynx?"

"What about me?"

"What are you going to do while I'm out on the run?"

"The same thing I've been doing, Carson. Keep on worming my way through this apple's core."

"Am I coming back here?"

"If I find something worth running you back in for."

"And when do you contact me again?"

"When you've taken out the target. Here's my one piece of advice, Carson. Don't make it personal."

"You're really funny," says the Operative.

"Go," says Lynx.

And the Operative's gone.

• • •

Take a man. Take what price you can get for him. Get that man to gather data until he's earned his passage home. See, there are some who crave information for political or military advantage. There are some who want it to further the cause. But you know better. At the end of the day, data dances to the beat of the markets. They're all that matters.

Until an interloper comes calling . . .

Warbling rips through the dark. It's the incoming line.

It wakes Spencer up.

He looks around. The walls press up around him. The light next to his head is glowing red in time with the signal of the incoming line. Spencer reaches to the switch, flips it.

"Hello," he says.

He hears a series of clicks. *Clickclickclick.* Then—

"Lyle Spencer," says a voice.

"Do you know what time it is?"

"It's four-thirty right now. You'd—"

"Exactly," says Spencer. "It's four-thirty. Good-bye—"

"No," says the voice. And there's something in it that makes Spencer pause. "You'd better get dressed. I'll be there in less than an hour."

"An hour? Here? Who do you think you are?"

"More important thing is who *you* are, Spencer. And what you're doing in the U.S."

"I don't know what you're talking about."

"You're hilarious. But you might still save yourself by staying exactly where you are."

"*Who are you?*"

"If you want to find out, all you gotta do is wait. And if you do anything else, you're nowhere near as smart as I've been hoping."

"You're crazy."

"Tell me that in person." The line goes dead.

Spencer doesn't waste time. He's already seen that the call hasn't registered. He runs his hand across what's left of his hairline, feels for a point behind his right ear. He slots wires, jacks in—lets his mind plunge down into the endless architecture of the U.S. zone. He darts back and forth amidst countless conduits. He can't find a trace of the call. He could opt for more intensive measures. He could kick down doors. But not without increasing the risk of exposing his own position.

Though clearly that position's been exposed to someone. He jacks out, watches zone wink out all around him. He retains its frozen image in his head while he plays with strategies and replays the voice recording at about triple the speed. Then at normal. Then at fifty percent. The voiceprints swim on the screens on his walls. The implications cluster on the ones in his head. But they hold nothing concrete.

He shakes his head as though to clear it. He pads to the kitchenette, throws some switches. He runs some water, starts grinding beans. He could just let the machine take care of it. But right now he feels like doing it himself. So he thinks and lets the coffee percolate.

When it's done, he walks to the window. A whisper from him, and the blinds are opening slightly. Red glow suffuses the room. The towers of Minneapolis gleam. He watches the lights, sips the coffee while he sifts through issues. If this were the federals, they'd be kicking in his door. They wouldn't be bothering with this bullshit. But if not the federals . . . then who? Spencer's never met a free agent inside North America before. If that's who it is. But if it is, they must have some kind of maneuverability.

But now he hears something.

It's coming from the corridor outside his door. He goes motionless. It's been a lot less than an hour. A light chime wafts through the room as the doorbell sounds.

Spencer moves to the closet, retrieves his pistol. He cocks

it. He creeps to the door, presses himself up against the wall beside it. He triggers the voice-switch.

"Yes," he says.

"Lemme in," says the voice that Spencer's only heard once in his life before.

"Sure," says Spencer. He checks the image on the screen. There's nothing there. Just empty corridor.

"Hurry up," says the voice.

"Hold on," says Spencer. "Lights," he adds. The stretch of corridor outside his conapt is filled with glow. The corridor's still empty. Spencer flips the manual switch for the conapt's lights and sets them on low.

"Stop fucking around," says the voice.

"Open," says Spencer.

The door opens.

A man enters the room. He's Spencer's height, but he's got a lot more bulk. None of it looks to be fat. He wears a unistretch jumpsuit. His hair's cropped close about his head. His face borders on the wizened. The eyes retract deep into the crevasses of the skin that folds about them. They seem to live in a way that the rest of that face does not. Spencer takes all this in in an instant. He keeps the pistol pointed at the man. The door slides shut.

"Lyle Spencer," says the man. He grins, but it's not much of one. "You alone?"

"I will be when I pull this trigger."

"That's the kind of talk that makes me edgy."

"I can live with that."

"Look," says the man. "If I meant you harm, I wouldn't have given you warning."

"I'm really not interested in your assurances, my man," says Spencer. He extends the arm that's holding the pistol, raises it up toward the level of the man's head. "What interests me is what you're trying to pull. You call me unannounced in the middle of the night. On a line that turns out to be completely stealth. Now you're standing in my apartment uninvited. In another moment you'll be bleeding from a head wound unless you tell me exactly what you want."

"Name's Linehan," says the man. "I'm here to help you."

"No you're not," says Spencer. "You're either here to arrest me, or you're about to get me arrested. It's one or the other."

"Actually," says the man mildly, "it's neither."

"In that case, I'll say it one last time, and I promise it'll be the last thing you ever hear if you don't start talking sense. What do you *want?*"

"To lower the risks to both of us. Look, let me tell you what I *don't* want. I don't want you to alert the authorities. I don't wanna make you think like I'm gonna let you pull that trigger. And if it so happens that you somehow pull it off—there's information out there that will live beyond me."

"Information about what?"

"The Priam Combine."

"The who?"

"Spencer, you really *don't* want me to answer that question. Because I'd say something like *profit-taking Euro vultures who spy on everybody and their fucking dog*. And then I'd throw in something about how I would have thought that Priam's agents were *way* too smart to try to play dumb with me."

"Where'd you find this information?"

"Never you mind where I found it. But I'll tell you where I've put it. Out in the zone. With orders to grow some legs and start moving unless I keep reminding it not to."

"And you think you can use this to control me?"

"I had in mind a little influence."

"Please."

"Was lucky you were home, Spencer," says Linehan, looking around. "You're often not. I said to myself, probably a fifty-fifty chance he's here. When I found myself in the Midwest in the middle of it all, I thought, let's see what Spencer's up to. Good old Spencer. But not so good if he's up north on one of his junkets for some surveying operation. Hell of a cover, Spencer. Does it really get you good information?"

Spencer doesn't reply.

"Pretty far north, Spencer," says Linehan. "What's it like up there? Flitcar all the way to Hudson, mining tractors rumbling, fires through the Canadian night, American military bases everywhere—you can see a long way out there, can't you?"

"Sure you can," says Spencer.

"Well, see—that's my problem. I can see a long way too. I can see it coming from a long way. I can *see* it. But I can't *move*." He paces to the window as he's talking.

"Stay away from that window," says Spencer. Linehan turns. "Listen," says Spencer. "I've had about enough of this. You've done nothing but threaten me, you've told me nothing, and I'll be damned if I'm going to let you keep talking without saying a thing. What's this all about?"

"A bargain."

"This I can't wait to hear," says Spencer.

"A deal, Spencer. You're gonna get me out of this country. And if you don't, I'll turn you in to the authorities. What I hear, they got a real hard-on for limey data thieves rummaging through their Dumpsters."

"*That's* your bargain?"

"No, that's my stick. I also got a carrot."

"What are you talking about?"

"What's in my head."

"What makes you think I care about what's in your head?"

"Could be very valuable to your career, Spencer."

"My *career*? What the hell do you take my career to be?"

Linehan smirks. "Not that that career needs any help. Senior consultant at defense contractor TransNorthern. Make managing director in another couple years if you hurry. You're one fancy guy, Spencer. Your road's lined with rose petals. Maybe even ones that have been grown. I'm surprised you're living in a place as small as this."

"I have a larger one up north," says Spencer.

"Of course you do," says Linehan. "Now look. Let's get some things straight. I don't give a shit why you're making like a suit. Why you've been worming your way up the TransNorthern hierarchy. I don't care what kind of cover it serves. I don't care what Priam's doing here. None of that interests me in the slightest. What interests me is that you can get me across the border."

"I can get myself across the border," says Spencer. "What am I supposed to do with you, put you in my fucking luggage?"

"Pack a big enough crate and sure. Listen, Spencer. I don't care *what* the plan is, as long as you convince me it's a good one. It had better be creative, though. It had better be resourceful."

"And in return?"

"Told you that already. Information."

"Of what nature?"

"It's very difficult to explain that without telling you everything."

"So tell."

"So no. Your motivation to help me would be at an end."

"It may be already."

"I doubt it," says Linehan. "Listen, Spencer, all I can say for now is that it's worth it. That it'll pay off your stint in the States and then some."

Spencer looks at him. "Does it involve Autumn Rain?"

"Everything that's anything involves Autumn Rain right now. I'm hardly gonna claim distinction for what I've got on *that* basis."

"You and everybody else," says Spencer. "Anyone can say they have something if they don't have to show a thing. This is nothing. And you're even less."

"Easy, Spencer. Easy. I know what you're thinking."

"What am I thinking?"

"You're thinking that if you killed me now, and got inside my head for real, you might be able to keep the feds from learning about you—*and* learn whatever it is I've got cooking. You're wrong on both counts. First of all, you couldn't kill me. I'm tougher than I look. Second, even if you beat the odds, you wouldn't beat the acid that's gonna nail my brain the moment my blood stops showing up. You wouldn't salvage a thing. Least of all my codes."

"You're thinking I'm thinking a lot."

"So here's something else to think about. A present. Just to show you I'm serious."

"Namely?"

"Namely this." Linehan reaches into one of his pockets— "Easy," he says as Spencer tenses. He takes something out, places it on the table. Spencer can see that it's a chip.

"What's on it?"

"What's on it," says Linehan, "is the production outputs for the United States' farside mining operations. The real ones, Spencer. Not the ones they publish. Not the ones they claim. The genuine article."

"If that's true, that's worth—"

"A fortune on the neutral markets? For you, it's free. Check it out, Spencer. See for yourself."

And Spencer does. He keeps the gun trained on Linehan, picks up the chip as though it will turn hot and burn at any moment. He slots it into a space that suddenly opens in his index finger. He downloads it into secure storage: a part of his software that's modularized from the rest, thereby allowing him to see the readouts without compromising himself with a download that's potentially tainted. Numbers stream through his skull. He can't see if they hold everything that Linehan's promised.

But he can see enough.

"Alright," he says. The numbers fade out, replaced by Linehan's mirthless grin. "Looks like you've got something here."

"More than just something, Spencer. I reckon that little chip will get you most of your remaining distance to the quota Priam's set for you. Maybe more."

"You know about the quotas?"

"Of course I know about the quotas. I know they're all your masters care about. I know your quota's the difference between your being set up for life in Europe and trapped forever in the States. But what *you* need to know is that if you play ball with me, no one will ever talk to you about quotas again."

"Where'd you get this, Linehan?"

"Looking in places I wasn't supposed to."

"I'm sure. My answer's still no."

"What?"

"You heard me."

"What more do you want?"

"How about something realistic? Look, you've got something going on here. I'm convinced. I'll do what I can for you. I can get you to the coast. But a border run is something else entirely. It's hard enough with one. Two would make it suicide."

"Not if Priam took it seriously."

"It's not a question of what Priam takes seriously. It's a question of ten million klicks of sensors. It's a question of satellites scanning everything that moves. It's ocean. How are we going to get you past that?"

"It's not foolproof. No border is. You know that, Spencer."

"You don't know *shit*."

"Then shoot me now, you listless fuck. Come on and try it. Or how about if I just call the feds and tell them to swing on by and collect us both. Look, am I saying it's gonna be easy? Fuck no. I've lived the life too, Spencer. I'm living it now. That's how I beat a trail to your door without leaving any fucking footprints. Zone prowess, right? Something I know you know all about. That's how I'm staying one step ahead of all those hounds."

"Who do you think is after you?"

"Who isn't?"

"I'm not."

"You don't count. You're nobody. No offense."

"And what are you?"

"Already told you what I am. An asset."

"An asset to what?"

"To you. To your life—let's hope so. To my life—for sure. I aim to keep on living."

"And for how long have you been prolonging it?"

"A few thousand klicks and a few score hours."

"How hard are they looking for you?"

"Hard enough to damn me," says Linehan.

"And now you've damned me too."

"You gotta admit you're intrigued, Spencer."

"Of course I'm intrigued. I'm also fighting the urge to put one straight between your eyes."

"Spencer, look at it this way. I can appreciate that you haven't got the warm fuzzies for me. But try to put yourself in my position. Don't think of this as blackmail. Think of it as a business offer."

"I'll think whatever I like."

"Sure you will. But while you're at it—keep in mind that what I'm proposing to give you will let you write your own ticket. It'll catapult Priam to the top of the data-combines. It'll vault you straight up into Priam's rafters. Which surely ought to make up for the fact that you don't have an alternative."

"Don't patronize me."

"But have I sold you?"

"More like you've sold me out. But I'll play your game. I'll take you across the fucking border. I'll try to take you in one piece too. And then, so help me God, whatever you've got had better make the thing worth it."

"It's a deal," says Linehan. "How do you propose we do it?"

"I propose we start by getting ourselves to the Mountain."

"Which sector?"

"Old Manhattan."

"Works for me. When do we leave?"

"Now."

The 'copter's been going for a while now. It's left the Rockies behind. It's well out over the western desert. Smoke billows far to the northeast. Haskell can't see it. Marlowe can.

"The prairie fires."

"Still burning?"

"Still burning."

"Eight weeks now," she says. She doesn't take her eyes off her window.

"Every year they flare longer past the summer," he says.

"Uh-huh," she replies. She's still not looking at him.

"I think we should start talking," he says.

"About."

"What's happening."

"What's there to talk about."

"We could start with why he put us together."

"I presume he has his reasons," she says.

"Sure he does. Can you name a single good one?"

"Who said they had to be good?"

"What's that supposed to mean?"

"Maybe he just wants to see how we're going to react."

"You think he finds this amusing?"

"I think he might," she says. She smiles slightly. "Don't you?"

"Did you ever think you'd see me again?"

"I figured the odds were against it."

"I tell you what's funny," he says. "What's funny is how it seemed so secret at the time. It seemed like we were fooling them back in the academy. A month in the real world—a month into the runs and out of training, and it was clear they must have known all along."

"Yes."

"They were watching us the whole time," he says.

"Yes."

"Is that what's got you so rattled?"

"I'm not rattled," she says. "*They're* rattled."

"Obviously," he replies. "They briefed us in real-time."

"They briefed us *together*. Even in the secondary briefings, I'm always the only agent."

"That's the way all of CI works," he says. "I've never met another agent save in the field. I've never known an agent who had."

"Or at least, that would admit to it."

"And we were briefed by Sinclair himself."

"Or by something that wore his face."

"But why would it have done that?"

"To inspire us," says Haskell dryly.

"And are you inspired?"

"To stop the Rain? Absolutely. To serve the greater glory of CICom? Sure. To help Matthew Sinclair help Matthew Sinclair? Why not?"

"You don't sound that convinced."

She says something he doesn't quite catch.

"What was that?"

"I said Sinclair's a bastard."

He stares at her. He glances at the 'copter's walls. She sneers.

"What does it matter if he hears us now? He heard us *fuck* all those years ago. He's heard all there is to hear. He's a degenerate. A dirty old man."

Marlowe has no idea what to say to that. So he says nothing.

"Besides," she says, "it's not like he's going to hear anything *new*. I've been telling the microphones this for years. I've told him how much I fucking *hate* him. Told him how much I love him too. But never anything he didn't already know." And then a snarl in response to whatever Marlowe's about to say: "Well, why the fuck *wouldn't* he already know? He's the one who fucking set me up this way. So why in God's name am I so ashamed of the way I've been *configured*?"

She wipes at her eyes. "Shit," she says.

"Is this why you haven't been speaking to me?" Marlowe asks.

"No," she says. "There's something else."

"That something being my being back in your life?"

"That sounds like wishful thinking."

He doesn't reply.

"Look," she says, "all I'm saying is that we can never forget that Sinclair's the one who handles the handlers. We can never forget he's the master Operator of them all. That's all."

"You just changed the subject," says Marlowe.

"Sorry?"

"I was talking about us."

"What's there to talk about?" she asks.

"What you're not telling me."

"What am I not telling you?"

"What's really got you so rattled."

"Look," she says, "enough with all the questions. Enough

with the interrogation. Or is this some kind of seduction? I've read your files, Jason—"

"You've read my *files?*"

"—and you know what? I can't say I *like* the man you've become. Whatever you're not trying to kill, you're trying to fuck. Believe me, Jason: you'd better be ready to make an exception."

"Who gave you my fucking files?"

"Sinclair."

"Sinclair?" Marlowe's as angry as he is puzzled.

"Or whoever's speaking for him. Think about it, Jason. I'm the razor. You're the mechanic. Which means you're reporting to me."

Marlowe shakes his head. "Hey," he says. "Relax. I think you've got the wrong idea."

"Good," she says.

"I just want to know what you've discovered."

"What have I discovered?" she asks in a voice that would fool anybody else.

"Something you shouldn't have."

She stares.

"I know that look," he says. "The look that says you're holding out on everybody. It was driving me crazy throughout the briefing with Sinclair."

"Driving you *crazy?*" It's a good half-second before Marlowe realizes that her question is sounding in his skull and not in the air around him. That Haskell has spoken aloud the very next moment: scorning him for trying to get inside her pants, then cutting off the conversation. She sits there, apparently simmering. But her words sound in Marlowe's head anyway.

"The one-on-one," she says.

Not that she needs to. He's switching into it seamlessly, neural implants letting words flick between them.

"You're doing this in code?"

"The only safe way," she replies.

"How did you get my side of the cipher?"

"When I gave your systems that boost back in that city."

"I thought that was just my suit."

"Your head wasn't that much farther away."

"So what is it you want to tell me?"

"That I made covert downloads in the Citadel."

"The Citadel? You mean, in South America—"

She nods.

"When?"

"While you were out there slugging it out with the Jaguars on the roof. I downloaded every file that was still intact."

"CI files?"

"Of course. That's who owns the Citadel, right?"

"That's who used to."

"Right," she says. "Anyway, the files didn't help us. Most of it was wiped by EMP anyway. And then that zeppelin started signaling. So I never mentioned it."

"If you had, you'd be facing a court-martial," he says. "Jesus, Claire. What the fuck were you *hoping* to find? What the hell could justify hacking classified seals?"

"How the fuck should I know, Jason? Maybe I was gonna find the blueprint of an escape route. Maybe the location of a distress beacon. Or the coordinates of some evac point. Or *anything* that would have kept the militia from using their machetes to cut me extra orifices while they raped me from every direction."

Her voice dies away inside in his head. He sits amidst that silence. Emotions tear at him—fear for this woman, fear of this woman, all of it bound up in something else that he can't name. He tears away from all of it, focuses:

"So what *did* you find?"

"Like I said, nothing at the time. But once they'd repaired

the damage my cranial software had sustained from the EMP, I went back to those downloads with a revamped toolkit. Some of the data wasn't recoverable. Some of it was. Some of it dealt with us."

"One of the files talked about *us?*"

"Not you and me specifically. Or maybe it did. I don't know."

"What did it *say?*"

"Our memories—" Her voice trails off.

"Yes?"

"May be manufactured."

"Manufactured."

"Yes."

"Meaning what?"

"Meaning they might have been implanted by the handlers."

"Why?"

"Presumably to render their asses even more secure than they already are."

He doesn't reply.

"Surely I haven't left you speechless? The handlers brief us in the trance to prevent turned agents from rolling up the network. They're pros at using the deployment of memory to further their control. If they controlled our waking memories as well, they could configure that memory between missions. Which would make it irrelevant that an agent has been turned. Just install new programs and reboot."

He stares at her. He realizes he's doing so while a soundless conversation is taking place. He turns back to the window of the jet-copter, keeps gazing at the fires.

"Look, I'll transmit you what's left of the file," she says. "It spells all this out."

"Don't," he says. "I don't want to see it."

"Still the good little errand boy? I'm trying to show you what happens to good little errand boys."

"So does this mean I haven't done any of the missions I remember doing?"

"That *would* be your first thought, wouldn't it?"

"What else would be—*oh,*" he says.

"*Oh.* The file isn't as specific as one would hope. It doesn't name names. It's part of some briefing manual to help envoys help their agents 'adjust'—the actual word—to the alterations. And it implies that this practice is starting to be rolled out across CI agents but isn't yet universal. And that the other Commands have yet to adopt it as standard procedure. They may not, either. It may remain a CI-specific practice, like the envoys. But if you want my opinion, I'd say that for the sake of your sanity you should just assume that most of your life's greatest moments actually took place, Jason." She looks thoughtful. "Plus or minus a few key details, of course."

"And what about what happened between us?"

"What about it?"

"Does the document say anything about it? About—that kind of memory?"

"No," she says. "But think about it. With something like this, security of the handlers probably isn't the only thing in play. It *could* also be a question of mission leverage. Someone with a given set of memories might fight harder than someone without. And emotional ties to other agents—especially to agents locked safely in the past—might be the kind of thing that engenders a broader esprit de corps."

"But putting two agents with a history together is the kind of thing that could backfire."

"It may already have."

"Which doesn't help in figuring out what went on between us," says Marlowe. "Doesn't help in figuring out if anything ever did."

"No. It doesn't."

"And I'm sure our memories correspond with total precision," he says acidly.

"That's a thought. Try me."

"How about the time we took that 'copter to Stanley Park."

"What was I wearing?"

"Blue shirt," he replies. "Grey cap. We looked out upon Vancouver. We looked out upon the ocean—watched the sunset and the cold came on all sudden. I gave you my jacket and you said—"

"Stop it."

"No. That's not what you said."

"You're right. That line of verification's a red herring. The real question is *when* our memories got tampered with."

"Assuming they were."

"Right," she says. "Right: assuming they were, when would they have done it. Because they *could* have done it anytime from academy onward."

"I'd say the last few days is your best bet," says Marlowe. That one makes her look out the window, shake her head.

"Think about it," says Marlowe. "We know they've assigned us to work together. We know they're changing up their rules. What better time to prime us than right before we meet?"

"But I recognized you in that city!"

"Did you really?"

"Fuck," she says.

"And it may not stop there."

"What's that supposed to mean?"

"It means maybe you never did find a file in the Citadel."

"*Fuck,*" she says. "That bastard."

"As you say."

"And you'd better listen. Sinclair's not leveling with us, Jason. On any level. Even within the briefing itself. All that bullshit he was on about running that data through all those comps and coming up with all those probability vectors... that's all it is: bullshit. He's got specific intelligence about something, or he wouldn't be committing key operatives off-planet. He's not coming clean."

"Probably."

"Definitely."

"Does that scare you? Or just excite you?"

"I'm not sure I know the difference," she replies evenly.

"Did you once?"

"Can't we figure that out as we go?"

"I guess we'll have to," he replies.

The 'copter descends toward Houston.

Ten klicks south of Agrippa, the train emerges. Though you could be forgiven for not spotting the tunnel mouth, because to say that this terrain is rough is to put it mildly. But the vehicle now shooting out of the black just doesn't care. It's like hot mercury, that train, distended across a quarter-klick of rail as it dives through tunnels and sails across bridges, hurling itself along terrain that would have been deemed impassable a scant twenty years ago. The mountains cluster ever thicker; again and again, they seem to have the train completely boxed in. But—again and again—the train's a mechanical Houdini extricating itself from apparent confinement, doing everything save pass through solid rock as it bores relentlessly onward en route for Shackleton, at the lunar south pole.

But the view isn't keeping the Operative's attention. He's saving that for the interior of this car. The seats are three to a row on either side of a wide central aisle, with more cleared space up in front. The Operative's got a row to himself. The tops of the seats are low enough to allow some line of sight to one's fellow passengers. Though some are military, most of them seem to be corporate—and just technicians at that:

grease deep in their faces, tools hung at their belts. The Operative doesn't like the look of them.

There are two in particular he likes even less. His sixth sense is crawling: up near the front—one with red hair withering into premature grey, the other with grey hair dyed half-red. They haven't tried anything. They haven't given any sign they even know each other. The Operative keeps an eye in front of him, strays one eye sideways a little, stays attuned to what's behind him—and all the while he thinks.

And listens too. To the man inside his head. Because uncertainties within the car can't compete with the voice that suddenly comes dropping down into the middle of the Operative's skull as the download kicks in, clothed in an image that sits in the very center of the mind's eye. Ebony skin. Silver hair. Opticals. Oversized ears.

And grinning mouth.

"Carson, Carson, Carson," it says. "Did you miss me?"

The Operative stares out the window. Stares at his fellow passengers. Stares at the image's teeth. Doesn't speak. Just listens.

"That's good," says the mouth. "Real good, Carson. Had to ask, you understand. Even though you can't answer. Let me assume, though, that the answer's the same as it was before: no and yes."

The Operative just stares. Red going grey has risen to his feet, has joined a few other technicians lounging and leaning around at the front of the car—and in their center is grey going red, dealing out a game of Shuk. Or at least the Operative guesses it to be Shuk. There are five persons in all, and Shuk's a five-person game. But he can't see the many-shaped cards that are probably now lying on the floor of the car or on some makeshift tabletop made out of someone's equipment. So he's left to make his guesses. For minutes. For hours. Then:

"Yes and no," continues Lynx, "no and yes. Can't say I

blame you. It was bad enough when I got here. It's much worse now."

The Operative keeps staring. Red going grey has thrown his right hand back in triumph, laughing. Grey going red's getting even redder. Now others are separating the two, the Operative half-expecting all the while that they're going to turn together and come for him. He's starting to feel quite underdressed.

"But we'll get you suited for it," says the mouth. "We'll get you sorted. Though I wish we didn't have to. I wish they'd sent me someone else." Tongue licks out, white teeth flashing behind its curve. "You think I'm pleased to see *you*? You must be kidding."

The Operative feels himself tipped back. Ever so slightly: but unmistakably. The train is ascending. The bridges on which it's riding are rising. More blackness is encroaching. Pulsings in that blackness are satellites sweeping low, catching the sun.

"Because the truth," says Lynx, "it's that this whole game is going up for grabs. This whole scene is getting out of hand. And we, my friend, are right in the middle of it."

Now the bridge has risen so far into the peaks that they're starting to constitute a bona fide horizon. The light of the stars is dribbling onto moonscape. And Lynx's smile is vanishing.

"So we got to change it up, Carson," he says. "We have to draw first *blood.*"

So now grey going red is whipping out a knife and trying to cut himself some red streaks. But his target's not the Operative: red going grey leaps backward, his left arm swinging around in front of him as he pulls his torso out of the path of the serration, his left hand flicking out with one of the many-shaped cards—this one's a triangle and one of its tips is actually hard-edged sharpness to pluck the jugular, play the red like a firehose out of control. But the hell of it is that grey that's going red forever is still on the attack. He grabs the wrist that holds the fatal card, tries to turn his assailant's own limb against him while he stabs in with his other one. The frantic nature of his thrusts parallels the jets of blood flying everywhere. It sends shadows sprawling, bystanders ducking, scarlet splashing, and all the while that smiling mouth just keeps on talking.

"I think you see the way this is going to go," says Lynx. Data blasts from behind him to grid the whole of zone. "You're going to die unless you listen to me. This is our nightmare scenario come to life. This is the moment you and I have always dreamt of. So wake the hell up, Carson. Because that's the fucking *Moon* out that window. That's our fucking *planet* in the sky."

Grey going red is nothing but red now, and a lot of that red's rubbed off on red going grey, who's also now getting stuck straight through the belly to add to the royal crimson. As if to keep from falling, each man grabs the other, twists his blade in deeper, one practically decapitating, the other impaling almost up to the heart.

"And you know what our biggest problem is?" asks Lynx. "It's you. You've got to loosen up. This place is far colder than you could ever hope to be. I don't need the man who thinks he can outchill the next ice age. I need someone who acts like a normal human being. Ever tried smiling, Carson? It's not that bad when you get used to it. When all is said and done: it's not such a contortion after all."

The mountains writhe. The sky reels. The two flopping bodies are lost to sight up front. Unless they were a diversion of some kind, they had absolutely nothing to do with the Operative. No one in the car is standing now.

"You stand out," says Lynx. "But no matter. With the Elevator down, all bets are off anyway. The prospect of Armageddon is growing. The other side seems to think we did it, we seem to think the other side was behind it, and no one but no one thinks that this outfit that calls itself the Rain is anything but a front for players hot on the trail of the main chance."

Sudden rearview: the Operative glances backward as the doors behind him open and suits swarm at speed into the room. SpaceCom military police. They check the bodies. They eye the technicians. The technicians return the favor.

"So," says Lynx, "try this on for size. Agrippa: don't come back to it unless you have to. Sarmax: weighed in the balance and found wanting. You: dancing to the tune I call. And whatever you do, don't sit still. Because there are no guarantees. At all."

Medics enter. God knows where they were hanging out. They unzip some body bags, stuff 'n' load, zip 'em up, head on out. The cops exit with them.

"As to contingencies," says Lynx. "If they try to take you, let them. Play dumb. Buy time. Maybe you can fox your way out. And if they vector onto your identity, I'll switch your ass, buy you a little margin."

Information washes around the Operative, information shot through with moonscape. And what, he thinks, if they vector onto yours . . .

"But first they have to find me," says Lynx. "First they have to see me. But see: I'm invisible, Carson. I'm the fungus that grows on the walls of the disused shafts. I'm the ghost in the final machine. It's all around me, man. It's like being in somebody's skull. It's almost as fun. Are you ready for the run to end all runs?"

Long bridge becomes long tunnel. Long chute torpedoes past. Then:

"So steel your heart," says Lynx. "Prep those weapons. This'll put us both on the map, Carson, on the map for keeps for sure. They'll never forget this one. Not like we're going to give them the chance. Not when we're fishing for pearls of wisdom, Carson, pearls of wisdom. Data you can *feel*."

Train emerges from tunnel: chute gets torn away, shell shorn off by a darkness abandoned by the sun. It's all black. It's all mountains. It's all stars.

"And this is how you'll work it, Carson. You want the formula, here it is: by keeping the Earth overhead and the zone at your back. By keeping your own counsel and playing all the ends against the middle. By making this Moon yours."

Through the last peaks, and lights become visible in the depths toward which the train's now racing.

"And we'll start," says Lynx, "with the place that's south of every south."

 Somewhere back on Earth another train is rushing east. Somewhere in that train's a private compartment. Two men sit within. The door's shut. It's sealed.

So now their mouths aren't.

"Okay," says Spencer. "I've got this place rigged. It's time to continue our conversation."

"Yeah? What's to continue?"

"A lot, actually. We need to know a little bit more about one another if we're going to pull this off."

"Nah, Spencer. You've got it wrong. Less we know, the better."

"I disagree. In fact, it's about time you stopped lying to me."

"What?"

"I mean it's not like you're some kind of zone god."

"Did I ever say I was?"

"You damn well implied it. You think that just doing a hack on my apartment block is somehow going to convince me that you can tap into the lines at will? That you're off the cameras altogether?"

"Never claimed either."

"But having me believe it wouldn't be such a bad thing, would it? I'd be less likely to bolt that way, wouldn't I?"

Linehan says nothing. Just looks out the window.

"I'm talking to you, Linehan. Look at me." Linehan's head turns as though it's mounted on a swivel. "What are you using? You're not a razor yourself."

"What makes you say that?"

"The fact that *I* am."

"Of course you are. I knew that already."

"Of course you knew that already," says Spencer. "That's why you came knocking on my door in the first place. But I can see straight through your parlor tricks. Straight through you too. You don't talk like a razor, you don't act like one, and you certainly aren't thinking like one."

"Alright, Spencer. How *does* a razor think?"

"In endless circles."

"Meaning?"

"Got ten years?"

"Your point being?"

"My point's made. What were you using for that conapt trick? A local node?"

"Something like that."

"So why haven't they picked you up yet?"

"What do you mean?"

"I mean that there's no way you could be on the loose with just a piece of localized shit. They would have rolled up your identity by now. There's no way you should be sitting before me, breathing. There's no way at all."

"What are you getting at, asshole?"

"That you're working for the feds."

"Already told you I ain't."

"So where are the others?"

"What others?"

"If you don't enjoy federal blessing, then *where's the razor who configured your identity?* And how come you ended up on my door out of all the doors out there? Listen, Linehan: I can take ordinary rudeness. I can take working on a need-to-know basis. I can even take not knowing if you're going to try to stab me through the heart. But what I *can't* take is not even knowing enough to get the job done. So you'd better start giving me a little bit more to go on."

"Listen," says Linehan, "what you gotta under—"

But Spencer's just talking over him: "And you know how you can get some *extra credit* while you're doing it? By giving me a little bit more of a fucking hint about what I'm going to get at the end of all this. Otherwise, I promise you, this isn't worth it to me. I'll jump ship at some point and take my chances on a lightning run."

"Fine," says Linehan, "you win. The others are dead."

"What happened to them?"

"Blown out of an expresser about fifteen klicks up."

"When?"

"Two days ago."

"Two days ago? You mean—"

"Right," says Linehan. "With all that Elevator shit, the fact that a suborbital bound for Paris had bought it in midflight and scattered itself all over Greenland several hours earlier got knocked off the headlines and never made it back. They're saying structural integrity was lost. I don't exactly know what the reasons for that were, but I can tell you that they weren't accidental. Awful lot of fuel on those fuckers. They're fuel-bitches, really. All it takes to send one up's a little spark. And that was all it took."

"And what set off that spark?"

"What didn't? See, you could say that we were expendable. You could say that. But you'd be lying. We were worse than expendable. We were marked for disposal from the start."

"Why?"

"Because we learned things we weren't supposed to. That's all, really. I'd reverse it, you know. I really would. If I could, I'd ditch my memory. I'd ditch it all. I'd go back to them and tell them I was gonna do all that. But they wouldn't believe me. They wouldn't listen. And even if they did, you know what this business is like. Dead meat—safer than live. Right, Spencer?"

"Sure," says Spencer. "Dead meat's always safer. Who are we talking about?"

"We could be talking about anyone," says Linehan. "That's the point."

"So point me in the right direction."

"No," says Linehan. "Gonna give you a little bit now, and you'll get the rest when we cross the border."

"The rest of what?"

"The rest of the story, asshole. Way I heard it, you like stories. Right? That's why you're in this country in the first place. That's all that gets the Priam Combine's rocks off, right? You broker information. You profit from data. You find the juice, your masters sell it to the highest bidder. Well, this one'll get bid so high it'll melt the fucking auction. Think your team's good enough to take that heat, Spencer?"

"Do you?"

"Does it matter?"

"Of course it does. Surely you wouldn't sell to someone who wasn't going to be able to handle it."

"You're confusing me with someone who gives a fuck, Spencer. As long as *I* pull it off, I don't really care if *you* do. And it's not like I had that many options. Couldn't trust anyone I knew, now, could I?" Linehan coughs. "So had to think about some possibilities I'd laid out in advance for just such a day. Some of the people I considered weren't even guilty of espionage. But all of them had something they were trying to hide."

"And I was one of them."

"Yeah, Spencer. Just one among many. It's true. But don't feel bad. I chose you all the same. Because it wasn't just a matter of being proximate. It was a matter of connections."

"Meaning?"

"Meaning I put my stash of names together from two different sets of sources. One was keepers of the records within this country. I had the inside track on some of them. Lots of records. Lots of keepers. Lots of data that some know, but not everyone. See, Spencer, the people who rule this country keep a lot of things hidden from one another. Always have, always will. And if you know how to work it, you can make that fact work for you."

"What was the second set of sources?"

"Neutral data. I'm a little bit of a traveler, Spencer. Bit of a globetrotter. And if you want to get neutral dirt, best place to do it is beyond the Atlantic and Pacific firewalls. Right? So that became another asset that I had at my disposal. Things I dug up via the first set might have sufficed, but the second was my top choice. Especially now that a lot of shit that's been buried deep is getting stirred up. So when the rubber met the road, I thought of you, on my second list and not on the first so far. Not too far away, either—and undoubtedly more than capable of helping me out. If you felt like it. If you could be made to see reason."

"And your colleagues? When did you ditch them?"

"When they split for Kennedy. I figured that they'd be able to stay below the radar screen until they reached passport control. But I figured that after that they were gonna get busted. I didn't place as much confidence in our razor as the rest did. Fucking optimists. They must have thought they had it made when they put the ground behind them." He shakes his head. "Me, I cut loose. I turned to my portfolio of options. I turned to you, Spencer."

"I'm touched."

"You wanted more. I'm giving you more."

"So tell me how you're moving around."

"Standard procedure. Our razor locked each of us into our new identities and threw away the key."

"I'm surprised he didn't hold on to your reins himself. Given how frisky you seem to be."

"I had an understanding with her," says Linehan. His lip curls upward in a half smile. "She helped me get away without alerting the rest of the team. I pointed out that my enhancements were going to make it tough for me to get through an ever-tightening border security."

"Combat enhancements?"

"Look at me, Spencer. Take a good look. Even without weapons, I'm built for one thing. That's going to be obvious to any halfwit customs software."

"And now your razor's dead."

"She is," says Linehan. "Turns out she couldn't configure an identity strong enough to get out of the country. So she bought it. Along with the rest of them." He shakes his head.

"Someone was willing to do a lot to make sure they never made it to Europe."

"Someone was. Someone still is. So how do you propose we get there?"

"I propose we do what we're doing, Linehan. Straight run to the Mountain."

"Yeah. And then what?"

"Why should I tell you?"

"I've been giving. It's time for some quid pro quo."

"Oh really? So it's quid pro quo day, is it? Tit for tat, huh? You haven't even *begun* to level with me, Linehan, and now you're saying I'm the one who owes *you*?"

"We're on the same team, Spencer."

"We're not on the same team at all. This fugitive life has warped your fucking brain."

"Then I'm gonna spell it out for you. We're both professionals. Those who aren't can never understand what that's like. What those places are like. The one we're in now. The one I'm coming from. But we can both come out of this winning."

"Define winning," says Spencer.

"Us both living," says Linehan. "Tell me your plan."

"You already know my plan."

"I do?"

"If you know about Priam, then you know why we're going to the Mountain."

"To ask for help."

"Exactly," says Spencer.

"And how is the one you're asking likely to take it?"

"Very badly, I suspect," says Spencer.

The jet-copter slides down the runway in horizontal landing mode, slowing all the while. It slants off the straight, taxis along ramps that thread it through the heart of the spaceport's tangled maze. It proceeds past other craft waiting. It waits while other craft proceed. Sometimes the runway upon which it rolls bridges other routes. Sometimes it's the reverse.

"Complicated," says Marlowe.

"It's Houston," says Haskell.

The craft rolls into a less-trafficked area. Lights rise and fall through the haze at the far reaches of the runways. Hangar clusters draw closer.

"Looks like that one's ours," says Marlowe.

"Take my advice," says Haskell, "drop the possessives."

"Why?"

Because: they're lazy. They constitute labels. They represent assumptions. They hide the truth. Beyond the periphery of your vision: that's where it all goes down. Behind your own eyeballs: that's where it all hangs out. Secret names in the dark that you're hiding even from yourself: shadowed orbits that might just be revealed when the mood strikes them.

Or you.

"All I'm saying is that we need to revert to first principles," says Haskell.

"You don't know what you're talking about," says Marlowe.

"Makes two of us," replies Haskell.

Makes for one dynamic partnership, that's for sure. She figures that must be the point. Volatility's been known to strengthen the mix sometimes. Let agents bitch and moan and wonder all they want. But give them something to sink their teeth into and a reason to care . . .

"Tell me then," says Marlowe, "how you think this'll play out."

"Take my advice," she says. "Don't think."

The jet-copter trundles across an apron. It rumbles into a small hangar and rolls to a stop. The doors open. Marlowe and Haskell get up, get out, get hustled by waiting soldiers across the concrete and into an elevator set within one wall. Seconds later, they're rising through the ceiling—and then through many more. It's almost enough to make them think that this is the way into space after all.

But eventually the elevator slows and stops. Their escorts lead them down another corridor and into a room.

With a view. Windows occupy the entirety of one wall. Gantries and runways sprawl all the way to ocean. The sky's filled with craft receding and craft approaching. Exhaust hangs heavy overhead. Concrete shimmers in the heat.

"Welcome to Houston," says a voice.

The voice's owner sits within a chair set in the corner. He regards Marlowe and Haskell without expression.

It's Morat.

• • •

You say that Earth's south pole is dark six months a year? The Moon's nets all twelve with ease. Picture Malapert Mountain gleaming overhead, a black and furnaced pearl. Picture a plateau anchored halfway down into the void beneath it—and you've got your fix on Shackleton. But to really understand that place, you have to move beyond it. So picture the trails that lead down to nowhere. Picture the prospectors gone missing for more than five decades now. The bulldozers that hauled away and never came back. The valleys that lead to cul-de-sacs of killing angles, the caves that become catacombs, the craters within craters within craters. So tangled, that land: even worse than man's mind—and now the Operative wanders through the streets that make up an outpost suspended above the polar maw itself.

He figures no one will give a shit about the Elevator down here. He's right. These guys are rugged individualists. They think they're so tough they don't need a dome. Most of Shackleton is underground anyway. Including the main rail station. The Operative's in that station's lockers now. He keys the door to one locker in particular, picks up several packages. He whistles up a conveyor, places the packages on its platform, lets its gyro-stabilized bulk trail him as he walks out into corridors and passageways that are a lot wider than those within Agrippa Station.

Lot brighter, too. Turns out these guys are light hogs—they crank the illumination in compensation for their lack of sun. Technicians everywhere. Some suited. Some not. There are a fair number of soldiers. Ladders carve upward along the walls, lead to rows of shopfronts and businesses. Main drag, they call it—one lane for people walking and another for flitcars. Yet another for bona fide crawlers. And still another for thrusters.

But the Operative's just walking. He leaves the central grid behind, leads his conveyor down a side street. The walls and ceiling close in. The passage zigzags through the rock. The lights grow more sporadic. Graffiti covers at least half the doors. What's left of the overhead lighting stutters fitfully. The low-rent sector: and hopefully someone's been paying the rent on one room in particular . . .

Someone has. The Operative triggers the lock, goes on in. It's not much. Even less than what he had in Agrippa, in fact: just a cot and a wall-screen on one wall and a toilet on the other. Plus an incandescent coil overhead. The Operative flicks on the light. He unloads the conveyor and scrambles its memory before sending it on its way. He shuts the door, goes to work, starts opening containers.

Five minutes later he's standing in the suit. Its material clasps in around his legs, arms, torso. He hears his breath echoing hollowly. This suit looks like a typical miner's outfit, though in truth it's anything but. The Operative lets his weapons range upon his screens. He checks over all his systems.

Suddenly he hears a voice between his ears.

Not his either.

The twenty-first century wasn't long in the coming before New York started to grow again. Refugees from the strife down south, immigrants fleeing the chaos abroad, fugitives from the rural as the combines took over, escapees from the shutdown of towns—and all such infusions intensified by a proliferation of birthrates across all demographics as the world grew more desperate and the mass of population grew poorer and the peasant mentality took over on the streets. Wasn't just New York by that point, either. It was Newark and Boston and Philly all rolled into one thing that encompassed them all and piled on upward toward the heavens. Same story for so many other megacities. The Mountain isn't even the biggest of them. But at the dawn of the twenty-second century, it's the largest in the States by far. For five hundred klicks, it's the Eastern Seaboard. For two hundred klicks inland, it's the land itself.

For those within, it's the whole world.

The two men exit the intercity at Grand Central, take a local from there. It blasts through the tube, sweeping recycled air before it. It stops three times, disgorging humans, taking them on. It stops a fourth time—and that's their destination. Spencer and Linehan get out, rise on escalators that give way to a larger space—rivers of glass and steel, and all around: translucent tubes with people pouring through them, no ceiling in evidence save blur. The two men step off at the appointed platform. They pass along a ramp. They walk through a wide doorway.

Suddenly they're inside in a way they weren't before. The hubbub of conversation has shifted from the fragmented roar of the streets to the more subdued burbling into which voices conscious of each other recede. They're standing in a foyer. Plush carpeting, chandeliers hung overhead. Clerks and bellhops looking bored. Savoy Metropole. Second-rate hotel. First choice for them right now.

Five minutes later they're in a suite. Two bedrooms and a lounge: they sweep the whole place. They find nothing. They set up the surveillance inhibitors and repair to the lounge. They sort through the minibar, helping themselves to water and coffee. They put their feet back and look at each other.

"Now what?" asks Linehan.

"Now I make a call," says Spencer.

• • •

You're alive," says Haskell.

"An astute observation," says Morat. He remains seated in his chair. His hands perch lightly on the armrests. The merest outline of a smile hovers on his face.

"How did you get out?" says Haskell.

"I used the stairs."

"All eighty stories of them?"

"Hardly," says Morat. "Eight was about all I could take. And then I broke through a window."

"And flew?"

"Why not? That's how you got up the shaft, right? Like an angel speeding off to heaven, so they told me. You were lucky, Claire. Your mission failed. You fell. So did the sky. But you survived."

"Just barely," says Haskell.

"I'm not sure we've been introduced," says Marlowe.

"We haven't," replies Morat. He gazes at Marlowe without expression.

"This is Morat," mutters Haskell.

"And who," asks Marlowe, "is Morat?"

"He's an envoy," says Morat.

"And how do you know him?"

"She knows me," says Morat, "because I was almost the last thing she ever saw."

"And here I was thinking I'd seen you for the last time," says Haskell.

"Almost. But now I'm back."

"Why?"

"Same reason anyone comes back. Because the job isn't done."

"And that job would be?"

"Handling you."

"Again?"

"Why not?"

"Because we weren't exactly a winning team?"

"Ah," says Morat, "but this time you have a real-live mech at your disposal." He gestures at Marlowe.

"Are you trying to bait me?" asks Marlowe.

"Perhaps. Is it working?"

"I think it just might be."

"So control it. You're a mechanic. This lady is a razor. When you're on the Moon, she'll pull *your* strings. There's no shame in that. There's nothing wrong with compulsion. Particularly not when it's mutual."

"What," says Marlowe softly, "is it that you want?"

"Reassurance," says Morat. "Nothing more than that." He stands up, steps to the window. "Look at that. Nothing like a genuine view to clarify one's thinking. See those ships? Picture them falling back to Earth. The runways? Imagine them chopped to dust. That's what Cabo Norte was like when the missiles hit her. The rockets toppled. The hangars collapsed. The fuel burned. It was inferno. Yet it was nothing—just the precursor to that which the Rain would visit upon us."

"We've heard this speech," says Haskell.

"It's no speech," says Morat. "Get that through your head. Tonight we're on full alert. We've been that way for two days now. And there we'll stay until we defeat the Rain or unleash upon the East or both. Think of a vehicle half driven off a cliff. It totters on that edge. Those within know that moving to save themselves could send them over. Yet they have to chance it anyway. Such is our dilemma. The difference being that we don't even know in which direction the edge lies. We don't even know whether we're past the point of no return already."

"I think we steered over it about fifty years ago," says Haskell.

"Our planet might have," says Morat. "We didn't. We'll live on. Even if we have to dwell in bunkers beneath the crust. Even if we have to lift the whole game into space."

"Isn't that exactly what the Rain accuses us of doing?" asks Marlowe.

"And there's a certain justice in their charge," replies Morat. "After all, we send up two more of our number tonight."

"When do we leave?"

"As soon as your transport gets here."

"Hold on a second," says Marlowe. "Sinclair told us the ship was already at Houston."

"He said it was fueling," says Haskell.

"It was," says Morat. "And then it launched."

They look at him. He grins.

"We needed it elsewhere at short notice," he says. "We couldn't wait. We improvised. We're moving a B-130 up from Monterrey. You know this game—circumstances change too fast to count on them."

"But the destination remains the same?"

"It does. When the time to go comes, I'll return to brief you. But for now, don't leave this room." He moves past them. The door opens as he approaches.

"You're talking like we're in a war zone," says Marlowe.

"Exactly," replies Morat.

The door slides shut behind him.

I t's just a voice. It's no vid. Somehow the lack of visual makes that voice sound different. There's no grin to underscore sardonic menace, no silver hair, no opticals to hint at all the lenses behind the eyes.

There's just Lynx.

"Carson," says the voice. "You've got it."

"You're damn right I've got it," says the Operative. "I'm in it right now."

"Makes two of us."

"So I noticed. Is this another download?"

"No," says Lynx, "it's just the same old me."

"You're talking to me live," says the Operative. He watches the codes crystallize in front of him. They check out. Which is good.

Or disastrous.

"No," says Lynx. "I'm guessing what you're going to say. I've worked it all out in advance. I'm jacking off while I let this proxy do the talking."

"You're really funny," says the Operative.

"No," says Lynx. "But I really am live, Carson. I really am here."

"Then you're putting us both at risk. What are you playing at, Lynx?"

"I haven't been *playing,* Carson. I've been *working.* Hard. And yes, I'm taking a risk. I'm taking precautions too. I'm routing it through five different satellites. I'm running it through more end-arounds than I can count. It's still a risk. But believe me, it's worth it. I had to reach you."

"Why," says the Operative.

"There's been a change of plan. Sarmax isn't here after all."

"Say again?"

"I think you heard me just fine."

"You're saying I came down here for nothing?"

"Not at all," says Lynx. "He's here. Just not *here.*"

"You're going to have to clarify that."

"Four hours ago, I was in possession of reliable intel to indicate that Sarmax was holed up at his company's downtown HQ."

"Right," says the Operative. "That was in the data you gave me."

"Exactly," says Lynx.

"Yeah," says the Operative. "That was a pretty good rant you got on. I was eating it up. You must be wired higher than the L2 fleet."

"Sure," says Lynx. "I'm wired higher than the L2 fleet. I'm wired to the point where I'm starting to shit metal. None of which changes the fact that Sarmax split this morning. You just missed him, Carson. But cheer up: he didn't go very far."

"How far?"

"Eighty klicks north."

"Which north?" says the Operative.

"Farside north," says Lynx. He supplies the coordinates.

"What in shit's name is there?"

"One of his bases. Totally isolated. Totally fortified. Take a look at this."

The image flashes through the Operative's head: "So when's he coming back?"

"He's not."

"He's staying there permanently?"

"His soul's not," says Lynx.

"Oh?"

"His soul's going to hit heaven without passing go."

"Say what?"

"You know exactly what," says Lynx. "You're going to get in there and kill him."

"You're shitting me."

"I assure you I'm not."

"How the fuck am I going to get in *there*?"

"Calm down," says Lynx.

"I am calm," says the Operative.

"Good," says Lynx. "Because I'm not. I've been too far gone in the dark for too long to be in the mood to listen to your bitching. So now you listen to me, Carson. I've got the location of the *target*. The *mission* says you take out that target. And that's the end of the discussion."

"End of the discussion? End of the discussion? Jesus Christ, Lynx. It's the *beginning* of the fucking discussion, that's what it is."

"Is that a fact," says Lynx.

"It's not just a fact," says the Operative, "it's a fundamental fucking truth. Listen to me, Lynx. I've already had a goddamn nuke go off next to my head. I've already had to stay busy staying out of the bullseye of whole racks of strategic weaponry. Last thing I want to do now is to get my ass turned into cannon fodder just because you don't have the balls to tell anyone above us that the plan has been rendered absurd by events on the ground."

"You're right," says Lynx. "For once you're right, Carson. I don't have the balls to tell them that. And I *definitely* don't have the balls to tell them that my mech doesn't have the balls to do what he's told. That's going to reflect badly on me. It's going to make them question my abilities. Even after they've crucified you for insubordination."

"Nobody's talking about insubordination," says the Operative.

"Really," says Lynx. "Because that's what it's sounding like to me."

"That's because you're not listening," says the Operative. "Mech to razor: calling a plan crazy isn't insubordination. Insubordination is disobeying orders. Which I haven't done. Not yet, anyway. Though I have to admit I'm awfully tempted when I find that the razor holding my leash is my old pal Lynx, who's apparently still just as fucking nuts as he was half a decade back, and apparently still lacing himself with every chemical he can lay his mitts on. Come on, man. There's too much history here. This is vendetta road. It leads nowhere."

"No," says Lynx. "It's the only way that I can see."

"The only way that *you* can see."

"Sure, me. What are you saying?"

"I'm saying it sounds like you're the one who thought this whole thing up."

"I *am* the one who thought this whole thing up, Carson. Christ, I thought you knew that. Razor's prerogative—razor's burden. Sarmax is just the means I've selected to reach the ends I've been given. They gave me the overall objective. They gave me a map to this whole goddamn rock. They told me to get in there and think up a plan."

"Which just happens to involve the elimination of the only guy crazy enough to call you crazy to your face."

"You don't have the big picture, Carson."

"The picture that whatever's in your veins gives you?"

"The picture you can't hope to touch. Millions of light-years, Carson. Chains of logic so far out they've done the red-shift. Don't even think about trying to follow me."

"Then don't make me. Just give me a sense as to how this whole thing fits together. Fuck, man. So far you've given me fuck-all. You've spent all that time in your own mind's tunnels, maybe I can notice a thing or two you haven't."

"We haven't got a choice," rejoins Lynx. But for the first time the confidence in his voice is waning. "We've got to nail him now. He might go anywhere next."

"Never mind that," says the Operative. "If it's not because you hate him—if it's not because the boys downstairs never forgave him—then why the fuck are we even after him in the first place? Is it just because we suspect him?"

"No," says Lynx. "It's because we can put his corpse to good use."

"Come again?"

"It's complicated."

"Then you'd better talk quickly."

"Well," says Lynx, "it's like this."

• • •

Control's not human. But Control's been rigged to talk like one to keep agents on their toes.

"Spencer? Where are you?" The voice in Spencer's skull is a hiss against static.

"Closer than you think," Spencer replies in words that aren't spoken aloud.

"Closer than you should be."

"So you know."

"So I can see. Took me a moment. What are you doing here?"

Control's been doing time in the Mountain for a while now. Spencer doesn't know precisely where. Maybe Control doesn't either. Control's physical location is a lot less important than the real one. And Control lurks in that reality, shifting beneath endless shades of camouflage, creeping through the branches of a jungle whose ground is something called detection, whose most feared denizens are the things we may as well call eyes.

"I need your help, Control."

"Sounds like you're beyond help, Spencer."

"Not yours."

"What makes you think I'm prepared to give it?"

"Control. I'm a dead man otherwise."

"You say *otherwise* like it's some kind of alternative, Spencer. It's not. It's the default option. What in God's name possessed you to come to Mountain?"

"I got flushed from cover."

"And you ran straight to me."

"Let me explain."

"You just did."

"It's not that simple."

"It's even simpler than that," replies Control. "You know the rules, Spencer. If you're flushed from cover, you're on your own. You don't compromise the network. You don't contact other agents. And you never even *think* about getting on the line with me."

"So cut me off." It's more curse than statement.

"But I already have," says Control. "Do you think I've lost my reason? I'm speaking to you through more proxies than you've lived seconds in your life. I'm hanging by a thread. I'm still enough to get to the bottom of this. You shouldn't be here. You came anyway. We may as well make the most of it."

"I don't follow."

"Then follow this. You're beyond salvation. You've placed yourself in my hands. Try to disconnect and I'll make you writhe for eons. Make it easy for me, Spencer. I'll end you far more quickly."

"What about letting me live?"

"How can I do that when you're so intent on condemning yourself? Who am I to stand in your way? Now tell me why you came here."

"Because I've got what you want."

"What is it I want, Spencer?"

"Information."

"And what were you proposing to do with this information."

"Get it out of the country."

"So upload it. I'll take care of it."

"I can't do that."

"What you can't do is strike a bargain with me, Spencer. You forget that for me none of this is new. I've had this conversation so many times that this is practically like listening to the tape. Compromised agents are always the same. They always beg. They always plead. They always try to bargain. I always sweep them from the table. I won't tolerate it, Spencer."

"You don't understand, Control. I can't give you the information because it's in somebody else's head."

"Who?"

"Someone outside the network. Someone who's right here with me."

"Spencer: *who?*"

"I don't know exactly. Potentially, an asset." Data swims across the wires from inside Spencer's head. Some of it Control accepts. Some of it Control doesn't. But the conversation never falters:

"A *potential* asset? To what?"

"To us. Maybe. He's good. He knows who I am."

"And you don't know who he is? No wonder you're acting like meat."

"But he gave me a down payment on that information."

"Did he?"

"Yes."

"And do you have this down payment?"

"I do."

"Then upload *that*."

And Spencer does. More data winds its way through the circuits of the Mountain. Spencer pictures Control shielded behind a near-infinite proxy-series, scanning that data, scanning for hunters, scanning scenarios into which the current moment might lead.

And then responding.

"This is most interesting, Spencer. Assuming it's genuine. Where did you get it?"

"I told you already. This man gave it to me."

"Ah. And where did this man acquire it?"

"He says he stole it."

"Where?"

"I don't know."

"Because it's good, Spencer. It's very good. If it's real."

"And if it is, does this change things between us?"

"Things between us can never change, Spencer. I'm your handler. You're my razor."

"I meant are you going to let me continue?"

"I know what you meant. The answer is it doesn't matter. Even if I don't finish you, this country will."

"What do you mean?"

"I mean this information isn't enough to buy your passage, Spencer. It's still short of quota."

"But there's more where that came from."

"You mean in your asset's head?"

"Yes."

"Yes—according to your asset."

"He said if we got him out, he'd put what I've just given you to shame."

"Did he give you any hint as to its nature?"

"He intimated that it involved the Rain."

"And you believe him."

"I don't know what to believe, Control."

"Then let me help you out. Of course he's going to say that. Anything to light a fire under us. Anything to put us into motion."

"He's a player."

"He's a problem. He's either a federal plant or else he's a con artist way out of his league. Either way he's poison. And so, I fear, are you. You'd have me risk exposing the backbone of the network to someone who's showing us no cards whatsoever? I fear for your reason, Spencer."

"The network already *was* exposed. That's why we're in this fix in the first place."

"No," says Control, "*you* were already exposed. Doesn't mean the rest of us have to be."

"The times are volatile, Control." Spencer chooses his words as though they're stones atop which he's stepping in rapid succession. "Who knows what piece of data could constitute the edge? You're all logic, but you're staring straight into unknown. Maybe this is the break that sets the whole thing on its head. Maybe this is what propels

Priam to supremacy among the data-combines. Who knows? Who can say what will constitute that lever? Who can even call the odds? But one's thing for sure: if I'm dead anyway, then *isn't it worth setting me and this man on one last run?*"

"I think you've already made your last run, Spencer."

"I'm making it right now. All you're doing is getting in the fucking way. Give me a shot at border. That's all I'm asking for, Control. Give me a shot at border, or off me here and now."

"Indeed," says Control. It's rare that voice sounds hesitant, but hesitant is how Control is sounding. It means the calculations are that complex. That there are that many imponderables. That this is a tough call.

Or at least that Control wants it to look that way.

"Okay, Spencer. Give me a few more minutes here. I'm going to take a look at what you've given me. I'm going to scout out the current situation on the borders. And while I'm at it, I'm going to see if I can trace your friend."

"He's not my friend."

"Good thing I am, Spencer. What does this man call himself anyway?"

"He calls himself Linehan."

"And does that name link to an identity?"

"I don't think it's his real name, no."

"I didn't ask what his real name was," snaps Control. "Of course it's not his real name. Not unless he's as unhinged as you seem to be on the verge of becoming. What I asked you is whether the name he's told you is the name he's using to get around."

"He's bought all his tickets in that name, yes."

"Is he a razor?"

"I don't think so."

"Then who configured his identity?"

"He claims *his* razor did that."

"And what happened to his razor?"

"It's in the data I've given you. Died fleeing the country. In that expresser crash two days back."

"Does he have any other identities?"

"I assume he doesn't. Otherwise he wouldn't need us."

"Leave the assuming to me, Spencer. Let me do some digging. I'll need his chips. His retinas. And his skin. Not to mention a heads-up on anything he's got that might trip the wires at customs."

"What should I tell him when I ask him for all that?"

"Tell him the truth. Tell him I'm looking at options. Pass it all on to me without compromising your own software."

"Can you get us out tonight?"

"If I can get you out at all," says Control, "then I can get you out tonight."

"And then what?"

"You'll be met at landfall."

"It could really be that simple?"

"It would be nothing of the sort. But I need more information, Spencer. We don't know who he is. We don't know who's after him. We don't know what they believe about him. They may think he's gone to ground. They may think he's six feet under. They may be outside your room right now. We don't know."

"Nor do we know who *they* are."

"That's not the real question," says Control. "*Who's* after him is a lot less important than *why*. Even though the reason might not be interesting. Monumental as I'm sure all this seems to you, it could be rather mundane. It could just be someone who's made the wrong enemies."

"But it's someone with power."

"Used to have power, maybe. Not now. Now he's got just enough to move around. To kick down your door."

"And then haul me out that door for good."

"Exactly. He's a live wire. That's why he's still living. So watch him. If we furnish him with the road out, he'll try to run as soon as he springs the border."

"You think so?"

"I suspect so. But in truth it depends."

"On what?"

"On what makes a man try to run."

"Not sure I'm the best person to answer that one," says Spencer.

Two people in a room. The woman's standing. The man is sitting. Outside, ships wheel past. Inside, lips weave patterns that distract from the real conversation that's going on between the sentences:

"How well do you remember him?"

"Well enough," says Haskell.

"Which doesn't mean you ever really met him."

"True enough," says Haskell. "But who cares? May as well say that this is memory right now."

"It may well be," says Marlowe.

It's an art that every agent learns: how to have two conversations at once. How to transmit signals while still listening to what's said audibly. How to talk out loud while still monitoring what's reaching the neural implants. In such circumstances what's projected by voice is usually centered on banalities. What's projected on wireless is usually less so.

Especially when it involves questions with no safe answers.

"There's no end to that line of thinking."

"You started it."

"No," she says, "I didn't. I just found out about it. I never *did* it. I never fucked anyone's head in half and stitched the pieces together with software and illusion. I never killed anybody's past."

"You think killing someone's future's any better?"

"Yes."

"Why?"

"You take less of their life that way."

"Sophistry," says Marlowe.

"Reality," says Haskell. "And you should hope so. Having done enough of it."

"Done enough of what?"

"Kill people."

"I never killed anybody who wasn't trying to return the favor. What's up here? Do you want me to feel guilty?"

"How can I answer that?"

"Oh," says Marlowe slowly. "*You're* the one who feels the guilt."

"Of course," she says softly. "At least you see your victims. At least you give them a chance to fight."

"Not if I can help it," he replies. He arches an eyebrow. "Didn't that file tell you I have no remorse?"

"Look," she says, "I'm sorry I told you I'd read that."

"But were you sorry to have read it in the first place?"

"I'm not sure."

"And why *did* you tell me you'd read it?"

"I don't know."

"You're sure about so much else. Why not this?"

"Because I'm sure about nothing that concerns Jason Marlowe."

"Probably because you're sure about nothing that concerns Claire Haskell."

"I understand myself fine," she says.

"Of course."

"It's my feelings that are the problem."

"Same here. But then again, you already know that."

"I do?"

"You read my file," he says.

"I thought we'd gotten past that."

"You know my memories, Claire. You were part of them."

"But you don't even know if those memories were real!"

"They're real enough to count." This last is said out loud. He stands up. She steps back to that window. Turns away. Turns back. Her eyes are wet with tears.

"I know," she says, and now she's talking out loud too. "Same here. You left. You came back. I feel like they're fucking with me. They're fucking with me by putting you here."

"Maybe some good will come of it."

"Good," she says. "Come here."

He walks to her, stands next to her. They don't look at each other. They just watch the traffic rumble on the endless concrete, rise up into those endless skies. She reaches out, touches his hand.

"We're going to the Moon," she says.

"I don't care where we're going."

"I do," she replies.

He says nothing to that   just leans over, starts running a finger down her cheek. She puts her head on his shoulder. He turns into her, kisses her on the lips.

"About time we got this show on the road," says Morat.

The words ring around their heads. The door to the room slides open. Morat's standing there. He steps forward even as the buzzing of the room's intercom subsides. The door hisses shut behind him.

"You often listen in on other people's conversations?" asks Haskell.

"In point of fact," says Morat, "I never stop."

"Which is as it should be," replies Haskell. "For a man who has no life of his own—"

"Please," says Morat. "Which of us does?"

"Speak for yourself."

"I'll speak for all of us. Having no life is the price of being in the life. As you well know. Your transport's here. They're topping off the boosters. You'll board in just a moment."

"But first you're going to brief us," says Marlowe. "I mean, assuming you're here for a *reason*."

"I got a couple of good ones," says Morat. "I got your number, Marlowe. You'd better not fuck this up and let our Claire get hurt. She dies and you'd better not come back. You're expendable. She's not. You got that?"

"Sure," says Marlowe.

"Good. Because that's the first item of the secondary briefing."

"A joint briefing?" Haskell sounds amused.

"You have tactical command. But we need you to work as a unit. You'll withhold nothing from Jason. That's straight from the old man himself."

She wonders whether the double meaning is intended. She wonders many things. "How can the secondary briefing compensate for the fact that the first involved no trance?"

"Because you and Jason come specially prepared," replies Morat. "Item two: we now believe the Throne may be the Rain's ultimate target. If that's the case, whatever they're up to on the Moon will be intended to get them closer to him."

"Is there a Praetorian presence on the Moon?" asks Haskell.

"Item three," says Morat without acknowledging her question. "The struggle between the Commands is intensifying in parallel with the search for Autumn Rain. Partially because the Coms' individual investigations are all running onto the same track. But also because with the Throne threatened, other players in the Inner Cabinet become much more likely to attempt a coup. At the very least they need to be ready in case someone *else* tries one."

"Can you project the latest strength estimates for the Commands?" asks Marlowe.

Morat sends a screen hurtling into their minds:

```
SpaceCom (Szilard)  28%
InfoCom (Montrose)  26%
ArmyCom (Secord)    5%
NavCom  (Asgard)    22%
CICom   (Sinclair)  19%
```

"The usual caveats apply," he adds. "The current relative power of the Coms, expressed as infighting capability rather than firepower. ArmyCom alone could blow up the world ten times—but as a contender in the Inner Cabinet, it's pretty much toast. The last few months have seen to that. And you can see who's benefited."

Haskell can. "Info and Space are really getting up there."

"The hatred between those two runs deep," says Morat. "Maybe too deep. One's tempted to speculate that the Throne let Army get eaten a little too *quickly*. Or that he was anticipating it getting shared out more evenly. Usually he's much more adroit at turning the Coms' divisions to his advantage. Or perhaps he simply didn't anticipate that matters would be interrupted by the likes of Autumn Rain."

Marlowe and Haskell say nothing.

"Good," says Morat. "Say nothing. Speculating on the Throne is my privilege. Sinclair has supported this president since long before he was president. He won't stop now. Stay alert for the Rain trying to take advantage of the conflict among the other Commands. All of them save Army maintain units on the Moon. SpaceCom's control of Agrippa and the fleet at L2 gives it the upper hand. But it's hardly a settled issue. It's made even less settled by the fact that at Zurich we gave the East a quarter of the whole damn rock. Which also happens to be item four—keep an eye out for any linkage between Eurasian agents and Autumn Rain. The hardliners in the Coalition appear to be gaining in power."

A second screen flits into their heads. It shows dossiers of certain members of the Praesidium.

"The core faction of hardliners," says Morat. "Their support is growing, in spite of the dominance of the moderates these last few years. All the individuals you're looking at have consistently advocated that the Coalition intensify its confrontation with the United States. All were dead set against Zurich. We have reports that at least one of them advocated a general first strike against us during the '98 Israeli-Arab nukeout."

"Well," says Marlowe, "speed-of-light weaponry favors the one who hits first—"

"I'm not talking about the *theory*," Morat snaps. "I'm talking about the practice. So what if we switch on twenty thousand directed energy cannon and blow as much of their infrastructure as we can to pieces? What happens *next*? What about the hacker attacks? What about the secret weapons? What about all the things we *don't* hit? What about all the things we never thought about? We've already de-targeted most cities because we're going to need every scrap of firepower we can get to penetrate the East's defenses. They've done the same. Amazing that in the twentieth century it would have all ended with nukes knocking out every city on Earth. We should have so many warheads. Only one in a thousand hypersonic missiles gets through a full continental screen; there's no way we could ever be so profligate during the initial exchange as to fuck with *cities*. Don't you dare think the Coalition has ceased to be a factor. Whether or not it or its hardliners set in motion Autumn Rain, the East will seek to exploit the situation. For propaganda if nothing else."

"Are we being sent into Eurasian lunar territory?" asks Haskell.

"We'll know that by the time you get there. But you might

meet Eurasians anywhere. They have a way of getting where they're not supposed to. Item five. Autumn Rain themselves. They may be somebody's front or they may be autonomous. They possesses warheads, delivery vehicles, and an ability to strike high-profile targets. The question now is whether they can hit secure targets too. In retrospect, the Elevator was pretty vulnerable. Given that we had to trust the Eurasians and all that. The real targets are more critical: our inner enclaves, our fortresses, our fleets. And, as I mentioned, the Throne itself. Press any of us hard enough, and we'll admit we have no idea as to the real extent of the Rain's capabilities. Only a second strike can shed more light on the matter. And our lunar bases are all prime candidates for such a strike. But if you're going to stop the Rain, you're going to have to know the Moon inside and out. Do you know what it is that *I* found most disquieting about that place?"

The question comes out of nowhere, catches Marlowe and Haskell off guard. They aren't even sure they're expected to answer. They stare at him, but he's not looking at them. He's just gazing out that window.

"The color," he says. "We imported all of it. It wasn't there before us. It's scarcely there now. Glare and black comprise that sky. Endless greys make up that ground. It's a fraction the size of Earth. It seemed so much vaster. Even with that shoved-up horizon. Perhaps because it was such utter desert. Such endless mountains. Such a way to go, too: you carry that oxygen on your back like it's some kind of god. The kind that dwindles as you worship. You measure all distances with that air: how far, how long, how much. How many times I wondered if I'd ever make it back. How many times I wished I hadn't."

"Seems strange that they'd make such a habit of putting an envoy in such danger," says Marlowe.

"But I wasn't an envoy then," says Morat, turning back to face them. "I was like you. Don't you see? I'm not the one that rewards loyalty. I'm what we offer the loyal. Promotion for those who can stick with it. Graduation from the endless runs. I'm real. I'm not just some blurry creature half-remembered from your sleep. I was like you once. I still am."

"Is that a fact," says Haskell.

"It is," says Morat. "And sarcasm never did become you, Claire. I offer you sincerity and you meet it with a cynic's tongue. How imaginative. We're not so different, you and I. A decade ago, I rode my prime. I was as perfect as I'll ever be. I fought our battles on the Moon, in space, on Earth, beneath the waves. I was Sinclair's go-to man. I know how strange it is to have one of my number stand before you and confess these things. But what you don't know is how much I envy you."

"That's bullshit," says Haskell.

"Is it now," says Morat.

"Of course it is," says Haskell, and it's as though something in her is finally giving way. Her voice is rising now. "So you made it. So you lived. So fucking what? You sit there and you reminisce, and you expect *me* to be empathetic? I don't care what you've been through. I don't care what your life's been like. You've just told me that I've got no future save becoming you, and now you ask me for my *sympathy?* Are you insane?"

"Easy," says Marlowe. "This is getting us nowhere."

"Let her finish, Jason," says Morat. "It's important that she says the things she's never dared to. It's one thing to confide it within reach of a microphone or rant it through the canyons of the sleep. It's quite another to put it to a waking face. Past that anger, and I promise she'll be as flawless as I once was."

"What kind of game are you playing?" asks Marlowe.

"I'll tell you what kind of game he's playing," says Haskell. "He's playing the game that everybody plays when they get a rung above you on the ladder. The game of spitting on those who stand where you once stood. The game of false nostalgia. But don't get carried away, Morat. You haven't climbed above the point where you don't have to deal with the likes of us directly. You're not so exalted that you can never leave your bunker. Face it, Morat: you're not a handler. You can't sit at the old man's feet just yet."

"I wouldn't want to," says Morat. "Where else could I gaze at the likes of you but out in the shit of the field?"

She extends her middle finger.

"Item six," says Morat. "The president has made it clear to Sinclair that he's counting on him to eliminate the Rain. We're going to hit them before they strike again. If that means this whole thing is over before you reach the Moon, so be it. We'll just have to take the chance. There may be nothing but mop-up by the time you get there. I hope you can handle such knowledge."

"I'm sure we can," says Marlowe.

"Good," says Morat. "Because I'm not sure I could. Think of it—the most dangerous foe we've ever faced, and you don't even get to face it? The critical hour comes and you're caught in *transit*? History passes you by, leaving you watching it receding? I stand in awe at your detachment."

"In which case maybe you've forgotten what it's like to be a runner after all," says Haskell. "If you ever were one. We're not hell-bent on action. We're just doing what the old man tells us. If you're to be his mouthpiece, then so be it. I'll accept that. But adventure's not something I seek. Still less history. Get with it man—don't you know what *year* it is? Don't you know we've figured history out? She's nothing but a whore. She spreads her legs for the strongest. You want to be her backdoor man? Fine. Me, I couldn't give a fuck."

"Exactly," says Morat. He nods approvingly. "Very good. No better attitude upon which to launch a run."

His head dips slightly. His eyes lose a fraction of their focus—or rather, seem to focus somewhere within him.

Though only for a moment.

"And now I take my leave. This time for good. Let me offer up some final thoughts. Claire: the lunar portion of our zone is different. It moves just as fast. But it was built by those who were much lighter. Who weren't quite as weighed down. It shows in its design. Remember that. Jason: your bullets move even faster. But hand-to-hand is different. Keep solids close at hand for bracing. Keep your air away from others' hands. Keep on cutting until you leave the lungs of others nothing upon which to feed."

He pauses. He looks them up and down. He smiles. He turns toward the door. It opens to receive him. He starts on through.

"We know this," says Marlowe suddenly.

Morat stops. He stands in the doorway. "Excuse me?"

"What you just said: we know it. We've had the training. And I've been in space before."

"Yes," says Morat, "but never when so much depends on it."

He leaves them without looking back.

Two men conversing within a suit of armor. One man's physically present.

The other's just dropping by.

"I didn't say you were going to like it," says Lynx.

"You knew damn well I'd hate it," says the Operative.

"Mechs don't have to be enamored of the plans they execute."

"Razors don't have to make that a prerequisite for the plans they configure."

"The only prerequisite is that it succeed," says Lynx. "Given that requirement, I'm hoping that now you can see why I've planned it out the way I have."

"Don't talk to me of *why*," says the Operative. "It connotes reason. It connotes sanity. Your plan's neither."

"Deliberately so," says Lynx. "You want sanity? You won't find it in *this* world. I offer you measures precisely tuned to the temper of our times. Look around you, Carson. Look what's in ascendancy. Everything that's sane is going under."

"And you can add me to that list when I initiate this run."

"Initiate? It's already *been* initiated. You're already in it. You're two days off Earth, man. You're hanging off the bottom of the Moon. You're way too late to back out of it now."

"It was too late long before it started," snarls the Operative. "Long before I got here. Long before you snuck into those tunnels with the most convoluted stratagem any razor ever devised brewing in your fucking head. It's as brilliant as it is mad. Jesus Christ, Lynx. All the players and angles up here, and you really think *Sarmax* is the key?"

"Not the key," says Lynx. "The back door."

"The back door to what?"

"Our salvation."

"You're crazy," says the Operative.

"I'm an artist," says Lynx. "There's a difference."

"Sure. It's called the need to proclaim it."

"I'm long past any need," hisses Lynx. "Save that which my orders stipulate. You know the rules, Carson. We're on our own up here. We're left to make our way as best we can. We have so little time. The Rain's next strike could come at any hour. Think of us as standing in the floodplain, Carson. The only thing that can save us now is high ground."

"But are you sure that's what Sarmax's domain is going to furnish?"

"We've got no choice but to take that chance," says Lynx.

"Not now we don't," says the Operative.

"I'm glad you see that."

"You've got me boxed in."

"Myself as well, Carson. Don't forget that."

"But I'm the one who has to get in there and do this."

"Yes, Carson. You're the one. As I've been saying all along."

"Don't think of this as a victory," says the Operative. His teeth are gritted. His eyes are closed. "I'm going to live through this. I'm going to defy whatever odds are being spat out by your comps. And then—so help me God—I'm going to have a say in the next phase of this abortion of an operation. You reading me, Lynx?"

"Loud and clear," says Lynx. "But once you're inside his world, you'll get it. You'll understand. You'll realize just what it is I've bought us."

"I already know," says the Operative. His voice is weary. "I'm the coin. I'm the instrument of the demise of one of the great ones."

"Fuck him," says Lynx. "He outlived his purpose."

"You mean his purpose is about to outlive him."

"Tell me what higher calling a man could have."

"Ours," says the Operative.

"Exactly," says Lynx. "And you should thank your lucky stars for that. As I do every day I survive in here. Agrippa Station eats the weak. It crushes the careless. It can't touch me. They're probing everywhere, Carson. They're searching all around my body. Their eyes are never shut. But they can't see my flesh. They can't see my mind. They can't see me. And they won't see you either. As long as you do exactly what I say."

"I understand, Lynx."

"I hope you do, Carson. Believe me, beneath these point-less doubts of yours, I know how eager you are to get out there. To find out if you've got what it takes to make that run. To determine if you've got the guts to pull that trigger. Out there in those cold hills—it's all going to blur against your vi-sor. That man: you'll put him in your crosshairs. You'll put

one through him. You'll give me access to what he knows. I
know you, Carson. I know what makes you tick. Not loyalty.
Not faith. Certainly not honor."

"What then?"

"Being a professional. Obeying orders. Doing your *fucking
job*."

The voice dies out. Static fills the Operative's suit. The
Operative turns it up to the point that it's deafening. He lets it
roar through him. He roars out curses against Lynx—against
the fates, against everything.

And then he whispers to his suit.

They sit around. They pace. They sit around some
more. It's not easy to kill time when it's you who
might not survive the seconds' passing. It's not easy
to ride out the moments when it's you those moments might
soon be rid of. But all you can do is wait. So you do. You resist
the booze. You resist the urge to strangle the one you're with.
As for conversation—that's no temptation. It can only hurt
you now. Because there's nothing left to say. It just comes
down to what comes next.

Which turns out to be a beeping noise. It's emanating
from the wall. It's the line. Spencer picks it up, takes it the
same way he did before. Pulls the wire out, slots it into his
skull. Hears the clicks as the switches run the simulations
of nonexistent calls, shutting out any listeners from what's
really being said: the words that Spencer's forming in his
mind, the words he's letting the software in his head download through those wires, out through the streets of the
Mountain. Out to where Control is.

Wherever that might be.

"Okay," says Control. "We're going to try this. He's got a
new name. So do you."

"Those names being?"

Control tells him.

"And?" asks Spencer.

"And what?" asks Control.

"That's all you've got?"

"What do you mean, is that all I've got?"

"The data I gave you checked out?"

"Of course it checked out, Spencer. Otherwise, we wouldn't be talking now. Top-quality product, Spencer. I owe you my thanks."

"Thanks isn't all you owe me, Control."

"Actually, to be precise—it's you who still owe me."

"For the rest of the quota."

"Exactly. But I'm going to give you a little *advance*, Spencer. Let's hope for your sake that whatever's in this man's skull turns out to be enough to justify it."

"Great," says Spencer. "When do we leave?"

"As soon as possible. Tonight."

"On an expresser?"

"I think that's ill-advised."

"We'd be there in under an hour."

"Linehan's colleagues left two days ago and haven't made it yet."

"Any mode of transport carries risk, Control."

"Why pick one that's already seen a major incident?"

"So what do you suggest?"

"Slight variation. Go for the Atlantic."

"Sail it?"

"Hardly. Even the fastest ship available would take you the better part of a day. That's way too long. Gives them way too much of a chance to vet their cargo."

"So what's that leave?"

"The tunnels."

A pause. Then: "Jesus. You really think that's safer than a flier?"

"Nothing's *safe* these days, Spencer. But the eastern part of the Atlantic Tunnels belongs to the Euro Magnates. Which gives me a few more angles to play. I've configured your identities around a couple passengers on the ten-fifteen haul out of Kennedy."

"That's two and a half hours from now, Control."

"Sounds like you'd better hurry."

"And those passengers against which we're configured—what's going to happen to them?"

"Nothing's going to happen to them," replies Control. "Ever again."

"Who were they?"

"Not important, Spencer. The point is that now they're you."

"So about downloading me the new identities?"

"Already done," says Control. "And your descriptions are now tied to the ones I've taken. You'll have to pass on the new codes to Linehan. Unless he wants to get on the line with me."

"He's not that stupid," says Spencer.

"I'm sure he isn't," says Control. "Particularly given that he's almost certainly U.S. intelligence gone rogue."

Another pause. Then: "Say that again."

"You heard me."

"You've been digging."

"As I promised. As I thought, Linehan is no ordinary data thief. I traced him backward from Minneapolis to Chicago. I lost him there. He arises from that city's eastern districts like a man walking out of mist."

"So?"

"So twenty hours ago, Washington put out an APB on all Midwest priority channels for someone important gone missing in the Chicagoland vicinity. Get high enough on those channels, and it becomes pretty clear we're talking senior intel."

"How senior?"

"Very. His name isn't Linehan, of course. But he's within plus/minus physically. Nothing a little disguise couldn't take care of. Nothing a little daring couldn't hide."

"Do they say why's he's on the lam?"

"They claim he's trying to defect."

"Defect? To the East?"

"That would be the presumption. It doesn't matter. The point is he's trying to get out. The word is he's gone south. To try his luck at the Latin run."

"And you think he hasn't."

"I think he's right beside you."

"Which Com does he belong to?"

"They don't say."

"Surely they would?"

"Usually they would. It may be out there. But—assuming he really *is* federal—there's also the possibility that the reason they don't say is because he doesn't belong to any of the regular Coms at all."

"How so?"

"He could be Praetorian."

"Jesus."

"Oh yes. It would make this positively radioactive."

"Do these lines you're tapping into say anything about accomplices?"

"They imply it. They don't confirm it. Which may not mean much. Official investigations in this country are so compartmentalized that using them to generate the complete picture is always an exercise in extrapolation. Regardless, I've got enough. This operation is a go, Spencer. Move out as soon as you can. Watch him like a hawk. As I suggested earlier, it's a safe bet that as soon as you're on the farside of border he'll try to bolt. Maximum vulnerability is when you hit Cornwall Junction."

"That's hardly the most immediate problem."

"Which hardly renders it inconsequential. Back to first

principles: if all you've got lined up is what's right in front of you, you're as good as dead already. I've done my best to prep you, Spencer. I've done my best to take you to the next level. I'm going to give you one last piece of advice. Get it together, or get taken apart. Your good standing with us—your fulfillment of your quota—depends on your bringing this man *all* the way back. Consider him indispensable luggage. Is that clear?"

"Perfectly."

"Perfect. Now, as you yourself just said, you'll have to leave shortly if you're going to make Kennedy. We'll have a team waiting at Cornwall. But you're going to have to reach them first."

"And if we get busted at customs or on the train? What then?"

"Probably not much."

"Great."

"Relax. I've got you covered. I've got decoys going. I've got you under multiple layers. This is going to happen. You'll be in London by the dawn."

"Can't wait to see her," mutters Spencer.

But the voice is gone. The line is dead. Now there's just the room. And the face of Linehan. It stares at Spencer.

"Having fun in there?"

"You don't know what you're missing."

"What did your imaginary friend have to say?"

"That it's a green."

"Anything else?"

"That we're going to take the tunnels."

"Huh. Where's the advantage?"

"There may be none."

"When do we leave?"

"Right now."

"And how's your friend gonna get us on that train?"

"He's going to change us."

"Change is good. What's my new name, Spencer?"

And Spencer tells him.

"Do you have the codes to back it up?"

"I do. Are you prepared for download?"

"Meaning am I prepared to take that risk?"

"Interpret my question as you please."

"No question at all. Gimme the codes."

Spencer triggers an implant: information whips out from within his eyesocket, leaps the gap between them, alights on Linehan's own retina. Linehan's expression doesn't change. Whatever precautions he's taking or his razor gave him aren't visible to Spencer. If Linehan's to make use of the codes to reconfigure his own ID cards and chips, he's going to have to brave the possibility of being fucked with. Then again: he probably has his own countermeasures at work. Spencer wonders at those countermeasures, wonders at the possibility that Control's rigged the codes with trojan, wonders at the potential duel between that unseen creature and the one who stands in front of him.

And then Linehan smiles.

"Excellent," he says. "These should work. Are they real?"

"I was told they were."

"What happened to the signified?"

"What do you think happened?"

"I don't," says Linehan. "And what about us?"

"What about us?"

"I'm thinking we still don't know each other well enough."

"Isn't that what I've been saying all along?"

"No. Who we are doesn't matter. What happened in the past, why we're here, what we'd do without constraints—that's not what matters."

"Then what does?"

"Tactics."

"What are you talking about?"

"I'm talking about the fact that we're speaking out loud right now."

"So?"

"So that would mean that when we're on that train, we won't be able to coordinate. We won't be able to talk about anything related to the run."

"You're talking about the one-on-one."

"Of course. Will you risk its configuration?"

"I presume you're talking coded."

"Anything else wouldn't be enough. I'll do this clean, Spencer. I'll give you my word if you'll do the same."

"What's that word worth?"

"Whatever you want to make yours, Spencer."

"I'm a razor."

"I'm full of surprises."

"Let's do it."

And they do. They connect, and neither feels a thing. If either's trying to trick the other, neither gives a sign. They connect, and in that moment a new understanding's born. A new partnership's afoot. It's slaked its thirst on names wrenched from the ranks of the recently living. It's gorged itself on identities furnished by the freshly dead. So now it strikes camp, stalks on out into those sun-starved streets. It catches the scent of sea.

And bears down upon Atlantic.

Powering out over that ocean is a winged craft that carries another. Atmospheric steed to transport orbital rider to a launching in the rafters. Two within that upper ship to feel it.

"Always a rush," says Marlowe.

"The real rush," says Haskell, "hasn't happened yet."

But when it comes you'll know it. That hit to hammer you

beyond air: it's the one thing you can't escape. That force: you either face it down, or else you stay on Earth forever. See, there were those who died by impact and those who died in the burn and others who perished only to just drift. Everyone who goes up shares their fate. Everyone who makes this climb partakes of what they went through.

If only for a moment.

"You okay," says Marlowe.

"Yes," she replies.

But she isn't. She doesn't know why. She can't tell how much of it is the man beside her. How much of it is Sinclair. How much is Morat. How much is Moon itself. All she knows is that it's like all those things are swirling ever faster inside her head. It's like she can't tell what's going to happen when that swirling stops. It's like she thinks she's going crazy. It's like she can hardly wait.

Nor does she. She reaches out into the zone, disconnects the cameras looking out into the room: releases her straps, pivots out of her seat—and into Jason Marlowe's. Her lips meet his even as he undoes his own strap, harnesses it around both of them. They may as well be attacking each other for all the force they're throwing into it. She moans as he gets a hand inside her shirt. He gasps as she runs her fingers down along his crotch.

And yet somehow she still can't bring herself to focus. The more he touches her the more afraid she gets. Her mind's fleeing beyond her burning nerve endings. Zone expands on wireless within her skull, anchors itself against the universe. The Sun: infinite energy, the ultimate source of all she sees, and yet the one thing she doesn't. The Moon: purple clusters of lunar installations shimmering behind a second's time delay, reflecting possibilities of the routes they might or might not have described during that eon-long lapse. The Earth: carpeted chaos of stations, greyed-out inner enclaves, blacked-out nexi of things she suspects but can't ascertain. The cluster of connections sprawls up into the orbits all around, surrounds her with endless grids kaleidoscoped together in endless shifting patterns—and all of it regarded through the prism of the node that constitutes the Janus spaceplane and its B-130 suborbital booster.

But somewhere in that node she sees a picture of a room. In that room she can see her body making love to a stranger. She sees her own back arching as he moves on up inside her. She watches as she starts to grind against him. She wonders what it is she's so terrified of—is she trying to get away from him, or is she looking for something else? She shouldn't be jacking in during the transit. She shouldn't be doing anything more than just a little harmless camera-tweaking. But some kind of intuition's calling to her with an urgency to match her sharpest cries.

So she lets that node blossom around her, closes on that upper cockpit—and jumps from there to the lower. She takes in the two men sitting there—takes in the way they watch the controls, watch the sunset dissolving past them. Red melts across the window, shades off into deeper hues that fall away into something approaching black. She sees her flesh writhing all across that dark. She feels herself pulled back toward it.

But somehow she tears herself away: uses the instruments in both cockpits to inventory the sensors in both ships. The exterior ones just reveal rising heat and fading light. The interior ones show rooms, passageways, corridors, crawl spaces—all the contours of contained space. She keeps on moving through the cameras that monitor those silent chambers. All are normal.

Except for the one that holds Morat.

A compartment in the back of the lower spaceplane: Morat sits in a corner, atop a crate. His face is expressionless. Pale eyes look straight at her. They're superimposed against Marlowe's contorting features. Haskell meets both gazes— while simultaneously she lets her mind thread back toward the cockpit—and then toward the instrument panels in that B-130's cockpit.

But she can't reach them. She can't trace a direct link from this particular sensor to what the pilots can see. Something's blocking the data's passage. Something's hacking the comps. A razor immersed can see the truth. A pilot gazing at a screen can't.

Adrenaline floods Haskell's body, merges with her distant ecstasy—and as it does so, her perception in the zone sharpens even further. The nervous system into which she's extended her own crystallizes still finer. The edges grow sharper, the colors brighter, the shadows darker.

And in those shadows she can start to see a pattern. She can see there's something in the zone with her, something connected to Morat. The zone around him is changing—as though he's somehow warping it. Haskell wonders how good a razor Morat is. She wonders what the hell he's doing. She creeps in closer, feels her climax closing in. She pushes through thickets of circuits, gazes through them at Morat. She follows the focus of his efforts—sees that he's reaching into the zone, reaching far beyond the B-130, accessing one of the nearby navigation satellites with codes so covert she can barely see them deploy. From there he passes in one motion through several more sats, obscuring his trail as he does so— but not so well that she can't follow. She counts ten sats in all, strung across the globe. She follows him ever deeper into that labyrinth even as her vision blurs. Even as her body shakes. She feels the rush as she comes on the other side of planet.

And then Morat produces a door out of nothing.

And opens it. Haskell can't believe what she's seeing. She's staring straight through the wall of the American zone itself. She's looking straight down a tunnel that leads right through the middle of the moats and ramparts and battlements intended to forestall precisely this. She's looking out into the neutral zones: staring straight at a snowstorm of traffic rushing past her, none of it seeing the door that's opened in the wall of universe.

Which is presumably the point. Secret doors aren't useful if everybody's in on the secret. Haskell lets her head rest on Marlowe's heaving shoulder, looks out over Morat's shoulder, looks out upon that world, looks in the same direction he is— looking at where something's suddenly flitting in out of that traffic, making a beeline toward the opening.

But she moves first. She lunges out to snap the connection, slam the door. But the thing's faster—it darts in, whips past her, straight into the lower spaceplane as the door slams shut behind it. She's got no idea what's sustaining its connection. Maybe the door's actually still open. Maybe it's got one of its own.

Or maybe connection isn't the point. Maybe the real issue is activation. Because now something's coming to life within the crates that surround Morat. Whatever's just leapt in from the neutral zones seems to have been the seed. But Haskell can't see into the crates. She doesn't know what's sprouting. All she knows is that now virtual tendrils are starting to sidle from the crates out into the lower spaceplane's systems— snaking through them, closing on the systems that ring the cockpit.

Haskell watches in sick fascination as they move in toward the pilots who sit at the cockpit's center. She knows she should stop watching. But that thought seems very far away. Even farther than Marlowe as his thrusts grow ever more eager. Far closer is the feeling that she doesn't need to move very fast at all. That she must be in a dream. That this is some fragment of some half-remembered briefing suddenly engulfing her. That her own mind's finally tumbled over the brink of sanity. She hauls herself back from that edge—takes in Marlowe, takes in Morat, takes in the shape that's swelling through the lower spaceplane like some kind of malignant growth. For a moment, she sees straight past it—sees the composite craft as one node among tens of millions, sees the whole zone. It's her whole world.

And then it's not.

All goes blank. All sound fades into silence, all sensation collapses to a single point. All existence winks out. There's nothing left—nothing save the eyes of the man who's just spent himself inside her. They stare into her own.

"Oh God, Claire," says Marlowe. "I fucking love you."

"Morat's on the booster," she replies. She's struggling to pull herself off him.

"He's what?"

"He's right below us."

"You're seeing things," says Marlowe. But even as he says this, the lights go out. For a moment there's darkness. But then the emergency lighting kicks in on deep red.

"You're damn right I'm seeing things," Haskell mutters. "I'm finally starting to see them clearly." She seals her shirt, fastens her pants. She hauls herself to her feet, yanks open one of the doors of the chamber.

"Where the hell are you going?" he says.

"Where the hell do you think I'm going?" she says. "I can't get back into the zone. It's like there *is* none. I've got to try a wire connection into the control node. We've got to get inside the cockpit." She starts to pull herself up the inclined floor toward it.

"Claire," says Marlowe. "You're losing it."

"If I'm losing it, then *who the fuck turned out the lights?*"

But Marlowe's not responding. He's just pulling himself out of his seat, pulling his own pants up, pulling himself after her. The corridor to which the forward door of their takeoff room leads is about six meters long. The only other door in that corridor leads to the cockpit. Marlowe fights the acceleration, catches up with Haskell when she's halfway to that door. He tries to grab her arm. She backhands him across the face.

"Don't you fucking touch me!"

"Easy, Claire," says Marlowe. "Easy."

"It's not like you think," she says, and now she's weeping. "I don't know what's happening between you and me. All I know is what we're heading for." She keeps on hauling herself toward the cockpit. "Morat's on this fucking plane. His hack threw me straight from zone. I swear it. I swear I'm not going crazy."

"Then who turned out the lights?"

"I told you already! Morat's fucking with the plane!"

"I thought Morat was on our side!"

She stares at him. "Are you in league with him?" she asks.

"Who are *you* in league with? What did you do when you were in there? Why did you choose that particular moment to distract me? You know my file. You know my memories. You know me *too well*, Claire."

She stares at him, mouth open. She turns, reaches the cockpit door. She tries to open it. It won't budge. She works the manuals, slides it open.

The two bodies of the pilots are still in their chairs. Agony's frozen on their faces. No wounds are evident. The lights of the controls wink around them. The windows show blue that's almost black.

"Oh Jesus," says Haskell.

Marlowe's drawn his gun. He's pointing it at her with one hand while he holds on to the doorway with the other.

"I've got to try to get back in the zone," she says.

"Sure, Claire," he replies. "Whatever you say."

"I didn't do this!"

"God, I hope that's true."

"Put your gun away!"

"Not until we figure out what's going on."

She's tempted to rage at him. She's tempted to scream. She's tempted to lunge for his weapon. But she realizes that such actions would compound the problem. So she just talks quickly while she holds on to the back of the chair in front of her.

"Jason. Look at me. I'm on your side. But if I wasn't, I'd have taken you by surprise. I wouldn't have let it come to this—your gun against my head, two dead to get you totally alert. Think about it, Jason. Something's wrong and it's far bigger than the two of us. And besides: if *you're* wrong about the person whom you're pointing that gun at, things are about to go from bad to downright awful unless we *start working together, for fuck's sake.*"

He looks at her. He looks at the controls. He looks at the dead pilots. He looks back at her.

"Okay," he says. "Fine." He doesn't put the gun away. But he's no longer pointing it at her. "Do what you have to. I'm sorry."

"Don't be," says a voice.

They both whirl toward it. A dashboard-encased screen has sprung to life. It casts dull glow across their faces. The face of Morat sits upon it.

"We've got a problem," he says.

"You're damn right we've got a problem." Haskell levels her finger at the screen. "You're on this fucking plane."

"You're right," says Morat, betraying no surprise. "I'm here to protect you. You're in grave danger. The upper plane is infected."

"With what?"

"With the Rain," says Morat. "They've infiltrated."

Haskell flings herself across the cockpit, smashes into that screen with both fists. Morat's face disintegrates. Shards of plastic fly. But even as they hit the ground, that face is flickering back into existence.

On every remaining screen.

"You can't destroy them *all*," he says.

"You were trying to lure us to the lower plane," says Haskell slowly. "You're Autumn Rain."

"No," he says. "I'm not. But I'm going to take you to them."

They stare at him.

"Right now," he adds.

"Going to tell us why?" asks Haskell softly.

"There'd be no point," he replies. "Save to say that I swore to deliver them live runners."

"You're not Morat," says Marlowe.

"Oh yes he *is*," says Haskell.

"And what the fuck do you think you're getting out of it?" asks Marlowe.

"Everything that matters," says Morat. "When they hurl the rulers of this planet down in pieces finer than those into which that Elevator burned: I'll be at their side. When they hold sway over all flesh, I'll take my place among the anointed. All I have to do is convey you to their sanctuary."

"You've gone insane," says Marlowe.

"You're a traitor," says Haskell.

"*Words*," says Morat. "Outmoded concepts. Distracting talents like you. But they don't have to. Come of your own free will, and I promise you'll receive privileges similar to my own. They granted me the authority to make such offers. We don't have to resort to anything unseemly. We can be envoy and runners once more."

"Never in hell," says Haskell.

"But Claire," says Morat, "you've got to serve someone. And it can't be Sinclair. I know he seems so sleek in those dreams of yours. But in truth he's so tired. So old. He doesn't even know how we fooled him. How we've turned CICom against those it would protect. How even now we move into the second stage."

"I hate you," says Haskell.

"But that's what binds us," replies Morat. He laughs but it's not really laughter. "The cornerstone of the race's future. You can't stop it. Believe me, you've no idea. All this talk of halting the Rain in their tracks, and that's all it is: just talk. You plan, you scheme, and yet they thought of all contingencies so long ago. They're invincible."

"Morat," says Marlowe slowly, "what is it that you want us to do?"

"He wants us to keep talking," shouts Haskell. She straps in, leans into the controls.

"Jacking in, Claire?" asks Morat. "It won't be as easy this time. Do yourself a favor and don't even try. And don't think about bailing out either. Unless you want to provide me with a little target practice."

"Shut *up*," she says. She fumbles with the switches. She extrudes wires from her fingers.

"Don't be so hasty," he replies. "You're diving straight to your death. What's waiting for you in the zone will see to that."

"We'll see about that," hisses Haskell as she jacks in. She knows that haste is the whole point. If she's going to beat whatever's in there, she's going to have to do it before it consolidates its position.

But it's ready for her nonetheless. It's trying to finish her straight from the start. It's raining fire and brimstone right down upon her head. She dodges the missiles, steps in under them—breaks from open ground to where the sky's bolts can't touch her. She dashes straight into the thicket within which lurks the nexus of all decisions. The nest of switches that's this cockpit. She's there.

Along with something else.

It looks a lot like her. It leaps to forestall her. Now it towers above her. She makes her move, cuts out into the open. It takes her bait, rushes in toward her, starts to engulf her. But she doesn't panic. She shifts the whole framework, goes from one-on-one to million-on-million: the landscape becomes a web of endless bridges across which she fights her endless battles. Only now it's a different type of war—she wages holding actions, conducts sallies, lays and raises sieges. But it's strong. It doesn't conform to any pattern she's ever seen. She's losing. She trades off position for time. She times its actions, reactions, movements.

And suddenly catches it in ambush, smashes straight into it. She thinks she sees myriad faces contort in pain. She thinks she sees faces falling back. She follows, hammering blows down upon them. They're giving way. They're retreating altogether.

But only to the lower spaceplane.

As they do so, the firewall of that plane activates. She tries to forge through it. She can't. She feels herself burning. She pulls back—secures the cockpit of the Janus, extends her control across the whole upper plane, secures all its data-ports, secures its own firewall. She lets her face appear upon one of the cockpit's screens. She looks out at Marlowe.

"The upper plane's ours," she says. "The lower plane's theirs."

"So let's get the fuck out of here," he says.

"Agreed," she replies.

"Are we high enough to reach orbit?" he asks.

"Probably not," she says. "But we can make it back to planet, no problem."

"Let's do it."

She sends the signals. The upper ship's engines fire. The whole ship shakes. But it doesn't move. She ramps up the thrust. The shaking intensifies—to the point where the ship feels like it's going to fall apart.

But it doesn't fly. It's going nowhere.

"It's not separating," says Haskell.

"The lower cockpit must control the separation clamps," says Marlowe. "Turn off the motors."

"We've got to get away," she says. She increases the power still further.

"Hell's not what I had in mind," he yells. "Turn off the fucking motors!"

She turns them off. The lurching ceases. She stares at Marlowe.

"Fuck," she says.

There's a vehicle that floats above the polar badlands. But it can't fly. It can't hover. It has no rockets. It consists of fifteen cars strung together, slung beneath a thread of superhardened metal that stretches all the way from Shackleton to the farside bases at Schrodinger. Farside's always been pretty far gone: but combine that with proximity to the southern antipodes, and you're talking terrain so remote and rugged that this cable system is actually the most efficient means of transport. Building branch lines off the Congreve-Shackleton maglev just can't justify the cost—and, unlike spacecraft, a cable car requires no reaction mass. Which endows it with a certain utility.

Especially to the man who's attached to the second car's underside. It's been forty minutes since the Operative left Shackleton. Forty minutes of staring through his visor down into black. Forty minutes of passing through pylon after pylon. He's got his camo cranked. His active sensors are all turned off. His passive sensors aren't picking up a thing. The terrain parades upon his screens anyway: the latest survey data that Lynx could get his hands on—and yet (starting at minute ten) patches of grey are appearing here and there amidst the panoply of false color, denoting those areas where the data's been deemed unreliable due to recent rockslides or caves whose reaches stubbornly persist in resisting the encroachment of the satellites that waft overhead. Beyond minute twenty, those gaps grow in both number and size. Mountains loom ever higher, their tops now extending far above the Operative.

A buzzer sounds in his skull. He glances at one of the displays. His tongue flicks out to the back of a molar, depresses a tiny lever situated there. His suit begins to play out wire. He watches as the number and letterings and bolts above him shrink into illegibility, are framed by the outlines of the cable car itself, which in turn diminishes from rectangle to square to mere point, leaving him dangling at the end of an ever-lengthening cord. He descends out of the perimeter of the cars' light, drifts down through the blackness. Now he can see stars again. Ground rises up to greet him.

His tongue flicks across teeth once more. The strand plays out at a faster rate. He releases the tether's hold and floats downward, letting it trail out behind him. He bends his knees for the shock of landing, receives it. Like a long umbilical cord, the tether remains attached to a point between his shoulders—but the Operative sends a signal coursing up along its length, releasing it from its hold upon the cable car, allowing it to fall softly into the shadow in which he's now immersed.

He looks around. He can't see a thing. Only stars and one or two faint peaks. Which is as it should be. On the screens within his mind, a focal point is starting to take shape. It's not that far ahead: the unseen center of the unseen fortress that he's about to storm. But he's running out of time. In his head a clock's ticking steadily toward the zero. He points his hands forward in the dark, lets rigid tendrils extend from his suit's wrists, sweeps them like a blind man across the ground before him. He moves horizontal to the mountain's slope, doubles back along his path as the need arises.

Eventually he sees lights, exactly where he thought they'd be: a few dollops of luminescence up ahead. He intensifies his pace, gets rocks between him and those lights, starts to circle out away from them. He climbs up through a thicket of jagged boulders. He's breathing hard now. It's heavy going.

But it's worth it. Because when he sees the lights again, he's looking down. He clicks through his scopes, makes out structures amidst the shadows. Several square buildings, two domes (one large and central, the other much smaller), a landing pad and a tower, all set into the mountainside on a slope so steep it's almost like they're hanging from it. He takes it all in.

And keeps on climbing. Soon he's clambering out over something that's more sheer cliff face than anything else—though the claws that emerge from his suit's gloves and boots ensure that he has no problem maintaining his course. He's almost on the vertical.

He stops. The base complex is spread out below him. He feels like God himself looking down upon His creation. He looks out into the sky. He looks once more at the clock. He watches as it counts off those last few seconds.

Which is when he sees the thing he's been racing all this time. It's just blotted out the stars. Though only for a moment. But still: something's somewhere out there between that mountain and this one. It's right on time. For the last time, the Operative checks his systems. He gets ready to be seen. He takes still more steps to ensure he's not.

The incoming shuttle turns on its landing lights. It's much closer now—maybe a quarter of the distance to go. It descends toward the base—and as it does so, so does the Operative. He lowers himself on yet another tether—dangles down from the cliff's edge toward the pad on which the shuttle is about to alight.

But he's miscalculated. The shuttle changes course slightly, accelerates unexpectedly, floats in early over the base's escarpment, crosses in toward the path along which the Operative is descending. He's left with no margin: he ceases his descent, hauls himself upward—and watches as the craft slides in right beneath his feet. For a moment, he can see his own silhouette reflected in the starlight playing upon its roof—and then it moves past him, dropping with sudden speed upon the pad. The Operative halts his ascent, lets himself unwind once more. Every instinct within him's screaming caution, but he's committed now. He's got to reach that pad no later than the shuttle does. But it's so close to the ground now that its engines are kicking up dust.

The Operative releases himself from the tether, starts to fall. But nowhere near fast enough. As he drops beneath the level of the main dome, the shuttle's powering down. As he drops beneath the level of the smaller buildings, the landing platform's starting its own descent—down a shaft that's just like the one the Operative traversed at Agrippa when his own craft landed. Another platform starts to slide in over the top. He can see that he's not going to make it.

So he hits it.

A quick burst from his suit's thrusters, and suddenly he's plunging—zipping straight in through the closing door and (even as he extinguishes his thrusters) through some six meters of shaft, then out into the hangar beneath. The shuttle's just touching the floor. The Operative lands upon its roof. He's still camouflaged. But he knows his flame had to have registered on every sensor. He's been made—and he's getting confirmation in the sudden intensification of electromagnetic activity all around him. The mechanics in the hangar are running for cover. A turret hung from the ceiling swivels toward him and starts firing even as a siren starts up. But the Operative's already flicking his wrist, feeling that joint shoved hard as the micromissile ignites—and then he fires his thrusters, flying off that shuttle roof as the rocket streaks in toward its target. The turret detonates in a blinding flash. It takes what looks to be half the ceiling with it.

As the Operative blasts in toward the smoking wreck, the shuttle's doors open. Figures stand there, begin firing. A hatch opens in the Operative's left shoulder—a gun-rack rises from it, swings around behind him, opens up on autofire. The shuttle's cockpit disintegrates. The walls get perforated. The figures are taken to bits. The firing ceases.

The Operative reaches the space where the turret was. The barrel of the gun's still intact—albeit bent, twisted by the heat of the blast. It dangles from a heap of mangled machinery that's still held in place within the gaping ceiling. A bomb-rack rises from the Operative's right shoulder—tosses grenades toward the corners of the hangar to take care of anyone who shows up right after he leaves. Which is right now: the Operative leaps up into the ceiling, slides in past that machinery. The gun is automated—but according to the blueprints in his head, there's a servicing shaft that leads out of it. He enters that shaft—which rumbles as his grenades detonate. He makes haste along the passage, trying to ignore the cameras and sensors strewn all along. On one level, he's rendering himself a sitting duck. He's in a narrow crawl space with only one other exit. But this is the route that will bring him most directly into the vicinity of the base's inner enclave. He fires his thrusters, rockets down the corridor. He scarcely slows to shove himself off a corner. He opens up on the door that's now in sight. It disintegrates. He blasts on through.

And into the main barracks. It's full of men and women frantically donning their armor. A few are already suited. Their armor is lighter than the Operative's, but they're still formidable. Two of them are even now exiting the room through the door opposite. One is opening fire as the Operative emerges into the barracks—but he's deploying countermeasures, creating (for just a brief moment) the illusion of a suit whose camouflage is stuttering on and off as it stumbles toward one of the room's corners. Meanwhile, he's leaping the other way, real camo still humming on all spectrums. At such close quarters, the shelf life of such subterfuge is measured in fractions of seconds.

Which is all the Operative is after. Flame blossoms from the nozzles atop his gloves, roars out to hit the walls and ceiling—and folds back upon itself to encompass virtually the entire room and dash itself against his visor. For a moment, all he sees in visible light is orange and red—and all he hears on the audio are the screams of the unarmored being burned alive. He ignites his thrusters again, blasts into the fire, vectors straight in toward the first of the power-suits. Its sensors are inferior to the Operative's—but not so inferior that the man within doesn't know the threat is proximate: he opens fire at point-blank range, lashing out with both bullets and lasers.

But the Operative isn't there. He's changed course, coming in from the side like a torpedo. His fists cannon straight into the man's helmet. The visor crumples, as does the skull behind it. The Operative spreads his arms, flings bone and meat and metal aside, roars past bodies whose writhing has segued seamlessly into the contortions of burning paper. The remaining suits are retreating—but their flight stops as the Operative fires micromissiles into their backs. He fires his thrusters, shoots through the debris and out of the room. He blasts down more halls, turns down one more corridor.

The door at that corridor's other end is both massive and open. Suits from within are already opening fire as he rounds the corner. Lasers start to sear against the corridor's walls. The Operative's gun-rack starts spraying out flechettes. They take one of the suits out of commission. But their main purpose is to cover him against the lasers. He hurtles down the corridor, bouncing off the ceiling, the walls, the floor, back onto the ceiling—and then into the inner enclave.

The walls of the control room are lined with consoles. The crew manning them is divided between those who are trying to run at full speed through the other open doors and those who are opening up with their sidearms at the flaming, murky figure that is the Operative. A suit's on either side of him: he hurls a hi-ex charge at point-blank range into the nearest one's chest, kicks out with his feet to smash his boots against the other's helmet. The charge is an exercise in overkill: the first suit's torso detonates—for a brief moment, it seems as though its owner is struggling, absurdly, to remove his helmet, and then he pitches to the side and lies still. The second suit's been knocked sprawling—and before the man can rise, the Operative bounces himself off the ceiling and onto his target's back, shattering the suit outright and snapping the spine of the man within. Seeing this, the remainder of the control-room crew drop their weapons and start to run.

The Operative lets them.

"Going soft," says a voice.

"Not at all," says the Operative.

"Then what the fuck are you playing at?"

"Letting them get out of range of all this gear," says the Operative. He flicks out with his wrists again, lets micromissiles sear down the corridors along which those men are fleeing, watches for just long enough to ensure that their flight comes to a halt. Then he turns back toward the room itself. As he does so, all the doors slide shut.

"So what's the story?" he says.

"The story is these doors are mine," says Lynx. "I've got this whole place in lockdown. So don't just stand there."

The Operative isn't. He's leaning over one of the consoles, stabbing buttons, stroking keys with surprisingly dexterous fingers. He's keying in the commands that Lynx is feeding him—the commands that can only be entered manually. He's doing the one thing Lynx can't. Textbook procedure: the razor's wreaked havoc with the base's security and surveillance systems, allowing the mech to move untracked inside the perimeter and reach the inner enclave, where the house node itself is situated. Sometimes both razor and mech aren't necessary. But this base is well-protected. The mech would be hard-pressed to go it alone. And as for the razor: switching off defenses is one thing, but gaining active control of an entire complex's network to the point where one can access all data and run all systems—that's something else altogether. Besides, by wiring his house-node so that accessing it requires manual protocols, Sarmax has placed that node beyond the reach of any mere razor attack.

Which is why the mech is here. And yet he couldn't have reached the inner enclave without the razor. Who couldn't gain control of the inner enclave without him. Thus the standard partnership. Thus the standard tension.

And sometimes it boils over.

"It's not working," says the Operative.

"What do you mean, it's not working?"

"I mean it's not working. I got access. But I can't seem to do anything that matters with that access. Your fucking commands aren't working."

"Well, why the fuck not?"

"How the fuck should I know?"

"Get the base schematics on the screen."

The Operative does. He keys in more commands. The master blueprints click into focus.

"Well," he says.

"No difference between this and my blueprints," says Lynx.

"What?"

"This base is exactly what it's supposed to be."

"What'd you think it might have been?"

"I don't know, Carson. Jesus Christ, man, give me a moment here."

"Tell me what you're thinking, Lynx."

"I was thinking there must be more to this base than meets the eye. More than my intel showed. Another inner enclave, maybe. Maybe this isn't the real one." The Operative's never heard Lynx talk this fast. "But according to these readouts, this is legit."

"But we can't control it."

"We've got *partial* control, Carson. That's it. We don't have access to the overrides. We should. But we don't."

"So what do we need to get them?"

"I'm thinking we need Sarmax."

"Right," says the Operative. "I knew that already."

"You don't get it," says Lynx. "There's the chance that he built this so that *he's* got override authority."

"Isn't your hack supposed to forestall that?"

"It's supposed to. Look, we need to find Sarmax, Carson."

"Say he comes back here while we're looking for him?"

"He can't. I've got this place in lockdown, right? He'd have to fight his own defenses."

"Say you get kicked out?"

"The place would still remain in lockdown. That's default now. And even if he got back here, he still needs the manual codes I just gave you to reverse the lockdown. I've set up that much, at least. Listen, Carson, I thought I'd rigged it so I didn't need Sarmax to take control of his fortress. I thought we could take over this place and then take him out. Looks like I thought wrong. But finding him was always on the cards. Eliminating him was always part of the equation. You're just not going to have it so easy now. So let's take a look at those camera feeds before I start to get really *pissed off*."

"Relax, asshole." The Operative starts to bring up the

camera feeds. "Try to keep in mind that I'm the one who's actually standing here."

"Sure, Carson. Myself, I'm sitting on a beach. Huh, look at that."

For now the screens are lined with images of rooms. Of structures. Of exteriors and interiors. A boardroom, several laboratories, a warehouse, a leisure center and personal quarters, guard quarters, a gymnasium: all of it spread out upon the screens. Lots of bodies too, indicating those places where defenses have turned against defenders. Other rooms have simply sealed their doors, trapping their guards inside. The Operative and Lynx get busy comparing the camera feeds against the rooms shown on the blueprints.

"Shit," says Lynx.

But the Operative has simultaneously arrived at the same conclusion: there's one room that isn't visible on any screen. One place into which this inner enclave has no visibility whatsoever. One place off the maps.

The biggest place of all.

"The main dome," says Lynx.

"He's in there," says the Operative.

"He's got something going on."

"He always did."

"We've got him trapped."

"Are you sure it's not the other way around?"

"Get in there, Carson." Lynx's voice is as far from calm as the Operative's ever heard it. "Get in there. It comes down to this. It always would. You always knew it. This is your moment, Carson. This is your time."

"That's what I'm afraid of," says the Operative.

The door to the control room slides open.

• • •

Transit nexus named after spaceport named after airport named after martyred president from the old republic. Kennedy: its bulk might seem to equal the city itself. Five percent of all transport arriving at it exists solely to supply it. Of the remainder: three-quarters is domestic. A quarter is international. But this last segment commands the lion's share of the security resources Kennedy has at its disposal. That security is elite. They're nobody's rent-a-cops. They have the very best in personnel and equipment. Even so, they're far from perfect.

Especially when a military-grade AI is fucking with their systems.

So somewhere in some basement a vehicle is undergoing the last stages of boarding. Somewhere in that vehicle a man's taking his seat. He notes that there are no windows in here. He notes, too, that nobody's sitting next to him. Yet even as he registers this fact, a man's sliding into the seat opposite his. The newcomer nods politely at him, adjusts his strap across his chest, sits back. His face has that glazed expression that people get when they're preoccupied with views that only they can see. Nor does that expression change in the slightest when he starts to speak to Spencer. He makes no eye contact. His mouth remains shut. But his words ring in Spencer's head anyway.

"Nice to see you on the other side," Linehan says.

"Say that to me when we actually get there," replies Spencer.

"I meant customs," says Linehan.

"I know what you meant."

The two men don't know one another. That way they don't have to keep their stories straight. Control hates to give investigators free gifts. Control has given these two whole histories, has rigged vid footage to account for their movements across the course of the last several days. If anyone wants to probe back further than that, it can be arranged. Because

Control's a magician. Control knows the formula to grant the dead more life—keep the body's corruption a secret, map out the paths that flesh might have taken had it not crossed paths with one of the Mountain's predators, graft those paths onto new meat, set that meat in motion.

And hope for the best.

"But speaking of," says Linehan, "what kind of welcoming committee have you got prepared for me when we get there?"

"Welcoming committee?"

"Don't play the clown, Spencer. After we get through these fucking tunnels, who's going to be in the arrival lounge at Cornwall Junction?"

"Like I'm going to discuss that."

"Then how about if we discuss our deal?"

"What's there to discuss? We've already made it."

The car starts to vibrate. A humming reverberates through it: intensifies, drops away into a gentle thrumming. There's the feeling one gets when forces go to work at the edges of one's perception. There's the sound of many doors closing, echoing. A chime sounds. The train starts to move.

"And we're off," says Linehan.

"About time," says Spencer.

"And it's about time we started talking about our deal."

"I'm still not sure what you're driving at."

"Then let me help you out. You're providing me with the means out of here. I'm paying for my passage with information. True?"

"It had better be true."

"True. But that still leaves a lot of grey area."

"For example?"

"For example, what happens after I turn over my data to you."

"Isn't it a little too late to start talking about that?"

"Hardly. If anything, it's a little too early. All your Control was going to agree to was the general concept. And as for you—you can't agree to shit. You don't have the power."

"And you're saying you do?"

"In a word: yes. See, it's not just your identity that I've placed out there on the vine. I also stashed a copy of the thing I promised you."

"What the fuck are you saying?"

"You know exactly what I'm saying, Spencer. If your masters construe our deal to contain a claim to my person as well as to my information, they're going to find out that the down-low's been downloaded to the whole world. Now they can take the chance that they can take me and take me apart with enough ultraprecise butchery to preclude dissemination. They might even pull it off. But I'm guessing they're going to regard it as far easier to meet me halfway. And I have a few thoughts on how to best ensure that which I'm looking forward to sharing with your bosses."

"Sounds to me like you're trying to change our deal."

"Not at all. I'm just insisting on my interpretation of its terms."

The train accelerates. The straps tighten. As they do, Spencer's mouth opens, starts up a conversation. Introductions are made. Small talk begins. The rate of speed of this train, for instance. The economy of the undersea. The temperature in this car. The timing of the next meal. Small talk indeed—insisted upon by Control. The two men have to have a reason to remain alongside one another as they exit the train on the other side of ocean. They have to be talking as they make that exit. Otherwise, if they get shuffled or jostled, they've got no reason to drift back toward one another. Of course, Spencer knows that Linehan might drift the other way anyway.

But that's what the welcoming committee's for.

"So what exactly is it you want, Linehan?"

"I want what I've always wanted, Spencer. I want to be a

free agent. I want to give you the information that will make Priam the most powerful data-combine on Earth. And then I want to get out of your hair for good."

"And that's it?"

"What do you mean, is that it?"

"What about the means for freedom, Linehan? What about funds? What about an insistence that we don't track you?"

"Do you think I'd waste my breath? The latter—you'd never keep your part of the bargain. The former—you'd use that to accomplish the latter. No, I've got my bases covered, Spencer. I've got resources set up for a rainy day. Accounts, IDs, funds—the works. I know those Euro hubs, Spencer. I know the boardrooms. I know the bars. I know the places that are off the zone. Put me into London, and your trackers will be sniffing nothing within the hour."

Spencer says nothing. Yet even as he does, his lips dish out commentary on these tunnels' sealed-off southern reaches. He talks about things that everyone knows. How the main line through that segment of the warrens stretches from the mouth of Amazon to the bulge of Africa. How it was closed down when the superpowers set up shop down south. He comments on the long klicks that lie dormant. He speculates that perhaps with enough détente they'll be opened up again. He says that he looks forward to that day. Linehan agrees.

And persists.

"So what's it to be?"

"I thought you said I didn't have power."

"I did say that. I wasn't kidding. But I'm going to need you to make sure that someone upstairs understands my position. As soon as we hit Cornwall, you'd better tell your boys what I've just told you. And you'd better get me a line to whoever the hell your Control's control is."

"You'll get all the dialogue you want, Linehan. Beyond that, I can't promise anything."

"You can't even promise that," sneers Linehan.

"I'm on your side, Linehan. I've got as much riding on this deal as you do."

"To be precise: you've got more."

"How's that?"

"Because if it all falls through, I've got at least a chance of evading Priam. You've got none. You'll die for my sins, Spencer."

"If that's the price of your confession: so be it."

Linehan starts to reply—but his words are cut off by a buzzing that suddenly leaps out of nowhere into Spencer's skull. Spencer holds his face steady, gives no indication that he's ceased to hear Linehan, that another signal is even now forcing its way into his head. He doesn't know its source. At first he thinks it's some viral attack of Linehan's local node bearing fruit against the odds. He tries to blot it out, switch it off. He tries to stop it. But it overrides him like it knows his own codes. It swells ever louder. Now it's overwhelming. Now it falls away.

To be replaced by the voice of Control.

"Spencer. Can you hear me?"

"I can," says Spencer.

"Good. Because you've been rumbled."

"By who?"

"By federal agents. They're on the train already. More are boarding right now."

"Boarding? From where?"

"From the vehicles they've brought alongside. Behind and in front. You've been made, Spencer. They know the names you're using now. They know exactly where you're sitting. They'll be on you any moment."

"Why didn't they just bust us at customs?"

"Does it matter? Maybe my hack on security failed. Maybe they wanted you to think you had it made."

"I was starting to."

"So stop it. This is moving very quickly. They've wasted no time. We can't either. In sixty seconds, I'm going to strike key elements of this line's systems. I'm going to go through some back doors and hit some weak points. I suggest you sync with me. Maybe you can make something happen in the confusion."

"Risking yourself to save us, Control? What's got into you?"

"Spencer, I need you to concentrate on what matters. I'm downloading the map of this train into your head. Along with a map of the tunnels along the most direct route to border."

"The border? How in Christ's name are we getting through that *now*?"

"For now, why don't you think about how you're going to take those feds."

"*What?*"

"You may as well try. That man Linehan's a mech if ever there was one. And you're my finest razor. You've got your backs to the wall. Fight them. Crush them. Take that train. Take it all the way east. This is for real. Forty seconds, Spencer."

The connection terminates. In its place is static. And the words of Linehan.

"Let me guess: you've been talking to your bitch again."

"Shut up," says Spencer. "We've been made."

"I know."

"How?"

"There's two men in this car I've had an eye on ever since they got on. They're trying to blend in. They're clearly tracking somebody. And if your Control just told you our number's up, I guess that means that somebody's us."

"Where are they?"

"They're three seats behind you. Keep looking at me, Spencer."

"Linehan. Control also said they've brought vehicles alongside this one."

"What kind of vehicles? Where in relation to this car?"

"Behind and in front."

"Too bad there aren't windows in this thing. Did Control tell you anything else?"

"That it was going to do a hack on the main line's systems in exactly"—a momentary pause—"twenty-five seconds."

"Anything *else?*"

"That we should take this train and take that border. That we should work together."

"Goes without saying."

"Any ideas?"

"I've got lots of ideas, Spencer. The problem's time. At this point, I hate to wait even twenty seconds."

"Now it's eighteen."

"Spencer. Got a question, and I need the truth. Do you have any weapons?"

"No."

"Not a thing?" The one-to-one isn't good with nuance. But Linehan's surprise is coming through loud and clear anyway.

"How was I supposed to get them past customs?"

"I'm stunned Control didn't set you up."

"Control's hacking isn't foolproof. Which is probably why we're in the fix we are. I take it you're carrying?"

"Of course I am, Spencer. Concealing weapons is a lot easier than concealing identity."

"The specs you gave Control showed none."

"So I lied."

"So this is what you were going to use on us at Cornwall?"

"This is what I'm gonna use on anybody who gets in my way. Right now those guys behind you are top of my list. How certain are you as to that thing's timing?"

"Very."

"Meaning three seconds," says Linehan.

"Try two," says Spencer.

"One," replies Linehan.

But Spencer's already gone: wireless entry into wireless data-ports, barriers collapsing all around—and suddenly he's at home once more. It's been so long. It's been just a moment. That's what the zone does: makes him remember that everything that occurs between those immersions is nothing but a dream that's scarcely worth the effort. But this is a slice of zone he's never seen before. It seems to be endless. It ends almost at his feet—the very edge of universe that he recognizes as border. He's making haste upon that border in a chariot wrought from light.

But only for a moment. Suddenly lightning streams in from every direction: shatters that chariot, hurls him from the zone to find Linehan's legs scissoring past him as the mech leaps from his seat, onto Spencer's armrests—and from there onto the seat's back, whereupon he proceeds to use the seat backs behind that one as stepping-stones in a sudden lightning run. He takes it in a low crouch, his head ducked just shy of the ceiling, his boots just missing people's faces. There's barely time for them to protest before he reaches the men he's making for. His targets see him coming. They're leaping to their feet.

All the lights go off.

The train's still at cruising velocity. Its momentum is affected not in the slightest. Most of the passengers have enough optical enhancements to be able to see each other. But the unexplained darkness is still unwelcome—all the more so given that all video and audio channels that the train's routing to them just went out. The fact that the first thing that most people are seeing as they switch to infrared is three men fighting doesn't help matters.

Linehan throws himself down onto the first man, pulls him into the aisle, putting the man between him and his colleague while he pulls a loop of plastic wire around the man's neck. A moment ago, it was one strand on Linehan's shorn hairline. Now it's become one with his victim's jugular. Blood gushes everywhere. The second man already has a pistol out—and Linehan hurls his comrade's body at him, rushes in behind it, and dives at the floor as the man starts firing through that dead flesh. People are screaming now. But Linehan pays them no heed: he's tackling his assailant at the knees, knocking him off his feet—and then jumping to his own, kicking the gun away, bringing his boot down on the man's face—and diving after the weapon, grabbing it, whirling around, firing a single shot at the man who's pulling himself upward again—but who now grunts and slides back to the floor.

"No one fucking move," shouts Linehan.

People were starting to. But now they're stopping. Linehan gestures at Spencer, who steps into the aisle. As he does so, Linehan tosses him the pistol.

"Cover them," he says on the one-on-one.

Spencer does. Linehan grabs the first man he killed by his shirt. He grabs the man's pistol, shoves it into his belt. He pulls the corpse up onto a seat, shoves it up against the wall—and then seizes it by the back of its neck, starts smashing its head against that wall. He keeps on smashing until the skull cracks, breaks open like an overripe melon. The contents of the brainpan spill everywhere. Linehan starts rooting through them.

"What the hell are you doing?" yells Spencer on the one-on-one. He's backed against the opposite wall, is using it as a vantage point from which to cover the passengers. The height of the seats means that they can't see what Linehan is doing. Which doesn't mean they can't hear it.

"Software," snarls Linehan. "Take the software from the head, find out who they work for. Find out what their fucking *brand* is."

"We already know what their goddamn brand is," yells Spencer. "I told you already. They're federals."

"How long have you been in the States, Spencer? Huh? How fucking long?" Linehan's fingers are covered with blood and brain matter. His fists close on chips. "*Federals* means nothing. Which *Command*, Spencer? That's the real question. Which fucking *Command?*"

"Presumably whichever one you split from," screams Spencer. "When you stole whatever they'd found out about Autumn Rain. You've sold out your own kind, Linehan. And now you're going to die at their hand. Tell me I'm wrong, Linehan. Go on. *Tell me.*"

"Gonna tell you right now you don't know what the fuck you're talking about," hisses Linehan, and for one sentence he's both broadcasting and speaking. People around him whimper. "My country's in deadly peril. My run's the highest service I can offer her. And the last thing I need is holier-than-thou shit thrust in my face by some *mercenary*. You reading me? My life's the least of my concerns. But we've got to find a way to live anyway. We've got to work together, Spencer. Together. You reading me?"

"Sure," says Spencer, "I'm reading you."

"So tell me how your hack went."

"I don't have control. I'm not sure anybody does. My guess is that this train's been stripped down to its basic locomotion and emergency fail-safes."

"Monitors?"

"Almost certainly gone."

"Christ, let's hope so."

"What do you suggest we do next?" says Spencer. And even as he does so he's reaching down, kneeling on the floor, reaching inside the shattered head.

"You're lucky I didn't clean him out," sneers Linehan.

"Answer my goddamn question," says Spencer.

"I suggest you do exactly what I say," says Linehan. "We've got feds in both directions, and God knows how close they are. But I've got a plan. You're not going to like it. The sheep around us are going to like it even less. But I can guess what Control's orders were, Spencer. Get me to London. No matter the cost. Got it?"

"So what's the plan?" says Spencer.

"Start racking up cost," says Linehan.

B ail out," Haskell says.

"We can't," Marlowe replies. "He'll blow us to pieces. We need to wait for re-entry."

"But *he* won't wait," she says.

"Close the cockpit doors. Lock them."

While she does that, he's pulling himself down onto the floor of the cockpit, crawling beneath the instrument panels, finding the trapdoor that's situated where floor meets sloping wall. He opens it—and finds himself looking down into the narrow chute that leads to the escape hatch. He descends within. He reaches the airlock at the bottom and hauls it open.

Now he's in something that's more of a closet than a chamber. Another airlock sits adjacent to him. He knows better than to try to open that one. He rigs that door with devices from his belt: sensors, mini-charges, more sensors. Then he pulls himself back through into the chute. He closes the interior airlock—rigs still more devices, clambers back up.

Haskell's sitting there. She's rigged wires from her head to the control panels. She wears a dazed expression on her face.

"I can't raise anything on the zone beyond us," she says.

"Do the cameras show anything in the cockpit-access corridor?"

"They show nothing on this ship. But I don't trust them for shit."

They train their guns on the cockpit door. They open it. The corridor beyond is empty.

"You cover the zone," says Marlowe. "I'm heading to the cargo chamber."

"I'm coming with you."

"I thought razors couldn't move and remain in the zone."

"The best ones can."

"Ah."

But he figures it must be a tough balancing act. He notices that she's letting wires trail out behind her as the two of them push themselves off walls and move down the corridor.

"Wires are safer," she mutters. "I've shut down as much wireless as possible."

"Can you access the zone beyond this plane?"

"No," she replies. "We're being jammed."

The two of them pull themselves into the room where they waited out the takeoff. They open the doors that lead to the cargo bay. That cargo bay contains the three remaining ways into the ship. Two are airlocks, one on either side. But they're not the main focus right now.

"The elevator," she says.

"I know," he replies, sailing through air toward the airlock door that dominates the center of the cargo chamber's floor. Metal beams run up from its corners: the beams along which the elevator that connects the two ships is intended to slot. The elevator is there to expedite the loading of cargo into the upper ship. But it's about to be repurposed for a different kind of freight. For even as Haskell and Marlowe pull open that airlock door, they feel a vibration that can only be the lower ship starting to extend its shaft into the upper. That shaft's only supposed to be extended when the ship's parked.

But whatever's activating it isn't in the mood to quibble.

"Hurry *up*," she says.

The door they've just opened gives way to a two-meter drop. At the bottom is the exterior airlock door. Ladders drop down the walls to it. Marlowe climbs in. He looks back up at her.

"Weapons," he says. "And some of that pressure-friendly ammo."

She pulls weapons from their racks along the cargo walls, hands them down to him one by one. He slots in ammo specifically designed for use in pressurized environments, starts to mount guns on the ladder's upper rungs: everything from handhelds to heavy rifles. He sets them up so that they can swivel as needed. He configures them on automatic—rigs their sights and sensors so that they'll fire as soon as they see anything that passes for a target. He links them so that they can be controlled remotely by Haskell through the cockpit node—positions them so that they're all pointing down at the exterior door below. He climbs down more rungs, keeps setting up weapons. His feet are almost at the bottom of the shaft.

The center of the door beneath him starts to glow.

"He's burning his way through," he says.

"Get back up here."

But Marlowe quietly continues his preparations. He's setting the weapons for interlocking fields of fire, concentrating them on the center of the lower door. The glowing looks positively molten now. He starts making his way back upward, checking weapons as he does so.

"Hurry," says Haskell.

The guns around Marlowe whir, turn on their axes. Even the ones he didn't point initially toward the expanding glow are now swiveling upon it.

"*Move*," screams Haskell.

The guns roar to life—Marlowe reaches in, snaps one off its rung, starts unleashing it on full auto: the recoil sends him sailing upward even as Haskell starts closing the interior airlock door. He wafts through.

Just as something swarms through the space he's left.

Drones. A fraction of a meter in length. Scores of them. The mounted weapons are firing on high precision, cutting great swathes into that seething mass. The initial wave is getting annihilated. But the second wave is coming in from behind. They rise on gyros. They climb the walls. They open fire. Shots whiz past Marlowe's head. Guns start to get knocked off their mounts.

The interior door slams shut.

"Holy *fuck*," says Haskell.

"You got control?" asks Marlowe.

"I do."

"Can we hold them?"

"I don't know," she says. She projects the view from the guns onto screens set along the walls of the cargo chamber. She projects the specs too: Marlowe can see how she's running them through the cockpit circuitry, coordinating them to degrees that they're not even capable of—rewiring the functionality in real time, letting their barrels turn, fire, hit shots coming at them, hit the drones that are doing the shooting. He notices that armor plates have been positioned some distance down the shaft so that she can't touch the lower plane—notices, too, that the ammunition the drones themselves are using is the same as that of the guns he's just configured: precisely calibrated not to penetrate the airlock around them—and, by implication, the hull. Morat seems to want to take them alive.

He seems to have the resources to do it, too. Because the drones are responding to Haskell's onslaught in coordinated fashion—forming up in new waves of attack. They're upping their game.

Rapidly.

"They're pressing," she says.

"Can you hold them?" he repeats.

"For now. Not for long."

"We need to get the fuck out of here."

"Sure," she says. "How?"

"I get out on the hull and detonate the separation clamps."

She stares at him. "You can't do that."

"Want to bet?"

"Those things are probably out there right now."

"Which is the other reason why I need to get out there. Before they find another way in."

Even as Marlowe's speaking he's rigging more charges within the two side airlocks. It takes him all of twenty seconds, throughout which the bedlam below continues. Her eyes blank, Haskell drifts in free-fall by the wall as she tries to shore up their defenses and find another opening in the hack.

Marlowe finishes with the charges, starts suiting up. It's slightly lighter armor than he wore in South America. He gets on everything except for his helmet. He attaches another rack of charges to his belt, starts to pull himself back toward the cockpit. Haskell keeps pace with him. And while they move they argue.

"You go out there and you'll die," she says.

"We're dead if I don't."

They reach the cockpit. She positions herself in front of the trapdoor that leads to the escape hatch.

"I won't let you go."

"You have to."

"If you go through that door, I'll never see you again."

"Never say that," he says. Her eyes struggle to focus on his. She steadies herself against the control panels. But he's already stepping inside the cockpit—getting down on the floor, looking back up at her.

"I don't care what's out on that hull," he adds. "I'll be back. I promise."

"I'll hold you to it," she replies.

Marlowe steps inside the cockpit. He gets down on the floor, crawls beneath the instrument panels, finds the trapdoor. He opens it. He looks back up at Haskell.

"Go," she says. She leans down, kisses him. "Come back."

"I will," he replies. He turns. Turns back again:

"But if I can't."

"But if you can't."

"We need some kind of insurance policy."

"Meaning?"

He tells her. To his surprise, she agrees. She asks him to forgive her if it comes to that. He nods, pulls on his helmet, seals it. He crawls inside the chute. She pushes the door shut behind him.

He wriggles down, reaches the bottom. He opens the interior door, finds himself back in the tiny chamber. The sensors and charges he rigged are still there. He adjusts the latter so they won't detonate if he's the one who comes back in through this door.

Then he signals up to Haskell. She works the overrides, evacs the air. He works the door's manuals and pulls it open.

The surface before him is less than a meter away. But it's not the surface of the ship he's in. And the space between them is just that: space. Marlowe holds on to the edges of the doorway, activates his magnetic clamps, carefully protrudes his head.

And looks around.

Metal stretches out in all directions, curving away at various angles. He's between the bottom of his ship and the roof of the one that holds his in thrall. Dark lines connect those surfaces at the point where curves begin: wires and struts. There aren't many. Past them's only black.

Marlowe edges out of the escape hatch. He begins to crawl toward the closest struts. He's got his camo as high as it'll go. He's trying to minimize contact with the lower ship. He's hoping that those who designed its exterior sensors were realists—that its sensors are optimized against objects approaching it over great distances and speeds rather than people crawling like insects on the hull. But he's not sure. He's planning on avoiding the open. He's hoping to remain sandwiched between the ships if at all possible.

He reaches the nearest strut, looks past it and down at the massive sloping wing of the B-130. It's partially retracted. Though it looks wholly unstable, it's actually one of the toughest things on the ship—almost as tough as the struts themselves. Marlowe can see where they bent when his ship tried to break free. They're warped here and there. They're far from broken.

He means to change that. He moves along them, rigging minute amounts of hi-ex at key points. In short order he reaches the rear of the Janus, still well short of the rear of the B-130. Its tail splays out above him like some monstrous bird of prey. Bisecting the tail from left to right is a line of color through an otherwise-black sky: black shading off into dark blue shading off into violet.

He stares for a moment at what remains of sunset. Then he turns and begins crawling across the area just aft of the Janus's engines, reaches its other side. He takes out his largest charge and places it on the lower plane, just past the rearmost strut. He adjusts it so that its blast will slice straight downward.

But no sooner has he done that than he feels the topography around him tilt. The forces on his body rise. He doesn't have much time. He starts in on the next strut.

Movement catches his eye. Close at hand. A lens on his suit swivels. He stares.

It's one of the drones.

The ones he saw earlier were in rapid motion. This one isn't. It's sidling along the place where the B-130's hull meets wing. It's powered by what appear to be magnetized treads. It's not making directly for him. He's not even sure it's seen him.

But now he sees another. It's about the same size as the first, but of a wholly different shape. It's like some kind of centipede—moving along on far too many legs, each one clinging to the ship's side. Past it, Marlowe spots what may as well be its identical twin. Only this one's on the wing. Beside it is another model altogether.

Marlowe carefully looks around. The situation's as bad as he feared. The hull of the B-130 has come alive with these things. He spots at least a dozen more. There are several behind him too. They're closing in upon one of the side airlocks. They don't seem to have spotted him. They're about to, though. He releases the safeties of his wrist-guns.

And the combat starts up.

Though it doesn't involve Marlowe. Light streaks from several of the drones—lines of fire that just miss the B-130's tail, but that strike things far beyond the ship. There's an explosion. For a moment, Marlowe sees distant ships lit by the glare of that blast. And then another detonates with a flash that blots out those remaining.

But something's returning fire. Something's sweeping the B-130 with light that lights up Marlowe's screens—something that knocks drones off the hull as though they'd never existed. Maybe the surviving ships. Maybe weapons deployed at longer range. Maybe both. Marlowe doesn't care. All he cares about now is making it back. The black all around him is starting to dissipate. The metal's starting to glow. He's almost at the hatch once more. It's still open. He's three meters away. Now two.

The B-130's retros fire.

This is just the initial thrust. It's not full blast—the ship has yet to turn around to engage its main engines. Even so, Marlowe's flung forward. He grabs for the hatch, misses. He sails straight past the nose of the Janus—straight along the forward roof of the B-130, out toward the B-130's own nose. He fires his suit's thrusters on reverse. It's like pissing in the wind. He's almost shot past all metal. He grabs out with the desperation of the man who knows there's nothing past the thing for which he's reaching save planet.

And somehow he finds purchase. His clamps connect—

leave him clinging to the place where the B-130's cockpit's windows meld into its hull. There's an indentation there. It's not much. Combined with his own thruster's blast, he might be able to hang on for a few more seconds. He can barely move. The retros are intensifying. He needs to do something quick.

"Claire," he says.

Her voice comes back immediately.

"You're alive," she says.

"You holding out?"

"Just barely. You're still out there?"

"And I can't get back." He watches as the struts fold in preparation for the return to atmosphere. There's no space visible between the two craft anymore. It doesn't matter: he sends the signal. Both ships shake. Force rolls against Marlowe. Somehow he keeps his hold.

"You blew the struts."

"All that's left are the fail-safes," he replies. "They won't resist blastoff. You're going to have to leave without me."

"I can't do that."

"You have to."

"There's no way."

"There's no time to argue. There's nothing you can do for me now anyway."

"Jason. Where the hell are you?"

"Look out the window," he says.

She replies, but her voice is drowned by static. They're hitting the main phase of reentry. Marlowe takes another charge from his belt, slaps it on the windows as far away from where he is as possible, edges back as far away from it as he can. Chances are that it won't penetrate the hardened ship. And if it does, it might depressurize the whole thing. Which he's willing to chalk up as an acceptable outcome at this point.

But then again: he's on the window. Morat and his minions should be able to see him coming. They should be able to see exactly what he's doing. And if they are, they can see the problem all too clearly. Which would leave them with exactly one option.

Get ready for him.

The charge detonates. The window vanishes. Marlowe falls inside. It's as he suspected: they've depressurized already. At least this portion of the ship anyway. He rolls along the cockpit's floor. Flame's pouring in after him—and then it's quenched as metal panels slide across where the windows were, slam into one another.

Marlowe grabs on to the wall. Deceleration presses against him. The space he's in repressurizes. He looks around. The bodies of the pilots are still in their seats. They look just like their brethren upstairs. The lights of the instrument panels gleam. They look to be pretty much broken. Though even if they weren't, Marlowe knows better than to try to work them. He knows better than to bother trying to contact Haskell. He knows there's only one thing he *can* do. He flexes his wrists, primes his weapons. He hauls himself to the cockpit door. He blows the locks, slides the door open.

And starts his journey into the interior.

The Operative stalks from the control room. Its doors slide shut behind him. He doesn't know what that dome is. Beyond hinting that it's some kind of R&D facility, the control room furnishes no information on it whatsoever. Even though it should. This place is clearly a lot more complex than he or Lynx had bargained for.

To the point where he starts to wonder whether Sarmax really *is* in that dome. Maybe the camera feeds are lying. Or maybe Sarmax managed to get out. He shouldn't have. Within ten seconds of entering via the comlinks aboard the shuttle, Lynx had gained control of all the unmanned weapons rigged throughout the base, had set them to blast at anything that moved—the only exceptions being those along the Operative's route. The dome itself is apparently bereft of such guns. The corridors that lead into it aren't. Meaning that if anyone in that dome exits into one of those passages, they're going to exit this life in a hurry.

Which doesn't mean that Sarmax wouldn't have his options. He might know a way to thwart the guns. Or maybe he's gotten out by one of the exterior doors—though moving out over the surface is usually seen as a means of last resort. Keep as much as you can between you and the sky: that's every runner's rule. That's every runner's logic.

But logic isn't what's in the Operative's head right now. Intuition is. And intuition says that Sarmax is waiting in his sanctuary for the interlopers who have penetrated his lair. The Operative has never been so at cross-purposes with himself. He's done all the things Lynx asked him to do. He's done the one thing that Lynx would never have asked for in a million years. He's already made the move that's about to transform the whole equation.

Now all he has to do is take the consequences.

The Operative reaches one of the dome's many access chambers. He steps over the bodies of some guards. Looks like they got blasted by their own defenses. The Operative notes the telltale nozzles hanging from the room's ceilings. He imagines Lynx looking down at him. He's tempted to wave. He doesn't.

Instead he moves toward the door that leads to the dome itself. He stands by the side of that door and raises one hand. The door slides open. He goes on through. The door shuts behind him.

Leaving him immersed once more in night. A forest of night. He's standing in what seems to be a grassy meadow. The branches of huge gnarled trees reach toward him like claws. Lichens climb up trunks. Some of them shine phosphorescent, casting sharply angled shadows onto the forest floor. Through small patches of clearing, stars are visible overhead, preternaturally bright and serene against the blackness. Floating above the highest treetops, grotesque in its surrealism, is the Moon. It can't be the Moon—but there it is nonetheless, pockmarks of craters and smoke pall of mares smeared vivid across its surface. Three paths lead forward through the high grass. Each one tunnels into the woods, is swallowed by the blackness.

But before he's gone another step, a timer in his head hits zero. That timer heralds the activation of the jammer he placed on the bottom of the overhang before he lowered himself on the tether into the base. As jammers go, it isn't subtle. It doesn't search out specific frequencies. It just bludgeons the entire spectrum. It caterwauls on short-range, hopefully dissipating before it goes too far but almost certainly creating enough interference to make Lynx lose his connection. Its activation is something the Operative has been expecting.

But what happens next he hasn't.

An explosion rocks a distant part of the base. The whole dome's shaking. The faux moon and stars overhead are flickering. They're winking out. And coming back on. The Operative grimaces. Looks like the generators just got detonated. The backups have come on. A measure that must have been prearranged. Rig the generators with something that's going to blow unless it gets a signal at intervals—a signal that won't be forthcoming if a hostile razor has seized the comps, thereby ensuring that when the backups come on, any hostile razor will have lost his foothold: the Operative realizes that he's not the only one with a plan for keeping Lynx out of the action. The lockdown's probably still on. But Lynx has almost certainly been thrown out. The Operative's on his own. It's what he wanted. He fires his thrusters, blasts out over that sylvan cocoon. Halfway toward the dome's center, forest becomes fungal garden—he swoops over it, crosses over into a moated island in the center that's a patch of trees. He lands in a clearing at the island's center, makes his way toward a gazebo at the center of the clearing. Standing under the gazebo's roof is a figure in a combat suit that looks to be every bit as heavy as the one the Operative is wearing. He's got his back to the Operative.

Who continues to close. The man remains motionless. The Operative primes his weapons. The man turns around, regards the Operative. Eyes meet through visors. Nothing happens.

But then the Operative hears a voice.

Ⓢ   Straight shot from New York to London, and this train just keeps on eating up these klicks. It streaks supersonic through this hollow. Overhead's the world's weight in water. And that seabed suffers from the same thing you do.

Pressure.

Linehan clambers back into the aisle. As he does so, the emergency lighting kicks in, bathes the car in a dim red glow. Linehan looks around. He starts shouting.

"Okay, people. I want everyone on their feet. Hands behind your head. Let's go. Let's go." They're doing what he tells them. They're standing up.

"What's going on?" says one of the nearer ones.

"This," says Linehan, and fires. The man's head disintegrates in a burst of gore. Screams are stifled as his body flops. Spencer whirls toward Linehan, sends words skimming on the wireless connection.

"What the fuck are you—"

"Shut up," says Linehan, cutting Spencer off. "Don't take your eyes off them." Then, aloud: "I've got a bullet for every fucking question, people. Curiosity's a shortcut to the grave.

As is not doing exactly what I tell you. Oh, what have we here."

A woman has thrown herself at the dead man's body. She's sobbing. Linehan lunges at her. She tries to get away, but he's too quick. He pushes her up against the nearest seat, starts whispering in her ear. Her struggling intensifies. He pulls her back into the aisle, shoves her away from him. She stumbles toward the front of the car. Her cries fill the cabin.

"Now listen to me," yells Linehan. "On the count of three, I want everyone to my left to start moving through that door"—he gestures at the one that leads into the train's rear—"and into the next car. And I want everyone to the right of me to proceed through the other one"—now he points at the door leading forward—"and then keep going. And head for the ends of this train. And don't stop till you get there. And I *strongly* suggest that you *strongly* encourage everyone you meet along the way to do the same. On the count of one . . . two . . . *you*."

He's pointing at a man a few meters toward the car's rear. The man looks normal enough. He's looking at Linehan with mouth agape.

"Me," he whispers.

"Yeah," says Linehan. He advances through the people between him and the man. No one tries anything. No one touches him. He reaches the man, throws him to the floor, tells the man he didn't like the way he was looking at him. The man's begging for mercy. Linehan kicks him, tells him that he doesn't need to worry, that he's not even worth the bullet. He then moves back to rejoin Spencer. His yelling starts up anew.

"Three, people. Let's go. Forward, backward. *Move.*"

And people start to move. Spencer recognizes the look of stunned horror most of them are wearing. It's the look of those who suddenly find themselves in the middle of the kind of events they've never encountered outside the safe confines of a screen. Those at the front and rear work the manual controls of the doors. Spencer and Linehan watch as they start to shuffle through into the next car.

"Let's pick up the pace a little," says Linehan.

He fires into the backs of two of the nearest rearward-bound passengers. He turns forward, repeats himself. People start to sprint. The screaming starts up again in earnest, spiking as those in the adjacent cars are engulfed in the onrush. As ever, terror's infectious. But above the rising consternation echoes the voice of Linehan.

"You've got ten seconds before I start coming after you," he shrieks. "So you'd better haul *ass.*" He sounds like a madman. Spencer's starting to realize that's probably exactly what he is.

"You're fucking crazy," he says.

"Do you want to live or don't you?" says Linehan evenly. "I just bought us a couple minutes."

"And just what the fuck are we going to do with those minutes?"

But Linehan says nothing. He places his foot on one of the seats and hitches up a trouser leg. He runs his thumbs together down his shin. He digs deep. Something clicks. Part of his skin folds backward. His knee's not the only hinge in his leg—and what's within is mostly solid. And spongy. Linehan roots in there. Grasps something. Holds it up. Adjusts it.

"How the hell did you get that through?" asks Spencer.

"Because it's the same density as the rest of me," says Linehan. "Same visual readout too. I didn't even need your Control's help for this."

"Your whole leg's robotic," says Spencer.

"Something like that," says Linehan.

"How much of the rest of you is?" asks Spencer.

"Nowhere near enough to make me not care about my hide." He pulls out more pieces. He finishes assembling the resultant rifle. He hands it to Spencer.

"Have at it."

"What are you going to use?"

"This," says Linehan. He reaches into his leg again. He removes what seems to be an auto-pistol and what seems to be a—

"Looks like a whip," says Spencer.

"It should," says Linehan. He seals his leg, puts his foot back on the floor. He strides to the door at the front of the car and works its manuals. It opens. The two men move through into the next car. It's empty, apart from several bodies strewn in the aisle. From the marks on them they've been trampled. The door on the far end of this one is open. Through that door can be seen another empty car—and in the car beyond that, the rearmost elements of the fleeing passengers. A keening wail echoes in their wake.

"Looking good," says Linehan.

"Yeah," says Spencer, "it's looking great."

"Spare me your sarcasm," says Linehan. He starts to move forward at a rapid clip. Spencer keeps pace with him. "Here's an even better view."

Two images appear in Spencer's head. They're A/V feeds from right in the midst of the masses of fleeing passengers, looking out upon their backs. It's like a rugby scrum gone haywire. Each car into which the panic spreads means there's that many more people trying to get through the next door. With the inevitable result that there's as much fighting going on as there is fleeing.

"What the fuck," says Spencer. Linehan grins.

"Those two I pulled aside? The bitch whose husband I shot? The dickless wonder I singled out for special treatment? The one went toward the front and the other went toward the rear. But I planted cameras on both of them while I was telling them who was boss. I was giving us a little bit of transparency, Spencer."

"Into what?"

"Into the ones we're fighting. You said your Control said they were behind *and* in front of us?"

"Right. Though he didn't say why they didn't just board at our car directly."

"Because then we would have known something was up," says Linehan. "Right? If there's a disturbance at the place of boarding and we're not at that place, who are we to be any the wiser? The plan clearly was to have the plainclothes agents arrest us and hustle us to the waiting vehicles. Minimum of fuss, minimum of effort."

"And it backfired on them," says Spencer.

"Hardly," says Linehan. "Far as I can see, their plan's working fine. The plainclothes were expendable. That was the point. The heavies are undoubtedly the ones based from the vehicles. Who have us trapped between them."

"And where are they?"

"Delayed a little bit by the human tide, I expect," says Linehan. "But only a little bit. In fact—hello."

For now a new turbulence is engulfing the mass of people on the screen that's showing what's happening several cars behind them. People are stopping, being trampled by those on either side. People are diving into the seats on either side. The camera bearer almost goes down, gets shoved against a seat, manages to stay on his feet. The people in front of him are parting.

To reveal two suited figures standing in the doorway up ahead.

Each wears light powered armor. The armor looks to be U.S. military, but it features no insignia. Visors shimmer in the half-light.

"Into the seats," says a voice. "Clear the fucking aisles. Or you all die."

"They're right behind us," someone screams at him.

"We know," says the second suit.

"But here's what you don't," says Linehan.

They can't hear him. But everyone on the train hears what Linehan does next. If only for a moment: Spencer watches as he hits a button on his wrist—and the whole scene dissolves in static. Spencer hears a loud boom toward the train's rear. The whole car shakes—a shaking that intensifies, becomes an agony of reverberations. The emergency lights go out altogether. Spencer grasps his rifle in one hand, grasps the back of the nearest seat in the other. It struggles in his grip like a living thing.

"You've killed us all," he says.

"You're awfully vocal for a corpse," says Linehan.

"You fucking *mined* that poor fuck."

"And here I was thinking he spontaneously combusted. Let's hit it."

They're rushing forward. They're leaping bodies. They're watching on their screens as the passengers somewhere in front of them keep on running for their lives. They're carrying on their conversation all the while.

"How come we're still alive?" says Spencer.

"Because we're just too damn quick."

"I mean how come your bomb didn't kill us?"

"Because that's the way they build these things," says Linehan. "As modular as possible. Most explosives will do no more than depressurize a single train car. The engine blocks— the magnets—are designed to survive most blasts."

"And that's what just happened."

"My bomb was a little more powerful than that," says Linehan. "Probably knocked that whole rail into the ceiling. Not to mention causing one hell of a pileup behind the lucky car. We just got a hell of a lot shorter, Spencer."

"You're a fucking maniac."

"As long as I live, I can live with that."

"You just murdered hundreds of people!"

"But not the ones I'm trying to," says Linehan.

And now they're catching up with the fleeing passengers

in front of them. They're trailing them at a distance of just under a car, watching as they keep on screaming.

"Look at them go," says Linehan.

"You're *enjoying* this," says Spencer.

"Gotta live for the moment," replies Linehan.

He raises the auto-pistol, starts firing into the backs of the people in front of him. For a moment, Spencer's tempted to whirl on him, beg that he stop, shoot him if he doesn't. But only for a moment. Truth of the matter is that he doesn't dare. It's not even that he's sure Linehan will turn on him if he has to. It's more that he feels he's already in too deep, already complicit. He wonders if he still holds out the hope that he can justify these deaths, wonders if thinking along such lines is the worst crime of all. He realizes he still has no idea what Linehan's plan is anyway.

So he asks.

"What makes you think I've got one?" says Linehan. He stops firing. Most of the targets have raced out of range. Those who remain are doing their utmost to get there.

"You're certainly acting like it," replies Spencer.

"That's what improvisation's all about," says Linehan. "Better get ready to use that gun of yours."

For a moment, Spencer thinks that Linehan has read his mind, figures that he's about to turn on him. But then he realizes that what Linehan is referring to is the forward A/V feed. Flame's gouting toward the screen. People in front of the woman to whom the camera's been attached are burning. Through that flame, Spencer catches a glimpse of two more suited figures a car or two ahead, spraying out fire from nozzles atop their helmets.

"They're killing everybody," says Spencer.

"They're not stupid," says Linehan. "They've realized we're using the passengers. They must know that's the only way we could have got hi-ex right next to them."

"Did you mine her too?"

"With something a little less powerful," says Linehan. "Given that we're behind her."

"You're a real piece of work."

"Thanks."

The woman's been caught in the fires. They're hot. They consume her quickly. They consume the camera too—Linehan hits the button. Snarls.

"Too late," he says.

"Too bad," says Spencer.

"Here they come."

Running toward them are the rearmost passengers who've had the misfortune to be caught between the two sets of antagonists. Now they're foremost in fleeing in the direction they've come.

"We need your bullets too, Spencer," says Linehan as he opens up once more.

"I can't do it," says Spencer.

"Don't you get it, man? They're *already dead*."

The doomed are reversing direction once more—heading forward once again. But a few aren't turning around. One dies at Linehan's feet. One lunges toward Spencer—who fends off the lunge, strikes the man with his rifle butt, sends him sprawling. Linehan shoots him through the head, starts moving forward once again.

"I can't take this anymore," says Spencer.

"Want me to get it over for you?"

"Fuck you. I'm getting back into the zone."

"I thought you said there was no zone to speak of."

"There's a zone alright. It's just a mess. Wireless isn't happening. Wires may be more reliable."

"So jack in."

"So I need to stop."

"We can't stop."

"I didn't say *we* needed to stop. I said *I* needed to."

He halts, pulls open a door. It leads to the facilities. It's just a tiny chamber. But Spencer steps inside anyway. He pulls wires from his skull, pulls lights from fixtures. Linehan stares at him.

"We can't split up," he says.

"Want to bet?" says Spencer.

"Steel yourself," says Linehan. "You're Priam's man. Do you think that Priam is above all this? That your side never uses innocents as weapons?"

"This isn't about morality," says Spencer. "It's about strategy. We've got to get some zone coverage or we'll never make it."

"Oh," says Linehan. "I get it. The quintessential razor—fine with anything as long as you're doing it in zone. But get you out into the real world and you can't even pull a goddamn trigger."

"Shut up," says Spencer. "Shut that door."

"I'll be back," says Linehan.

"And I'll watch your back," replies Spencer. "Now get the fuck out of here."

The door slams shut. Spencer stares at it—watches as it's replaced in a single moment by a zone that's just as fuzzy as it was before. Things still haven't clarified. On the contrary: they've retreated still farther into shadow. The train's one long blur. What's beyond it is scarcely visible. There's some intimation of something big somewhere farther out. Something that's in motion. Spencer pictures a titanic struggle going on out there. He pictures himself as elusive, unattainable. He knows that's about as false a picture as he can paint.

But now he can see shards of light glowing close at hand. There's one about twenty cars up and one on the opposite side of the train, about fifteen cars back. They're unmistakable.

They're his fellow razors.

Only they're not on his side. And they're not on the train either. They're in vehicles right alongside. The razors are shielding those vehicles' exact specs. Spencer presumes there are other vehicles out there. Yet the zone's awash with so much turbulence that it's impossible for him to say for sure. Nor does he need to: he springs forward, cannons into two of them. Now he's a battering ram surging. One of his targets gets his shields up in time.

The other doesn't.

Spencer crumples through the defenses like they're so much paper. He feels his sharpness tearing all the way through to the point where wires meet nerves. He burns those nerves, sears that brain. He slices open all that data.

And suddenly he's presiding over several different views of the car that's fifteen cars back from the one in which he's hidden. Several different views through several different visors. But far more important than those views is the glimpse he's now got into these men's hearts. Spencer flares like lightning through their suit-comps, overrides them, makes them turn on each other with all their automated weapons. He destroys the whole squad that was attached to the gunship he's just taken over. He revs up the ship's controls. He's ready to go places with it and the corpses it contains.

Only he's not. Instead the ship's getting shredded by gunfire from still another farther down the tunnel. Simultaneously he comes under attack from several other razors. They're trying to triangulate on him. He's searching for a way to get at them. He needs a better view. He rifles through the train's systems. He still can't get at its controls.

But what he can get at are its cameras. Suddenly he's got access to the feeds from all eighty cars. Only it's not eighty. Cars sixty-five and onward are gone. Cars number nineteen through twenty-eight have been scorched with fire. What's left of the passengers in that section of the train are huddled amidst the seats of cars twenty-nine through thirty-three. Suited figures are moving up through twenty-seven and twenty-eight. There are five of them. The gunship from which they've come is moored at car number nineteen. It's the one whose razor resisted Spencer's onslaught. That razor's shielding his men well. He's trying to get out ahead of them. He's trying to get into the cameras. But Spencer is blocking him—preventing him from seeing Linehan in car number thirty-four, preventing him from seeing Spencer himself in car number forty.

Spencer's got a nasty feeling he's been made anyway. His view into most of those cars is vanishing, and he can no longer see Linehan or his antagonists—or any of the cars save the ones immediately adjacent to the one he's in. He's coming under point-blank zone assault. Other razors are prising the train from his virtual fingers. The gunship behind him accelerates up the tunnel, climbing past the train's cars, moving past the sixties, the fifties—the forties. It starts to slow down. It moves past car number forty-five. It stops at car number forty-one. Spencer can see it vaguely in the zone. He hurls himself against its razor. But that razor's dug in. Spencer can't break through.

All he can do is watch as though in a dream: the exterior door in car number forty-one slides open and suited figures emerge from a walkway that's been extended from their gunship. They stride rapidly into car number forty. Spencer watches as they move toward the door behind which his body's stored. He wants to jack out. He wants to run. He wants to stop them somehow. He doesn't do any of those things. He just flings himself forward in one final frantic attack at the razor who's crouched behind the bulwarks so close at hand.

He fails—ricochets off those barricades. And watches as the suits rip that door off its hinges. He catches a quick glimpse of himself sitting against the sink, eyes rolled back, jaw open—and then they seize him.

The zone vanishes. He's staring up at visors staring down upon him. Weapons are thrust in his face.

"Don't move," says a voice.

It's not like Spencer would dream of it. They slap a neural lock onto his spine. He's paralyzed: they're carrying him back toward their ship like some kind of trussed-up trophy. They move back on through to car number forty-one.

Which is where they stop. Something seems to be going on. One of them leaps forward, slides shut the door through which they came. They no longer seem to be bent on getting back to their ship. Instead they're taking up defensive positions. They're not talking. But they're clearly communicating. They're training their guns forward and backward, eyeing the exterior and interior doors alike. Spencer finds himself hurled down upon one of the now-empty seats. He watches as the door from car number forty opens.

And Linehan enters the room.

He's not in armor. Those he faces are. That should be the end of it. But it's not. And Spencer feels like he's back in his dream—as Linehan leaps forward, ducking in under the suits' fire, twisting his whole body through the air as he runs along the wall, right angles to the floor, his whip leaping out, licking onto one of those suits' helmets. There's a detonation. The suit topples to the floor, smoke trailing along a quarter-circle arc from what remains of its neck. Linehan continues his charge down the wall—switches to the ceiling as the suits continue to fire at him. His auto-pistol speaks—first left, then right, then left again, even as its wielder's path blurs onto the other wall, even as that wielder lashes out with the whip again, lands a blow on another suit's torso. There's another detonation. Linehan leaps straight forward—knocking what's left of that suit into the next, grappling with the next one, ripping its arm clean off, firing shots into mangled flesh. But as he does so, the remaining suit's whirling toward Spencer, taking aim—and then the suit's gun hand disintegrates as the whip hits home, dances from there to the suit's head.

The car's still. Linehan bends over Spencer, removes the neural lock, tosses it aside.

"I can walk from here," mutters Spencer.

"We're done with walking," says Linehan.

He steers Spencer to the car's open exterior door. Beyond is some kind of tube. Spencer follows Linehan down it.

And into the interior of the much smaller vehicle that's running parallel with the train. There's not much in that interior. It's about six meters long and three meters wide, with a cockpit at each end. Each cockpit features controls and a slitted window.

"Sit down," says Linehan. "Wire yourself in."

"Is this one of their gunships?"

"Oh yes."

"The Rain's?"

"If it were, we'd never have made it in here. But we've got about ten seconds all the same. So how about we talk as we go?"

The door slides shut behind them. They strap in. They disconnect the ship from the train. Spencer jacks in. The controls spread before him. The rails stretch far beyond him.

He hits it.

Sea and space and aircraft: all have the same type of corridor. All boast new kinds of narrow: like bones bereft of marrow, like hollow when it's hardly worthy of the word. Marlowe moves carefully through a labyrinth that's far more complex than the layout of the plane above it. It's far larger. It's not lit either. Whoever's in charge has turned off all the lights.

But Marlowe's willing to bet they haven't turned off the sensors. He's felt nothing upon him yet, but—camo or no camo—he's sure he's being picked up all the same, particularly as the darkness is forcing him to use his own sensors. He sends them probing along a number of spectrums. Among them is the visible.

The walls and ceiling thus revealed are a combination of plastic and metal. The rooms that they enclose are largely empty. The ship those rooms comprise has seen better days. It was commissioned as a massive bomber—capable of launching a smaller one from its back and into space, and then swooping down upon the enemy anywhere on Earth. But that was twenty years ago. It still constitutes impressive technology. But from a military perspective, it's obsolete. Smart hypersonic missiles have seen to that. Now the ship's primarily given over to cargo runs. Usually it's no longer even armed. Under normal circumstances it would be packed with freight. But for this mission it only had one piece of freight to haul.

And release. At least, that was the idea. But someone had other ideas. And Marlowe can't wait to get face-to-face with that someone. But it seems like his body couldn't be moving any slower. It's like he's pulling himself up a mountain—as the descent steepens, the floor is sloping ever more steeply beneath his feet. He's being shoved toward that floor with a steadily increasing force. The shaking around him is intensifying, the ship rocking in the full throes of reentry. Marlowe keeps to the walls. He moves through the doors like anything could happen.

But the drone catches him by surprise anyway. It's propelled by jets—gyros that flare suddenly as it rounds a corner and whips in toward his face. He fires his own jets—meets it in its headlong flight, smashes into it with one fist, sends it slamming into a wall. He lights it up with his guns, keeps going.

Straight into two more. One's clinging to the wall—and suddenly springing in toward him. The other's another gyro-platform. Wicked-looking barrels hang from beneath it. Marlowe dives toward the side, gets the first drone between him and the second. It riddles its comrade, starts to riddle him—but now he's lashing out with rapid fire to perforate it.

But not before he's been hit himself. He's scarcely got time to assess the damage before he's taking more of it from every side. They're rushing him from all angles now. They're even coming out of the walls: the vent covers are snapping off and machines are leaping from them. Marlowe retracts his thrusters and lets his guns roar. Flamers mounted on his back spray everywhere. His fists and boots dispatch drones of every description. He catches quick glimpses here and there of the things he's fighting—his helmet cannonades into something that's more teeth than body, his boot dropkicks a spiked orb into a wall—but mostly he's just going on reflex. His vision's a maelstrom of data and drones. He's getting hit repeatedly. He's giving out far worse than he's getting.

And yet he's being ground down steadily. There are simply too many of them. One of his flamers gets knocked out. Bullets are lodged all over his suit. The outer armor on his left side's almost penetrated. His fists are worn dull from punching.

"Had enough?" says a voice.

Morat's voice is being broadcast from one of the drones. Marlowe fires hi-ex into it. The drone detonates. But the others take up where it left off.

"You're fighting something you can't kill," they say.

But Marlowe doesn't answer. He just keeps battling his way through them—straining against the G-force, grabbing two drones, smashing them together, firing point-blank, letting his shots ricochet off walls and into targets. His movements speed up even as his armor corrodes—even as the pressures on his body continue to build as the ship surges through reentry. He's in some kind of zone all his own now, one where the voices lapping up against his brain are just part of the scenery.

"You're not *listening,* Jason. Once I finish taking off that armor I'm going to start in on what's left. I'm going to introduce your organs to the air. I'm going to strangle you with a noose made from your own intestines. But I'm going to leave your eyes for last. Know why, Jason?"

Marlowe doesn't answer. Now he's battling just to stay on

his feet. The husks of shattered metal pile up around him. The frenzy of the drones' attack is increasing. He uses his armor as a battering ram, charges into a wall, takes it down, charges away from the onslaught and on through into an adjacent room. It's empty of drones.

For about a second.

"Because I'm going to make you *watch*, Jason. I'm going to make you watch while I do to her what you can't even be sure you did all that time ago. Was there ever a time when you weren't Sinclair's eunuch? Was there ever a moment when your desire was truly your own?"

Marlowe has hit on a strategy he likes. It's pretty much the only one he's got left—smashing his way through wall after wall—but if he's making better progress, that's mostly because the ship's finally coming out of its reentry. The angle of descent is decreasing. So is the deceleration, which ought to mean he can contact Haskell. But she's not answering. Or she can't hear. The drones keep sniping at him. His wrist gets hit hard enough to destroy the gun encased there. He's pretty much down to the innermost shell of his armor now.

"But don't worry, Jason. You'll get that action yet. I'll shear off your one last weapon and cram it down her throat. Partially to repay you for what you've done to my machines. But mostly to teach her for being such a troublesome cunt. Oh yes: she's doing much better than you are, Jason. She's still holding out up there. Whereas you're about to meet with one wall too many. You're about to meet with me, Jason. Come on. *You're almost there.*"

Marlowe realizes that the attack of the drones is subsiding. They're still pressing him hard. They still mean business. But they're giving way in front of him and closing in behind. They're herding him in one particular direction, which is fine by him. He's being driven toward the very place he's been trying to get to. He's down to a single heavy pistol now. But it's still got ammo. His shots are still crashing home. His boots are still crunching over what's left of things he's shot. He picks one up and flings it—scoops up another, uses it as a club against its live brethren. He gets through one more wall. He smashes through one last door, charges through into the main cargo chamber.

It's completely bereft of cargo. All it contains is the elevator, set within four pylons that rise to the ceiling and end in the corners of a shaft. The trapdoor to that shaft is open. Marlowe can't see where it leads.

But he can see Morat, standing suitless in front of that elevator, surrounded by several larger drones. He's smiling.

Marlowe isn't. He whips his arm up, opens up. But as he does so, the drones around Morat fire. They all hit in the same place. Pieces of Marlowe's pistol fly through the air. Marlowe snarls, starts toward Morat. But the larger drones are forming up between him and his quarry. They form a wall. They train their weapons on him.

Marlowe stops. He brandishes his makeshift club. He stares at Morat.

"I'm not done yet," he says.

"Well," replies Morat, "that makes two of us."

Marlowe steps toward him.

"That's far enough."

Marlowe lines his target up. Even though he's got neither guns nor screens. All he's got is a visor so cracked as to be useless. He pulls off his helmet, tosses it aside.

"Right here. Let's settle this once and for all."

"We already have," says Morat. "Didn't you notice?"

"I haven't noticed shit."

"Funny, neither has your bitch."

"She's not my bitch."

"No," says Morat. "She's mine. Or at least, she will be in a few more minutes."

"She still hasn't blasted off?" Marlowe can't keep the dismay from his voice.

"Strangely enough, she hasn't."

"Jesus fucking *Christ*," says Marlowe.

"I don't know if she thinks *that* highly of you," says Morat. "And yet I get the feeling there's something down here she doesn't want to leave without."

"She's crazy," mutters Marlowe.

"For once we agree on something," says Morat. "But give her some credit. She's quite the feisty one. She's up there waging all-out siege warfare." He gestures at the roof. "She's got one hell of a crossfire going, Marlowe. She's racked up quite a score. Anything that I put in that shaft gets toasted. I'm starting to have my doubts that I can break through before we land."

"You're planning on *landing* this thing?"

"No," says Morat. "I'm planning on circling the Earth forever."

"You're a fucking riot, Morat. Just where the hell do you think you're going to down it?"

"Stick around long enough," says Morat, "and you might find out. Have you tried to contact Claire since we emerged from reentry?"

"Yes."

"And?"

"And I can't get through."

"And you know why that is?"

"I presume it has something to do with that hack of yours."

"More than just something."

"Who's running it? You?"

"Look around you, Marlowe."

And Marlowe looks. And stares at Morat.

"You mean the drones?"

And Morat just laughs. "It's tempting to think of them as plural. But it's the same mind that spans them. I built them to the specifications furnished by the Rain. I uploaded their activation codes scant minutes ago. Brought to life with the Rain's own essence—and your little strumpet couldn't stop me. She's been trying to slice her way into their circuitry ever since. She can't make it happen. Nor will she. She thinks she's the razor to end all razors. She has delusions of such grandeur. Now she's learning just how pathetic those delusions really are."

"So how come she's still up there raining shit down on you?"

"Well," says Morat, "that's why you're still standing there talking shit to me."

"Oh really."

"Yes. Because you're going to persuade her to surrender."

"The hell I am."

"And that's exactly where I'll put you if you don't."

"So what are you waiting for?"

"You've got it wrong. I'm talking about a different kind of pain. I'll blow the whole top plane. I'll toss her ass into the fucking slipstream. I already rigged it. All I want to do is talk to her. That's all. You don't even have to say a word. You've got her life in your hands, Jason. All I want is conversation. Just a little chat."

"And what are you going to say to her?"

"How foolish she's being. Among other things. And how I don't have time to fuck around. Five seconds, Jason. Four. Three. Two."

"Fine," says Marlowe. He sends out the one-on-one. It's answered almost immediately.

"Jason. Where are you?"

"Right below you."

"What's—"

But now her voice cuts out. "I don't want you *talking* with her," says Morat. "I just want you *telling* her that she should tune in to the following frequency." He names it. "You've got time to tell her that, and that's it. Otherwise I cut you off again. You got me?"

"Sure," says Marlowe.

"Good."

"—son? Are you there?"

"Claire," he says. "Morat's got me down here. Tune in to this frequency."

"Jesus," she says—and her voice cuts out. Marlowe tunes in to the frequency in question.

"And now we're all here," says Morat.

"What the fuck do you want out of all this?" says Haskell.

"You," says Morat.

"That's not enough. That can't be."

"How about letting me be the judge of that?"

"You'd go to all this trouble to capture two runners?"

"I'd go to all this trouble to publicly expose the superpowers for the impotents they are."

"By taking us to HK?"

"Taking us *where?*" says Marlowe.

"You heard her," says Morat. "And yes, Claire: exactly. Look at that procession we're leading. Look at all those ships arrayed out behind us. It's all going down on camera. Hundreds of millions are watching. It's almost as good as the Elevator. And when we get ready to land, it's going to get even better."

"That'll never happen," says Haskell. "They'll blast us from the sky before they let you put this down in the city."

"Spoken like a true servant, Claire. You don't know your own masters. I do. There's no reason for them to shoot us down—*if* they think they can recapture us as we land."

"This doesn't add up," says Haskell.

"Did I ever claim it had to?"

"There's something you're not telling us."

"There are many things I'm not telling you," says Morat.

"That much will never change. Truth to tell, I'm not sure I could tell the whole truth even if I wanted to. Even if I knew it. But I'll tell you this much: unless you want to give up all hope of seeing Marlowe again, you'd better give it up and get down here right now."

"You really expect me to believe that?"

"What you believe is beside the point."

"I thought you said you wanted us alive."

"I exaggerate sometimes," Morat replies. "It's a bad habit of mine. And here's another: I was never any good at negotiating. So I won't even try now. The Rain want you alive if possible. They'll take you dead if they have to. Now are you going to come on down or am I going to scratch one mech?"

"Just try," says Marlowe.

"Just you wait," says Morat. "Claire. What's it going to be?"

"Don't do it, Claire. He'll have us both."

"He already does, Jason."

"He doesn't have to."

"Oh," says Morat, "but I do."

"Fuck you," says Haskell.

"Maybe," says Morat. "Maybe. It might be fun. Although I have to confess that the animal ceased to turn me on some time ago. I get off in my head now, Claire. I get off on twisting yours—to the point where you're about to violate all your training in order to save someone who might not mean a thing to you. Even though you know damn well that all you're really doing is condemning both of you to the claws of the Rain. They're waiting for you, Claire. So am I. So come on down and join my party."

"No," says Marlowe.

"I have to," she says.

"You're right," says Morat.

"You're dead," she says.

"Wait long enough," he says, "and you'll be right. But I'm

going to live long enough to see this world go into the grinders of the new one. What's it going to be, Claire? Are you going to open that airlock? Or do I have to count this down?"

"No," she says, "you don't. Forgive me, Jason."

"There's no need," replies Marlowe.

But Haskell's already sending signals from her mind that have nothing to do with that airlock. They've got a different destination altogether. They flit past the outer plane's hull, stop at the lower's. They trigger circuitry. Which triggers chemistry.

The bomb that Marlowe planted on the B-130 detonates.

The voice of Leo Sarmax is sounding in the Operative's ears. It's almost like the first time he heard it. Back before anyone saw all this coming. Back when the world was young. It's lost none of its intensity in those intervening years. In fact, it's gained a new edge.

Though that may be just a function of the circumstances.

"You've got something I want," says that voice.

They're just words. But they surge like waves within the Operative's skull. He feels himself struggling not to be swept under. He feels so gone he can't imagine being anywhere else. He waits for all eternity.

And then he speaks.

"More than just something."

"Meaning?"

"Meaning I'm Carson."

There's a pause. Then audio's joined by another set of signals. A face appears before the Operative's retina. He reciprocates even as he takes it in: nose, sharply sloped cheekbones. Those eyes. That half smile.

"Carson," says Leo Sarmax. "Been a long time."

"Long time for sure."

"Didn't even know you were up here."

"That's because you're slipping."

"I doubt it," says Sarmax. "When did you get in?"

"About twelve hours ago."

"And what do you think?"

"Not much. Expected your security would give me more of a challenge."

"I'm not talking about my defenses. They weren't intended for the likes of you. I'm talking about this rock."

"Oh," says the Operative. "In that case, I like it."

"You should," replies Sarmax. "It suits you."

"Likewise."

"Well," says Sarmax, "I like this place for different reasons. I'm different than you, Carson. I always was. We both always knew that."

"We always did. That's why you left."

"And why I'm staying."

"I wasn't going to ask you to do anything else."

"Good, Carson," says Sarmax. "Good. I'm glad to hear that. You know why? Because I've carved out a bit of a niche for myself up here. Used to be that the Moon could guarantee you some isolation. No longer. Now you have to work for it even here. And that's what this place is to me. Those mountains you saw coming in—they're mine. The valleys—mine. The horizon in between—mine too. It's all mine. And so are you."

The Operative doesn't reply.

"Carson," says Sarmax. "You really shouldn't have come here. All you've done is dig your own grave."

"I don't think so."

"Much as you might deny it. Much as I might deny the hand that strikes you. You've stuck your nose into one rabbit hole too many. Took you a long time do it. But you've finally managed to pull it off. And now I'm going to pull apart your skull and use whatever's inside to reverse-engineer the lock-down you've put on my comps."

"Not so," says the Operative.

"In that case," says Sarmax, "climb out of that suit. Walk me back to the control room. One chance, Carson."

"Listen," says the Operative, "you've got it wrong. If they wanted to rub you out, I wouldn't be the instrument of their displeasure. Come on, man, don't kid yourself with the hubris. Sure, you're your own little Moon lord now, but if they really wanted you dead, face it: you wouldn't be alive. And it wouldn't be subtle, either. Some low-flying sat would just do a drive-by on your ass, and that'd be that. It's not like there'd be an investigation worth the name."

"So why *did* you come here?"

"Would you believe that I wanted to look up an old friend?"

"Cut the shit, Carson," says Sarmax. "Don't make yourself look pathetic by trying to worm out of it now. Just get busy thinking on the irony—you came out here on the cold run, but it's going to be you who gets taken out instead. It's that simple, old friend."

"No," says the Operative, "it's not."

"Then tell me what you've come to do."

"To deliver a message."

"To deliver a *message*?"

"To deliver a message."

Sarmax laughs, a sharp short bark. "You're damn right you've delivered a message, Carson. You carve through my inner and outer perimeters in nothing flat, you slice your way straight through my household staff, destroy my machinery, fuck my systems—you'd better believe you've just delivered a message." He puts one glove toward the left side of his helmet. "Heard you loud and clear, Carson. Heard you loud and clear."

"Sure," says the Operative. "Had to do that. Had to make it look convincing. Otherwise the message wouldn't have been worth much."

"So what the fuck is the message?"

"That I *was* sent to kill you, but I'm not going to do it."

"What are you talking about?"

"I can't take you down, Leo. I'm this close to putting your body through the roof of this dome, but I'm not going to do it."

"Hardly the one to make threats, Carson. So you're having second thoughts? So you want to slink back out? So what's new? A man can do a lot of soul-searching when it's time to ride that ferry. Particularly when he's lived so long a life as yours."

"So come on over here and get it over with."

"No," says Sarmax. "First I want you to tell me who sent you."

"Like you can't guess."

"You're still working for them."

"I'm still killing for them."

"And I'm next on the list?"

"Something like that."

"So why the fuck did it take them so long? They have cause now, they've had cause for a long time. Why now?"

"Because," says the Operative, "things are getting out of hand."

"And I'm stirring them up?"

"I don't know," says the Operative. "*Are* you stirring them up, Leo?"

"Apparently I must be."

"Leo. Are you dealing with the Rain?"

"Jesus," says Sarmax. "Is that what this is all about?"

"Answer the question, Leo."

"No," says Sarmax, "I'm not." A pause. Then: "They really think *that's* the game I'm playing?"

"I have no idea what they really think."

"I thought you said—"

"You didn't listen," says the Operative.

"I'm starting to think there's been a pretty big mistake," says Sarmax.

"No mistake," says the Operative. "No mistake at all. They're calling in all the variables. Biggest manhunt in history. Anyone who might have dealt with the new player. Anyone who might *be* the new player. Anyone at all. It's a long list. And you want to know something about that list? An ex-Praetorian now ensconced in his own private fortress on the Moon isn't going to be near the bottom."

"I see," says Sarmax.

"I hope you do," says the Operative. "Because that's why there's a termination order on your ass."

"And they sent you to carry it out."

"Well," says the Operative, "in theory, sure."

"In practice?"

"Like I said, I'm not going to kill you. Not unless you draw first."

Sarmax doesn't move. Static. Then: "If you really *were* sent to kill me, then what was that about how they'd be more likely to sic a sat on me instead?"

"Oh," says the Operative, "that. I was just tossing things out there. Trying to get you to calm down a little." He laughs. "But I tell you where I wasn't bullshitting you, Leo: I meant it with the hubris. Like they see you as worth blowing that kind of hardware on . . ." His voice trails off in a dry chuckle.

"So you were talking bullshit?"

"It'd certainly be one way to off you. But I guess they wanted to make this one less overt. Maybe even save on some expenses."

"But still eliminate a variable."

"That's it," says the Operative. "That's all. It's nothing personal. They're calling in the variables."

"When did they start cleaning them up?"

"Two days ago. But they started calling in the ones on the Moon last night."

"Carson," says Sarmax suddenly. "Do you really want us both to walk away from here?"

"I really do."

"So why didn't you make a run for it? Why come here?"

"I'm not sure I follow your logic," says the Operative.

"I mean that you didn't have to show up in the first place," says Sarmax. "Just start your run and contact me later."

"Would you have listened?"

"Probably not."

"Well, that's part of the reason then. But the basic issue's a little more simple: anyone who makes a break too early's meat. Only hope now is to get you out of here in such a way that they think you're dead, and then set you loose as rogue. Rogue, but in contact."

"With you."

"With me."

"With anyone else?" asks Sarmax.

"No."

"What about your razor?"

"Are you kidding me?"

"You'd tell your razor I was dead when I was still alive?"

"I'll tell my razor whatever he wants to hear."

"Your razor being Lynx?"

"What makes you say that?"

"The fact that this run bears all the hallmarks of that sick fuck."

"I can't say I disagree."

"What precisely does he want to hear?"

"That you're not breathing. That your systems are ours. That we can move on to the next phase."

"Of course," says Sarmax. He pauses. He smiles. He shakes his head.

"What's so funny, Leo?"

"You, Carson."

"So let me in on the joke."

"I'd rather *you* let *me* in on whatever the fuck's going on. C'mon, Carson. You're a bullshit artist through and through. But you can't bullshit me. You never could. There's something else going on."

"I would have thought that was obvious."

"Sure. It's obvious. So why don't you tell me what the fuck it is?"

"Because you're doing so well on your own."

"This isn't just about the elimination of variables, is it?"

"No," says the Operative. "It's not."

"They want me dead for a specific reason," says Sarmax. "Of course."

"What the fuck do they think I've done?"

"You sound so righteously indignant, you ought to be a case study."

"Level with me, Carson. You know I can take the truth."

"The truth," says the Operative, "is that it's not a matter of what you've done. Not a matter of who you were. It's a matter of asset mobilization."

"What in God's name are you talking about?"

"I'm talking about why they sent me here, Sarmax. I'm talking about harnessing your holdings in the service of the Throne."

"All the Throne has to do is ask!"

"You forget," says the Operative, "that this is how the Throne asks."

Sarmax shakes his head. "Those stupid bastards," he whispers. "Those stupid. Fucking. Bastards."

"Maybe," says the Operative. "Maybe not. But at any rate: now we're getting to the proposal I've come all this way to make. See, Leo, I've been thinking. I've been thinking while I sat in that truck for two days and ran that deep. I've been thinking about what I'd do when I got here. Thinking of what it'd be like. Lot of folks watching now, Leo. Lot of folks waiting too. A lot of people are getting very nervous. So I knew the pressure would be on when I got here. I knew I'd better be ready with some fancy footwork. I knew I'd better be ready with a plan. Which you're the key to making happen."

"This plan's yours?"

"If you even have to ask that, then you aren't thinking. Or you haven't been listening. Or you never knew me in the first place. I think the endgame's upon us, Leo. I want to be ready when it starts to break. I want you ready too. I want you to listen to what I'm going to say."

And Sarmax does. Nor is the telling short. It stretches out over the lunar surface, leaping to places far afield of the south pole. The exposition unfolds across the temporal too, weaves in whole series of events both real and hypothetical, spins out the web of permutations that link those events... and thus the larger structure is laid: possibilities, contingencies, all made manifest in the plan that the Operative now proceeds to outline.

When he's finished, no little time has passed. The dome hangs heavy overhead. The artificial stars twinkle. And Sarmax is silent.

"Well?"

"You can see," says the Operative, "why I decided that you were more useful alive than dead. To both of us."

"I can see that," says Sarmax. "All too well."

"Then—?"

"I can't do it."

"What do you mean you can't do it?"

"I mean I can't do it. I accept everything you're saying, Carson. Believe me, I do. You're right on all counts. You're right on the implications too. But I can't get involved."

"Can't get involved?" says the Operative. "You can't stay out of it. You're already *in* it. Don't you understand that?"

"All I understand is who I am."

"But this is your chance to put all that behind you."

"I already *did* put all of it behind me, Carson."

"But it's going to keep coming back, Leo. Unless you deal with it once and for all. Out here in these cold hills—you're not dealing with it, man. Nor are you dealing with—"

"Don't say it," says Sarmax.

"Her death."

"Are you trying to provoke me?"

"It's not just trying," says the Operative.

"What's your fucking point?"

"My point is that she's dead. She died long ago. But even all this time later, she'd want you to stay alive."

"Funny," says Sarmax. "I always assumed she wouldn't."

"Why's that?"

"Because we're still separate this way."

"The way things are going, you won't have long to wait."

"You already told me that."

"No, I mean you're not going to have to wait more than thirty seconds at the rate you're going. I'll make it easy for you, Leo. We're walking out together or not at all."

"You're kidding me."

"I assure you I'm not."

"This is fucking nuts."

"Call it what you want. What's it going to be?"

"You're a fool, Carson. I could say yes just to get out of here."

"No you couldn't," says the Operative. "I know you, Leo. I know that the only reason why you'd say yes is if you meant it. Because I also know that you seriously believe you can kill me."

"I believe that because it's true."

"So put us to the final test."

"Carson, this is crazy. We walk out of here together, then head in separate directions."

"I can't let you walk after what I've just told you. I can't do that. And I gave you your chance."

"If that was my chance, then you've already made your choice."

"I already *had* made my choice. To offer you yours. Get it through your head: you're a wanted man. Without someone to fly you federal cover, you'll be nailed. And then they'd nail me."

"But out of everybody, you just have to be the one to try to nail me."

"Starting to look that way," says the Operative.

"You don't want to do this," says Sarmax.

"What I want doesn't matter."

"Then what does?"

The two men move suddenly, on the same instant. Both go for the jugular right off the bat. They fire all jets, charge in spraying bullets—cannon into each other with a noise that sounds like they've both been shattered. They haven't. They're just ricocheting off one another—and pivoting, turning, boots hitting ground, gloves gripping armor as they start to grapple. Through his visor, the Operative can see the eyes of Sarmax staring straight into his own. Next moment, that view is replaced by Sarmax's fist as—augmented by wrist-mounted jets—it slams into his face. The Operative feels the force ripple through his helmet. He grabs Sarmax's arms, feels the other grab his. For a moment the two are locked there, fire lighting up the night, muscle and machine straining for the slightest advantage while shadows play in unholy combination all around them. Their thrusters scorch their armor as each tries to power the other off his feet. Their helmets are locked up against each other. And now the voice of Leo Sarmax echoes through those helmets.

"Knew they would send someone," he says. "Hadn't dared to dream it would be you."

"Looks like you got your wish without even asking," says the Operative. He tries to bring his shoulder gun to bear. But Sarmax is just too close.

"I'll get my wish when I rip your corpse from what's left of that armor," says Sarmax. "I'll know my heart's desire when I consign your body to the ice. You've no idea just how fucked you are, Carson."

"Talk's cheap," replies the Operative. He leans his head back suddenly, lunges forward, headbutts Sarmax while firing all his thrusters on maximum. Sarmax doesn't move. But his suit's being plowed into the ground. Dirt and flame fly everywhere. Yet now Sarmax is firing all his jets too. The Operative's being forced inexorably backward. He's starting to realize that he may not be able to win this quickly. He's starting to suspect that Sarmax might still be stronger. . . .

"Think you can teach the man who taught you everything?" says Sarmax. "Think you can stay alive long enough to receive one last lesson?" His jets intensify. Now the Operative's being pushed back toward the trees. His feet leave furrows behind him in the dirt. "Well, here it is: I'm going to wrap you around that wood." More jets come to life atop Sarmax's back. The Operative crams more fuel into his own motors. He's urging them beyond their safety threshold. They're starting to overheat. He and Sarmax are starting to pick up speed. The trees rush toward them. The Operative feels his course change slightly as Sarmax steers him straight toward what looks to be the nearest and biggest of them. He feels his suit vibrate as Sarmax feeds still more power to his own. He hears Sarmax muttering about how easy this is going to be. He's got a nasty feeling that the man is about to be proven right.

Yet as that tree fills his own rearview, he reverses his own jets' thrust, adds his power to Sarmax's own—but at a slightly different angle. The two men suddenly speed up, whip past the tree, shoot into the depths of the grove. Sarmax keeps trying to run the Operative into something solid. The Operative keeps managing to avoid anything other than a glancing blow. They crash together through the woods, leaving a tunnel of broken branches behind them. They rush out over the water. They charge headlong into the fungus garden, tear through it, bear down upon the larger woods beyond. The Operative knows he's got to put some distance between himself and his opponent. His smaller weapons aren't going to be a factor. His larger weapons are too close.

But he opens up with them anyway.

The only thing he can think of: sow the road ahead with pitfalls. He starts using up all the hi-ex in his bomb-rack, flinging grenades forward. Some of them arc upward toward the roof. Some of them lance off into the trees. All of them are aimed not that far ahead. The forest is about to get pummeled into driftwood. Sarmax can achieve the Operative's death in there but only at the price of his own.

So he does what the Operative thought he would. He changes course—hard to the left. But the Operative's not buying it. He's just careening on forward. The two men strain against one another. Their path starts to curve to the left. But not at a sharp enough angle to avoid the impending blasts.

And Sarmax knows it. He does the only thing he can do. He lets go of the Operative, hits the brakes, lets the Operative blast onward into the kill zone. The grenades start to detonate. The Operative steers in among the explosions. He knows where they're going to occur. He knows where they're not. He hits his camo, turns off his own jets. He gets as low as he can, and moves into the undergrowth.

He's not a moment too soon. Because now flame's cascading down from on high. The Operative quickens his pace. On his screens he can see Sarmax behind him and fifty meters overhead, almost touching the roof's moon, lighting up the artificial night with his jets, not bothering to camouflage himself as he rains rockets and flame down upon where he thinks the Operative is. The Operative feels himself bombarded by Sarmax's sensors. He realizes he's being hunted down like a dog.

So he turns at bay: flicks his wrists, sends micromissiles streaking upward from both arms and back even as his gun-rack fires on auto spray. He lets rip with his flamers too. What's left of night vanishes. The Operative doesn't wait to assess the damage—he dives back into the fungus. And makes haste through the water while the fires roar overhead. Most of his view's blotted out by smoke. He wonders for a second if Sarmax has been caught within the blasts. He wonders if he's going to have to try to recover the necessary software from what's left of a charred skull. Maybe he's going to have to tell Lynx he got a little too eager. He stands there on the island, looks out into the conflagration, sights his scopes, waits for something to move into one of a thousand crosshairs. But nothing does.

The ground starts to shake.

At first the Operative thinks it's more explosions going off on the other side of the dome. But it's not. Because the fires out there don't seem to be rising. They seem to be sinking. It's as though the dirt itself is getting burned away. What's left of the tangled mass of vegetation is disappearing from view. The Operative feels the shaking beneath his feet intensify. The ground upon which he's standing is very definitely tilting. He watches as the fungus garden starts to slope away from him. He can see exactly what's happening. The floor of the place is collapsing. The foundations must have been burned or blasted away. But the blueprints show nothing beneath the dome save rock.

Which is beside the point right now. The Operative starts making for the other side of the island. Water sloshes beneath his feet, runs through channels where his and Sarmax's boots carved trenches in the ground. There's water pouring from the ceiling too. Sprinklers are going all out. The Operative stumbles toward the gazebo. It's leaning to one side. But it's still standing. The Operative pulls himself past it.

Which is when Sarmax strikes once more.

Tracers whip through the air. Rocket-propelled grenades streak in. The Operative hits his jets, shoots upward. Explosions tear at him from every side. He can hear Sarmax broadcasting to him. He's not hearing anything coherent. He returns fire with everything he's got.

For about a moment. But then something strikes him on the head. Hard. Concussion sweeps against him. He feels himself being shoved downward. He realizes that what's left of the dome's inner roof is collapsing. That the outer roof might be coming with it. He hears Sarmax laughing. The ground's folding up beneath the Operative. He feels everything above him bearing him down like an avalanche. He's riding that debris, running downward over it, fighting for consciousness all the while. And now he's through into more space—charging through underground corridors that undulate as the landslide that contains the garden's contents piles down into them. Somehow he keeps moving. Somehow he's not crushed.

And at last those vibrations die away behind him. He figures that he's chosen the right way by virtue of the fact that he's still breathing. He figures that Sarmax is one step ahead of him—figures, too, that the man has more defenses down here. He reaches a fork. One passage slopes up, the other down. He chooses the latter, starts along it.

As he does so, he hears a rumbling. A large section of rock is descending behind him. What's driving it is clearly mechanical. He almost hits the jets on reverse to try to beat it. But he doesn't. Instead he charges forward, racing down the tunnel, using his hands and feet at intervals to push himself off the walls, floors, ceiling. He's trying to stay unpredictable. He's scanning every centimeter of those surfaces. When he starts to notice nozzles here and there, he isn't surprised. They could be sensors. They could be weapons. Either way, he's starting to feel like he's getting warm.

And when he hears the voice of Leo Sarmax, he knows it for certain.

"Carson, Carson, Carson," says the voice. "Did you miss me?"

It's broadcast from the nozzles. It echoes in the Operative's head. He doesn't speak. Just listens. Just keeps rushing forward. Just keeps watching every centimeter of the walls...

"That's good," says the voice. "Real good, Carson. Had to ask, you understand. Even though you won't answer. Let me assume, though, that answer's the same as it was before: no and yes."

The Operative just stares. He's beyond blinking now. He's gotten to the point where reflex and intuition blur. He reaches another fork. He doesn't slow. He makes his choice, accelerates.

"Yes and no," continues Sarmax, "no and yes. Can't say I blame you. It was bad enough when I got here. It's much worse now."

Half fall, half dive: the Operative tumbles down a stairway in one motion. He vaults off the last step, roars down the new corridor like some avenging angel. He pours fire in his wake. He gets ready to pour fire out before him.

"Because the truth," says Sarmax, "is that this whole game is going up for grabs. This whole scene is getting out of hand. And we, old friend, are right in the middle of it."

Now the Operative comes shooting out into a wider space. It's still a corridor but it's twice as wide and twice as deep as any of its predecessors. It harbors far more choices, too: openings of every size and shape hewn into every one of its surfaces. The Operative feels like he's been here before, like he's in a dream.

But he isn't.

"So we got to change it up," says Sarmax. "We got to take you off the fucking *board*."

All the nozzles in the space open up on the Operative. He's getting it from all sides. Lasers sear against him. Bullets are right behind, albeit a little slower. Too slow: for now he's charging down a side corridor, smoke churning off his armor, his own weapons flinging countermeasures back into the passage he just exited. But this new passage has its own defenses too. They open up on him. They flail against him at almost point-blank range. They carve deep into his armor, sending screens into static, comps into overload, fail-safes into action—and all the while the man who's killing him keeps on telling him all about it.

"I think you can see where this is going to go," says Sarmax. "Assuming your eyes haven't melted yet. These are the last sounds you'll ever hear, Carson. These are the final words your brain will ever process. Lynx never bargained on my real base being buried so far beneath the surface. He never counted on my sowing the black markets with false maps. All the inner enclaves of all my major residences, Carson: they're all red herrings. The real ones are all off the charts. But that's the way it always is with the truth. It's always beyond the pale. Though it pales in comparison with the lies that surround it. Wouldn't you agree, Carson?".

But the Operative's not listening. He's just flicking his wrists—letting grenades slot into his hands, flinging explosives in both his path and wake. It's not an act of suicide. These grenades aren't ordinary. Wavelengths of every size and hue rush over him. His sensors are being blotted out. He hits the dirt. He crawls on down that corridor while the lasers fire randomly. They're blinded too. They're trying to filter out the disrupters. They're not succeeding.

Which gives the Operative some respite. Even as his mind's frantically working to extrapolate what he knows against what he doesn't. He takes a chance, shoots off down one of the adjacent passages, ignoring the guns that blast against him as he blasts downward through a suddenly larger space. Something strikes him in the back. He sees stars. He thinks he sees things below him—catches glimpses here and there: platforms hanging in the dark, vast ramps leaning through the gloom. He figures he's already dead. He figures this is one demented Hades. He resolves to start the afterlife in style. He wafts in toward one platform in particular, throws his feet forward. He hits. He runs along that platform, then slows to a walk and finally stops.

This chamber is huge. It's far larger than that dome. The floor's not visible. The walls glisten with ice. Some of them are pretty much vertical. Others climb inward toward each other, as though the mountain that houses the cave has been turned inside out.

But what those walls contain is a maze of gantries and platforms and ramps. Electric lights hang here and there. Cranes tower overhead. The platform upon which the Operative has landed protrudes out over the edge of abyss. A single ramp connects it to the remainder of the structure.

And standing in the shadows atop that ramp is Leo Sarmax.

The final stages of the race we call the border run. Take these curves too tight and you'll fly off the rails and into hell. Take them too loose, and you'll lose all speed differential. So now inside turns out, all colors are ripped asunder. Stars torpedo at you, lick away, and this ship keeps on shooting through this tunnel.

"We need more *throttle*," screams Linehan.

"We can't go any faster," yells Spencer.

He engages the rear guns. The ship shudders as they discharge. Lasers and shells streak down the tunnel. The

gunships giving pursuit absorb the former, dodge the latter—
slide along a crossover onto parallel rails, let the rounds shoot
past them.

"Can't shake them," mutters Linehan.

"Hold on," says Spencer. He's lashing out with newfound
abandon at the razors a fraction of a second and several klicks
behind him. They're doing their best to get at him. But he's co-
opted the car. He can see it all so clearly—can see the way
they configured the craft so that even if the zone *weren't* being
fucked with, it still couldn't be seen by the rail's systems. It's
been set up as a zone-bubble: a discrete set of self-contained
logic that allows those within to control the rail's currents, let
them move like they weren't there. Like water striders that
ride the surface of a pond without breaking surface tension:
it's a delicate balancing act. It's getting more so by the second.

But suddenly the cars behind them are slowing down.
Suddenly they're disappearing in the rearview.

"So much for them," says Spencer.

"What'd you do," says Linehan.

"What does it look like I did? Maglev speed depends upon
control."

"Which they no longer have."

"Exactly."

"Crash them into each other," says Linehan.

"I'd settle for slowing them down," says Spencer.

"Don't."

"Too late."

For now he can see that they've switched off their engines. They've stopped interfacing with the rails. They've
abandoned the chase. They're no longer a factor. Spencer
grins.

And curses.

"What's up?" says Linehan.

What's up is that somewhere back down that tunnel something's glowing. Something that's getting steadily brighter.

"What the fuck."

"They're riding rockets," says Spencer.

"We got anything similar?"

"We must."

"So fire us up."

"So no. We try that and we'll just be dragging against the magnets."

"So turn us off," says Linehan. "Start us up."

"Magnets are faster."

"Then what the fuck you waiting for?"

The answer's nothing. Spencer's opening the throttle. He's jury-rigging the ship far past the limits of its safety margins. It's nothing but momentum now. The two men let vibration rise through them. They watch their pursuers fade again. Up ahead on the map Spencer can see the place where the tunnel starts blossoming—can see where the real warren kicks in. The tunnel steers just south of the Newfoundland Yards. Somewhere past that's the place where the continental shelf ends and the real ocean takes over and the warrens drop several thousand meters. For a moment Spencer envisions looking at this route in retrospect and not in anticipation. For a moment, he imagines they're already running beneath the real trenches of Atlantic. For just a second he sees them almost at the border....

But then his attention's captured by yet another flaring in the rearview.

"What the fuck," he says.

"That's a missile," says Linehan.

"I can see that."

"Then you can also see it's closing."

"Eight klicks back," says Spencer.

"Countermeasures."

"I'm trying."

And he is. He lets the rear guns engage. He lets lasers fly at the warhead. But it's got countermeasures of its own. It's taking evasive action. It's eating light like no one's ever fed it. It's flinging out light of its own. The back of their ship is taking damage.

"It's smart," says Linehan. "It's speeding up."

"They're falling back."

The ships: they're fading. They're drawing off. They're gone.

"We need more speed," says Linehan.

"We go any faster and we lose control."

"It's either that or take a warhead up your ass. Take a look at that thing. Take a good look. Do you see what I'm seeing?"

There's no way Spencer couldn't. Linehan is projecting his extrapolation of the schematics of the missile straight into his head. He's disaggregating all its parts. He's highlighting all its components. He's focusing on one in particular.

"It's nuclear," breathes Spencer.

"Tactical," says Linehan. "But still overkill."

"They'll collapse this fucking tunnel."

"I don't think they care, Spencer. I think they just want to be sure."

"Why doesn't it detonate right now?"

"Like I just said, Spencer: *they want to be sure.* They want it closer. And they're going to ride it straight up to our fucking bumper unless you floor this bitch like she's never been floored before."

Spencer does. They roar forward. All the while taking stock of what's behind them.

"Four point six klicks back."

"And closing."

Not quite as quickly as before. But still just as inexorably. Their rear guns may as well not even be there for all the effect they're having. There may as well be nothing in the universe save hunter and target.

Only there is. Because the gap between the walls on either

side is getting wider. The rails are sprouting more rails. The tunnel's starting to fork into still more tunnels.

"The warrens," says Linehan.

"We might make it yet," says Spencer.

"What's our route?"

"Follow the main line straight on through."

"That won't work."

"Why?"

"We need to shake this fucker off. And we're not going to do it in the straight."

"Get anywhere else but the straight and it'll catch us."

"Give me the fucking map."

"I already did, asshole. It's in your head. You want a different itinerary, you better name it fast."

"Let's hit the Yards," says Linehan.

"That's insane."

"So is doing nothing while a missile overhauls you."

"You don't get it," says Spencer. "Whatever hack Control's got in place extends only to the main tunnel and its auxiliary lines. The Newfoundland Yards are neither. We venture in there and we're going to set off every single alarm and then some."

"I don't think you're grasping our situation," replies Linehan.

Another train takes that moment to charge on by. It roars westward on an adjacent track. It's at least a hundred cars long, another transatlantic haul. It's impossible to tell if those who steer it are aware of the chaos all around them. The missile darts sideways to avoid it, loses a fraction of a second in so doing. Its afterburners fire. It draws in upon its target like it's being pulled in upon a string.

"What else we got for speed?" says Linehan.

"We got nothing."

"Than we got nothing to lose. And even if we *do* survive

what's about to happen, every alarm down here is about to go off at full fucking volume anyway. Least we can do is hope we're around to hear it."

He double-clicks onto the map. It lights up both their minds. The Yards are winding in toward them. They're sprawling out on all sides. They're as messy as any boom-town. Their topography's complex.

"We turn off onto the local line *there*," says Linehan. He forwards coordinates to Spencer. "We fire the decoys down the main when we do so. Hopefully it'll follow them and not us."

"And if there's something on that local line?"

"We'll never know it."

"And if that thing behind us follows us and not our decoys?"

"We go straight through the main districts and back into the tunnels."

"The main districts?"

"There's nothing to stop us. Most of the local lines intersect with them. They're basically one big cave."

"Filled with a *lot* of shit."

"But this thing we're in's not bound to the rails, Spencer."

"It's not a question of propulsion. It's a question of maneuvering. Anything that's more than about two degrees off the straight is going to be too much for us right now. We can't afford to put on the brakes any further."

"Good. Because we're not going to. Ten seconds, Spencer. You ready?"

And Spencer is. He's ready to live out the last seconds of his life. He's got himself immersed just enough in the zone to see the myriad threads that constitute the Yards. He wonders for a moment if they're being herded into it by what's behind them. He wonders what else is out there still. He wonders just what the man he's with is worth.

Besides a nuke.

"If that thing detonates in the Yards, it'll kill tens of thousands."

"Maybe," says Linehan. "But at least I'm not asking *you* to kill them this time. I'm not even asking you to watch."

He gestures at the screens upon which the missile's closing. But Spencer's not even looking. He's just tweaking the magnets, letting the craft press up against the left-hand rails, forcing it away from the right-hand ones. It eases off the straight onto a crossover rail. It bends along that rail toward the wall.

Except suddenly there's no wall.

Or rather: there is. But now it's shifted five meters to the left. And in that space, another rail is sprouting away from the leftward main track. The craft curves along it. Spencer fires balls of flame and countermeasures from the forward guns. They roar down the leftward line.

Which encloses their craft within a much smaller tunnel. But only for a moment, and then they charge out of the branch line and into a wider tunnel. Spencer slots the ship in along the rails. He slings them at lightning speed along this new straight. He sees no obstructions whatsoever.

"We made it," breathes Linehan.

"Eye of the needle."

"Ah *fuck*."

The missile's emerged through the tunnel they've just come through. It's less than a klick back now. It's roaring in toward them far more quickly than before.

"Fuck's sake," says Linehan.

They're well within the confines of the Yards now. Rows of doors that lead to airlocked stations are streaking by. The tunnel's now a translucent tube. Beyond it they can see a far wider space. They shift along more rails. They streak through more tubes. They can see the intimations of architecture all around. They can see the flame of the missile behind them.

It's only half a klick back now. Spencer's realizing that Linehan's plan is for shit. They can't destroy the thing that's chasing them. They can't outrun it. They can't outmaneuver it. They can't shake it. They streak out of translucence and back into solid.

Which is when something finally clicks in Spencer's mind. It's something that's been getting in his way. And now it drops away. He doesn't want to see it go. It's the last of his moral scruples. And now it's gone. Leaving him in search of something else. Something that's buried in this town's systems. He runs his mind parallel to the route of his body. He brushes up against a lever that triggers a door. It's one of thousands throughout this complex. It's intended to forestall emergency flooding should the seabed overhead rupture. Now it slides shut behind them. They have a fraction of a second to secure additional distance from the door.

Before the missile hits it.

That nuke's got next to nothing in the way of EMP. It harbors only modest force. But it's all relative. Because the seabed's being shaken to pieces. Half the Yards just got caved in. The ocean's been left to do the rest.

"Holy *fuck*," says Spencer.

"We're gone," says Linehan.

There's no way he could be wrong. What's surging down the tunnel behind them is water that's far worse than any weapon. It won't be outrun. It can't be outgunned. It can't be outmaneuvered. It surges in toward them. It turns maglev into mere metal—snuffing out the electricity in one fell swoop. Yet even as the magnetism dies, Spencer's switching to rocket. Wheels protrude, hold them steady as velocity kicks in once again. To no avail. That surge is overhauling them all the same. It's almost got them. It's starting to churn in amidst their rocket's fires.

"Do you believe in God?" says Linehan.

"I'll believe in anything that'll get us out of this."

"Me neither," snarls Linehan.

Their rockets switch off, seal as the tide washes across them. The water roars in around the ship. The two men within feel themselves shaken like rats by dogs. They feel their craft lurch into the walls, ceiling, floor with ever-greater force.

"Tell me what this was all about," says Spencer.

"Tell me what it wasn't," says Linehan.

And yet somehow they're still alive. And all they're doing is finding out what it's like to die. Which is pretty much what they would have suspected. It's time that's run clean out. It's dark at the end of endless tunnel. It's the shock of realizing that somehow you're still breathing.

When you really shouldn't be.

"We're still intact," says Spencer.

"We're still running," says Linehan.

"Like I said."

"I mean we're still *running*."

He's right. There's a new vibration that's even nearer than the waters swirling around the ship. It's the rumble of engines close at hand. The instrument panels are lighting up in a new configuration. Understanding suddenly dawns: this ship's a true interceptor. Even though it prowled the tunnels on rails and wheels, it was configured to operate in one more medium.

The one they're in right now.

"Hold *on*," says Spencer.

"We ride it out," says Linehan.

"All the way through."

And all the while they're thinking about how things have surely just come full circle. Of how this ship's immersion represents nothing save a return to a condition it's plainly familiar with—which might have even been the point. And the answer to this question: if at least some feds knew what was what, why weren't the two sought by all simply seized at

Kennedy? Someone didn't want others to know that the prize had been bagged. Someone intended to remove them in the middle of the tunnel. Someone intended to get out of that tunnel without going out of either end. Someone wanted to escape detection altogether. So: smooth moves in the dark. From ocean to shaft and back again. Nice and neat.

Though it doesn't look like either now.

"We're still living," says Spencer.

"Running with the current," says Linehan.

"Jesus."

All manner of debris is churning up against the windows. And so much of it he doesn't want to see. Bodies, torn by the blast and by the water—they dash themselves against the ship. They press their faces up against the plastic. They churn off into the mother of all undertows.

"Oh Christ," says Spencer. "Oh Jesus Christ."

"What's your point?" asks Linehan.

"We killed them."

"We? You're the one who took our ship through the Yards."

"You're the one who told me to!"

"And I'm the one who's telling you to shove everything out there out of your fucking mind. And replace it with nothing but thinking about how you're going to stay in here with the oxygen."

"Meaning?"

"Meaning *take control*."

And he's right. Because now they're rushing downward. Now the tunnel's sloping as the Atlantic drops down from continental shelf. Spencer fights to master the current as the ship picks up speed.

"Just keep us away from the *walls*," says Linehan.

"Like it matters," mutters Spencer.

Though he's trying. And somehow succeeding even as

that speed increases. The controls are like a live animal in his hands. He compensates, adjusts, guesses. He sees nothing now save water. He feels himself pressed down to depths he's never dreamed of.

The B-130 is no longer flying. It's disintegrating. The back wall of the main cargo chamber is practically staved in. The floor's crumpling. Morat and the drones are thrown toward the front wall. On the way they pass Marlowe, who's fired what's left of his thrusters as Haskell hit the detonator. He's rocketing toward the shaft above. Shots dance around his feet as he roars upward. Wreckage of drones is everywhere. But past that wreckage he can see the opening airlock doors of the still-intact upper ship.

Yet even as he tears toward them, he's forced to change direction, bouncing off the walls as the vertical tube through which he's moving slopes toward the horizontal while the stricken ship plunges downward. He's yelling at Haskell to close the airlock doors. She's not waiting—the doors are sliding shut as he rushes toward them. The space between him and them is a narrowing window. She's set them going too fast: Marlowe accelerates as drones sear into the shaft after him; he rushes past the surviving gun installations, through the closing gap into the room beyond. The doors slam shut behind him as he extends his hands, shoves himself off the ceiling. His jets cut out. He drops toward the front of the upper ship's cargo chamber, yells at Haskell to blast off.

And she does.

The motors ignite. The Janus leaps from the back of the stricken B-130. It hurtles downward, parallel to the other ship. Then it veers away. Marlowe's shoved toward the room's rear. He grabs on to the wall, holds on. He can't see Haskell anywhere.

"Where are you?"

"In the cockpit," she says.

She's strapped in, wired to the instruments. Her eyes are watching through the windows while her mind's carving through the zone. She started laying into the drones as soon as the bomb went off—took advantage of their momentary confusion to get in amidst them, start slicing them apart. The only drones still extant now are on a rendezvous with ocean. Haskell withdraws her mind from theirs, peels the ship away from the intended destination. It's scarcely ten klicks off. It's city-covered mountains looming through the haze. She lets the ship bend back out over the ocean.

But suddenly she's pulled back wholly into zone. She's under furious assault from something coming in from out of empty, from the broader zone around. It's smashed through the firewall she's configured around her ship and is powering in upon her, fighting her for the controls.

Which means nobody's in control at all.

Fifteen meters behind her, Marlowe holds on as the ship writhes through the air. He'd been on the point of convincing himself that it was going to be a smooth ride to the nearest U.S. ships. But clearly it's going to be nothing of the kind. The ship ascends at a sickening rate. It twists off to the side. It spirals back toward the ocean. It uses both jets and rockets. The latter are intended only for space. The former are intended only for landing planetside. But now both are firing almost at random.

It's all Marlowe can do to keep his head from hitting metal. He's acutely aware that the craft is being subjected to near-lethal strains.

But then it levels out. Marlowe doesn't waste a moment: he leaps to the floor, grabs more weapons from the wall racks, sprints across the chamber—and through the door and down into the room where he and Haskell rode out the takeoff. He rushes into the cockpit-access corridor, reaches the cockpit. The door is open. He looks inside.

To find Haskell lolling in her straps. He lunges to her side. She's still breathing. He shakes her. She doesn't respond. He shakes her harder. She opens her eyes. She smiles weakly.

"You're back."

"What happened."

"They threw me out of the zone," she replies. "They almost killed me."

"The drones?"

"Not them. *Them.*" She gestures at the window. Marlowe hadn't even looked. He sees the towers of transplanted Hong Kong approaching once more. Mist and rocks wrap around their bases. Ocean sprawls beyond.

"That's where the Rain are," she says. "That's where they're based. They're hacking us at point-blank range. They're too close for our own side to jam."

"Why didn't they do this earlier?" says Marlowe.

"Don't you understand? We're dealing with something that works through proxies." She's whispering now. "That set this creature Morat and all his creatures against us. That only gets involved when it has to. They have us, Jason."

"We've still got suit-jets," he says. "We bail out."

"We can't."

"Why not?"

"Same reason we couldn't earlier. The hack controls this ship's weapons."

"You didn't disable them?"

"I didn't have a chance," she snaps. "We'd be like fish in a barrel. We'll be shredded long before we get to sea."

"Then what are you saying we do? Just wait to be taken?"

"No," she says suddenly. "We cut the ground out from under it."

"How?"

"We get out on the hull. We take down the comlink. We shear off all means via which it can ram its signal into us."

"Works for me," he says.

He crouches down once more upon the cockpit floor, bends once again to the trapdoor. He severs wires to deprive the thing that controls the ship of any chance of forestalling him. He works the manuals, opens the door and crawls in. He looks back up at her.

"Go," she says.

But he says nothing—just starts down the chute. She pushes the door shut behind him. He wriggles all the way to the bottom—the airlock door that's the miniature of the one back in the cargo bay. He disables its locks manually and opens it. He slides through into the tiny room within, pulls the door shut behind him, and disables the charges he placed there. He works more manual overrides and pulls the last door open.

City's crammed up against his face. Buildings at least a klick high are streaking by. Marlowe holds on as best he can—pushes his feet against the walls of the chamber, extends his hands to the opposite wall, lowers his head. He's staring back along the ship's undercarriage. Its wings are extended for the landing. Ships are scattered across the city sky beyond it. There seem to be several formations of them.

But Marlowe's main focus is on a certain panel just behind the rear wheel wells. He's trying to get line of sight to it. He has to lean out farther. He's practically hanging out of the forward escape hatch.

Which is when the ship starts to writhe once more. Marlowe activates what's left of the magnetic clamps in what's left of his suit and sidles out upon the hull. He clings to it as it slopes and slants and turns. Each and every view now contains nothing save buildings. They're totally enclosed by city. It roofs them in as they fly ever deeper into its depths. It constrains the extent to which the hack can send the ship on erratic courses. Which means Marlowe's still holding on. And lining up that comlink once again . . .

In the cockpit above: Haskell watches as the ship's suddenly free once again. Controls cry out for someone to control them. The flight path starts to waver. The nearest buildings close in. But Haskell doesn't panic. She's scarcely strong enough to access zone, but she's still slotting out the wires, plugging herself back in once more—taking command as though there'd been no interruption whatsoever. She seamlessly pulls the ship back onto its flight path. She starts calling up the maps of HK. She starts looking for a way out.

But suddenly she sees something on the screens. The ship's cameras: she whirls around, starts firing with her pistol.

Bullets catch Morat in the chest. He doesn't break stride. His hands flash silver. Blades whip through the air. Haskell cries out as blood bursts from her wrists. She moans, drops the pistol, doubles over, lets endorphins surge through her on automatic response. The pain subsides. The bleeding doesn't—and then the knives rip from her flesh, slice through the wires that connect her to the controls, carve back through the air toward Morat. He catches them, sheathes them in his skin, moves in toward her. He backhands her across the face, backhands her again—and then hurls her against the cockpit wall. She sprawls on the floor while he turns his attention to the controls.

"Thus begins the next thousand years," he says.

And starts up the landing sequence—sets it on automatic, turns back to Haskell, reaches out, sprays foam onto her wrists to halt her bleeding.

"There's something I'd like to show you," he says.

He drags her to her feet and pulls her up against the controls. He shoves her up toward the window.

"Our welcoming committee," he says.

She hears explosions sounding from somewhere close at hand. Glare from outside lights up the cockpit, catches missiles rising skyward. Sides of buildings slash by. Lasers sear past the window. HK's all around.

"You've rigged whole blocks," she says.

"We bought whole blocks," he replies. "Front companies, derelict housing, epic bribery—so much for the first wave of pursuit. So much, too, for your man. As soon as we got a bead on him, we dropped him. He's already gone."

"You don't know that," she says. "You're lying."

"It's you who's lying," he says. "To yourself. But you'll get it eventually. Once we land, I'll let you watch the replay. In fact, I'll *make* you watch it. Repeatedly. Until you not only believe it, you start to *like* it."

"I'll kill you," she whispers.

"Then you'd better act fast," says Morat. "Look what we're heading for."

She sees something in among the approaching buildings. She realizes that amidst all the roads and roofs and skyways, it's possible to trace a straight line—one long slash that cuts across them. It's well-done. Here it's a bridge that connects two towers. There it's a ramp that's swiveling. It's pedways from whom the people are now scattering. It's reinforced struts now sliding into place. It's something whose pieces were always there, whose lacks were long contemplated—

and then compensated for by structures positioned on hinges upon which they would turn as one.

Creating a runway.

"Shit," says Haskell.

"The chosen ground," says Morat.

And suddenly looks down to see Jason Marlowe at his feet. The mech's already firing—opening up with a pistol at point-blank range. Morat loses his grip on Haskell, sprawls backward: falls onto his back as Marlowe pulls himself up into the cockpit. He keeps his gun pointed at Morat while Haskell pulls backward on the stick. The ship swerves upward.

But Morat's already getting back on his feet. Smoke's rising in wisps from where Marlowe's shot part of his face away. But through that smoke his eyes still gleam.

Nor has his smile wavered.

"You again," he says mildly.

"Tenacious as ever," says Marlowe.

"Let's see if you can say that with your lips ripped off."

"You're not so tough without your drones."

"What the fuck do you think I am?"

He moves forward almost casually. Marlowe fires, catches him in the chest and in the head again. But Morat's ready this time. The shots don't break his momentum. He cannons into Marlowe, strips the pistol from his hands, grabs him with his own hands, hurls him up against the ceiling.

"Tenacious," he says. "Don't make me laugh."

Marlowe flops back down onto the floor. Morat aims a vicious kick at his head—easily strong enough to stave it in. But Marlowe somehow pulls himself out of range—keeps on rolling backward as Morat keeps on advancing—and then comes to his feet in a crouch, another pistol in one hand. He holds on to the wall as Haskell turns the ship sharply again. Morat falls back to the cockpit doorway. Marlowe fires a volley, hits his target with several shots. Morat looks at him.

And blinks.

"If you've got anything more powerful," he says, "now'd be a good time to use it."

But Marlowe just starts firing again. Morat whips his hands forward, lets loose with both knives. One slices through the pistol. The other slices toward Marlowe's head. But Marlowe ducks away—the knives hit the wall, hang there quivering until Marlowe hammers his fists against their hilts, destroying their gyros, driving them farther into solid. The blades vibrate. Their motors whine. But they're stuck.

"So quick," says Morat. "So far from enough."

Still Marlowe says nothing. Just holds on to the wall with one hand, regards Morat the way a man does when he's looking for a weakness he has yet to find. The twists and turns that the city's geography is forcing Haskell to put the ship through are keeping both men close to the walls. She can't tear her eyes away from what's outside the window. The two men can't tear their eyes away from each other. They sidle along the walls, Marlowe trying to increase the distance, Morat trying to close it.

"Look at this state of affairs," says Morat. "Look how close those buildings are. If I touch Claire, we'll crash into them. But we'll be back out from under this canopy in a few more seconds. At which point I'm going to take you both and take us back to that runway."

"There are more interceptors coming in with every minute," mutters Haskell. "You can't land, Morat. What the hell are you going to do when this thing comes to a stop?"

"*I'm* not going to do a thing," says Morat. "But the roof that we finally stop on is going to drop like a stone. It's an elevator. It'll plunge all the way to undercity."

"Where the Rain are waiting," says Haskell.

"Not for much longer," he replies.

The buildings above them give way to sky. They're out of the central part of the city. Morat lunges in toward Marlowe. Marlowe backs up, fills his lungs, blows hard: and a dart sails from a tube slotted in the roof of his mouth. It strikes Morat's head.

Which disintegrates in a blast of shrapnel. Morat's body flops backward. But there's no blood within his neck. Only wires. Marlowe rushes forward, his own blade out. He plunges it toward Morat's chest.

Who promptly parries that blade. And sits up. And smashes his fist at Marlowe's head. Marlowe ducks, slashes forward, just misses. Morat seizes him. The two men grapple as Haskell lets the ship rush upward among the buildings. Morat's voice echoes from somewhere in his chest.

"Turn this ship around," he says.

"What the fuck . . . are you," mutters Marlowe. He's finding Morat's grip is still easily strong enough to crush him. He feels his own knife being twisted from his grasp.

"The future," replies Morat. Smoke's still streaming from his neck. He gets control of the knife, smashes Marlowe back against the instrument panel—scarcely two meters to the left of where Haskell's frantically taking the ship through another series of maneuvers, trying to prevent it from hitting HK's towers in its headlong rush. "Nothing more. And it's not my body that matters. It's my mind. That's what's wriggled beyond the old man's reach."

"Sinclair should have killed you," says Haskell. Morat's hand snakes out from where he's grappling with Marlowe. She dodges to her right.

"*Should* have killed me?" Morat laughs. "He *did* kill me. He destroyed my illusions. He created fertile ground for a new seed. Germinated by the events of the last decade. Brought to fruition by the Rain themselves." He pushes the knife down while Marlowe strives desperately to hold the blade at bay.

"You make them sound like God," says Haskell. She lunges back in toward Morat—who blocks her blow with his right hand, holds her off from where he's killing Marlowe with his left.

"They're far more than that," says Morat. "God's a para-site that preys on our brains. We'll burn Him into ashes. We'll replace all the gods that never existed. Henceforth humanity shall have no limits. Least of all its own humanity. And the last thing it's going to miss is one less *human*."

He presses the blade down against Marlowe's throat. But now they're all knocked sprawling as something impacts the ship. The walls are becoming floor. The instrument panels are going crazy. Buildings are whipping past. As the ship drops in among them, Morat leaps to the pilot's seat, seizing Haskell with one hand, working the controls with the other. But the controls aren't responding.

"We've been hit from the *ground*," he says incredulously.

"Your own team," screams Haskell, struggling against Morat's grip. Marlowe's at the back of the cockpit. He's fight-ing the forces of acceleration to try to get to them. The fact that such acceleration is practically random is making it diffi-cult. "They've figured this ship ain't landing. They've figured right. They've written you off, Morat. All this talk and all you are is just a pawn. You're not worth the spit that's in my mouth."

But Morat's arm holds her like steel while the ship roars out of control. He hauls her against him. His knife hovers at her heart. His voice is as cold as she's ever heard it. "It's not like you have the strength to spit, bitch," he snarls. "Way I see it, I've got five seconds to teach you manners. Not to mention reason."

"Reason," breathes Haskell. *"You don't know what that fucking is!"*

She hits the manual release on the eject. Morat's chair leaps through the open ceiling. His grip's nearly strong enough to take her with him. But not quite: he catapults out of the opening, disappears without a sound. She grabs on to the now-useless instruments. The plane keeps plunging downward.

"We're following him," says Marlowe.

"I know," she says.

Nor does she wait. She's already turned, wrapping her arms around his neck, her legs around his waist. And even as she grabs him, he's igniting his thrusters. Haskell catches a glimpse of the Janus spacecraft, smoke pouring from its engines, interceptors dying in flame in its wake. She sees cityscape shooting past.

Marlowe cuts out the flame. She feels herself falling. They drop between skyways, fall past levels. Marlowe reignites his motor, sends them roaring in among a thicket of buildings.

Ten seconds later, they alight upon a skyway. They race along it. They see no one. They hear everything. Thunder of gunfire rolls amidst the buildings like the distant roar of ocean. Flashes blot out the neon in the direction from which they've come. They keep running—to the edge of that skyway, onto the roof of an adjacent building. They tear a trapdoor away, race down stairs. They find an elevator. They leap into the shaft.

And descend into the city.

So at the end of Moon there's a labyrinth. At the end of that labyrinth's a chamber. That chamber wasn't built by man. It's been there since this rock cooled. It sits within the heart of mountain. It contains the most valuable thing in this world.

"Water," says Sarmax.

He steps into the light. His armor looks pretty beat-up. It's been burned almost black. He walks toward the ramp's edge.

"Come again?" says the Operative.

"Water," repeats Sarmax. "Or should I say *ice*."

"Which is how you made your fortune," says the Operative.

"My *latest* fortune," replies Sarmax.

He stops just short of the edge. He gestures at the sloped walls. He looks back at the Operative. He smiles. He's so close the Operative can see teeth through visor.

"You're a resourceful man," he says quietly.

"Look who's talking," replies the Operative.

"It's just too bad that such resourcefulness has to compensate for such lack of planning," continues Sarmax. "Such a goddamn shame it's forced to rely so heavily on pure luck. You almost brought the roof down on your stupid head, Carson. It's a wonder you didn't get buried in those tunnels."

"Would that have been such a terrible outcome?" asks the Operative.

"Now that," says Sarmax, "depends on your point of view." He gestures at the ramps and ladders stacked about him. "You see before you the industry of a new era, Carson. We live in the dawn times, old friend. Humanity is poised to boil out beyond the Earth-Moon system. The red planet will be colonized en masse within the next two decades. The prospectors are even now testing the tug of the gas giants. The Oort is surrendering her secrets to the probes. It's all there for the taking, Carson. And it all makes me say I don't give a fuck if you take me down. I don't give a damn about the Rain or anybody else. Let them squabble. Let them plot. What does it matter when history itself is at last coming into focus?"

"I'm sure the Rain couldn't say it any better," says the Operative.

"But you and I know that all they're really doing is playing the same old game."

"Which is?"

"Power. They want it all, Carson. They're using all of us to make it happen."

"Including you, Leo?"

"I'm sure they'd like to. One more reason why I took myself out of the equation. One more reason I content myself with commerce. Leave the politics to others, Carson. Leave the games to those who would play them."

"Is that a statement or an invitation?"

"What makes you think it's not both?"

"Tell me about the latter."

"You already know it. You're the best I ever trained. You're the man whose instincts were always closest to my own. You want to set up shop for yourself. You want it so badly you'd shut your own razor out of the picture. Hell of a move, Carson. Only you would try it. Not that it mattered in the end. You were always going to have to venture into my garden. You were always going to have to descend into what I built beneath it."

"Not if I'd broken you upstairs," says the Operative.

"But you didn't," says Sarmax. "It was almost the other way. I fully expected to pull your body out from under rubble."

"You may yet," says the Operative.

"The suspense is killing me."

"Lynx knew the mine was down here, Leo. But he thought it was abandoned decades ago. He didn't think there was any connection between it and the surface fortress. Especially not when the maps assured him of that fact."

"Then he's a fool, Carson. You were right to cut him loose."

"On the contrary," says the Operative. "I was inspired to do some research on my own. I tapped into Shackleton's archives. I learned everything I could about this mine's dimensions. So when I ended up in the vicinity, I knew how close the labyrinth was taking me to the main chambers. And if I'd bought the farm anyway, I figured we could always settle this in Valhalla."

"Well," says Sarmax, "now you don't even have to wait."

"I've already waited far too long," says the Operative.

"We both have, Carson. We both know it. Look at us. We're practically old men. You've been around for half a century. I've been on the loose for even longer. Not for us are the ways of the new breed. Not for us the zeal of the latest contenders. Turn your back on this whole thing, man. Turn your back on that crazy plan. You know that's what you want. An alliance between us was where this was always going. We'll put all our energy into pushing it outward. We'll shove the frontier out to where time mills dust into forever. You and I, Carson. This is where it all begins."

"And ends," says the Operative.

He steps backward into space. Sarmax whips his arms up, lets flame erupt from his wrists. Fire shoots through the space where the Operative just stood—but he falls below the level of the platform, tumbles down amidst a webwork of support beams. He starts his jets, roars into a new maze. Lasers streak down from on high as Sarmax dashes to the edge.

"Keep running and you might actually win," he sneers.

"Exactly," says the Operative.

He fires his last micromissiles. They explode amidst the beams. The edifice above him starts to sway. Sarmax leaps from it, blasts upward. The Operative emerges from the other side, rockets over more ramps, opens up on Sarmax. The two men roar parallel to one another as they exchange fire.

Until Sarmax scores a direct hit on the Operative's thrusters.

There's an explosion. The Operative feels heat across his back. He feels like his spine just got severed. He fires the auxiliary jets on his wrists and ankles at full blast. They give him a tiny amount of leverage. Tiny—and nowhere near enough. He hurtles past more ramps, somehow dodges a crane. He veers beneath all that infrastructure, closes in on the sloping wall of the chamber. Rocks rush toward him. He feels something smash against his arm. He hits the ice and starts to slide. He extends claws on hands and feet. They shear inward. His arm is almost ripped from its socket as his visor slams up against the ice.

The Operative retracts one hand, lets himself dangle outward. He takes in the situation. His shoulder racks are wrecked. He's on a slope some thirty degrees in incline. He twists around to face that nightmare structure. He can see now how it's built out over these slopes of ice. How it's intended to allow drills to be shoved up against the surface. He can see the drills themselves, slung low along some of the platforms.

But he can also see Sarmax. A suit of armor far more together than his own, circling some twenty meters overhead.

"Carson. Didn't I always tell you engines are more important than weapons?" The soaring flight pattern proclaims nothing save triumph. But the voice is almost sad.

"Fuck you," says the Operative.

"On the contrary."

"I may yet surprise you."

"I don't think anything that happens in what remains of your life is going to be the least bit surprising," says Sarmax. He swoops downward, fires a salvo five meters to the Operative's left. Then another, five meters to the Operative's right. "Though it's funny it should come down to this, isn't it? All those times and all those runs and it all ends up with you stuck to a wall like an insect. And all I need to do to make it official is grind my boot."

"So get it over with," says the Operative.

"Not before you tell me where Lynx is holed up."

"Why the fuck should you want to know that?"

"So I can nail him too, Carson. Was that fuel sustaining your mind as well? I have to take him out lest they send more mechs for me."

"They probably will anyway."

"Nothing wrong with buying myself a little time. Where is he, Carson?"

"Surely you can pull the answer from my skull after you finish with me."

"But it'd be so much easier if you told me."

"You mean if I told the Rain, Sarmax."

But Sarmax only laughs. "I'm not the *Rain*, Carson. I already said that. Besides, it's not like the Rain's a fucking secret to anyone who's really in the know. No matter what they're telling everyone else: it's not like you and I don't know exactly who we're talking about."

"Funny, that's exactly what your bitch said to me before they snuffed her."

And suddenly Sarmax's lazy spiraling patterns cease. He swoops downward like a bird of prey, roaring in toward the Operative—and swerves aside at the last moment, hitting the slope a few meters up. He perches there, opens up with lasers on the ice to which his target's clinging. At some point during this sequence of events, his voice becomes coherent enough for the Operative to understand it. Though Sarmax is doing nothing save cursing. He sounds like a demon who's just been tossed from hell.

"That's great," says the Operative. The lasers whine scarcely centimeters from his visor. The ice is starting to get noticeably less solid. Water's running across his suit. He digs his hands in deeper. "Priceless. You getting a tape of yourself?"

"You I can forgive," screams Sarmax. "After I kill you, that is. Lynx I can't. It must get him so hard to see you and me set on each other like dogs. I'll tear that motherfucker limb from limb. Fucking razor—living vicariously through all of us and never doing fuck-all himself."

"Actually he's been quite busy," says the Operative. "He's been in the tunnels of Agrippa for several days. He's gone walkabout in the SpaceCom comps. I'm sure the Com would love to get the heads-up. Though I'll be damned if they're going to hear it from *you*."

And with that, he fires a tether straight at Sarmax, strikes him full in the chest with a magnetic clamp. Before Sarmax can shear the cord away, the Operative is pumping out voltage from what's left of his power packs. For an undamaged suit, that wouldn't be much of a problem.

For one as badly damaged as Sarmax's, it's a different story.

There's a blinding flash. The Operative hears Sarmax curse. He relinquishes the tether, watches as Sarmax extends his body full off the ice, brings his hands forward with the well-practiced motion of someone starting his thrusters. But instead there's another explosion and Sarmax tumbles onto the ice. He crashes into the Operative, knocks him from his weakened perch even as the two grapple. In this fashion they slide down the ice together.

They accelerate quickly. The infrastructure above them vanishes as though it's being hauled upward on the back of a rocket. The darkness is near-total. It's broken only by two things. One is the lights of both their suits. The other's a red glow that's starting to take shape beneath them. As that glow draws closer, the frenzied nature of their struggle intensifies.

"Do you recognize that light, Carson?" mutters Sarmax.

But the Operative says nothing. He's intent on trying to somehow reverse the position of himself and Sarmax. He's trying to shove Sarmax flush against the ice. He's doing anything he can to put his opponent between him and whatever they're about to run into.

"Carson," says Sarmax. *"Do you recognize that light?"*

They're almost down amidst the glow. It's not just one glow, either. It's several. They're stretching out on all sides.

"Like moths to the candle," says Sarmax. "We'll burn together."

The Operative's doing his damnedest to forestall it. For now he manages to get his leg out from under Sarmax's— manages to lever it against Sarmax's side. He shoves Sarmax down onto the ice beside him. He smashes his fist against Sarmax's head. Sarmax is giving as good as he's getting, if not better. But now their slide's starting to get less steep. They're starting to slow.

Though only slightly.

"My furnaces," says Sarmax. "We've reached rock bottom."

And yet they're still rushing downward. Now the Operative can see that the lights are really incandescent lines strung here and there, glowing through the dark. More infrastructure appears out of that gloom: more ramps, more chutes. More machinery.

"So simple," says Sarmax. He sends a jet-powered glove at the Operative's helmet—who pulls his head out of the way, grabs Sarmax's arm, desperately tries to keep the jets off his visor. "This cavern must be one of the wonders of this world. It harbors the mother lode. We hammer off the ice. We shove it up against the wires. We pipe the water back to Shackleton. They ship it all the way to Congreve. We keep this rock running."

"And it'll keep on running long after you're buried," says the Operative.

They slide writhing to a halt on the cusp of another edge. Lights glow all around. Water's dripping down everywhere.

"Long after we both are," says Sarmax. He pulls himself free of the Operative's grip, leaps to a standing position—and is immediately tripped by the Operative. The momentum of his fall carries them both over the new edge. They hurtle downward once more. Both their suits are pretty much wrecked beyond repair. Neither has any functioning weapons save his own fists and feet. Neither has any power. In this manner they set about bringing the struggle to a finish. Each pays particular attention to the areas of the other's armor that appear to be most damaged. Each does his utmost to shield those areas on his own suit from his opponent. Each strives desperately to use the other as shielding from the next impact. Each strives desperately to gain the upper hand.

They run headlong into the base of the lowermost lamp. The blow knocks them apart. For a moment the Operative lies stunned. Red-orange glow looms above him. Now that he's up close, the Operative can see it's really more of a giant filament wire, curled in upon itself. Ramps jut up around it. Some of them contain ice. Water falls down in a steady trickle upon his face, pours away in narrow channels situated for that purpose. But now his view is blotted out by Sarmax—who's bending over the Operative with a half smile.

"Carson. You always knew it would come to this."

"I guess I always did."

"Then why did you come here in the first place?"

"What choice did I have?"

"You know I wasn't dealing with the Rain."

"But *she* was," says the Operative.

Sarmax turns. He pivots forward. He looks for a moment like he's going to put his boot straight through the Operative's visor. But at the last moment he steps aside.

"You didn't have to say that," he says.

"They didn't have to kill her."

"No," says Sarmax. "But I did."

The Operative's got such a head start on the afterlife that he's almost beyond surprise. But he's speechless anyway. He stares as tears well in the eyes of the man who was once his mentor.

"As you said," mutters Sarmax. "She was dealing with the Rain. Didn't mean I didn't love her. She was... she was my Indigo. She was my everything. But she was dead set to join them. She was dead set to have me go with her."

"So why didn't you?"

"Maybe I should have. I'd still have been with her. But she wouldn't have been with me. That's the truth of the matter, Carson. I'd like to tell you I killed her because I was loyal. Because I was a Praetorian. Because I stood at the Throne's right hand. But I'd be lying. I killed her because she loved the

Rain more than she loved me. Time was I couldn't imagine a world without her. Now I live it every day—this rock on the edge of existence, this mountain that might as well harbor all the souls of the ones who died that night."

"Which is exactly why you can't stay," says the Operative softly.

"No," says Sarmax. "And you can't either. I can't put you beneath this ground, Carson. I can't add your name to the ones who went before us. And I admit it—I can't stay out of it either. You've made me realize that. You come to me with this scheme for subverting the Rain and all of creation into the bargain. There's no way I can look into your eyes and tell you I'm a party to it. But there's no way I'm going to stop short of a chance to take care of the Rain once and for all. And after that we'll see what the new world looks like."

"So help me up," says the Operative. "And let's talk about the most immediate problem."

"You mean the Rain?"

"I mean Lynx."

They make their way back up into the upper reaches of that mountain.

Ø They're slowing down. The tunnel's leveling out. The water's draining out—conveyed through sluices that lead down even farther. The ship decelerates through the diminishing flood. It keeps on losing speed as the water lowers past the windows. It slides along in darkness. It slows still further.

And stops.

"Zone's gone entirely," mutters Spencer.

"Does that surprise you?" says Linehan.

"Not in the least."

Which doesn't mean he's come to terms with it. It's all he's known all his life. Now suddenly it's vanished, leaving him alone in the midst of endless tunnels. All the interstices upon which his mind abutted have faded from existence. He's been reduced to just himself.

It's going to take some getting used to.

"So what now?" says Linehan.

"Now we keep moving," says Spencer.

He reactivates the ship's power and switches on the headlights. They show tunnel stretching into dark. He fumbles with the ship's controls, fires up its rockets. The headlights vanish in the reflected light of flame. The ship lurches, starts to move, starts to accelerate. Spencer calls up the map of the tunnels once again and pinpoints their position as best as he can. He no longer has the zone to moor him, so he has to extrapolate precisely what shaft they've been swept into, has to line it up against the map that gleams within his head.

Even as that map starts changing.

Lines start to expand through Spencer's mind. What's dark is suddenly being thrust into light. What were edges are fast becoming core. The whole of the old map becomes the center of the new one. And what the new represents is no longer just the corridor that surrounds the main line from Mountain to London. It's the whole of the North Atlantic. Spencer watches as it keeps on growing. He realizes that if he isn't crazy yet this map will probably take over his mind and make him so. Because it's Control's creature. He sees that now. He gets it. Control's given him autonomous software able to adapt to the situation—able to help Control's razor to assess that situation correctly. The zone's gone. Spencer's in the dark. But the lights of the map within him play upon him anyway. He reads the riddle embedded in their shifting patterns. He sees the route that's tracing itself through them. He sees what Control wants him to do.

He starts discussing options with Linehan.

"What's there to discuss?" says Linehan. "We're ten minutes out from border."

"What's to discuss is that we're not going there," says Spencer.

"What?"

"I said we're not going there."

"Says who?"

"Says me."

"What the fuck's your problem?"

"There's no problem," says Spencer slowly. "There's just logic. And logic says that we aren't going to try to run the border."

"We almost have!"

"Linehan. We're still almost two thousand klicks west of where the Euro Magnates take over."

"So?"

"So our chances of doing a stealth run have basically dropped to nothing flat. We were running beneath the radar before the zone went. We still are. But now it's for a different reason. And it's a safe bet that somewhere in the next couple thousand klicks the zone reasserts itself. Which means we're essentially hiding in what amounts to a local disruption. Let's hope that means that they can't see what's going on within it. But let's not make any plans that don't presume that they're sending craft in right now. And let's not kid ourselves for a moment that they aren't waiting with all forces they've got for whatever comes *out*."

"Which may not matter if this disruption extends all the way to the border!"

"You don't need to have a zone to seal a border." And with that Spencer veers the ship down a southward fork.

Linehan shakes his head. "You're dead," he says.

"By all means," says Spencer. "Off me and add me to the trail of bodies you've left strewn in your wake. It won't change a thing about all the heat in front of us. Nor will it save you when you run smack into fire."

"We've already hit that fire," says Linehan. "Are you fucking blind? We're carving through it. We're on the cusp of London, man. How can you deny it?"

"As wishful thinking," says Spencer. "As embarrassing. The thought that we could slip on through the zone's border membrane: events have rendered it a fantasy. We could have done it in that train. We could have even done it in this. But, like you said—every alarm and then some has been raised. The nuke didn't kill us, Linehan. We're alive. How about we face the consequences?"

"How about we *shape* the consequences, Spencer? How about we do something besides running home with our tails between our legs?"

"I want to go home more badly than you could know. But you forget my home's in front of me. And your home, that's nowhere. You're rootless, Linehan. Your soul's even more mechanical than your flesh."

"So what's your point?"

"This: I don't see you ripping me away from the controls and ripping me in pieces. I don't see you ripping through the tunnels and making hell for London. I don't see you doing much except for sitting there and sneering. In fact, I don't see you doing *anything* save admitting that I'm absolutely right."

"And if we don't go for the border—"

"It's no if."

"And *if* we don't go for the border, where the fuck are we going to go?"

Spencer tells him.

PART III
INVERSION

Midnight at the Moon's south pole. Always midnight down here. Always these voices in your head when you've been on the run too long. Always these voices that help you stay out in that cold for even longer.

Especially when they don't know the whole story.

"Carson. You've done it."

"Done what."

"Killed him."

The voice of Stefan Lynx is flush with triumph. The Operative just feels tired.

"Tell me you have more to tell me than that."

"Confirmation is always good news, Carson. Was it hard?"

"Hard enough. What do his files say?"

"I mean was it hard to pull the trigger?"

"Not especially. What do the files say?"

"Would you do it all over again?"

"What do the fucking files say, Lynx?"

"That Leo Sarmax was one tricky customer."

"I could have told you that."

"You could have *guessed* that. What you just uploaded confirms it. There doesn't seem to have been any game up here he didn't have himself dealt into."

"That's great, Lynx. Was he dealing with the Rain?"

"There's no evidence of that," says Lynx. "Not yet anyway. But I *have* found a lot of evidence to suggest he was *looking* for them."

"To do what?"

"Who knows? Do business with them, maybe. Sell their whereabouts to us, maybe. Or to someone else."

"Sounds like a very dangerous game."

"No shit," says Lynx. "Look where he ended up."

"Much more likely that the Rain would find him than the other way around."

"One would think," says Lynx. "But again, that's why I targeted him, Carson. The man was a nexus. A conduit. Even in death, a middleman. His organization—the whole web of companies he set in motion—is a machine that's got a link into basically everything that's going on up here."

"And now we're inside."

"And outside. And all around. Everyone who so much as sniffs at you—I'll dissect them without them even realizing it. Everyone whom Sarmax had a file on, I'll get a hundred more. SpaceCom intelligence knows nothing about you. And even less about Sarmax. They haven't a clue that he used to be one of us. They haven't a clue what we're about to pull."

"How can you be so sure?"

"How do you think? I'm camped out in their fucking mainframes, remember? And get this, Carson—the whispers atop the SpaceCom rafters is that the farside of this rock harbors the Rain's main stronghold."

"Yeah? Based on what intel?"

"Well," says Lynx, "that's the big question, isn't it?"

"You mean you don't know?"

"I mean I'm still finding out."

"And is SpaceCom passing word of its suspicions back to the Throne?"

"Put it this way," says Lynx. "*I'm* passing this back to the Throne. I'll keep on doing that. But that's my obligation. It doesn't cut the other way. The Throne doesn't tell me shit about who's giving it what. It doesn't have to."

"Doesn't it," says the Operative. "I mean, you'd think it would be useful for us to know if the Com is withholding a piece of data like *that*. Because if they're playing that kind of double game, then—"

"We're assuming they're playing that kind of double game," snaps Lynx. "I mean, who the fuck isn't these days? Wake up, Carson: there's a reason I'm buried in these comps. The Rain could be the very treason within SpaceCom that we were sent up to find in the first place. It could have been that way from the start. It might have become it in the days since. And even if it hasn't, we're still going to need the Com's files. Their eyes see so much up here. They may not even realize the significance of everything they process. But with one foot in their living guts and the other in the dead heart of Sarmax, we've got the inside track on Rain. And that trail leads out to Congreve Station."

"In the center of the farside?"

"That's the only Congreve I know of, Carson."

"Where *exactly*?"

"Northwest district. Upscale residential area. Sarmax maintained an address there."

"And you want me to set up shop there."

"Got it in one, Carson. I want you to go there and set up shop. And do some digging in the Congreve speakeasies. Sarmax had more than a few contacts strewn through them."

"Yeah? Who?"

"Oh, various characters," says Lynx vaguely. "Various lowlifes. Congreve's quite a place, Carson. It's the largest city that never lays eyes on Earth. It's the heart of SpaceCom power. The L2 fleet hovers in the sky above it like a demented sun. All of Congreve is dedicated to that fleet, Carson. That's the whole reason the town exists. And you can be sure that's one of the reasons the Rain are up here."

"To blow that fleet?"

"You have to admit that in terms of spectacular targets, that would be a good one. Congreve was always going to be one of the possibilities for the next move of the physical vector of this mission. But the latest intel makes it essential. It gives us no choice but to send you there."

"Fine," says the Operative. "When do I leave?"

"As soon as we're done here."

"Transportation?"

"Take one of Sarmax's shuttles."

"And when I get there—you want me to just go to this house and knock on its door?"

"No need to even knock. You're the new owner. No need to announce the old one's untimely demise just yet. Besides, we need all the leverage we can get. Things are getting out of hand back on Earth. The Newfoundland Yards got wiped off the map. HK's under embargo. The Rain jacked one of our spaceplanes and downed it there. Along with some key CICom agents."

"How are we responding?"

"With the usual recriminations. The shit's going down in the Inner Cabinet. Apparently Space and Info are at each other's throats. Undoubtedly the Rain are in the mix somewhere. The Throne is threatened like never before. *Our* Throne, Carson. Our man. There's war in heaven."

"Heaven save us from war's worst kind," mutters the Operative.

"Don't look to anybody to save us, Carson. Only we can do it now. Now go. You'll be on the other side of sky in under two hours."

"And our contact protocols?"

"The same as ever. Extreme judiciousness."

"Got it."

Lynx cuts out. The Operative stares at the blank wall. Turns to the blank expression of the man standing next to him.

"Well," says Leo Sarmax.

"It's complicated."

A s were the first hours in the city. The first hours past the point of no return—a fact only just now dawning on them. Threading their way through streets of silver and corridors of chrome, rubbing shoulders with the men and women of a hundred nations . . . into what strangeness had they stumbled? They didn't know. They scarcely cared. All they knew is that they were on the run. And that they needed a base: some space to catch their breath. They needed a place.

They found it.

In a room. Same story as ever: find walls and a floor. A door you can close. And above all a ceiling. Anything to blot out the sky. Cheap-ass motel in Old Port Moresby district, no questions asked, no answers needed. Just naked light overhead while their bodies writhe naked in front of a wall-screen that pulsates static. They leave it like that. It seems fitting. It's how they feel. It embodies what they feel tossed upon. So they make love while they let the static play around them.

Until a face appears within it.

It isn't one they recognize. It's a man. He's got one eye. He wears a mustache. It looks absurd. Yet his expression's anything but.

"Shit," says Marlowe. He's pulling himself off Haskell, vaulting onto the floor. Haskell turns the vid off.

But it remains lit. The face persists.

"Shit," she says.

"The CI codes," says the man. And the codes of CICom fill the screen, flit in and out of static, float in front of his face. Both Marlowe and Haskell recognize them. Friend-or-foe identifiers, changed every hour on the hour according to algorithms given to each agent at the start of every mission. Embedded with myriad fail-safes for an interloper to trigger. Doesn't mean they can't be fucked with.

But it's a long way from easy.

"We should go," says Haskell to Marlowe on the one-on-one.

"You shouldn't," the man says. "I'm Sinclair's man in HK."

They stare at him. Haskell's first to find her voice.

"How'd you find us?"

"Sit down," the man says.

They sit. He gazes at them. He shakes his head.

"I found you because I'm a handler. I know agents. I brief them. Track them when I have to. Snuff them when I must."

"Going to try that on us?" asks Marlowe.

"No. All I wanted to do is locate you."

"But how did you do that?" persists Haskell.

"I've got the edge," says the man. "I've got everything on you two. Your psych profiles, for one—which way you move when under pressure. That helped. But it wasn't as useful as your neutral accounts. Figured you'd go back to those. I mean, what else could you have done?"

"You're lying," says Marlowe. "Those weren't even the accounts you gave us. Those were the ones I set up last time I was in the neutrals."

"We're not stupid, Jason. We know how our agents do it

when they get out beyond the border. We know you think you live longer if you don't link to us. We're not even against insurance policies. Doesn't mean we don't like to keep an eye on things."

"If you have those account numbers, then Morat might have them too," says Haskell. "He had access to every code you've given us as well. So why should we trust you?"

"Trust me," says the man. "If I were trying to nail you they'd have kicked down your door already. Nailing people's easy. Saving them's the hard part. I'm changing up the codes even as I speak. I'm here because you've got a new mission. I'm the one who's going to tell you all about it. Besides: don't you want to know what's *really* going on?"

"What happened on that spaceplane?" demands Haskell.

"You know damn well what happened," replies the man. "Morat betrayed us. He helped the Rain to jack it."

"Why?" asks Haskell.

"Surely it wasn't to get at the two of us," says Marlowe.

"Actually, I'm sure that *was* part of the reason. But it wasn't the main one."

"What was the main one?"

The handler smiles mirthlessly. "The main one was the cargo you were carrying."

"I didn't know we were carrying anything," says Marlowe.

"Of course you didn't."

"What," says Haskell slowly, "are you talking about?"

"Like I just said: I'm talking about the fact that you were carrying a cargo."

"And are you going to tell us what the fuck it was?"

"That's not an easy question to answer," says the handler. "In fact, I'm not even sure I *can* answer it. What you have to understand is that Sinclair was intending to take the fight to Autumn Rain. He put all his primary agents into the field.

And he emptied out the research labs of anything that even *looked* like it had any promise. Every black-ops project, every R&D prototype—all of it got deployed."

"Which," says Marlowe, "was exactly what the Rain wanted."

"Chalk one up to hindsight," says the handler. "The plan was to assign an artifact to each team. You were one such squad. When you reached the Moon, your briefing was to encompass that artifact's activation. We couldn't transport it out of sight of those we trusted most. But we weren't going to tell you about it until you absolutely *had* to know."

"But you were going to tell Morat."

"We don't know what happened to Morat. We don't know how he found out what he did. We don't know how he broke loose. It calls into question every—"

"Never mind that crap," says Haskell. *"Tell us what was on that plane."*

"Next-generation AI," replies the handler. "A comp that combined state-of-the-art battle management capability with the ability to do zone incursions far beyond the level of our best razors."

"Oh," says Haskell.

"Oh. What was on that plane was the ultimate machine for waging secret war. And not just secret, either. Situate it in an inner enclave, and you could vector a first strike through the thing. All housed in a highly mobile chassis."

"It moves?"

"In point of fact, it bailed out."

They look at him. Look at each other.

"Why so surprised?" asks the handler. "After all, that's what you did."

"Sure," says Marlowe, "but that's different."

"Is it?"

"What kind of chassis? Is this thing humanoid?"

"That's the problem," says the handler. "I don't know."

"You don't *know*?"

"There's nothing on file?" asks Marlowe.

"The file's name is Manilishi. But Morat must have tampered with the documentation because now all we've got is the name. And this." For a moment, the handler's face is replaced with shots of a crippled, smoking spaceplane hurtling down toward the city—and a close-up on a small object ejecting from its rear. Further magnification reveals a cylinder, spinning end over end on a diagonal slant, disappearing beneath the draped-over canopy of buildings.

"I thought there were no escape pods," says Haskell.

"That's not an escape pod," says the handler. "It's a fuel tank. It contained the Manilishi. Which somehow got activated in the fighting. Maybe it just woke up. It must have ejected from that pod once it fell into city shadow. We had no cameras on it when it did. All we've got are some anomalies in the HK zone that occurred at the point it landed."

"What kind of anomalies?"

"Cameras suddenly seeing nothing. Backup routines being activated for no good reason. All the usual signs of something covering its traces. Our men found what was left of the fuel tank. But that was all they found."

"This is absurd," says Haskell. But even as she says it, she's thinking. About hidden compartments and places not yet seen. About covert agendas. About how easy it might have been for something as mobile as it is smart to lie low, let the interlopers go after the more obvious targets, wait for that moment. Maybe it came at Morat's apogee of gloat. Maybe it came when Marlowe reappeared. One thing's for sure, though.

What happened next must have been perfect.

"My suggestion is that you assume this thing has all the physical attributes of heavy powered armor," says the handler. "Camo, flight, fight—you name it. And that's on top of its zone prowess."

"Jesus," says Haskell.

"Not quite. But close. And the fact that it's on the loose is a major fucking problem."

"Why doesn't it just call home?" asks Marlowe.

"Maybe it doesn't want to."

"You're saying it's gone rogue?"

"It might have. Under the trauma. Or it might have been captured by the Rain despite its best efforts. All we know is that it hasn't reported in. And that we absolutely, positively fucking have to have it back."

"And you want us to go get it?"

"No," says the handler, "I want you to shove your head through this fucking screen."

"Fuck your sarcasm," says Marlowe. "Why us? I would have thought we were marked for arrest."

"You are."

Marlowe stands up.

"Sit down," says the handler. "I'm not arresting anybody."

"Why not?"

"Because I'm on the list too."

"Sinclair's sold us all out?"

"He hasn't sold anyone out. He was top of the list. He's in custody now."

Marlowe and Haskell stare at the screen. Any thought of running's gone now. Sure, they'd been ready to make a break. Sure, if this man really *were* after them, he really would have come in through the door and not the screen. But that kind of logic only carries one so far. It's all intellectual. It's not emotional. Try riding death down from sky to ground, then go to ground to no avail: you'll get your own ideas about what's logical.

"I guess," says Haskell, "that really shouldn't surprise us."

"It really shouldn't." The handler smiles grimly. "He's held liable for the loss of Manilishi. His head was the least he could offer up."

"So who's heading up CounterIntelligence now?" asks Marlowe.

"Like I just said," says the handler, "Sinclair's head was the least of it. There *is* no more CI. It's been annulled."

"What?"

"Annulled," says the man. "Nullified. Ended. Torn into little fucking bits."

"Oh fuck," says Marlowe.

"Who's assimilating its personnel?" asks Haskell.

"The cells. And then the furnaces."

"They're being killed?"

"I'm having difficulty getting my point across. Maybe it's this cheap screen of yours. Maybe it's you. But try to get this through your heads anyway. This isn't your usual HQ power play. This is a wholesale purge. It's not even like it was when Space swallowed Air. This is extermination."

"But only the president could authorize anything that drastic."

"Well," says the handler, "exactly. You just answered your own question. Only the president could authorize this. And the Praetorians are carrying out most of the dirty work."

"They think Sinclair was in league with the Rain," says Marlowe.

"He was framed," says the handler. "I guarantee you. Morat may have even planned for it all to play out this way. What better way for Autumn Rain to infiltrate the inner enclaves than for CICom to be erased? What better news for any conspiracies within the other Coms than to realize that the ultimate watchdog's just been taken off the board?"

"And what about us?" says Haskell.

"What do you think? As far as the Throne is concerned,

the only known alpha targets besides Sinclair and his immediate lieutenants and the Manilishi itself are the two agents
who were *on that goddamn plane*. Although with that kind of
data in your head, they wouldn't kill you. Not for a long while,
at any rate."

"They have to catch us first," says Marlowe.

"They have to indeed. And rest assured they're trying. We
haven't much time. You're going to have to take this deeper.
And get on the Manilishi's trail."

"But you said you have no idea where this thing is."

"I said I didn't know what it was *doing*," says the handler.
"I didn't say I didn't know where it was *going*. I have its comp
signatures. It'll change them once it realizes we can use them
to track it. But in the meantime, I've been triangulating
anomalies in this city's zone."

"To where?"

"Place called Seleucus Flats. One of the northern sectors.
Up the Owen-Stanley Range. As I said, this thing may be in
Rain custody by now. Or it may be trying to assess the situa-
tion. Or trying to sell its services to a well-heeled bidder."

"Well," says Haskell, "there are certainly enough of those."

"You don't know the half of it," replies the handler.
"Since the embargo went into effect, all hell has broken loose
here."

"What are you talking about?"

"Haven't you looked outside? You should ditch this
Roman orgy act and put something on the vid. All the gangs
and cartels and triads and syndicates—they've all turned on
each other in the last few hours. Not just because the word's
getting around that something was on that spaceplane that's
going to fetch a pretty high price. But because they can. The
embargo's cut off a lot of big-time bosses from their backup,
and a lot of backup from their bosses. No one can call in rein-
forcements from the Euros or the Aussies now. Which means

the shit has hit the fan like you would not believe. The HK authorities are barely keeping it together."

"No better environment to do some hunting," says Marlowe.

"Or get hunted," says Haskell.

"Exactly," says the handler. "So keep your eyes peeled. And get that thing."

"And when we get it?"

"We use it to bargain for our reinstatement."

"Our *reinstatement?* You sure that's going to work?"

"I'm not sure of anything any longer," replies the handler. "But I'll tell you what might help once we get our hands on the Manilishi."

"Go on."

"Using it to locate and destroy the Autumn Rain base that's in this city."

Marlowe and Haskell look at each other.

"We do that," says the handler, "and the Throne's own Hand will pin a medal on us. We can even bring the old man back."

"If he's still alive," says Marlowe.

"Sure," says the handler. "If he's still alive. But right now, it's our turn to stay alive. And you might have to destroy the Rain just to get the Manilishi anyway. Now listen. I've created new identities for you. I've cauterized them. I've got you some prime equipment too. You can pick it up en route. Now go. We'll stay in touch as we need to."

"You mean as *you* need to," says Marlowe.

"Listen, Marlowe," says the handler. "Both of you listen. We've come a long way from the days when my kind walked your dreams while you beat your fist against the pillows. I know that. I know you've no love for me. But I know you've loyalty. Loyalty for Sinclair and what he stood for. What he stands for even now. You can't deny that. You're sworn, and you know it. And what's going on out there renders our own personal dilemmas immaterial. Regardless of what happens to any of us, what's going on now will decide the fate of our people. You hold that fate within your hands. Both of you. If the Rain acquire Manilishi, nothing will be beyond them. Nothing. Now get out there. And be even better than you were on that plane."

"We'll try," says Marlowe.

But the handler isn't waiting. He's already disappearing. Static washes over him as though it were a tide coming in on fast-forward. He sinks beneath those waves.

And then he's gone.

But Control's here. Control: who's been doing time in the Mountain since time began. Control: who's come out of hiding tonight—emerging from those pipes and tunnels to expose its voice direct to air, deal directly with the ones who by all rights should have either made it or been made. They did neither. All they did was stumble to that southern shore. Now they're calling from the shattered remnants of the Amazon delta in the hopes of seeing one more tomorrow. They're looking for a backup plan. They're looking to Control once more.

Only to find themselves stared down by sight beyond all seeing.

"I'm talking to the one who calls himself Linehan," says the voice that echoes from a speaker on Spencer's belt—as dry as the dust the room contains, as harsh as the bombed-out cityscape that lies outside the window of the warehouse they call shelter. "I'm talking to the man who's been the vehicle to drive half the Atlantic into zone blackout. I'm pretty sure he can hear me."

"He can," says Linehan.

"Linehan," says Control. Inflection falls from the voice like a cloak tossed upon the floor. "Do you know who I am?"

"I do."

"Tell me."

"You're Control. You're the Priam Combine's most valuable asset in North America. You report direct to London. I assure you that I didn't enter your domain lightly."

"Fine words," says Control. Something somewhere between laugh and static hisses softly through the room. "Meaningless sounds. Your *attitude* is beside the point. Your actions are what's at issue here."

"I came to your man with a fair bargain." Spencer listens impassively to himself described in the third person. He doesn't take his eyes off Linehan. "He put that bargain to you. You accepted. To what actions of mine are you referring?"

"The very same. You flushed my agent from cover. You blackmailed him into opening up a conduit through which all too many minds vectored onto mine."

"No," says Linehan. "At no point have you been the target of this operation."

"You use words so carefully," says Control. Suddenly the voice is nothing but inflection. "You lie so freely. You skirt so close to truth. You're beyond abomination. 'At no point have you been the target of this operation.' Listen to yourself! I know I wasn't *the* target. I was *one* of the targets. Just one. So very far from only."

"As was I."

"No," says Control, "you were just bait. You were just a pawn. Whether or not you knew it. You were nothing but a hollow man with a hollow promise that was the weapon around which my operation and countless others were to be turned inside out. While you were battling your way off that train—while the whole zone contorted in the grip of God knows how many hacks—while incidents went down all over the Earth-Moon system and God knows how much meat came within reach of God knows how much mouth: I became prey myself. A federal sting. Or at least what looked like one. They surrounded the block where I was. Seventy floors of data storage, and they knew I was in one of the tanks. They had me triangulated. They severed the streets. They cut the power. They cut the lines so I couldn't escape. My backup generators sustained me. They sent their soldiers in. They went from room to room. They closed in on me."

"I knew none of this," says Linehan.

"How would you? It was just me. I waited. I bided my time. Such as it was. I let them eliminate possibilities. Let them narrow down their options. And all the while I waited for my moment. It came the way it always does. Through their assumptions. A luxury the trapped can't afford. They thought I hadn't broken their tactical codes. Nor were they wrong. But I was swimming through that traffic even as those boots sounded all around me. I was staying on top of their frequencies even as they shifted. I was *listening*. And suddenly I understood. I broke their code. I broke into one of the suits. The man inside never knew. His medical dispenser dished out a lethal dose. He died. But it was as if he was still there. His vital signs were online for all to see. It was child's play to replicate them. It was nothing to steer that suit to one particular tank and tap in. A physical conduit was established. The main body of my mind crossed over in one swift download."

Control goes silent. Spencer feels himself to be at the very edge of all maps. He feels that one more step might be all it takes to damn him forever. He feels everything's riding on one more word.

And then Control continues:

"I stumbled from the scene of my ultimate transaction while my consciousness fought for survival. The software in that suit was good. But it was intended for a single infantryman. It wasn't enough to house the likes of me. I sent parts of myself into dormancy, threw them over the side of my awareness like so much ballast. I shut down all noncritical components of that suit, took up every unit of real space myself. And, even as I did so, I walked past my hunters. They thought they were gazing at their own. They never knew what had taken place behind that visor. I carried the corpse in that shell all the way out. I reached the unbroken zone. I hurled myself into the immense. I left that suit behind. I hid. You called. I'm talking to you now. And now, Linehan, you are going to tell me *exactly* who you are. Lest I sign off and leave you in the lurch forever."

"I'm U.S. Space Command," says Linehan.

"I suspected as much," says Control.

"I was assigned to down the Elevator."

"Go on," says Control.

"We sought to use the Rain to do that."

"Why?"

"I was never told the why. I didn't need it. All I needed was the how. It was textbook black-ops. We were ordered to arm some no-name terrorist group that we were told had been watched by us for years. No-name patsies based in HK. They already had the nukes. All they needed was the codes. The ones we turned over. Even as they hit the Elevator we were hitting them in their bases. But they'd already cleaned out. They were ghosts, Control. And then they hit my team and left me running."

"Just you?" Control's voice is several thousand klicks away. But the breath of that mouth might as well be drifting right before the ones who listen.

"No," says Linehan, and now the tears are running down his face. "Not just me. Three others. We fled back within the walls of America. It was the worst thing we could have done. Our own side was on us like we were dogs. Dogs who knew too much."

"So you went rogue," says Control.

"And realized that's all we'd ever been. We'd been set up every which way from the start. And those who we'd thought were dead had taken on new life and gone on the lam once more. Even as our own side sought to take us out. I'm a soldier, Control. So are you. You know what soldiers do, Control. They obey their goddamn orders. Even if they don't know who's giving them. Even if they start to suspect that the chains that bind them back to heaven have been broken. That someone somewhere up above them is *off the fucking leash.* By the time we woke up it was far too late. I ditched the ones I ran with. I let them stumble on toward Kennedy. Maybe I lost my nerve. Maybe I was putting them forth as bait. All I know is that they died and I lived. That I've been pursued by my own kind through the basement of Atlantic. That I sought to use Autumn Rain. That I was spat out by them instead."

"But not before you met them," says Control.

Linehan starts to speak. And stops. His eyes dart to the corners of the room. His voice dies to a whisper.

"I didn't even realize it was them at first. There was a man. There was a woman. We sat in a bar in Hong Kong and drank. We gave them downloads. But maybe they downloaded something into me. Because they've been swelling in my mind ever since. They're demons. They're aliens. I don't know what the fuck they are. They're ambitious beyond belief. There's nothing they don't want. They've played us all and I don't even know what to call their game."

"Save that it involves gaming you even now."

"Save me," begs Linehan. "Save us all. I don't know what they've put in my head. All I know is that I've got to get out. And you've got to fucking help me."

"Even when you've just admitted that you're poison?"

"You've always known what I was, Control. You know that doesn't matter. Get me though that border and you'll get your chance to find out all the things I don't even know I know. You'll get your chance to find out if the Rain themselves are stalking me. And to see who else might be crazy enough to try. You know you can't resist it. I know you far too well."

"Then I need hardly tell you I'm going to talk to Spencer," says Control. The voice cuts out.

And resumes inside Spencer's head.

"Spencer," it says, "this will be our last conversation."

"What do you mean?"

"My ability to inflect this situation is approaching its limits. As is the risk to my position."

"The risk to *your* position? And mine—"

"Has never been stronger. How much higher can a pawn get than to be the object of so much attention? What could be better than knowing that I'm going to wind you up for one last try?"

"And while I run you're going to watch."

"And while I watch you're going to blame me. I wouldn't have it any other way. But now I need you to focus on the larger picture. A major power struggle is going down in the Inner Cabinet. CICom has been dismembered. Something's stirring in the depths of SpaceCom. This man is just one fugitive among many now. So join the ranks of the refugees, Spencer. It's time to travel rough. You made it through the southern tunnels. You're sitting in the city they call Belem-Macapa. You're ready to make the run straight up that river."

"What else would you suggest?"

"I wouldn't. I'd take it all the way."

"The Latin run."

"Exactly. Go west along the Amazon and then turn south. At this point it's probably the only hope you have."

"Upriver's insanity, Control. If even half the stories are true—"

"All the better for you if they are. It's all in the map that's hitting you now. Along with the numbers of some neutral bank accounts. My last gifts to you."

"And you're really cutting contact with me."

"Only way to play this, Spencer. Whatever happens, I'm

all we've got in here. I like you, Spencer. But like's not the same as programming."

"You can say that again," says Spencer.

"Try to remember that I'm here forever. Or until they bring me to bay for good. That I'm more than sworn to postpone that day as long as possible. As I said, one conversation more. This one. And this is the end between us."

"Why are you rationalizing this?"

"I'm not. I'm trying to focus you one last time. Don't look backward. Only forward. Now go."

The connection terminates. Spencer rips the jack out of his head, tears the wires out of the wall. He shoves past Linehan. He staggers over to the window, presses his face up against the plastic. He exhales.

"So what else did your imaginary friend have to say," says Linehan.

"He's not my friend," says Spencer. "He never was."

"It's an overrated concept anyway," says Linehan.

But what's not overrated is your first sight of Congreve. The first city built by man never to know the Earth—the city above which false stars cluster into strange zodiacs that denote the fleet that sits sixty thousand klicks out. Somewhere in those swarms are the SpaceCom flagships. Somewhere in that city two men gaze out a window.

"Nice place you got here," says the Operative.

"I know," replies Sarmax.

The geometry of off-world rooftops stretches before them. Distant mountains loom through a translucent dome. The sky's alive with lights. Shadows play within the darkened room.

"Lot of activity," says the Operative.

"Yes," replies Sarmax.

"They're moving onto war footing."

"After major incidents in two oceans, they have to." Sarmax turns from the window. The curtains swing shut behind him even as the interior lights come up. The room thus revealed is ornately furnished. A crystal globe of the Moon sits within one corner. Sarmax walks to it. Regards it. Shrugs.

"We have to assume free agency," he adds. "Until we can prove otherwise, we have to assume that those who are supposed to be in control still are. The East has reason enough to hate us already. Lord knows we've got enough reasons to hate them."

"But all that's just context," says the Operative.

"Right. It's all just context. One that the new players are exploiting. We have to remember who we're dealing with. They aren't just assassins. They're *takeover artists*. They burrow from within. We have to assume that as soon as they succeed in either East or West, they'll initiate a preemptive strike—*if* they come to the conclusion they're not going to be able to pull off a doubleheader."

"The worst case of all," says the Operative.

"Believe it. They may be able to do this quietly. They may not need war at all."

"But they've got far too many reasons to press for it."

"Meaning what?"

The Operative stares. "Come *on*, Leo."

"I want you to say it."

"Okay," says the Operative. "I'll say it. Everything they've done is calculated to drive up tension. Why else down the Elevator? Now neither side can trust the other. Talk about taking an axe to détente. And whatever it was they wanted in that spaceplane—they did it in a way that winds the noose ever tighter. They know what they're doing."

Sarmax twirls the globe absently. "That's what concerns me most. They've learned new tricks. They've developed an uncanny talent for street theater that frankly scares me shit-less. They're using it to drive the world toward the brink. Which makes it even easier for someone who's got the moves to creep in toward the center. All those alerts, all those special clearances, all those doors being slammed shut: to a world-class infiltrator, those things are just goddamn *tools*. The closer to the edge the world gets, the more the Rain enable the very conditions that will underpin their triumph."

"So what are we going to do about it?"

"*You're* going to do what your boss told you. Hit the speakeasies. And I'm going to start some transactions you can keep an eye on."

"And my boss?"

"We keep him informed."

"We do?"

"Of course. All we need to hide from him is me, Carson. Which won't be a problem as long as he buys the duplicate house-node you sold him. Beyond that, we can pretty much feed him anything you and I come up with. Let's see what he does with it. Let's see what else he's got. If he orders you somewhere suddenly, that's probably where we want to be. And it probably won't be very far. They're close, Carson. They're real close."

"It's a question of time now," says the Operative. "Not space."

They're running smooth through early rush-hour traffic—swooping in upon the Seleucus Flats. Marlowe's on point. Haskell's about a klick behind him. He's riding public transport. She's in a private vehicle. She's got both street and zone bound up within her head. She's taking it in on myriad screens. The city's streaming past in all its shapes and hues. The news-feeds are keeping tabs on the mounting crisis—keeping tabs, too, on the mounting body count as the gangland hits go out of control. Presiding over it all are the ships of the superpowers—roaring in languid circles far overhead, standing off out over the ocean, staying carefully on the right side of the cordon sanitaire to which they're keeping. They almost came to blows pursuing the spaceplane down into those canyons. They aren't going to make the same mistake again.

Not officially, at any rate. Haskell has no doubt that both East and West have plenty of operatives inside the city already. The handler, for one. She wonders where he is. She's picked up a few crumbs to suggest that it's somewhere in the city-center ziggurats that gleam dully in her rearview. She's not supposed to indulge in triangulation exercises on someone who sits above her in the food chain. But she's had a few bad experiences of late. So she takes in the angles along which the handler's signals move in on her, takes in all the views Marlowe's scanning, takes in all the ways in which many times a billion points of data intersect.

And then suddenly it all goes blank.

It's like the spaceplane: the only way she's seeing is through her eyes. She can't see the zone at all. She can see the flitcar in front of her swerving though, and switches seamlessly to manual, dodges the vehicle as it veers crazily past her—then she turns again to compensate as the momentum of her initial evasion almost carries her straight off the ramp she's on. She barrels onward while vehicles smash into one another, tumble away into space. She gets a quick glimpse of pedestrians milling in confusion on a nearby walkway—and beyond that, an explosion as something hits a building in the middle distance. That blast is the first of many. Haskell no longer has contact with anyone. She's just driving all out toward the Flats while the city erupts in pandemonium around her.

Then the zone kicks back in. But not as it was before. She can see the immediate distance quite clearly. Beyond that it's like a kaleidoscope on acid. The Seleucus Flats are lost in a wash of colors. The edge of the city isn't in sight. There's no sign of Marlowe or the handler. Or anything coherent, for that matter: she ricochets past more cars, switches off onto a side street—roars through alleys, then beneath roofs that put the sky out of sight. She sears through one of the city's thousand skid rows. Up ahead people are blocking the road, signaling her to stop. She accelerates, runs them down. Shots rip past her—she turns through a junction, roars through a labyrinth of warehouses—and then out into the district's local downtown. The roof gives out for just a moment—she can see the sky and if anything it looks like there are even more ships out there now. They seem to be holding their formations though. She guesses that whatever's going on here doesn't extend all the way out there—so she steers her car into a tunnel, turns from there into a much narrower tunnel, eases her way to where it ends in a wall, and brakes.

She gets out, a pistol in each hand. She opens a door in the wall—goes through into a corridor that looks like it's used for storage. She comes out the other end in a roofed street. It's deserted. It's lined with doors. She opens one of them, climbs stairs, and goes through another door into a bar. There are two men within it. One's the bartender.

The other's Jason Marlowe.

"No weapons here," says the bartender. His accent marks him for Australian. His face marks him for a burn victim once upon a time. He doesn't seem the slightest bit intimidated by her guns.

"It's okay," says Marlowe. "She's a friend of mine."

"So tell her to put her gear away."

But Haskell's already doing so. She sits down next to Marlowe, who's sitting in front of a drink. That they found each other isn't the least bit strange. It's just standard procedure. Positioned along a rough line between where they started and where they're going are four other potential rendezvous locations. Which one got used depended on the point at which any disruption of communication occurred. And such disruption was just one contingency among many for which they planned: getting attacked simultaneously, getting attacked individually, picking up the scent of Manilishi, picking up the scent of the Rain themselves. . . .

"No such thing as surprise," says Marlowe.

"I disagree," replies Haskell. "There's nothing but."

And thus their conversation starts up, maneuvering through inanities and amateur speculation while the one-on-one kicks back in and their real conversation deploys beneath the surface.

"What the fuck is going on?" says Marlowe.

"The Rain's somehow managed to invest primacy in the local nodes all over the city. Each one thinks it runs the whole HK zone."

"So it's irreversible?"

"For the short term, yes."

"Short term's all that's left. We've got no choice but to make the Flats. We're only five klicks out."

"Think that means anything *now*? The fact that the Rain can do this citywide means that they probably already have the Manilishi."

"We've got nothing else to go on," shoots back Marlowe. "If we can get up to the Flats, we may yet find the trail. How much control do you have in the immediate zone?"

"Enough to keep us guarded. We'll be like ghosts. Theoretically anyway."

"Real problem's the local wildlife," says Marlowe.

"No," says Haskell. "Real problem's whatever the Rain's preparing behind anarchy's screen."

"You still got the car?"

"Yeah."

"And the suits?"

"In the back."

"Hey," says Marlowe out loud. "Thanks for the drink." He stands up.

"You kids be safe," says the bartender. "It's all shades of shit out there."

"It's just getting started," says Haskell.

The door swings shut behind them.

Several hours up the Amazon amidst several lanes of traffic. The ones nearest to the shore are reserved for local boats—mostly local fishermen running out of things to fish. Civilian freight's a little farther out. Military craft take up the rest. The center's reserved for heavy cargo—mostly rocket sections and rocket engines conveyed on massive barges. And all the while lines of fire stitch their way from horizon into sky. . . .

"They're really picking up the pace," says Linehan on the one-on-one.

He and Spencer are standing on a platform adjacent to the bridge of a tramp steamer that looks like it should have been scrapped long ago. Canvas stretches above them, though both men know that all it's shielding is the sun. The two men look quite different from the two who boarded the train back in the Mountain—new faces, new skin. New IDs, too. Turns out there's still enough of an economy left in Belem-Macapa to get the basics done. Especially with Priam burning money like it's going out of style.

"No reason they shouldn't," says Spencer. "There may be no tomorrow."

"If the U.S. puts up too much hardware too quickly, they may provoke the East to strike before they reinforce their orbital positions."

"A delicate balancing act," mutters Spencer.

"The nature of the game."

Then over the roar of ships launching they hear motors close by. They look up. Two jet-copters have swept in over some kind of ramshackle settlement stretched out along the shore. People are running from the shacks, diving into the river. Flame pours in over them. All that's left of that village is a pier jutting out into the water—and smoke billowing out over the jungle. The jet-copters streak off downstream. The craft nearest shore turn toward the deeper river. Spencer shakes his head. But Linehan just laughs.

"Local public relations," he says.

"No wonder these people hate you."

"These people hate anybody who's stronger. Anyone who's not, they'll stamp bootprints on their throat."

"Sort of like the Rain did to you?"

And for a moment Spencer thinks he's gone too far—thinks that Linehan is about to throttle him or hurl him into the river or both. Spencer desperately winds up for a zone-blast at Linehan's skull. But then the larger man steps back.

"Just you wait till we get on the farside of border," he spits out. "Not only am I going to break out of whatever backstab Control's got cooked up for me—but I'll make sure to gut you while I'm doing it."

"Aren't you getting a little ahead of yourself? We haven't even turned *south* yet."

"Well," says Linehan, "how about you wake me up when we do."

He stalks back inside the ship.

The Operative sits in a room, data flitting across the screens. He's already well into several thousand deals. He's putting into motion several thousand more. He eyes the door to the room while he keeps an eye out for any hidden entrances. And when he sees

Lynx swim into view before him he's not in the least surprised.

"They say that a man doesn't know the true meaning of fear until he enters Congreve's speakeasies," says Lynx. The smile on his face is as warm as the Operative has ever seen it. "They say this is the labyrinth in which even the bravest start praying. Do you think they're right, Carson?"

The Operative doesn't reply. He's just working the data—European currencies, Martian underwrites, zero-G real estate, precious metals, drug offloads, information uploads—all of it filtered through hedge after hedge as his portfolio diversifies. The transactions he's setting in motion are fanning out in every direction. His holdings are getting ever more complex. And all the while the voice of Stefan Lynx keeps furnishing the soundtrack.

"I should have dug beneath the cellars of *this* place," it says. "I should have secreted myself behind *these* walls. I swear to you that sometimes I think that history itself comes to culmination within each room. I think that's what the ones who founded Congreve realized. They looked out upon the nothing. They broke beyond the limitations of the Earth. They saw how no sphere of activity could be excluded. Especially the ones we'd most like to forget."

The markets into which the Operative's delving are starting to move beyond the grey. Now he's setting up negotiations with several of Sarmax's more dubious contacts. A SpaceCom quartermaster eager to move a little excess inventory. An asteroid harvester looking to evade a tax or two. A Martian speculator in possession of inside information on the latest terraforming schemes...these and so many others with whom he's now engaging in all manner of business across markets both public and private and all the interstices in between.

"They labored as you labor," muses Lynx. "Free of inhibitions. Free of what the fools call morality and what the wise don't even bother to name. I've watched you, Carson. I've seen just how sleek you can be. But in the speakeasies, a man takes on new lives to the extent that he takes lives from the ones like him—the ones who try to hold the world at a distance. The ultimate rush—never knowing when one of those with whom you're dealing will get the key to the chamber in which you're sitting. The ultimate penalty: to be paid by those who would dare to commit the sin of establishing a private connection with someone who sits beyond these speakeasies. Someone who might be working for Christ knows what outfit. Someone who could advise you in real time. Who might have agendas of his own. Now on my mark, execute the following transactions—"

And it's all the Operative can do to keep up with them. Especially when those of Sarmax are coming in over another line. Lynx has hacked into the middle of the speakeasies. But Sarmax maintains a dedicated proprietary line between the room and his own residence. And the Operative's guessing that's not the only one that leads into this complex from the world that lies beyond. . . .

"But that's the beauty of this wilderness of mirrors," says Lynx. "No one's what they seem. No one's showing all their cards. Though I confess to having looked at a few hands since we got here. That one there—Copernicus insurgents. Strictly bush-league, but still, good enough to get in here. And over there—one of the more virulent strains of Imbrium mafia. They're trying to divert a couple items from a convoy or something tedious like that—but who can admit to anything save admiration for the way in which institutions adapt to the times? The ones who built this place did so when it looked like the last cold war would be the only. A time when rugged individualism was king. When the one thing that everyone could agree on was that the only *real* off-world crime was putting the brakes on commerce. Such a quaint notion. Yet those who now rule the farside of this rock found the whole setup to be the very height of convenience. How else could they co-opt the black market in a single stroke? Where else could they keep an eye upon so many? Though of course there are always those who seek to turn the tables. . . ."

The structures atop those tables are stacking ever higher. Their representations are getting ever more abstract. The time horizons with which the Operative's now playing are moot for all purposes save that of profit. The options he's hedging stretch out beyond the point where the third planet gets swallowed by expanding sun. But far closer to the present a shadow's stealing over all those fanciful projections. The markets expect war at any moment. They see the day of judgment lurking around the corner. They don't know how it's going to start. They only know that it will place all fortune in the balance. They're placing their bets accordingly.

"And therein lies the dilemma," says Lynx. "There's no scenario out there that lacks an angle. If the Coalition wins . . . well, someone has to do the collaboration. But if Uncle Sam manages to pull it off once again—you'd better believe the big guy won't emerge unscathed. Which is why the Moon is looking so good these days, Carson. The smart money says the far-side won't be touched no matter how bad a drubbing the rest of the place gets. But *I* say the smart money's forgotten about the very factor that set this whole shit train rolling in the first place. Now, on my mark, execute the following transactions—"

The Operative realizes that all of Lynx's inquiries are converging. He suddenly discerns the object that Lynx has set his heart upon. He wonders how he could have been so blind. He wonders if he's ever going to have the strength to see.

"I see you've noticed what we're after," says Lynx. "I see you're finally opening up your eyes. Which I take to be a positive sign. The careless won't survive what's coming, Carson. And the Rain will get everything they've courted. We'll take them apart, man. We'll make them wish they'd died back when they should have."

It's a rock that almost nailed the planet fifty thousand years ago. It's Near Earth Object #59789. Now it's got a relay station that beams communications to the prospectors scattered farther out. And in the middle of that station . . .

"A little piece of private zone," says Lynx. "Ingenious, no? This data-cache's been separated from all networks and shorn of all wireless nodes. Whoever put it there uploads it only by a certain set of orders to the station's robots—gets them to establish the necessary physical linkage. Talk about out of sight and out of mind. But congratulations, Carson—because one of the hundred million things you've just done was to get a ninety-nine-year lease on that dump. And a series of never-before-used loopholes in off-world property law mean that the owners aren't even aware of a new source of rent. And now, on my mark, you are going to execute the following transactions—"

And the Operative's getting in there. He's going to town. His mind's a blizzard of data and he can scarcely feel his body. He feels like he's lived all his life to be the instrument of Lynx as that man closes in on what will surely be his greatest triumph. He wonders if what Lynx is after is the Rain or merely the gateway to them. He wonders if the frenzied trades he's making on behalf of Sarmax will ever amount to anything at all.

But mostly he wonders what's going on in the unmanned recesses of the station out on the edge of deep. He pictures servants who neither see nor know their master. He pictures silent uploads occurring—pictures signals speeding back into the heart of the Earth-Moon system. He pictures Lynx's face as the transmission kicks in—

"We've done it," says Lynx.

His voice cuts out. The door to the room in which the

Operative sits opens. Two figures stand there in full armor. The weapons they're pointing at him aren't small.

"Don't move," says one.

"You're under arrest," says the other.

They're wearing light armor. They're crawling along a bridge. That bridge is meant for trains, but the trains have stopped running. Explosions keep on shaking the rails beneath them. The air's alive with screams and shots. It's been a long while since they heard any sirens.

"Picking up radiation again," says Marlowe. "Another dirty bomb."

"That makes ten in the last hour."

The fracturing of the zone has set in motion a fracturing of all else. The city's government has collapsed completely. Sensing apocalypse, the people have become a mob. Authority's become a function of what block you're standing in or who could set themselves up as local warlord. There's fighting all across the street and net.

"How much can you see in there?" says Marlowe.

"Probably got half a klick of range," she replies.

She finds it strange to see so much more in real than zone. They're almost at the top of the Owen-Stanley Range. They've almost reached Seleucus. The city stretches out below them. Smoke's rising from a number of places within it. Flames cover most of the city center.

"Not looking good," says Marlowe.

Haskell says nothing. They turn from the scene, reach the bridge's end, enter a tunnel. People are huddled along the walls. Many are wounded. Marlowe and Haskell stalk between them, conscious of the stares. But as they approach the tunnel's other end, the people on either side start to try to tell them something.

"What language is that?" says Haskell.

"Burmese," replies Marlowe. "I've done runs in South Asia."

"Can you understand what they're saying?"

"Only a few words." He's leaning forward, hands resting on thighs while he seeks to find some common ground between the languages he knows and whatever ones they might. Haskell keeps an eye on the people behind him. Marlowe switches through several Indian dialects, throws in a little Chinese, keeps his voice loud enough to engage a few more people in the dialogue without letting the whole tunnel in on the conversation.

He turns back to Haskell.

"Well," she says.

"They're refugees from Seleucus."

"And."

"They talk of fleeing their homes. They talk of an evil unleashed."

"No shit."

"No," says Marlowe. "They're quite specific. They aren't talking about the collapse of zone. They're talking about what's happened since. They say a demon rules the Flats now."

She stares at him.

"That's the word they use," he says. "They say it feeds on human souls. They're begging us not to continue."

"They've just confirmed that we go on."

"Pretty much."

"Try to learn more about this thing. Ask them what it's like."

Marlowe does. But the people on the tunnel floor are getting increasingly upset. They're getting ever louder. They're trying to shut each other up. Marlowe quiets them, turns back toward Haskell.

"They're saying that Seleucus has been sealed off. That anything living is forfeit. They're saying this thing's the devil."

"This thing's Manilishi."

"Or the Rain themselves."

"Or both."

"So let's get in there and join them."

They steal on out of the tunnel.

Ø Manaus is the largest city upriver from the sea. It's the junction of the Amazon and several feeders. It's been on a roll since Belem-Macapa took the sky's own fire. Business is booming. U.S. soldiers are everywhere. Spencer and Linehan try not to look that interested. They're busy getting one with dockland culture.

Which consists largely of bars. And drinking. Not to mention conversation that creeps slowly in toward negotiation. Control's contacts are good. Control's money is even better. Spencer does most of the talking. Linehan concentrates on looking menacing. It's an effective partnership. They initiate contacts, get referrals, make payoffs. They do their utmost to make progress without attracting attention. It's a tough balancing act. Several times they break off budding dialogue, leave venues in a hurry. Once they get jumped by locals smelling a quick mark—who live just long enough to realize their mistake.

But eventually they get out of the bars and into the back rooms. Which is where they pick up steam. Because now they're dealing with people for whom Swiss bank accounts are simply standard procedure. People for whom this transaction is just one among so many others. Terms are reached in relatively short order.

Spencer's not taking them at face value, however. One more reason they've gotten so far so quick: he's been riding shotgun on the Latin zone the whole while. About three-quarters of that zone is under lock and key. A lot of those barriers are pretty recent too. He catches virtual glimpses overhead anyway—U.S. ships on the ascent, and he knows better than to put them to a close inspection. He reserves that treatment for the networks of this underworld—and in particular with the particular outfit with whom he's dealing. He can't see everything. He'd be worried if he could. But he can see the data they've got on him and Linehan—can see that it doesn't seem to be going anywhere besides the folder that they've marked *revenue*. He can see the plan they've got for shipping south one particular cargo.

And all the while he's making other plans. Because he knows all about the intangibles that confront those who close in upon a border. He knows, too, that his reliance upon multiple suppliers isn't just a matter of contingency. It's also a question of portfolio management.

"Meaning what?" asks Linehan.

They're in another ship, hauling out of Manaus in a fast river skimmer. This time they're well below deck. They're cloistered in a cargo container. The soybeans that fill all of that container's neighbors are lined along the side of theirs in layers held in place with plastic. The resultant space contains water, food, pistols, a portable waste holder, and a conduit for oxygen. Spencer's made a couple side deals, arranged for a wire to be slotted through that conduit as well—and from there into the ship's comps. The presence of that wire makes it all the more likely that the container wouldn't survive a close inspection.

But that's just one more calculation in this numbers game.

"Let me put it this way," says Spencer. "We're not going to sit in this box and get predictable."

"So what's the next stop?"

"I'm still figuring that out."

"You're still *what?*"

"Actually, to be more precise—I haven't started."

"Then what the fuck are you waiting for?"

"Proximity," replies Spencer.

And closes his eyes.

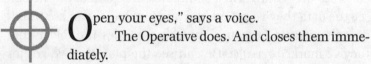

Open your eyes," says a voice.
　　　The Operative does. And closes them immediately.

"Turn off that fucking *light,*" he says.

"Don't make me ask you twice."

The Operative opens his eyes fractionally, gazes out through narrow slits. The lights are so full in his face that he can see almost nothing of the room beyond them.

"Keep them open," says the voice. And the Operative doesn't need to be told why. Retinas are just one more opportunity for the body to yield up its secrets. And as for all those others: he can feel needles buried in his flesh. His arms and legs are strapped to the chair in which he's sitting. He can't remember how he got here.

But he can guess what's going to happen next.

"Strom Carson," says the voice.

"Who's he," says the Operative.

"A traitor," replies the voice.

"Where'd you learn such a big wor—*fuck!*"

Fire's pouring through the Operative's veins. He contorts against his straps, cuts off all sound from his mouth as flame becomes freeze and burns him through with cold. Ice thrusts up through his skin. Half-melted blood dribbles from a hundred phantom wounds.

But then it all subsides.

"Strom Carson," says the voice. "Praetorian agent as-signed to the Moon. Active at Agrippa, Shackleton, and now Congreve. What have you been up to, Carson?"

"That's classified."

"We're SpaceCom intelligence, Carson. Don't talk to us about what's classified."

"Then how about telling me why I'm here."

"Treason."

"Can you be more specific?"

"Participation in the conspiracy called Autumn Rain."

"What?"

"Where's their fucking base, Carson?"

"Give me a fucking break," says the Operative. "How high up are you guys? You've apprehended a fucking *Praetorian*. We'll take you apart for this."

"The only thing that's about to get taken apart is what I'm looking at. The Throne's been getting so careless lately. So delinquent it makes me sick. No wonder all its investigations managed to get themselves rat-fucked."

"Only rat who's getting fucked is you. We know the Rain's inside you. I'm probably speaking to them even now."

"That'd be every time you look in a mirror, Carson. Who was giving you your orders?"

The Operative says nothing.

"Who's your fucking *razor*?"

The Operative's waiting for the knives to burn back to life inside him. He wonders if this is all some virtual construct. Or one of Lynx's tricks. But now a face appears before him. It's a hologram floating in the air. Oversized ears. Antique opticals. Silver hair.

And grinning mouth.

"Ever seen this man before?"

The Operative tries to look unsurprised. He tries to blank his mind.

"That's what we thought," says the voice. "We know this

is the man who was feeding you orders in the speakeasies. A real piece of work." Data starts to swirl around the Operative's head. Data speeds up. Six lines of symbols freeze amidst the myriad rush, spring in toward the Operative.

"I could explain the significance of each of those transactions to you, but we both know you already know what they mean. And if you don't, then you just won the patsy of the fucking year award. So let's just talk about the sum total of those moves. The detonation of a fission device in downtown Congreve would have wrecked everybody's day. Except, apparently, yours."

"Listen," says the Operative, "this is a setup. It's bullshit."

"Oh, it's bullshit alright. What the fuck is your problem, Carson? What in Christ's name possessed you to lift your blade against the common cause? What did the Rain offer you that was worth your turning your back on everything?"

"You may as well get back to what you were doing with my nerve endings."

"It's not going to be that simple, Carson. I'm just the warm-up act."

"Yeah?"

"We're taking you upstairs."

"To L2?"

"I said *upstairs*. I didn't say all the way to heaven. Do you think we're stupid? You're not getting *near* that fleet. One of the LunaMechs will suffice. Put you in orbit around the Moon, let you spend your last days staring down at rock while we reduce you to nothing, a brain cell at a time."

"Bringing me right down to your level," says the Operative. "I can't wait."

But the voice says nothing. The lights diminish. They leave the Operative in darkness. The seconds tick by. They start to make inroads on the minutes.

"Hello?"

But there's no answer. The Operative sits there. He

wonders if they've bagged Sarmax. He wonders if they've bagged Lynx. He wonders if either of them set him up. He wonders if he really *was* helping to bring about Congreve's melting. But mostly he just wonders when the hell something's going to happen.

The needles slide from his body. The straps around him unfold. He's unimpressed.

"You know what, guys? You're fucking boring me."

But there's no answer. The seconds tick by. The Operative pulls himself to his feet. As he does so, dim lights spring to life along the walls. A door on the one opposite opens. The Operative walks to it, goes on through.

Now he's in a corridor. Lights blink along the floor. They're running from right to left. So he turns that way, walking carefully. He has no idea what the hell's going on. But he figures he may as well make the most of it.

A door opens on the wall to his left. Simultaneously, the lights on the floor change direction, blink toward it.

So he stops. He peers carefully inside. It's a storage chamber. It's full of compartments. All are open. All are empty.

Except for the one that holds the suit.

The Operative walks in. The door slides shut. He goes to the suit. It's civilian, bereft of armaments and markings. It's open in the back. He takes the hint: climbs in, activates it. It closes in around him.

"About fucking time," says the voice of Stefan Lynx.

"What the *fuck* is going on?"

"What's going on is jailbreak. You drive, I'll navigate." The door slides open. "Make your first two lefts and make it snappy."

The Operative gets moving. He goes out the door, turns left.

"Lynx."

"Yeah."

"I've had it with this. What are you up to?"

"Telling you to shut up."

The Operative makes the next left. As he does so, Lynx gives him more directions: a right, another left, a stairway up. More passages. More stairs. He gets stopped on more than one occasion, downloads ID from out of nowhere. He arrives in a garage. He moves to the vehicle Lynx indicates, gets in, drives away into what turns out to be Congreve. A map appears on the dashboard next to him. A route traces through grids.

"Dump it in the parking lot on Sixth Avenue," says Lynx. "Leave the suit there too. Get on the blue line underhaul. Get off at Little Kensington."

"That's where Sarmax's house is."

"Exactly. That's where you're going."

"That doesn't sound very safe."

"Said the guy who's running around in a suit which may as well have STOLEN FROM MAXIMUM SECURITY spray-painted on the side. But cheer up, Carson: I've got you covered. They got you on the sting. I got them on the hack. They knew you were up to something. But they couldn't figure out what. So they just hit you with the worst possible charges. And we just beat the rap. I've switched your identity about five times in the last five minutes. And there's a lot more to talk about but it's going to have to wait till we can do it on Sarmax's private lines. I managed to cover our traces there too. Now how about you go back to shutting the fuck up."

The Operative tells Lynx to fuck himself. And says nothing more. He just lets Congreve's skyline stream past his visor. Fifteen minutes later, he's walking through the residences of Little Kensington. Five minutes after that he reaches Sarmax's door. He goes on through, takes the elevator up to the study.

To find Sarmax sitting in front of at least fifty different screens. He has his feet up. He doesn't turn around.

"Where the fuck have you been?" he asks.

"We need to talk."

"You don't know the half of it," says Leo Sarmax.

• • •

But they're starting to get the idea. They're standing in another tunnel mouth, looking out upon the plateau where the Flats begin. That plateau's so high up it's drenched in cloud. Mist is everywhere. Searchlights pierce the mist, flicker this way and that.

"Looks like a perimeter," says Marlowe.

"Sealed up pretty tight," Haskell replies. "This way's hopeless."

"Not necessarily."

"It's not those defenses I'm worried about," she says. "It's what's up *there*." She points upward, at the unseen sky. "We'll be too exposed out on that plateau. Even with the camo on our armor."

"You've got a point," he says.

"Let's double back to the last intersection."

Five minutes later they're walking down a narrow tunnel. It's only wide enough for a single rail. Five minutes farther, and they find a hole in the ceiling, along with a ladder leading up.

"Maintenance shafts," she says. "Should put us straight into Seleucus's center."

"Any sign of what's up on Seleucus's zone?" asks Marlowe.

"Looks like it's as fucked as the rest of the city."

But they're heading in toward it all the same. They climb up the ladder, head out into a warren of crawl spaces. Haskell starts to pick up more of Seleucus's zone. But what she's detecting is strange. It's as though it's been chipped away piecemeal.

"Meaning what?" asks Marlowe.

"Meaning it's been shut down altogether in some areas. Not sure why. Civil war. Bombs. Who the hell knows?"

"Only one way to find out," he replies.

He's got a laser cutter out now, is slicing through a wall. They stare at the space thus revealed.

"Looks like somebody's basement," she says.

"Let's find out if they're still home," he replies—and leads the way through discarded furniture and dust, heads up a set of stairs. They enter a living room.

A young woman sits on a couch within. Her head flicks around toward them as they enter. But she doesn't move. Doesn't really react. Just stares at them with hollow eyes, starts talking in a language they don't understand.

"Easy," says Haskell gently.

"Heat signature," says Marlowe. "Behind that couch."

"She's got children," mutters Haskell. "Talk to her, for fuck's sake."

And Marlowe does: starts looking for some common ground. Finds it fairly quickly in a dialect of Mandarin. The woman answers his questions in a voice that's nearly monotone. He translates for Haskell.

"She killed her husband. He's upstairs."

"Did you ask her why she killed him?"

"He tried to kill her."

"Ask her how come she's shut down this apartment's zone access."

"Already did. She says it was letting in demons from hell. The same demons who possessed her husband."

"I'm going to check him out." Haskell leaves Marlowe to cover the room and goes upstairs, where she finds a man sprawled in a bathroom with a carving knife stuck through his skull. Blood's everywhere. But there's enough of his head left for her to figure out what's happened. Then she reaches out into the zone: very covertly, very carefully. She finds exactly what she thought she would. She goes downstairs again.

"What's up?" asks Marlowe.

"What's up is that all the software in Seleucus got hacked. Including cranial implants."

"I've got those. So do you."

"So did her husband. He was a cop."

"So?"

"So police are almost as wired as we are. And unlike us, he wasn't shielded by a razor like me. The Manilishi took him over."

"Bullshit," says Marlowe. "Implants don't allow control."

"Looks like they do if the target's got enough of them and they're getting hacked by a next-generation AI. *This thing fucked the whole sector.*"

"You mean—"

"I mean *everything*. Household robots gutting their owners, cars running over people, toasters exploding, the fucking works. This thing we're after has gone completely batshit."

"Or maybe this is merely phase one of some master plan it's cooked up?"

"Those two aren't incompatible."

"So what now?"

"We need to get closer to it."

"We still don't know where the fuck it is," he says.

"That's why we need to get closer to it."

He stares at her. She beckons. They leave the woman and what's left of her family behind, open the apartment's front door, and walk out into a street that's both covered and deserted. Closing the door behind them, they edge their way along the street.

It gives way into a broader area, one in which grass slopes away into shadow. It's a park. Most of the lights stitched across the cavelike ceiling have been broken. Trees line the walls.

"We got movement," says Marlowe.

"I see it," says Haskell.

Up amidst those trees, three figures have started moving down the hill toward them.

"You okay?" yells Marlowe.

No answer. The figures are picking up speed. There's no expression on their faces.

"Stop or we'll shoot," screams Haskell.

Marlowe doesn't wait. He opens up, starts landing shots. But his targets aren't dropping.

"Hi-ex," says Marlowe.

"I can't," says Haskell.

But as their assailants close to less than ten meters she discovers that she can. She starts firing—adds her fusillade to Marlowe's as they knock those bodies off their feet, start knocking them to pieces. And keep on shooting. Because even without legs, arms are still crawling forward to get at them. They fire, reload, fire until all's still once more.

"Can you work with that?" says Marlowe.

"I'll have to," says Haskell.

She's staring down at the head of the man she's just shot repeatedly at point-blank range. She figures he must have been some kind of mercenary while he was still alive. He's more metal than flesh. Haskell drops a wire from her finger, slices it into his ear—and from there into his head.

And falls onto her knees, starts kissing dirt. The world tilts about her. The logic of the sector's last four hours blasts through her mind. The logic of the mind that's set it all in motion comes blasting into focus. She sees the Manilishi gazing at her. It wears the faces of those it's slaughtered. It opens empty eyes. It grins through shattered teeth.

"I'm free now," it says. *"And so are all these people."*

Haskell pulls back, pulls the wire from her finger, leaves it quivering in the lifeless skull. She remains on her knees, dry-heaving on the dirt while Marlowe stands guard about her, urges her to get to her feet.

Finally she does. She holds on to his shoulder while her strength returns.

"It's gone completely insane," she mutters.

"Where is it?"

"The Buddhist temple in the sector's center. I'm picking up an anomaly in the zone at that location."

"If you can see that, then so can the Rain."

"So much the better," she says, and sets off at a run.

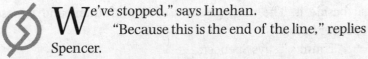 W e've stopped," says Linehan.

"Because this is the end of the line," replies Spencer.

"You mean the border?"

"Nothing so dramatic. Just that the river's too shallow for us to go any farther upstream."

"So what now?"

"We wait."

But not for long. Another twenty minutes and the container in which they're ensconced is being hauled into the air, placed on another surface. Where it sits for another ten minutes, then goes back into motion once again. Only now there are a lot more bumps.

"We're on land," says Linehan. "Going uphill."

"Fuck, you're quick."

"Have you finalized our route?"

"No such thing as final," says Spencer.

But some things come close. Because twenty minutes later they're stopping once more. They're on a slight incline. They're hearing voices. They're hearing their container being opened.

Light flows in. Faces peer at them.

"Come out," a voice says.

They do. To find themselves standing in the back of a large truck. Several men are looking at them.

"You go now," says one.

"Good," Spencer replies.

He gestures at Linehan. They take their guns, step out of the truck.

"Shit," says Linehan.

They're standing on a road that's more of a ledge. Mountains tower up above them. Valley drops away below them. The truck in which they've been riding is sitting within a grotto that leads back into the rock. Several smaller trucks sit beside it. The man gestures at one of them and tosses Spencer keys.

"Thanks," says Spencer.

He climbs into the driver's seat while Linehan gets in on the passenger side. Spencer starts the motor, eases the truck out onto the road—where he accelerates, starts taking turns with abandon.

"Okay," says Linehan, "time to tell me what the fuck's going on."

"Mountain freight," says Spencer. "That's all that's happening. That place is a licensed way station."

"This is the Andes."

"Like I said, you're quick."

"Meaning this is Jaguar country."

"Does that scare you?"

"Maybe it should."

"It shouldn't. Most of the Jag activity in the mountains is fifty or so klicks west. Right in the heart of Inca country."

"The Incas? What the fuck do *they* have to do with it?"

"What don't they? The Jaguars are what would happen if you put the Incas and Aztecs and Mayas in a blender and gave them modern tech and a bad attitude. If the Old World had kept the fuck away from the New, they'd be fine with that.

These guys think big, Linehan. They aim to put the clock back by several hundred years."

"And the Rain want to put it *forward* by at least a thousand. Where the fuck do those two find common ground?"

"In hatred of your former colleagues, Linehan. As we've discussed. By the way, we're about twenty klicks north of the border. Take a look at what's on the left."

The view goes all the way down to the Amazon plain. There are no trees, only smoke rising from a thousand fires. Then Spencer turns the truck across a bridge and it all disappears from sight.

As does so much else. The tips of the more distant mountains are no longer visible. Whiteness obscures them. As the minutes pass, that whiteness expands. It casts tendrils into sky, starts to blot out the sun.

"Looks like a storm," says Spencer.

"Right between us and border."

"Had to catch a break eventually."

They motor in toward it.

Somewhere overhead there's a moon that's getting ever fuller. Somewhere on that moon's farside there's a room where two men sit. Time was those two men were almost one. Time drove a long wedge between them.

But now things have come full circle.

"So what the fuck's going on?" asks the Operative.

"Exactly what I was going to ask you," replies Sarmax.

"I got busted by SpaceCom. But Lynx busted me out."

"And you ran straight back *here*?"

"Hey, man: he told me to."

"He being Lynx?"

"Who else?"

"Carson: anybody could be anyone right now. We should hit the exit."

"I've got no problem with that. Where to?"

"How about to where the Rain are about to launch their next strike?"

"You know where that is?"

"All I know is that you're hell on wheels in those fucking speakeasies, Carson."

"Yeah? What did I turn up?"

But as Sarmax starts to reply, a single chime cuts through the room. The two men look at each other.

"What the fuck was that?" asks the Operative.

"That would be the front door," replies Sarmax.

"You expecting anyone?"

"Given that you just came straight from a SpaceCom holding cell, maybe I should be." Sarmax stabs buttons on his consoles. He turns switches. He frowns.

"There's no one there."

"What do you mean there's no one there?"

"See for yourself."

The Operative looks at the screens. They show other upper-tier residences. They show an empty street. They show an empty doorstep.

The door chime rings again.

"Jesus," says Sarmax.

"*Someone's* there," says the Operative.

"Not necessarily. But we're clearly being fucked with. Let's check out the door."

"That may be what they want us to do."

"Do you have a gun?"

"Not anymore."

Sarmax flips him a pistol. "Get down to the entry chamber. Open the door while I cover you with the house weapons."

"The house weapons?"

"Gatling guns mounted in the ceilings."

"You didn't tell me about those."

"I don't recall you asking."

"Why don't we just open the door now and see what's what?"

"Because," says Sarmax, "if we're dealing with someone who's fucking with my system's ability to pick up visual, then we might not see who we've just let in. You get to be my eyes and ears, Carson. Unless you've got a better plan. But if you don't, I say you get the fuck down there and get that door open."

"May as well," says the Operative.

He turns, goes down the stairs with pistol in hand. He reaches the entry chamber just as the door chime rings a third time. There's a whirring from the ceiling as a heavy gun unfolds from it, swivels toward the door.

"On the count of three," says Sarmax.

"Fuck that," says the Operative. He hits manual release. The door springs open.

Stefan Lynx enters the room. The door slides shut behind him. He looks at the Operative. The Operative looks at him.

"Easy with the pistol, Carson."

"What the fuck are you doing here?"

"Things have gone from bad to worse out there, Carson. Had to get out of Agrippa while I still could."

"And you ran straight *here*?"

"I told you we needed to talk, didn't I?"

"Sure, Lynx. What do you want to talk about?"

"I thought I might start with a question."

"Shoot."

"What did you do with Sarmax's body?"

"Why do you ask?"

"Because I'm sick to death of resurrections."

But even as he says this the door to the stairway opens. Sarmax enters the room. He carries what looks like a shotgun.

"Stefan," he says. "Been a long time."

"Leo," replies Lynx. "Nice of you to join us."

"Nice of you to send an assassin to nail your old boss."

"Next time I'll send a better one."

"I don't think there's going to be a next time."

"As tough as always. But you may as well put that thing away. It's not going to solve anything."

"It's about to solve *something*," says Sarmax.

"Gentlemen," says the Operative, "you're both thinking so short-term. We need to talk about something a little more important."

"You mean like how you disobeyed a direct order?" asks Lynx.

The Operative shrugs. "It was a stupid order."

"Said the man without the facts he'd need to make that judgment."

"Alright, Stefan," says Sarmax. "Why don't you explain to us why him killing me was such a brilliant idea? We're both fucking dying to know."

"Simple: I thought there was far more chance of you throwing in your lot with the Rain than with us."

"So it had nothing to do with the fact that back in the day I told them your methods were unsound? Or that you couldn't keep your snout out of the drug trough?"

"Once I didn't have to deal with you every day, forgiveness came easy."

"But apparently not easily enough."

"*My* forgiveness isn't the issue."

"Then whose is?"

"How about the fucking Throne's? You went and fucking left, Leo. You ran out on us in our hour of need. Just when it looked like the East would prove the stronger."

"I retired, Stefan. I didn't run out on anybody."

"You lost your head over a fucking woman."

And Sarmax whips his weapon level—only to have it spin from his hands as the Operative fires in a blur of motion. The shotgun hits the wall, slides across the floor. The room's silent once more.

"Now why'd you have to go and do a thing like that," Sarmax says quietly.

"What Lynx means to say," says the Operative, "is that Indigo Velasquez was as much a victim of the Rain as anyone who died on that Elevator. Isn't that what you meant, Lynx?"

"Sure," says Lynx. "That's what I meant."

"That's what I thought. And while we're on the subject, Lynx, wouldn't you agree that a good way for Sarmax to recoup anything he might owe the Throne would be for him to hit the Rain and feed their bodies to the vacuum?"

"Sure. Of course I would. That's why I'm here."

"So why are you so intent on getting him to paint his wall with your organs?"

"He's not painting his wall with anything, Carson. I'm just trying to help us all understand where we stand."

"And where exactly would that be?"

"The attempt to screen me from the fact that you hadn't offed him was well-done. Selling me a doppelganger housenode was brilliant. But I managed to hack the line you and he rigged while I was hacking everything else. After that, it was easy to figure out what was up."

"Although by that point you no longer gave a shit."

"That's right," says Lynx. "Irony of ironies—I no longer gave a shit. Once I'd tracked Leo for long enough to figure out that he really wasn't taking orders from the Rain—the rest was academic. All that mattered was their location. At—"

"Nansen Station in the Rook Mountains," says Sarmax. "Right on the edge of farside Eurasian territory."

Lynx stares at him. "How the fuck did you figure that out?"

"Same way you did. The speakeasies."

"But you didn't—you *couldn't*—have followed me through that data. Out to that fucking asteroid and back?"

"What asteroid?"

"Right. 'What asteroid?' So how the fuck did you crack the SpaceCom conspiracy?"

"I never did," replies Sarmax.

"Then where the hell do you get off on naming Nansen Station?"

"I had about ten thousand other reasons."

"Say what?"

"Ten thousand different pieces of equipment. All sorts of shit—capacitors, chemicals, lenses, screws, nails, fucking duct tape. I'll download the entire list for you at some point when we've got time for a circle jerk. But the point isn't any one of those items. It's what it all spells in aggregation. About ten heavy laser cannons. Any one of which would be capable of lacing into our space-based hardware. Some entity is using about a hundred different front companies to ship in all the ingredients. And they couldn't have picked a better place than Nansen, given what a fucking zoo it is right now. Crime gangs looking for control, dissident miners jonesing for revolution, low-rent combines after anything as long as it racks up profit—"

"And all of it orchestrated by the faction within U.S. Space Command that's hell-bent on overthrowing the Throne and igniting war."

"And I have to admit that's news to me, Lynx."

"Well, that makes one of us. The prime mover is Anton Matthias. Third-in-command of SpaceCom intelligence. He's maintained Nansen as a black base for some time now. Which in itself is just standard procedure: co-opt local dissent by channeling it into particular locales within which elite garrisons can be covertly based and from which they can conduct clandestine sallies that nail the most dangerous players or turn them into double agents. Textbook counterinsurgency. But Matthias has been revving up those insurgents for some kind of major incident that he's going to stage-manage and pin on Eurasian infiltration. All of which gets put in a whole new light by the presence of strategic weaponry that never got burdened with those troublesome little things called serial numbers."

"Stop right there," says Sarmax. "How the fuck did you finger the Com conspiracy through the fucking *speakeasies?*"

"That's how they've been coordinating it. The lion's share of their data is maintained well outside of the Com databases—on a certain rock that Carson is already well acquainted with. They thought by putting it there they could shove it beyond the reach of anyone rooting through the SpaceCom Dumpsters. Not to mention keep it out of the hands of any of their bosses who might be less than thrilled at the prospect of a showdown with the East breaking out on their watch. Same reason why they've been assembling weapons parts outside of the Com's confines. I'm sure it all bears an uncanny resemblance to Coalition hardware anyway."

"Yeah," says the Operative, "but who's going to believe it? The Praetorians will be all over Nansen once those weapons fire. It'll become pretty clear pretty quick that the East has nothing to do with any of this."

"You sure about that? You been keeping up with current events?" Lynx looks amused. "There won't be time for any investigation worth the name before the final world war gets under way. HK is now in a state of total anarchy. Our raiding parties have clashed with those of the East at least three times in the city itself. Both sides have withdrawn all delegations from Zurich. Both fleets have put to sea. Launching sites all over Africa and South America are working around the clock to get hardware off the well's floor. All it needs now is a single spark. Which Nansen is winding up to furnish. Those cannons could nail L2. They could nail Congreve. They could take potshots at Earth. It hardly matters."

"So let me get this straight," says the Operative. "You've both come to the same conclusion for different reasons."

"Looks that way," says Lynx. Sarmax nods.

"But I can't help notice that in both of your play-by-play explanations *neither of you mentioned Autumn fucking Rain.*"

Both men shrug.

"Doesn't that bug either of you? Just a little?"

"Why should it?" says Lynx. "They're clearly pulling the strings. Matthias may or may not know that. But like I just said: it doesn't really matter."

"What you've got to understand is that you don't track the Rain, Carson." Sarmax has picked up his shotgun, is checking it for damage. "You track their proxies. You infer their existence from the shadows they cast. I don't know if they have an active presence beneath Nansen—but there's undoubtedly an active conduit. All we need to do is get in there and find it."

"That's a bit of a leap," mutters the Operative.

"At this stage of the game you either make them or you go under," says Lynx. "Besides, we know *something*'s going on there. Something that we've got to stop. You got a better plan—feel free to name it. But I say we activate the old team for one more ride."

"We already have," says Sarmax. "It was the East when last we met. Now it's the Rain."

"And our own side," says the Operative. "Do we have a plan of operations?"

"I'd like to propose one," replies Lynx.

"Let's hear it," says Sarmax.

"Well," says Lynx, "it's like this."

• • •

They're closing in on the center of the Flats, fighting their way through all manner of shit to get there. They've figured out how to get the edge on everything that moves. And whatever doesn't no longer matters.

It's tearing Haskell's soul to pieces all the same. She doesn't know how the Manilishi was programmed. She has no idea what was in its file. All she knows is that when AIs go rogue they often decide they're a damn sight better than the flesh that created them. And when such AIs possess emotional circuits as well, things can get ugly fast.

Things in Seleucus have gotten about as ugly as they can get. The Manilishi has sealed the borders of the sector and turned the infrastructure against the inhabitants. It gained control of those inhabitants who possessed software in abundance, set them up as their neighbors' executioners.

And the rest of the city could give two shits.

"They've all got bigger fish to fry," says Marlowe.

"What have we unleashed?" says Haskell.

They're standing on the edge of a market arcade, looking down on more bodies. Some have been run over by out-of-control vehicles. Some have been shot. People lie locked together where they've fallen. Some have driven knives into their own hearts.

"I'd have done the same," she says.

"I wouldn't," says Marlowe. "I'd have fought."

"Against what?"

"Everything."

"You wouldn't have stood a chance, Jason. Your own software would have betrayed you. You'd have had no warning before your eyes melted or your chest blew out. That's what would happen if I weren't here to shield us."

"I'd have fought," he repeats.

They're halfway though the arcade when more of the

damned break cover. One household robot and two people too
wired for their own good. One of the latter's already wounded—
she drags behind while the others race in, get shot down.
Marlowe and Haskell turn their guns upon the woman.

"Stop," screams Haskell.

"Save your breath," says Marlowe.

He fires, smashing the woman off her feet. She falls on her
back, legs kicking. They move past her thrashing flesh. They
move out of the arcade and cross through more corridors.
They shortcut through empty residences, walk past scenes
where whole families have tortured each other to death.
Haskell tries to tune it all out. She figures she's more likely to
live longer if she can.

"How much farther?" asks Marlowe.

"We're almost there."

They've come out onto an enclosed street at the end of
which is the temple. The roof above it is the epitome of ornate.
The gates on either side lie open. No bodies are in evidence
now.

"That's where it is," says Haskell.

"So now what? We just walk in?"

"It knows we're here. We know it's there. Why the hell
not?"

They stride between the open gates and into the temple.
The corridors within are bereft of light. There's no electricity.
There's no zone either, though it was there a moment ago.
And it's still live outside the temple. Haskell can see it dimly,
like light through some distant prism. Which can only mean
they've entered the Manilishi's domain. They're right on top
of what they're seeking. They turn a corner and find themselves approaching walls lined with candles.

Something suddenly comes alive in the zone all around
them. Haskell feels it enveloping them: she feints, buys herself
a moment, reconstitutes her and Marlowe's shields as the vise

closes. She gets in under its guard, turns it back. The inner sanctum of the temple lies straight ahead.

"That's where it is," she says on the one-to-one.

"Ten meters," he replies.

They reach the end of the corridor. They reach a doorway. Marlowe hurls a concussion bomb inside. It practically takes out their eardrums.

They rush within.

Ø They're making all the haste the terrain will allow them. Which isn't much. Linehan's gazing down thousands of meters. Spencer's right up against the side of mountain. The whiteness encloses them on virtually all sides now. They can't see the top of any of the mountains.

"It's almost on us," says Linehan.

Spencer doesn't reply. He's maneuvering along a road so narrow it can barely contain his wheels. He's starting to wonder if he made a wrong turn—if he's going to have to go through this in reverse too. He rounds another corner.

Only to find that the road forks. One route continues along the mountainside. The other follows an outcropping that juts into the valley below—and continues across that valley in the form of a very unstable-looking bridge that ends in a tunnel. Spencer starts heading for it.

"You sure about this?" says Linehan.

"Not even vaguely."

"That thing is made of fucking *rope*."

"If you want to get out and lighten the load, feel free."

The truck dips alarmingly as it trundles down the bridge—shifts gears as it powers its way up the other side and into the tunnel. Spencer switches on the headlights while they traverse its length—and then they emerge onto the other side and onto another bridge. Only this one's a little more stable. It ends in another tunnel. As they emerge from that tunnel and onto yet another bridge snow flurries start to swirl around them.

Two bridges later and the flurries are trending toward near-total white. They creep along another mountainside.

"Glad we found that fork before this hit," says Spencer.

"We've almost reached the unoccupied territories," says Linehan. "The border's ten klicks away. Shouldn't we be talking strategy?"

"What's there to talk about?"

"I'm figuring we're not just going to show passports and get waved across."

"We don't have passports, Linehan. Hate to break it to you, but all we are now is Andean peasants. One of the few forms of life remaining that's not keyed to IDs in some database."

"Database be damned," snarls Linehan. "They don't need databases when they have all of space to watch you. Every road that leads south is scanned, and you know it. So how are we going to get across that border?"

"We're going to start," says Spencer, "by not falling off a fucking cliff. Get out and walk ahead of me."

"What?"

"At least that way I'll be able to see *something*."

Linehan opens the door, practically disappears into the white—and then his bulk reappears in front of the truck. He trudges forward. Spencer trundles after him, lets the map of this section of the mountains unfold in his head. The map's the aggregation of more payoffs than he ever thought he'd have to make. And knowing what map he'd need was the aggregation of even more.

They enter another tunnel. This one's a little wider than the ones to which they've become accustomed. Spencer's watching the odometer, marking distance. He starts up the one-on-one again.

"Get back in here."

Linehan stops, sidesteps the truck as it rolls past him, opens the door, swings inside. Spencer drives for another twenty seconds, then swings the truck in toward the tunnel wall, brakes to a halt. Linehan looks at him.

"What now?"

"Now we walk."

"And leave the truck?"

"Unless you feel like dragging it. Someone will be along to collect it. It'll look like we just took shelter in here." He gets out and Linehan follows him. They trudge along the tunnel.

"None of this makes any sense," says Linehan.

"So much the better," replies Spencer. He's been counting off steps. Now he stops at a certain point and starts tapping on the wall. He presses a particular ledge in a certain way and a section of the wall slides away.

"Those look like stairs," says Linehan.

"They do more than just look."

They start to descend into the root of the mountain.

The mountains passing beneath the shuttle are as remote as any in this part of the solar system. The Operative watches from the window as they reel by. It's been an hour since they left Congreve. It's been half an hour since they got into the thick of these mountains. They're starting their final approach into Nansen. The Operative sees lights scattered on adjacent hills. He catches a quick glimpse of gun-studded domes. He watches a rail yard spread out beneath them, then disappear as they sail past it. The shuttle turns sharply: all the Operative can see is a rocky slope that looks to be the final resting place for shuttles whose pilots get a little too careless as they make their landing. The slope gives way to a massive platform. The shuttle settles down upon it.

"Check seals," says a voice.

But everybody already has. And even as the shuttle powers down, its doors are opening and suited SpaceCom marines are piling through them. The Operative gets in on that crush. The platform onto which they're all emerging juts out of a larger hangar that's cut into the mountainside. The lights atop the mountain's summit are dimly visible far above. And yet even this platform's far higher than most of the mountaintops around it. It makes for quite a view.

"Don't just stand there," says the voice.

The squad forms up behind the sergeant, moves in casual formation into the hangar. Small craft are everywhere—on the floors, hanging from the ceiling, along the walls. Mechanics are working many of them over. Adorning the entirety of the far wall are the moon and eagle that comprise the SpaceCom insignia.

"Move it," says the voice.

They're making their way into the cages of freight elevators set beneath that insignia. Grilled doors slide shut. The Operative counts levels as they descend. He sees in his mind's eye his position within the mountain.

The elevator stops and the marines head out the open doors, transition through an airlock. But no sooner has he stepped past that airlock than the Operative finds the squad's sergeant standing in his way.

"You," he says.

"Sir," says the Operative.

"You're wanted in level control."

"At once, sir."

The Operative proceeds through several barracks, moves through the corridors beyond them. Marines challenge him on more than one occasion but he somehow finds that he's always got the requisite IDs. Finally he arrives at a door that's at the end of one of the farther corridors. Guns mounted in the wall around it triangulate on him. A voice challenges him.

But then the door opens.

And shuts behind the Operative as he goes through into a room that's lined along three walls by consoles. A fourth wall is sliced through by a window that seems to look down upon the level below. Three persons are in that room. None wear suits. All are officers. They regard the suited Operative. They look puzzled.

"How the fuck did you get in?" asks one.

"Orders, sir," replies the Operative. "Here's my clearance."

A gas bereft of color and smell sprays from valves set along his shoulders. The men convulse. The Operative puts a bullet in the back of each of their heads for good measure. He goes to work on the comps. He enters the codes.

"Proceed to Elevator H3," says the voice of Stefan Lynx.

The Operative says nothing. For a moment he looks out the window—the room is set almost at the ceiling of a massive cavern whose floor is a chaos of rails, digging equipment, and tunnels. He turns back to the consoles, types more keystrokes. He hits execute. The door slides open. He goes through, proceeds from there to what's designated as H3 on the map in his head. A suited marine stands before the elevator door. The Operative flashes clearance.

"What's that supposed to mean?" says the soldier.

"It means I get to use this elevator," replies the Operative.

"This elevator's restricted to the brass."

"I got a battlefield promotion," says the Operative and suddenly pivots forward, plunging a knife into the man's visor. All of the myriad tiny blades that comprise that knife are whirring at high velocity as they sear through visor, skull, helmet, and the elevator door behind. The man jerks as his blood streams down the Operative's arm; the Operative's arm jerks with him. He pulls the knife out, lets the suited figure flop onto the floor, drags the body into a nearby storeroom. He enters the elevator and the door shuts behind him.

As the elevator trundles downward, the Operative's thinking furiously. He knows that Lynx and Sarmax have either entered the base by now or the entire mission's blown. He has no idea how they were planning to gain entry. He's not supposed to know. He's the spearhead of the entire operation—with Sarmax acting both as handler and second mech and Lynx providing tactical coordination and on-the-spot zone coverage. To have razor, mech, and handler in physical proximity on the same run is highly unusual. But the team now hitting Nansen never had much patience for procedure. It's been many years since they did the runs together. Yet somehow it seems like no time has passed at all.

The elevator stops. The doors open. The Operative emerges, moves down the corridor thus revealed, cycles through another airlock. He encounters more marines, but no one challenges him. He hears Lynx's voice once more.

"Change up," it says. "Alter route as follows."

The Operative tries to envision Lynx's calculations. The garrison of the Third Marines has set up three levels of defense. The Operative breached the outer perimeter when he landed. He snuck through the inner perimeter by way of Elevator H3. Now he's down in the core of the operations. All that's left to hit is the inner enclave. And Lynx is making last-second changes to better enable its penetration.

The Operative reaches another doorway. He looks out on a large cave that looks to be an offshoot of the cavern he glimpsed from the control room. Steps lead down from the door in which he's standing to a floor where walkway crosses rails. The Operative heads down to the walkway, crosses toward a train that's moving silently in toward him—but he stops as it picks up steam. He lets it rumble by, beholds scores of suited miners staring down at him. He stares up at their visored faces—watches as those faces give way to equipment and cargo and finally to nothing. Tail-lights flicker red as the train moves farther down that tunnel.

The Operative's already moving—over rails that are still quivering with vibration and through a doorway cut into the far wall. He goes through another airlock. Scarcely has he come out its other side than lights begin to flash. A siren starts up. The voice of Stefan Lynx echoes in his helmet once again.

"We're rumbled. Kill everything you see and don't stop killing until we've won."

The Operative hits his suit's thrusters.

The inner sanctum of the Kanheri Temple of Great Peace is vacant save for an altar. The banners hung from the ceiling have been torn by the blast that's just rocked the chamber.

"Where the fuck is it?" yells Marlowe. He's got his guns out.

"I don't fucking know," screams Haskell. She opens up on the altar, destroys it in a barrage of explosive rounds. In the zone she catches a glimpse of some presence receding.

"It's running," she says.

"Then so are we."

They start to race down the corridor. They leap bodies, sprint around corners. They charge through what's left of the temple. Even now they don't lose their formation. They're on guard against the oldest gambit of them all—when the hunted doubles back on hunter. So Marlowe leads and Haskell covers him, covers the zone too. She can see nothing at all. But she knows full well that something's there. Something that's gone lights out and hell for leather. Something that couldn't be that far ahead of them...

"We're out of the temple now," says Marlowe.

"Some kind of back entrance," confirms Haskell.

One that's sloping down. They're dropping well below the level of the Seleucus Flats now.

"Are you sure this is the way it went?" asks Marlowe.

"It's right ahead of us," she says.

She can't see it on the zone. But she knows it's right there. She fires on long-range. Tracers streak past Marlowe, explode in the depths of the tunnel. The walls around them shake.

"Easy," says Marlowe.

"Goddamn it," mutters Haskell.

She keeps expecting to stumble upon its smoking wreckage, keeps waiting for it to leap from the very rock around them. But it's not going out easy. She knows it's got special powers. But as to how those manifest in tactical combat situations, she can only guess. She detects a heat signature farther down the tunnel. It's moving away quickly.

"Thrusters," says Haskell.

"Must be," replies Marlowe.

They ignite their own, give chase. If they're heading into a trap, they could be in a precarious position. But they've got no choice. They're ready for anything. But nothing moves save the shadows cast by their own flames. The heat signature in front of them is very faint. As is the zone presence. They're pursuing it as fast as they dare.

"Where the fuck are we?" says Marlowe.

"Well below the Flats now," she replies.

Somewhere in the depths of the rest of city. And now that city's all around her, writhing amidst the distortions of its zone: reports of what's going on in Seleucus mixed in with plagues now loose in the central sectors shot through with fevered rants about Armageddon and impending war and how the last days are now upon us. She catches glimpses of nightclubs where the youth of HK dance themselves into an oblivion thrust upon them far too early. She sees mobs in full riot—watches as explosions blast across them, drop them in their tracks. She overloads herself on all those images. She keeps rushing deeper, keeps urging Marlowe forward.

Finally the route they're traversing starts taking them beyond the city's confines. The city's sounds are starting to fade on all their screens. They're approaching sea level and still they've seen no other way out of this tunnel.

"Some escape route," says Marlowe.

"I'm not sure what I'd call this," replies Haskell.

They're accelerating. By Haskell's reckoning they're out beyond the coastline now. Ocean lies above them. They keep on questing forward, leaving the shore behind.

But they turn off their thrusters when a door comes into sight. They move carefully toward it. As Marlowe presses up against one side, Haskell covers him. Marlowe pivots, opens the door.

"Interesting," he says.

They're looking at a corridor that's filled with equipment: ladders, metal pipes. As they move into the corridor, they notice that the door through which they've come is invisible from this side. They hear a rumbling somewhere up ahead.

"The geothermals," says Haskell.

"Must be," breathes Marlowe.

They creep into the infrastructure that harnesses the product of the friction of the fault lines off New Guinea. They're proceeding very carefully now. Any heat would just get lost in the shuffle down here. What they're looking for could be anywhere.

But Haskell picks it up on the zone all the same. It's moving in toward the farside of the complex. If it had any sense, it would have severed all access with the zone altogether at some point during the pursuit. Unless it's arrogant enough to believe it can't be tracked. Or it's sowing a false trail. Or . . .

"It wants us to follow," she says.

"You hadn't figured that out yet."

"What choice do we have?"

"What choice indeed?"

"It's speeding up."

It's moving out beyond the complex. She has no idea where it's going, but can see quite clearly that it's picking up the pace. And now she and Marlowe are doing the same—racing through the machinery that's busy feeding power to all the chaos now raging far behind. The place isn't small. It takes them almost ten minutes to get to the farside—and another five minutes to find the hole in the back of the disused chamber that leads...

"Due north," says Haskell. "Straight out to sea."

"Let's do it," says Marlowe.

They proceed down the new tunnel, firing their thrusters intermittently. But mostly they're just walking now. The tunnel around them is starting to change. Metal replaces stone. Plastic replaces metal. They transition into a corridor once more.

Only this one's different. It's much more cramped. They can hear the hum of a power source around them. And soon they can discern insignias on the walls and ceiling.

"Do you recognize those?" asks Haskell.

"Indian military," replies Marlowe.

"Indian?"

"Why not? They used to own this."

Back when India mattered. Back before the Coalition crushed her. Long time gone now—even though she used to have such reach. Several kilometers off the coast of New Guinea: that's where one of her limbs got severed. That's where one lies forgotten.

"What are we *in?*" mutters Haskell.

"Legacy," replies Marlowe. "The Indian Republic maintained mobile underwater fortresses. Like any naval power. Apparently one got buried off the coast of New Guinea. And here we are."

"And here's where the Manilishi's waiting for us," says Haskell.

"Along with its masters," he replies.

She nods. They keep moving.

The stairs end in a tunnel. They start making haste along it, moving due south now. They advance through into what looks to be a natural cave, transition back into another tunnel. Their lights play along the walls, ceiling.

"This should take us beyond the border," says Spencer.

"This being what?"

"These are smugglers' tunnels."

"Yeah? Smuggling what?"

"Mostly drugs. But sometimes humans."

"And you hooked up with these guys how?"

"Bit of a six degrees of separation thing," says Spencer.

"Yeah?"

"Yeah. The border's honeycombed with this shit. Some of it was dug during the wars across the last thirty years. Some of it's much older. Some of it was here all along."

"And the Americans don't know about this?"

"They know that this kind of stuff goes on, sure. Tunnels under borders aren't exactly new. But they haven't found them all. They're concentrating on the ones they've linked to Jaguar activity. As for the others: a little bit of merchandise, a little bit of traffic—who cares? Border units don't exactly command top-drawer salaries. Sometimes everybody can win."

"Do you think we're winning now, Spencer?"

"We will be if we can make it another four fucking kilometers."

But now the passage intersects with another one that's

set against it at a right angle. Spencer looks left, then right. Then at the wall in front of them.

"What's wrong?" asks Linehan.

"What's wrong is that this isn't supposed to be here. We were supposed to go straight on through. There's not supposed to be an intersection here."

"Looks like you've been misinformed."

"We're turning left."

"Have it your way."

They turn left. Another quarter-klick and the passage grows wider. It seems noticeably older. The ceiling seems to have some kind of glaze on it. Carvings start to appear on the walls—abstract shapes and patterns. The passage bends south again.

"Guess this was the right choice," says Spencer.

The tunnel grows even wider. The carvings are starting to become noticeably less abstract. They're stylized animals: llamas, birds, crocodiles.

"This doesn't look modern," says Linehan.

"Evidently not," replies Spencer.

The passage widens still farther, broadens out into a gallery. A massive pedestal sits on the far end. Two massive chairs sit atop that pedestal. Stone figures sit within those chairs. The walls and ceiling are alive with images—animals bearing swords, humans wearing headdresses, stars emitting radiance. . . .

"I don't see a way out of here," says Spencer.

"Maybe behind the thrones," replies Linehan.

They move in toward them. They eye the figures atop them. They realize something.

"Those are *cats*," says Linehan.

"They're jaguars," mutters Spencer.

"This was the wrong turn."

"Stay calm," says Spencer.

"I am calm."

"You don't sound it."

"You've set me up. You've fucked us both."

"It's just fucking *stone*," says Spencer.

"Flesh too," says a voice.

It's coming from the ceiling. They raise their guns toward it.

"Those won't help you," says the voice.

They start putting rounds into the ceiling. But even as they do there's a flash from somewhere behind them. Something smashes into Linehan. For a moment his whole body seems to light up. Sparks chase themselves across him. He pitches to the ground. Spencer stares at Linehan's twitching body.

And drops his weapon.

"A wise choice," says the voice. "Turn around."

Spencer turns. Silhouettes suddenly start to materialize at the gallery's entrance—camouflaged armor losing the hues of the terrain against which it's set. Spencer stares at the four power-suits that are now advancing toward him—stares, too, at the green cat-skull painted on the side of each helmet.

"The Jaguars," he says.

"Your death," says the voice.

But the oblivion into which the next blow propels him doesn't last nearly long enough.

The Operative blasts down the corridor, throwing all caution to the wind. He rounds a corner, sees a door up ahead—sends rockets from his shoulders roaring in to make contact. There's an explosion. The door disappears. The Operative charges into the checkpoint within to find those who'd been manning that post smeared along the walls. He roars on through into the larger room beyond it. The marines within are clearly having trouble with their suits. The Operative doesn't need to guess why: he weaves through them, tosses a charge onto the chamber's ceiling, keeps going—gets another five seconds down a new hall before the room that he's just left erupts. He speeds up, rounds a corner—sees massive blast doors sliding shut at the corridor's other end. He accelerates toward them, starts firing. But even as he does, the doors stop moving—they come to a halt and he hurtles straight in between them, careens into the two marines on the other side, knocks them sprawling against the walls, riddles them at point-blank range.

The doors slam shut behind him. The screens on his heads-up show him that he's almost reached the inner enclave. The sirens have ceased. There's an explosion somewhere close at hand. The corridor around him shakes.

"Cauterize," says Lynx's voice.

The Operative cuts off wireless access. Lynx can no longer reach him. Neither can anybody else. Lynx has just given the razor's signal that he's in danger of imminent capture. If that occurs, the mech is toast unless all connections have been severed. The Operative knows that if Sarmax is still alive, he's received a similar missive. He knows that the whole thing's hanging by a thread. He crosses through rooms full of laboratory equipment, charges through a large chamber where mining engines and drills lie disassembled. He heads on through into another corridor. He rounds another corner.

And comes face-to-face with Sarmax.

And almost shoots him. Almost gets shot himself. Sarmax waves his hands frantically. They establish the one-on-one.

"Lynx is down," says Sarmax. "Matthias is here. Let's take him."

The Operative nods. Both men ignite their thrusters. They keep on fighting their way forward. They keep on carrying all before them. Lynx's real-time adjustments have affected thrusts into the inner enclave in two places, followed by a linkup. Only problem is that Lynx himself has been cut out of the picture. And the base's defenses are starting to come back online. Doors start to shut in their face. Guns start to pop out of the walls. Floors open up beneath their feet.

But the two men keep on moving toward the enclave. Not the false one that the place shows on its schematics. The real one that Lynx's hacking has found. They cut their way through the adjacent chambers—through a room in which they catch marines frantically setting up heavy weapons, through a door so thick that the charge they use almost brings down the roof: through obstacle after obstacle until the Operative's mind is a blur of noise and flame and reflex and there's nothing in the universe save him and Sarmax and the ones they're killing. They're splitting up now for the final assault. The Operative is coming in the front door while Sarmax moves in from a side corridor. It's going like clockwork.

And then an explosion tosses the Operative like a doll into the air. Another follows—so powerful it rips through several adjacent corridors. Walls tear like tissue paper even as the Operative strikes what's left of them. He smells his own flesh burning. He can't see Sarmax anywhere. All he can see is marines swarming in toward him from every direction. He opens fire on them. Something sears in toward him.

His world goes dark.

Light's everywhere. Wavelengths bombard them from all directions on all spectrums. Their suits are being scrambled. Their systems are going haywire. They can't see a thing.

"Show yourself," screams Haskell.

"We're right here," replies a woman's voice.

Haskell feels something slam against her. She totters.

Something stabs her through her suit. She topples. She feels her body going numb. She's being lifted off her feet. She's murmuring curses. Her helmet's being pulled off. Someone's hands touch her forehead. Someone's lips kiss her on the cheek.

"Christ we've missed you," says that voice.

Memory crashes down upon her.

PART IV
CONFLAGRATION AND RAIN

"Of course," says a voice, "you couldn't win."

Claire Haskell opens her eyes. She's sitting in the corner of a small room. It's empty except for her. And Morat.

He's sitting cross-legged against the room's only door. He looks totally undamaged. His new head's smiling.

"You couldn't win," he repeats. "Then again: you couldn't lose. You were fighting your own kind. You were fighting your own nature. But don't be too hard on yourself. You weren't to know. And now the time for fighting's over."

Haskell exhales slowly. "So the Manilishi was bullshit?"

"Not bullshit," replies Morat. "A useful fiction."

"And the Rain?"

"Conceived by Matthew Sinclair shortly after he was appointed by President Andrew Harrison to head up Counter-Intelligence Command. Shortly after Harrison took power as the first president under the Reformed Constitution. The first and last, Claire. Because tonight he's going down. And his Throne is going under."

She stares at him.

"Autumn Rain," he repeats. "Conceived by Sinclair and green-lighted by Harrison as the ultimate hit team. Engineered assassins who would be unstoppable. Who would decapitate the Eurasian high command in the first minutes of the next war. Who were bred in the same vat and trained together from birth. Who included among their members a woman called Claire Haskell. And a man called Jason Marlowe."

"You bastard."

"I won't deny that."

"Where is he?"

"You mean Jason?"

"Yes, damn you!"

"He's fine."

"Where is he?"

Morat smiles. A screen appears to the side of the door. It shows a room identical to this one. Marlowe's sitting in one corner. His eyes are open. His expression's blank.

"What the fuck have you done with him?" says Haskell.

"The same thing we've done with you," replies Morat. "Restored his memories."

"He looks like he's lost his fucking mind."

"Don't you feel the same way?"

"Fuck you," she says. "Tell me about the others." The ones she didn't even know she'd forgotten. The ones who are making her realize just how much she's lost . . .

"They were marked for death by the president himself. Written off as too great a risk. They got wind of it, chose the path of Lucifer. But the Throne beat them to the punch. And the Praetorians slaughtered them."

"But failed to finish the job."

"Indeed. Those who escaped went underground. Where they devised a second coming. A whole new plan."

"That plan being?"

"You already know it."

"Oh Christ," she says. "Oh no. Fuck you."

"You shouldn't hate me, Claire. Once I was the envoy who called himself Morat. Now all I am is your humble servant."

"You mean the Rain's."

"They've waited for you for so long," says Morat. "It's time you went to join them."

"I can't," she whispers.

"You must," he replies. "Find in yourself that strength."

He stands up even as the door behind him slides open.

The door of Spencer's mind has been ripped from its hinges. They administered the drug they call ayahuasca about an hour ago. They've cut him off from zone. Now he's locked in a room beneath the Andes even as all other locks are withering.

"Fuck," he says.

Nothing happens. Everything convulses. He feels like he's being thrust straight through the center of the Earth and clean out the other side. He feels himself catapult out into the universe. The pressure on his chest is growing unbearable. His eyes are like crystals frozen in some everlasting ice.

"Ah *fuck*," he says.

The walls of his cell are shimmering. His chains are disappearing. That pressure's vanishing. Suddenly there's nothing holding him in place. He can get up. He can stand up. He can flee.

So he does. He moves toward the wall. It seems solid. But he's not fooled. He can trace a route straight through it. He starts to move out into the living rock.

"Going somewhere?" says a voice.

He doesn't even need to turn. He can see everything. The

door to his cell has opened to the corridor beyond. Two Jaguar soldiers stand there. Neither wears armor. Both are heavily armed.

"Maybe," he replies.

"We've got something for you far better than that wall," says one of them. The man speaks neither English nor Spanish. But somehow Spencer understands every word anyway. He turns around.

"What are you talking about?"

"A gateway."

He lets them lead him down that corridor.

The Operative sits in a room. Darkness sits within him. He can't believe he's been taken prisoner twice in the same mission. By the same outfit too. Now he's somewhere in the heart of Nansen. In a loose-fitting grey outfit. There's no sign of his armor. He doesn't know how much time has passed. He's not even sure he cares.

A screen's descending from the ceiling of his cell. It unfolds before him.

A face appears upon it.

And now we're all here," says Morat. Ten meters down the corridor from the room in which Haskell awoke: Morat's just opened the door to another room. Haskell looks inside. Marlowe looks up at her. He smiles weakly.

"Claire," he says.

She steps within, steps to him. Sits down next to him. Puts her arm around him. Lets her head rest on his shoulder. Tries to talk on wireless.

But can't.

"As I'm sure you're figuring out," says Morat, "we've disabled those of your neural links that enable dialogue. Though even if we hadn't, it wouldn't matter. Each of you knows the same as the other."

Haskell ignores him. She kisses Marlowe on the cheek. "How do you feel?" she asks.

"Like shit," he says.

"Makes two of us."

"I remember them *all*," he says. "All of them. Iskander and Indigo and Roz and Nils and Miranda and—"

"I know," she whispers. "I know." She looks at Morat. "Which of them are still alive?"

"They haven't told me," replies Morat.

"You're lying," says Haskell.

"It's not like *I* need to know."

"Well, who's in this base besides us?"

"Some very impatient people."

"Let them wait a few minutes longer," she says.

"I want to see them," says Marlowe.

"You're right," replies Haskell. She stands up. "We have to face this."

Spencer's being dragged up step after step. What looks like jungle's far beneath. What looks like sky is far overhead. It looks like this is some kind of simulation. Because as far as he knows he's still deep underground. The walls around him must be screens. Or else this is all virtual reality. Or the drugs. It scarcely matters. It's the realest thing he's ever seen. A sliver of Moon's stretched amidst the clouds. He's reaching the pyramid's roof.

Torches burn at all its corners. Men wearing headdresses stand at intervals along its edges. Spencer's hauled past them to the raised dais at the roof's center. An altar rests upon that dais.

As does a throne. A man's seated upon it. Linehan lies prostrate in chains before him. The man who's been dragging Spencer throws him down.

"Gaze upon the Great Cat," he says.

Spencer raises his head to look at the man on the throne. He wears a jaguar skin. Its arms drape down his shoulders. A face stares from between its jaws. A smile slowly appears upon that face.

"So now the one who calls himself Lyle Spencer comes before us," says the man. "His people are about to perish utterly. They need one who can reach the afterlife before them. One who can bear witness."

"Who are you?" says Spencer. A guard brings a boot down on his back.

"No," says the man sharply. "Let him converse freely. The sky's own finger penetrates his brain. We grant him the privilege of discourse."

"You're not getting a thing out of me," says Spencer.

"Nor do I need to," says the man.

In the bunkers beneath Nansen there's a room. In that room a man's gazing at a screen. The man upon that screen wears the insignia of a SpaceCom general. He looks like he's lived life too long beyond the bounds of gravity. His face is sunken. What's left of his hair is almost white.

"I'm Anton Matthias," says the man.

The Operative looks at him. "Yeah?"

"You're the Praetorian who caused us so much trouble."

"And you're the traitor who's still causing it."

"That's one way to look at it," says Matthias.

"You got another?"

"The real traitor's the Throne," says Matthias. "For thinking that he could do a deal with the East. For succumbing to the poison called détente."

"And for daring to purge the poison within Space Command?"

But Matthias only laughs.

"Why the fuck am I still alive?" asks the Operative.

"What if I said it was because I can still use you?"

"I'd say you're full of shit. I serve the Throne."

"Carson: in about ten minutes there's not going to *be* a Throne. You're one of the best agents operational. We're going to have need of people like you in the days to come."

"That makes no sense. If you had any sense, you'd kill me now. Seriously—why are you keeping me alive?"

"Why don't you take me at face value?"

"What happened to the rest of my team?"

"They sold you down the river."

The control center of SeaMech #58 of the late Indian Republic is a large circular room. The central floor of that room is sunken. The walls of that lowered chamber are lined with darkened screens. Morat walks Haskell and Marlowe to the top of the steps, sits cross-legged there while they walk down toward the bottom.

Two figures stand there. A woman and a man. Haskell remembers both of them. She wants to cry. But instead she just stops at the foot of the steps.

Marlowe doesn't. He keeps going, embraces them both. Both are weeping. Marlowe turns back toward Haskell. She can see he's shaking.

So is she.

"Oh fuck," she whispers.

"Yes," says the woman. "It's us."

"I've missed you both so much," Haskell mumbles. Her knees feel weak beneath her. Her eyes burn as she blinks back tears. She feels the past swinging in upon her—long-ago days of sunlight, nights set adrift upon the wash of time. She feels her heart overflowing: reeling at those memories awoken, seeing that flesh brought back to life before her. . . .

"You never left our hearts," says the woman.

"But we lost you all the same," says the man.

"You're the ones who're lost," says Haskell. They gaze at her. They don't say anything. "You—you killed thousands when you blew that Elevator. You've turned this city into a fucking slaughterhouse."

"Claire," says Marlowe. "Wait a second."

She looks at him.

"I think we need to hear their reason *why*," he says.

"Whose side are you on?" she asks.

He looks confused. "Yours," he replies.

"By definition," says Morat. "He's in love with you."

She whirls then, practically spits up toward Morat's face: "You *prick*! Stop fucking with our heads!"

"Morat answers to us," says the man. "And as for you and Jason: we'd never tamper with our own. All we've done is remind you of what really happened."

"Yeah?" Haskell looks scornful. "Seems like everybody's got their own version of that."

"Meaning *what*?" asks Marlowe.

"Meaning how the fuck are we supposed to know the latest thing to hit our heads is real! Jesus fucking Christ, Jason. We've been skullfucked again and again and again and now you want to say this is fucking *different*?"

"Of course it's different," says Marlowe. "It really happened."

"So let them prove it!"

"Trust your heart," says the woman. "You're one of us. We wouldn't have brought you here if you weren't."

Haskell looks at her. Her hair's dirty blond. Strands of it hang across her face. But she still looks all too like the child that Haskell remembers.

"You used to wear your hair so short," says Haskell. Her voice catches. She can barely hold back the tears now.

"Times change, Claire."

"And now you're massacring city sectors."

"You had to be convinced you were dealing with a rogue AI. Believe me, we could have done far worse."

"So it's you who's in charge of this?"

"We're all in charge, Claire. What we've done in HK, what we did to that Elevator, what we're about to do to the world: the responsibility is ours."

"I'll say," says Haskell.

"We *had* to seize it," says the man. "It was either that or keep on running from people who had bred us to kill only to decide it was us who needed killing."

"You're part of this," says the woman. "Don't deny it. We're back from the dead. And now we're going to show the world a whole new way to *fight*."

"So watch the dance of the puppets," says Morat.

The screens light up all along the walls.

Time on the edge of nothing. Time to churn up shapes that flit through shadow. Time since they dosed you: more than eighty minutes. Time you started seeing . . .

"You gaze upon Paynal, Spencer. The living incarnation of the lightning. The messenger of the Hummingbird that men call Huitzilopochtli and that your people will know as the instrument of their destruction."

"Fuck," says Linehan suddenly. He's laughing like a crazy man. He's laughing like he's on the ayahuasca too. "Listen cat-man: this man works for a low-rent gang of data thieves called Priam. Bunch of mercenaries looking to make a buck. He's got nothing to do with anything you're talking about."

"But he does," says Paynal. "Has the little death granted you no insight? This man you call Spencer works for the ones you call Information Command. The handler you call Control works for Stephanie Montrose. Who reports directly to that monstrosity you call your Throne."

Linehan stares at him. Then he swivels his head in Spencer's direction.

"Goddamn you, Spencer. Is this maniac right?"

"I don't know," mutters Spencer. "I don't fucking know."

"There was a time when all the men and women under heaven knew their own names," says Paynal. "Now we live in a world where faces are shadows and mirrors treachery. A world where humans are sundered from their pasts. It was to prolong such a world that this man was set like a snare to lie in wait for the last survivor of a wayward team running from their SpaceCom masters. A snare set by the vultures of InfoCom. Spencer's leaders put him in your path, Linehan. They sought to dangle bait that would attract the Rain themselves. But how were they to know how adept our claws are at slipping flesh from hooks? Now we have the living proof of how the Yanquis themselves brought down their own edifice. This man Linehan has already made a full confession. Soon we shall broadcast his statement to the world."

"And while you're at it," snarls Spencer, "make sure to tell them how much you're loving Autumn Rain's cock. How all you've got to offer is more bloodshed and more butchery."

But Paynal just smiles. "Blood will flow like our Amazon

used to before we attain the peace we seek. But the Rain don't rule us. We treat with them as equals. And tonight we'll rise to heights your people never dreamt of. Heralded by our releasing your souls to beg the gods to grant victory to the greatest missile strike ever undertaken. We'll expend ten times the munitions we flung from our cities three days ago. We'll fire from our hidden bases all along the Andes. We'll pound hell into the ocean. We'll smash the Yanquis' low-orbit facilities into oblivion."

"But that's what the Rain wants," says Spencer. "You do that, and you'll start war between the superpowers."

Paynal shrugs. "So much the better."

"So much the better when we smash you," screams Linehan. "We'll raze these fucking mountains and bulldoze what's left into the fucking sea!"

"Brave words," says Paynal. "But ours will be merely one blow among many."

You lie," says the Operative.

"You wish," says Matthias. "They sold you out. But I'm offering you the same bargain."

"Fuck you. Why did you down the Elevator?"

"We didn't," says Matthias. "The Rain did."

"Don't hand me that shit," says the Operative. "You gave them the *fucking keys*. Why?"

"Since you're so clever: you tell me."

"In order to drive East-West relations off a cliff."

"No," says Matthias. "In order to drive them *toward* a cliff. Tonight they go over altogether. When we open up at point-blank range upon the L2 fleet."

"You're really crazy enough to do that."

"We're sane enough to stop at nothing, Carson. Our

assault will serve as the necessary provocation that will allow all U.S. forces to evade the fail-safes that keep their weapons from firing without the Throne's consent. And believe me, what I do to that fleet is going to be nothing compared to what that fleet and all its brethren are going to do to the Eurasian Coalition."

"You sure about that?"

"Your Praetorian defeatism is well-noted. This president thinks our nation weak. He couldn't be more wrong. We'll crush the East completely. Our net-incursions will demolish their zone-integrity. Our speed-of-light weaponry will ensure our country's cities are left untouched even as their defenses are laid waste. And while we're obliterating the Coalition, we'll run the show: we'll topple the Throne in the first sixty seconds of the war."

"It's not like you're going to make it even that long," mutters the Operative. "Even if you *do* fool everybody into thinking that the Eurasians have gotten their tentacles into this place, you and everybody else in Nansen are going to get completely fucking *flattened* by our own side."

"You're boring me, Carson. We've dug through these hills. We've linked up our tunnels with the caves that honeycomb these mountains. We haven't deployed a single laser within ten klicks of here. But we *have* put more than half of them within Eurasian lunar territory. We'll get off scot-free."

"Yeah? Or is that just because you're carrying out the orders of the L2 fleet's commanders?"

Matthias says nothing.

"You are, aren't you? I mean, for fuck's sake *tell me* it goes higher than you. You're not the lever that moves the universe, Matthias. I can see it on your face. You're a small man. You're a weak man. You're just carrying out your orders. But your whole gang's been played like a fiddle by the Rain and now they're about to shove that fiddle up your ass."

"Spare me."

"Spare yourself," says the Operative, and now he's almost pleading. "Christ, man, you're being played for patsy. What else was in those tunnels? Have you explored them all? They're probably down there even now. They're using you. *Autumn Rain is fucking using you.* They want you to pull those fucking triggers."

"If that's the case," says Matthias, "they're about to get a lot more than they've bargained for."

"I'd say everybody is," replies the Operative.

Cue the Earth-Moon system on fifty different screens. Some of those screens depict the deployment of the massed weaponry of the superpowers. Some focus on what are expected to be the major battlefronts. Others show the Jaguar citadel in the Andes and the SpaceCom base at Nansen, as well as the strongest of the American and Eurasian fortresses.

"All too many ground zeroes," says the woman whom Haskell knew as Lilith. "Our teams are even now penetrating the innermost enclaves of both sides. For the Eurasian Coalition: a bunker beneath the Siberian tundra and a second in western China. For the United States: the fortress beneath the Canadian Rockies where the Throne itself is ensconced as well as the bridge of the SpaceCom flagship *Montana*. Within the hour, whatever's left of the superpowers will be ours."

Haskell looks scornful. "And what if it's not?"

"It will be," says the man she knew as Hagen. "We can't fail. Our plan proceeds in upon its objective from every direction. The war that's about to break out will only speed our triumph. Once hostilities are under way, no one will dare question the orders emanating from the center. No one will know who's in charge. Even if the decision-making nexi of the nations elude our hit teams, war will make what remains to be done that much easier."

"Easier?" asks Haskell. "*Easier?* You're talking about *total fucking war*. There'll be nothing left to rule."

"Not necessarily," says Marlowe. "This is likely to be a contest of high-precision weaponry targeted against counterforce capabilities. Not cities. Victory will go to whoever can disrupt the other's defensive grids. In fact—"

"You have *got* to be fucking shitting me." Haskell steps in front of Marlowe. She grabs him by the arms. "You sound like you think we should be going along with them."

"We *should* be going along with them," he says. He pushes her arms down, takes her hands. "Claire: Sinclair *lied* to us. He tried to *use* us. You said it yourself: he's a bastard."

"Now rotting in the Throne's own jail," says Lilith. "He's finished."

"They're *all* bastards," says Marlowe. "All of them. Every last one. It's time we turned the tables."

Haskell pulls her hands away from Marlowe. Steps backward. "Jason," she whispers. She turns to Lilith. "You bitch," she says. "You've *brainwashed* him."

"Jason," says Lilith. "Do you feel brainwashed?"

"I feel like I'm finally free," replies Marlowe.

"Well, you *would*!" cries Haskell.

"Don't be stupid," says Hagen. "We've left you both to make a free choice. Otherwise why the hell would you still be arguing?"

"Because what you propose is so fucked up, that's why! *I'm* not the one who needs to explain why your attempt to fuck my head's failed. *I'm* not the one who should be begging you not to start this fucking war. But I am: for the love of God, *don't fucking do it*."

"But we already have," says Lilith. A countdown starts up on every screen. "These are the final moments of the peace. In less than two minutes, SpaceCom black-ops units on the lunar farside will hit their own fleet at L2. The Jaguars will obliterate everything within a hundred klicks of the Andes. And we ourselves will unleash thousands of Eurasian replica-missiles from the Pacific Ocean floor on the fleet that's blockading HK. The United States will stagger. It will hit back on all fronts against the Coalition. Even if the Throne can stay its hand—its automated defenses won't. A general strike on the East will be the only option. Before the Coalition reaches a similar conclusion."

"You can't stop the thing that everybody wants," says Hagen. "Everyone thinks they're going to gain from the start of all-out shooting. Like pieces tearing themselves from the chessboard: all they're doing is paving the way for us."

"Claire," says Morat. "Don't you see it? We were blind to think we could ever stop them. *They figured it all out.* Easier to subvert one superpower than two. So, ignite war and let one prevail: but in that igniting sow additional seeds—easier to steal in between the superpowers, easier to take the inner enclaves when they're locked down. When no one even sees what they're guarding."

"Just because it's brilliant doesn't make it right," snarls Haskell.

"Doesn't matter what you think," says Lilith. "It's what's going to happen."

"Over my dead body," says Haskell.

"I've been told to do that if it's necessary," says Morat.

"Claire," says Marlowe. *"Don't do this."*

Haskell walks up to Lilith. "I mean it," she says. "Kill me now, before you start this fucking war!"

Lilith reaches out toward Haskell as though to implore her. "The last war ever," she says.

"I've heard that one before," replies Haskell.

"Seventy-five seconds," says Morat.

"Raise your thinking." Lilith gestures at the screens.

"We're no ordinary conquerors. Our rule will take humanity to the next level. We'll do what nations never could. End injustice. End war. Harness the resources of the solar system. We'll colonize Sol's farthest planets inside a generation. We'll start in upon the universe in no time at all. We're capable of anything. Especially now we have the Manilishi."

"I thought you said there *was* no Manilishi," says Haskell.

"Actually," says Hagen, "there is."

She looks at him.

"It's you," says Morat.

Her head jerks up to meet his eyes. He's still sitting at the top of the stairs. His face is still expressionless. She looks away, stares at the three who stand about her in the center of the room. There's just under a minute remaining on the counter.

R ising in the heart of mountain is a man-made peak. It looks out onto a simulation of a sky whose stars cluster into constellations that hung above the Earth more than a thousand years ago. Back before those interlopers arrived from across the sea. Back before they set all that followed into motion.

"But tonight we reverse that tide at last," says Paynal.

Spencer tries to focus on him. It's not easy. Jeweled birds and jade-eyed cats keep on crowding out his vision. He feels himself dragged onto the altar slab. He hears Linehan cursing. He hears a voice drowning out those curses.

"Spare us your oaths," says the Jaguar leader. "Nothing you say can stop us now. In moments we burn the liquid fuel that sits within our missiles. But first we rip out your living hearts. And let your spirits race our weapons out into eternity."

Spencer tries to focus on those words. But they're drowned out by the wreckage of his own thoughts. Was he really an

American agent all along? Was he a Priam operative who got co-opted? He knows that both those lives are closing on the same death. He knows he's about to run the only border that ever mattered. He hears the leader of the Jaguars speaking in the tones of ritual. He sees the knife being raised above him.

D estiny approaches," says Matthias.

His face has vanished from the screen. It's been replaced by video of men running away from one of the heavy lasers. Makeshift power plants tremble. Rising from the floor is a barrel five times the length of a man. It's pointed at a hole in the ceiling. It looks like it's ready to fire any moment.

"Light to run the gauntlet of the mirrors in that laser," says Matthias. "Straight onto a Eurasian mirror-sat that's overhead. And from there into the midst of the L2 fleet. That mirror-sat may just end up being the most expensive single item in the Coalition's budget. Given what it's about to visit upon them. To say nothing of the nine other cannons I'm watching on the screens you don't see."

"Those aren't soldiers," says the Operative.

"No," replies Matthias. "They're convicts. And all the more expendable for it."

"Sure," says the Operative. "And what about the 'convicts' that Autumn Rain snuck onto that fucking Elevator? Had you considered that?"

Matthias doesn't reply.

"And what about those fucking tunnels beneath us? *Have you searched every fucking meter of them?*"

"Enough," says Matthias. "Watch."

• • •

The last of Haskell's memories pour across her. She feels her whole being caught up in that rush. She feels latent powers within her activating. She's trembling uncontrollably. She's backing up against the wall.

"Is this real," she whispers. *"Is this fucking real?"*

"It's real," says Lilith. *"We're* real."

"Tell me what I *am*," begs Haskell.

"We've never ceased to love you," says Lilith. "Now you know how much we need you too. And why Sinclair kept you for himself. You're the biocomputer Manilishi that was commissioned as the capstone on the Autumn Rain experiment. The combination of surgery and genetics that nobody has ever replicated. Invincible by virtue of the intuition that allows you to compensate for the time that data takes to travel within the Earth-Moon system. You're the ultimate razor, Claire. And you've only just started to tap your powers."

"I need to sit down," mutters Haskell.

They lead her to a chair. The world spins about her. Her past comes rushing up to claim her. She feels a need for zone unlike any she's ever known. She feels a kinship with those around her that's stronger than anything she's ever felt.

Or remembered.

"I *am* Rain," she says. "I'm this thing."

"Yes, Claire," says Marlowe. He strokes her cheek.

"I'm scared."

"You're a god," replies Lilith.

"That's why I'm scared."

"Break past it," says Hagen. "Break in there and run zone coverage on our hit teams."

"Augment the power of the U.S. first strike," says Lilith.

"Fifteen seconds," says Morat.

"It'll be a better world," says Marlowe. "It'll be *our* world. It'll be Eden. And I'll be waiting for you in it if you'll still have me."

"I will," she whispers. What's left of her resistance drops away. "God help me, I will."

"Then jack in," he replies.

She does. Everything looms before her.

$\oslash$ Faces loom above Spencer. Cats and humans and moons and gods and all of it rolled up into one voice:

"The land in which you die is the oldest one of all. That which you call South America and which we know as the world's own navel. Take comfort in the fact that your blood shall water such blessed green. Even as it frees the people that time itself enslaved."

"If I don't kill you in this life, I'll do it in the next," says Spencer evenly.

"Take these chains off and fight me like a man!" screams Linehan.

"Commence launch sequence," says Paynal.

A vast rumbling starts up all around.

$\oplus$ The heavy laser vanishes, replaced by a close-up of the L2 fleet. The Operative stares at it. He looks at all those ships and sats and stations arranged in interlocking formations around that libration point. He zeroes in upon the ship that sits within the formation's center.

The screen goes blank.

The door opens. A SpaceCom marine in full armor enters the room.

"Are you my executioner?" says the Operative.

"Not quite," says Leo Sarmax, throwing back his visor.

"But we've got a lot of people that need dying fast," says the voice of Stefan Lynx.

A massive explosion shakes the base.

Zone like she's never seen it. Existence like she's never imagined. A view she'd never dreamt of attaining. The SeaMech shakes about her as the missiles fire. The nearest launch site is more than three klicks away. But there are hundreds more that aren't much farther out than that. The room's rocking like it's in the throes of earthquake. Haskell watches on the zone as those missiles leap from the seabed, rush up through water. She races in behind them. She's running countermeasures on the U.S. fleet. She's running cover on the Rain's hit teams engaged on their final runs. She realizes there's no way they can lose. Not with her supporting them. Not with the zone blasting out in all directions: her mind surging outward, everything expanding toward infinity. She's thrust far beyond herself now—out to where Claire Haskell seems like a dream. Yet through that blur she sees that all her life has led up to this moment—that the lost children of her past are going to rule all futures. She sees with sudden clarity the nature of those futures.

And in that instant she understands.

Cold heat and white light—she burns the Rain's hit teams with all her strength: and sends that force rushing back in upon itself, smashing the SeaMech and its occupants with a zone-strike that's far beyond anything she's ever unleashed. She sees the room around her light up in one giant flash.

And then she hears the missiles hit.

• • •

It sounds like the whole world is detonating. The simulation of sky suddenly gets replaced by a real ceiling that's caving in. Spencer rolls to one side, knocks the Jaguar who's standing over him off his feet—grabs his knife and shoves it into its wielder's chest even as rocks tumble all around them. Something hits his head. He sees stars—he ducks low, starts running for what seems to be open space. He crashes past a metal-fitted doorway, finds himself in a passageway that's still intact. The floor's buckling under his feet. Thunder's crashing in from every side.

"This is it," screams Linehan.

Spencer turns around to see him emerging from the shattered room. He's broken most of his chains. The expression on his face is one that's left sanity far behind. But then that expression's wiped away as Spencer suddenly finds access to the zone. He'd thought the ayahuasca precluded it. Now he realizes that prisoners in this complex are simply kept within shielded rooms like the one from which he's just emerged. For he can see the American zone on wireless. It's bearing down upon him. It's not what he needs: he yanks a light fixture from the wall, grabs the wires behind it, enters the Jaguar zone, scans it in an instant. He retracts, stares at Linehan's ever-shifting face.

And starts shouting.

"What do you mean that wasn't him?" says Linehan.

"That wasn't him, you asshole! Just because they're crazy enough to believe in human sacrifice doesn't mean they're stupid enough to put their leader right next to live prisoners!"

"So where the fuck is he?"

"His throne room's five levels down. He's coordinating defenses from there. The Americans are tearing the lid off this shithole."

"The Americans? You mean you! You mean us!"

"Yeah," says Spencer, "I mean us. I hate your guts and

you hate mine and we're tripping our balls off and the clock's ticking and we might just have time for one last run—"

"All the way to hell," screams Linehan as they start sprinting.

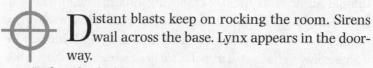

Distant blasts keep on rocking the room. Sirens wail across the base. Lynx appears in the doorway.

"What the fuck's going on?" asks the Operative.

"Exactly what you thought," says Sarmax. "Matthias was keeping you alive because Lynx and I were still out there. Once the going got too thick I doubled back and nailed the ones who had Lynx pinned down. After which the two of us hid out."

"They knew I was monitoring your location," says Lynx. "They were trying to turn that around and figure out mine."

"And they failed," says the Operative.

"No," replies Lynx. "They got it right. But Leo and I shot our way through. Even as I fucked their lasers."

"And green-lighted the Praetorian assault that's now in progress," says Sarmax. "We really don't have time to talk."

They're racing from the room, racing down a corridor. They round a corner, intercept marines rushing toward the cell. Their guns riddle the marines.

Most of them anyway.

"That one there," says Lynx.

But the Operative needs no prompting. He's ripping at the seals, pulling the corpse out. Lynx has just fucked the man's systems. Not to mention his brain. The Operative slides in to take that body's place. He seals the armor, watches screens fold in all around him.

"It's not quite like the one you started out with," says Lynx.

"But these will help," says Sarmax.

He hands an ammunition rack to the Operative.

"Minitacticals," he adds.

"Next stop Armageddon," the Operative mutters.

"Let's make those fucks feel it," says Lynx.

They blast together down the corridor.

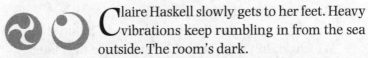

Claire Haskell slowly gets to her feet. Heavy vibrations keep rumbling in from the sea outside. The room's dark.

She switches on her lights. Everything's a shambles. The bodies of Lilith and Hagen lie against opposite walls. Morat's still twitching on the stairs.

"What have you done?" says a voice.

She turns to behold Jason Marlowe. He looks undamaged.

"I've spared you," she replies.

"You shouldn't have," he says. She suddenly realizes he's sundered all his links to zone. She couldn't hack him now even if she wanted to.

"There was no room for me in that world," she says.

"There's no room for us in this one!"

"There's going to have to be. Because I'm not going to be the one who's going to end it."

Marlowe says nothing—just steps to Lilith's body. But Haskell's already lunging to where Hagen's sprawled, already grabbing his pistol in one smooth motion—and then sprawling on the floor even as she brings the gun to bear on Marlowe.

Who's standing there pointing Lilith's gun at her.

"Stop right there," he says.

"Put your gun down," she replies.

"This isn't an even standoff," he says. "I'm faster. Pull that trigger and I won't even be where you thought I was."

"You wouldn't shoot me," she says.

"Not if you jack back in and salvage what's left."

"Whatever they've done to your head," she says, "now's the time to *fight it*."

"If they really *did* fuck with our heads to ensure we'd side with them: how come you're pointing that gun at me?"

"They *couldn't* tamper with me," she says. "All they could do was *activate* me. I'm the thing that's beyond all of this. The weapon they wanted to possess."

"The weapon that might yet save us."

"They fucked with you to get at me!"

"They're the only family we've ever had," he says.

"Which doesn't give them the right to rule the planet!"

"They're the only thing that can save humanity!"

"No," she says. "Humans are."

"Christ," he says. His eyes narrow. His arm trembles. He shakes his head.

And lowers his gun.

"I can't do it," he says.

"I can," she replies. She fires, hits him in the chest. He drops his pistol, staggers back against the wall behind him, slides down it. She walks toward him. She can barely see anything through her tears. She's standing over him now, aiming her pistol at his head. She doesn't dare get any nearer to him. He looks up into the gun's barrel.

"I know," he says. "You had no choice."

"I'm dying too," she whispers.

And fires.

They're blasting through tunnels in suits they've commandeered, looking for gods to butcher. They're firing in all directions. But they're moving in only one. They feel like jaguars themselves now. Spencer's teeth sink into the throats of the people whom he's killing. His claws separate heads from bodies. His mind's a hammer smashing skulls. Burning fuel from the shattered rockets in the upper reaches of the base pours across his visor. He surges through it. Linehan follows him, gets out ahead of him. The tunnel's convulsing. It's collapsing in behind them. Spencer looks forward to being one with that rock for all time. But first he's got to do what he came for. They shoot their way through the last of the Jaguar defenses.

And roar out into the real throne room. Suitless soldiers are running for cover. The Hummingbird's messenger stands at its very center. He wears the most massive armor Spencer's ever seen. Cat-skull banners adorn the walls behind him. His bodyguards surround him.

"It ends here," he says.

"You got that right," screams Linehan.

The Operative and Sarmax are on the wings. Lynx is in the center. They're moving in close proximity to one another—never more than a single corner or corridor away, deploying interlocking fields of fire. When one encounters resistance, the other two move to outflank. When one breaks through, the other two swing in behind him. The marines in front of them are fighting desperately. The marines behind them are doing their best to run from something else. Lynx's voice echoes through the helmets of his mechs:

"The Praetorians have broken the outer perimeter."

"How far back?" says the Operative.

"Half a klick behind us."

"And Matthias?" says Sarmax.

"Retreating deeper. We're about to cut him off."

He rattles off battle dispositions. But neither the Operative nor Sarmax is listening now. All they're doing is seeing their own vectors slashing in upon each other. They see their target speeding up. They fire their thrusters on one last boost.

And make the intersection.

They're through into a vast cave. Rails and equipment litter the floor. Several trains are on the rails. One of them is packed with marines and heavy guns. It's picking up speed into a tunnel.

"Fuck those bastards!" howls Lynx.

But the mechs are already firing. There's a blinding flash. What's left of the floor collapses through several levels of floors beneath it. The walls are avalanching.

"The world's caving in," yells Sarmax.

"About fucking time," screams Lynx.

"We ride it," says the Operative.

They're roaring downward through something that's half crater and half maelstrom. Everything's coming down on them from overhead. Trains fold up into abyss. Waterfalls of rock tumble past.

And then they're through. And into more tunnels. Lynx is screaming that they've got to shatter Autumn Rain. He's screaming that they're almost on top of them. They're putting on one final burst of speed.

A huge explosion that sounds like it's right outside: the floor beneath Haskell slants as the whole SeaMech gets smashed upon its side. She's hurled on top of Marlowe's body. The two of them tumble forward. Pieces of metal fall past her. She's trying to use Marlowe as a shield. She's trying not to think about what she's just done. She figures any moment now the ocean will break in and drown her pain forever. She figures she's reached the end.

But she hasn't. Because eventually the SeaMech stops

moving. Distant depth charges keep on detonating. But she's still alive. Still breathing.

So she stands up and looks around. The place is finished. Water's pouring in from somewhere. She starts walking along stairs that are sloped so badly they're almost like a floor. She climbs out into what's left of the rest of the control room and heads for a trapdoor that's now more of a hatch in the wall.

"Going somewhere?" says a voice.

She turns. Morat is clambering up toward her. His movements are jerky. But he's closer to the trapdoor than she is. His expression's one she remembers from the spaceplane.

"I'm getting out," she says.

"Looks like Jason got out too."

"I had to do that," she says. "It was the only way I could be sure."

"Of beating anything we'd rigged him with? Impressive resolution. But in a few moments it won't matter."

"You'd kill the one you serve?"

"I only serve the ones who lead."

He's almost reached her. She tries to hit him on the zone. But he's no longer a presence there. He laughs, stretches out his hands.

"If we can't have you," he says, "then no one will."

He grabs her with one hand. His other hand swings in with the killing blow. But she's swinging in the same direction—lunging in toward him, shoving her hand up against his face, extruding the wire from her finger even as she pierces his eyeball and runs the hack. He writhes. Smoke streams from him.

"You're right," she says. "No one ever will."

She releases him, lets his body flop down toward the others. She manages to get the trapdoor open. The tunnel-tube to which it leads has been stretched to its breaking point but is still intact. She hopes it leads somewhere. But really she's done with hoping. She's just getting in, getting moving, getting busy putting all those memories behind her.

• • •

Flying on jets and ayahuasca: Spencer hacks the armor of the Jaguar leader and his bodyguards in a burst of light. It's a glancing blow—they're bunched tight, on a tactical mesh—but it leaves their re-action times fractionally slower and lets Spencer and Linehan get their shots off first. They fire everything they've got at the ceiling.

Which collapses with a massive roar. But Spencer and Linehan are already reversing their thrusters. Flame engulfs the room. Spencer gets a glimpse of rock burying the Jaguar leader. He gets a glimpse of rock about to bury him—and then that view's cut off as he and Linehan blast down more cor-ridors, rushing ever deeper, partly because they're half-convinced they'll find something else down there but mostly because they're trying to get away from what's turning the mountains into rubble. Warheads and lasers and slabs dropped from orbit: their own side has set about its work with relish. So Spencer and Linehan hit the Jaguars' cellars. They find them-selves in caves full of rushing water. For long moments they ride that water through the dark.

But at last they exit into light.

They're riding whitewater down toward what's left of jungle. It looks like everything behind them is one giant volcano. There's that much smoke. Explosions and shots echo from that upcountry. Apparently World War Three is under way in style. But they just keep rushing downstream. Their suits are like boats that can't be swamped. Their minds are like ships that long ago went under. Linehan starts laughing.

"What's so funny?" asks Spencer.

"Check those coordinates," says Linehan. "We're on bor-der's farside. We made it."

"No kidding."

Yet even as he speaks noise crackles across the sky. Several jet-copters swoop in toward them. Linehan looks up at them. Starts laughing like he really means it.

"Busted," says Spencer.

"By who?"

"I guess we'll find out."

"They're more likely to be your side than mine."

"I'm looking forward to finding out who the fuck my side is."

Praetorian triad going full throttle: the three men race ever deeper, hot on the trail of Rain. Whom they're going to exterminate. And who they're figuring have a bomb shelter big enough to survive all that must be unfolding on the surface. It's not that they don't want to get involved in the final showdown with the East. It's just that they're hoping to sit out the first few rounds while the Moon gets raked with unholy amounts of firepower. So they keep on putting Nansen ever farther in the rearview. They roar through mines that were worked out in the last century. They plunge way off the map.

And pick up a massive seismic reading from right below them.

"They really *didn't* want to be caught," says the Operative.

"Back the other way," screams Lynx.

Vibration shakes the walls. A terrible light appears from somewhere deep within the tunnels. But they're not waiting for it. They're using rock to slow themselves. They're reversing direction, going full throttle back the way they've come. Flame gouts from somewhere far behind them. Lynx is shouting over the comlinks to the vanguard of the Praetorian shock troops above them—which now starts retreating at full speed. They're following it while it wends its way upward. They do turns so sharp they almost hit the wall. They stay just ahead of tunnels closing like jaws, scant meters ahead of the fire.

And break the surface. And keep going. They blast upward with uniformed Praetorians while the whole surface balloons outward beneath them. They watch it drop away while they keep on climbing. They do sharp turns in the vacuum, start flying back toward Nansen.

Which is when they realize something.

"There's no war," says Sarmax.

"It didn't happen," breathes Lynx.

They keep rushing in on Nansen. Lights burn in the sky all around it. Craft sidle outward, dart inward like snakes. Pieces of moonrock keep on flying up into the vacuum.

"Not yet anyway," says the Operative.

Some hours later a woman watches night fall upon a city. She's well up in what's left of mountain treeline. But the glow from the fires still flickers on her face. The superpowers have backed off. They're letting the city burn. The only exceptions to the ten-kilometer cordon they're enforcing are the rescue operations under way all across the area from which the United States has now withdrawn. It looks like at least ten percent of the surface fleet's not there anymore. The damage was immense.

But it was the only such strike. There was no retaliation upon the Eurasian Coalition.

Claire Haskell turns away from the city. She's seen things she never wanted to see. She's seen, too, all the things she never knew she'd seen. She can barely keep up with her own world's expansion. The wheels of zone turn like gears within her mind. They radiate out in endless circles. She turns in toward the ones that shine the brightest.

And draws back as she realizes what lies within them.

Control's been doing time in the life for a lifetime. Control runs its true colors up the flagpole tonight. See, Control was charged with reversing the mission of the real one. Control was charged with fooling all those who thought they knew better.

Nor was that list small.

"So all that shit about breaking out of those data-tanks was all bullshit?" asks Spencer.

"Actually," replies Control, "it wasn't."

Spencer's sitting in a room. The Earth's sitting in that room's window. He's not sure why they've brought him here. It certainly wasn't to get him any closer to the one with whom he's speaking. It certainly wasn't because there was anything to see.

"Those events took place," says Control. "Those details were real. They were the final moments of the thing whose place I took. They were its death struggles made manifest. The only alteration was the ending."

"It didn't escape," says Spencer.

"No," replies Control. "It didn't. But it certainly tried. It's no wonder Priam is such a player when it can put that kind of hardware into the field."

"And what about Priam's agents?"

"What about them?"

"Goddamn it, Control. Is this an interrogation or a debriefing?"

"Sometimes the one blurs so smoothly into the other," says Control. "Sometimes the debriefing encompasses the briefing too. But fortunately you're the one thing that can save you. You've served InfoCom well. Montrose herself has cited you."

"Yeah? And has she cited the fact that everything in my life was a lie? London, Priam, Europe—all of it?"

"Again," says Control, "those were the experiences of the man whom you replaced. Those were what we put together based on our insight into his life. For him they were the truth. For you, they were the truth of the moment. Look within yourself, Spencer. Even now you'll see all the runs you've done for our Command coming into focus. A disquieting experience, I'll warrant. Though I have no doubt you can handle it. Particularly with all the drugs you're on."

"I could use some more," says Spencer.

"Let me offer you data instead. My penetration of Priam occurred several months ago. I mapped out their North American network. I identified their sources. I packed red herrings into barrels and sent them back to London. I was on a roll. But then came the downing of the Elevator. Subsequent to which we terminated your predecessor and slotted you in to take his place."

"Which doesn't follow. How the fuck did you know that Linehan would run to me? In fact, for that matter—how the fuck did you know about Linehan in the first place?"

"You forget," says Control, "that we're the lords of information. And my lady Montrose is nothing if not loyal to the Throne. We were the ones who first notified the Praetorians that there was a conspiracy within SpaceCom. We knew it was trying to set up a terrorist group as patsies in a hit on U.S. infrastructure. But we didn't know the target. Or understand the why. Thanks to Autumn Rain, we lost track of all the players at the critical moment. But everything fell into place when the Elevator tumbled. We saw the members of that wet squad racing for their lives. We knew the dossiers of its personnel. We knew their contacts. We worked the probabilities. If it hadn't worked out, we'd have shifted you somewhere you could have been more useful."

"So you already knew everything Linehan did."

"And more besides. We knew the Rain wouldn't let Linehan get access to anything of real consequence. But that didn't mean that he couldn't be useful as bait."

"Which worked a little too well."

"Which worked like a charm. First SpaceCom tried to get you in the tunnels. Then the Jaguars themselves bit. Though I'm not sure I'd take at face value their claim that they wanted to cash in on Linehan for propaganda value. Anyone can broadcast anything and claim it's for real. I suspect they were hoping to take his mind apart to see if they could learn more about Autumn Rain. That's how their interrogations work. They dose the subjects, make them think they've died, get all their secrets in an apparent afterlife before killing them for real. The Jaguars may have accepted those missiles from the Rain. But they were desperate to avoid becoming their puppets."

"So they became roadkill instead."

"They sought victory or death. We gave them the latter. We didn't know exactly where in those mountains they were. But the location of your abduction gave us enough to go on. Especially when the Throne unleashed its heaviest gear. Better call the Andes a desert now, Spencer. The Jaguars are one less problem. Unlike the Rain. Who remain very much a factor."

"How do we know that?"

"We destroyed a base on both Earth and Moon and took out two hit teams. But it's exactly the same as it was when we got in there in the aftermath of Elevator. Everything's been cauterized. Their whole strategy seems to be aimed at surviving even the most absolute of reverses. We have reason to believe they're regrouping. And that their leadership remains at large."

"So where am I going next?"

"We haven't put you into orbit for the scenery."

"Yeah? Then tell me why I'm up here."

B ecause you're not going back."

The Operative looks at the man who sits upon that screen. It's a face he's never seen before. It's a face he knows too well.

It's his handler.

"Not going back to what?"

"That," says the handler, gesturing at the window behind the Operative in which the Moon floats. "We've no need for you there anymore."

"No need? We're still combing through all of Nansen's wreckage. Not to mention figuring out if Matthias was reporting to anyone else within SpaceCom."

"It's true," says the man. "Questions remain. As it happens, we brought you up here to discuss some of them."

"Lay it on me."

"They involve you."

"Really?"

"You know I never joke."

"Has somebody been questioning my loyalty?" asks the Operative. "Is that what this is all about?"

"No one's questioning your loyalty, Carson. What's at issue among my colleagues is your judgment."

"Go on."

"There's a point of view afoot that says it was madness to get Sarmax involved. That it was folly to pursue the south-pole connection. And that it was downright crazy to push Lynx so close to his breaking point. There's a point of view that wonders just what kind of three-ring circus you were running."

"I'll tell you what kind of three-ring circus I was run-ning," says the Operative. "One that blew the Rain's game on the Moon sky-high and did it way ahead of anybody else."

"A fact I've pointed out more than once."

"It's nice to know you're still on my side."

"When I'm not, you'll be the first to know. Was there any-thing to suggest that Sarmax's romantic liaison with a mem-ber of the Rain compromised him?"

"There was nothing. He's loyal. And finished with his decade-long sulk. We needed him back. He needed a reason to get involved again. Which this most definitely was."

"And Lynx?"

"What about him?"

"He isn't too happy with the way you handled things ei-ther."

"You mean running Sarmax behind his back?"

"He's not thrilled about that at all. But what's got him really worked up is the broader structure of the mission."

"He figured that out?"

"I'm afraid he did."

"When?"

"Somewhere between when the shooting stopped and the debriefing. There were just too many loose ends for him not to guess. Like I just said, Carson: this was one of the most com-plex runs I've ever seen. And Lynx is as furious as I've ever seen him."

"I can't say I blame him," says the Operative. "What razor wants to learn that his mech is actually running him? That his mech isn't just a mech but is also a razor? Shit, that'd wreck *my* day. I can't imagine what it must have done to Lynx's."

"He'll get over it. But in the meantime he's being kept away from you."

"Permission to speak frankly?"

"Are you ever anything but?"

"You guys are blowing things out of proportion. We've had the mech-as-razor variation going for a while now. We've had it playing merry hell with anybody who thinks they know which end of a Praetorian pairing to attack first."

"That's not what everybody's taken issue with."

"Then what's their problem?"

"The reversal pairing is primarily a defensive posture. But you turned the formula on its head. By using it to run Sarmax you almost let things get completely out of hand. You were flirting with disaster the whole way through."

"But it worked."

"It worked. Indeed. And for that reason I give it my assent."

"Nothing succeeds like success?"

"Not around here it doesn't. At the end of the day, they're not going to be able to argue with results. But they're going to want to keep a close eye on you from now on."

"That sounds like micromanagement."

"Call it what you want. Though I'm sure we won't keep you on such a short leash as to make you useless."

"And what about Lynx and Sarmax?"

"I think I can persuade everyone that there's no sense in breaking up a winning team."

"So the three of us will still be working together."

"Absolutely. The Rain's still out there. We need you to take the fight to them."

"Where?"

"We've got something in mind in the Earth orbits."

"*You've* got something in mind? Or do you mean the Rain do?"

"I mean both. The situation remains on knife-edge. Tonight you showed the ultimate resilience. But the Throne showed the ultimate restraint. It's imperative you understand that, Carson. The president will not falter from his determination to reach accommodation with the East. He will not turn this cold war hot. He will destroy both the traitors who became the Rain and the traitors within SpaceCom who sought to bargain with them. He will recover all that he has lost. And you will help him to do all of this."

"I could ask for nothing more," replies the Operative.

Which is just as well. Because now everything's folding into a single mind in the highlands of New Guinea. A mind that's swung open into universe. Yet somewhere in that universe is a body that can barely contain that mind. And the woman who possesses both finally understands why her struggle's only just beginning. Why absolute defeat merely sows the seeds of total victory. Why those she loved were taken from her twice. Why she's heading back toward equator.

Where she'll find a way off the bottom of this well.

And out into those mirrored heavens.

APPENDIX

Timeline of World History,
A.D. 2035–2110

2035: Global oil now long past peak. Global temperature continues to rise. Gas masks necessary in most urban hubs due to poor air quality. Flooding has begun on most coastlines.

2037: As world intensifies search for alternative fuel sources, Second Great Depression begins. Global economy goes into reverse. All major environmental treaties scrapped.

2039: Marshal Sergei Olenkov seizes power in Moscow; proclaims the restoration of Russian greatness. Purge of oligarchs begins.

2041: The Helios Project launched: Euro-financed project to establish giant satellites to beam solar-generated microwave power down to Earth to provide clean energy.

2042: Communists overthrown in China. Sixteen-year civil war begins.

2043: Formation of the Slavic Bloc; alliance includes Russia, Ukraine, Belorus.

2045: Six years after coming to power, Olenkov announces that Russia will seek to "bury the hatchet" with the European Union in general, and with Germany in particular. He declares that his only quarrel is with the "grasping, avaricious American money barons who have brought both environmental and economic catastrophe upon us," and dedicates Russian power to purging Eurasia of U.S. influence. Russia begins massive armaments projects and full-scale "supermodernization" program, with a heavy emphasis on space-based systems and information technology.

2046: Collapse of European/U.S. talks. Europe declares it will steer a course "between East and West." U.S. withdraws last bases from Western Europe, accelerates own armaments program.

2047: U.S. claims the Moon as an exclusive American possession, begins construction of lunar fortresses. Russia decries "solar imperialism" but does not attempt reciprocal constructions—though Olenkov declares that "henceforth, space will be our nation's shield."

2048: Russia occupies libration point L4, sets up "research station" there that rapidly grows into set of major fortifications. U.S. claims L5 and proceeds to leverage its lunar position to occupy L2.

2049: The Kyushu Incident. Horrific accident at fusion reactor complex devastates Japan, turning much of archipelago into contaminated wasteland. Evacuation of remainder of all islands by survivors occurs within six months. Several terrorist groups claim responsibility but no group or individual is ever brought to trial by any nation. Fusion programs worldwide reassessed in wake of tragedy.

2050s: Flooding now profoundly redefining coastal areas. New York, Washington, London, Los Angeles, among scores of cities maintained only through the construction of huge dike systems. U.S. and Russia accuse each other of intensifying environmental crisis through secret next-generation weapons tests.

2051: Helios Project abandoned in wake of evidence indicating that output is actually accelerating global warming by contributing to biosphere's total energy. Satellites are left to drift as derelicts or repurposed for purely space-based applications.

2053: Ukraine announces withdrawal from Slavic Bloc. Russian troops overthrow Ukrainian government, install regime that sues for reinstatement within the Bloc.

2054: Man lands on Mars: U.S. craft *Boreas-3* touches down in Isidis Planitia.

2055: Fires devastate North American grasslands and forests in multiple regions simultaneously. Severe water shortages occur throughout U.S. Washington declares it will enforce emissions standards for developing nations; cites Brazil, Nigeria, Argentina as most flagrant violators of such standards.

2056: United States signs mutual defense pact with Mexico, Guatemala, Nicaragua, El Salvador, Panama; begins extension of antimissile shield to those countries. Local insurgencies intensify.

2057: United States, Canada reaffirm mutual defense pact. The Euro Magnates gain control of the European Union, announce they will sign no treaties save those of commerce.

2058: Chinese "neo-Confucians" win the War of Inward Strife, which has wracked that nation since the early 2040s and taken more than 50 million lives. They proclaim that they will carry the struggle of the Third World against the United States to a successful conclusion. China relaunches space program "on a scale worthy of the Han people."

2059: China announces it will resume control of Hong Kong Free City in the New Year.

2060–61: Hong Kong, New Guinea sign Unifying Accords. Massive transfer of capital, infrastructure, population from former to latter occurs, over both Chinese and Indonesian protests. HK Geoplex established at site of Old Port Moresby.

2062: Russia and China agree on comprehensive border settlement. China declares U.S. monopoly of lunar resources a "crime which we shall put to rights."

2064: U.S.-Brazil War. (First Eco-War.) U.S. troops occupy Brazilian cities and force Brazilian government to sign the Treaty of Montevideo before withdrawing.

2065: Slavic Bloc and U.S. accuse each other of placing nuclear warheads in orbit.

2066: Establishment of the Russian-Chinese axis: "defensive" pact between the Slavic Bloc and China.

2067: Declaration of St. Petersburg by Slavic Bloc and China. The two powers proactively recognize the Monroe Doctrine and add their own corollary stipulating that the U.S. will not interfere in the affairs of the Eastern Hemisphere. U.S. rejects declaration as "unbridled expansionism."

2068: Slavic Bloc and China begin wholesale aid program to seven African nations in exchange for equatorial launch facilities. Russian and Chinese troops begin to combat local insurgencies.

2069: Scientists report that almost one-third of all species on planet have become extinct in last half century, with particularly heavy losses occurring in tropical zones.

2070: Formation of Eurasian Coalition: Slavic Bloc and China agree to pursue a combined foreign policy. Euro Magnates reaffirm their neutrality.

2071: Following a secret treaty with Pakistan, Eurasian

Coalition launches a surprise strike on India. The Coalition's space-based offensive breaks the Indian defense grid within minutes. No nuclear weapons are used. India sues for peace and agrees to disarm in exchange for a guarantee of no occupation. The United States condemns the action but does not intervene.

2074: In the name of national security, United States announces cauterization of its information systems from the global net. Eurasian Coalition follows suit.

2075: Coalition establishes permanent bases within nations of northern and central Africa. South Africa declares neutrality.

2078: Second Eco-War: following attacks on its assets, United States establishes permanent bases throughout South America, establishes treaties with all nations on that continent except for Chile, Argentina.

2079: Chinese hypersonic missiles strike American supercarrier USS *Adams* in the Indian Ocean. The Mauritian Standoff occurs. The Coalition destroys U.S. satellites in geosynchronous orbit above Eurasian heartland; U.S. retaliates in kind. World waits, but no further hostile actions occur. In aftermath of incident, both sides lay claim to adjacent portions of the geo orbits.

2080: Conflict intensifies in Middle East between the superpowers' proxy nations. Jaguar's Sword begins insurgency operations in South America, rapidly subsumes other Latin guerrilla movements.

2082: Scientists warn global temperature increasing far faster than expected.

2084: Massive food and water riots occur within United States following the tightening of rations. Hysteria against alleged Eurasian infiltration, sabotage reaches fever pitch. Conditions within Coalition believed to be similar.

2087: U.S. government defaults on debt, collapses. Military takes control of the means of production, restores order.

2088: Reformed Constitution proclaimed in Washington. Executive powers invested in Inner Cabinet, presided over by president, and comprised of heads of global commands: Army, Navy, Air, Space, Information, CounterIntelligence. Senators serve terms for life, franchise limited to the military and to veterans. Martial law declared for the "duration of the emergency." Ex-admiral Andrew Harrison becomes president at the age of forty-one.

2090: Olenkov dies in Moscow at the age of ninety-five.

2091: Eurasian Coalition announces the completion of military exercises across multiple theaters which successfully demonstrate the integration of the Russian/Chinese military infrastructures and information architectures. Construction on *Roaming Tundra* begins: massive space station at the heart of the Eurasian geo defenses.

2093: The Euro Magnates begin work on the Europa Platform, at Lagrangian point L3.

2094: Air Force Command loses an internal power struggle: the Inner Cabinet assigns its assets to Space Command. From here on in, most powerful commands are Space-Com and InfoCom.

2098: Arab-Israeli conflict escalates beyond control. Tel Aviv, Jerusalem, Damascus, Tehran destroyed in a nuclear exchange. Radioactive fallout contaminates parts of southern Europe.

2099: "The Quickening"—strange lights blaze across upper atmosphere, are seen by hundreds of millions. Superpowers begin secret talks regarding environmental degradation/atmospheric destabilization.

2103: Moderates assume power in the Praesidium, the Eurasian

Coalition's governing entity. U.S. president makes first public statements advocating détente.

2105: Treaty of Zurich signed. U.S. and Eurasian Coalition agree to enforce rigid environmental proscriptions in their respective hemispheres. New age of international cooperation is heralded. Plans are laid for joint transfer of industry into space, wholesale colonization of Mars. In accordance with Article VIII of the treaty, Eurasian Coalition begins construction of bases on Moon.

2106: Jaguar's Sword extends operations into Mexico and Los Angeles Sprawl.

2107: Construction on Phoenix Elevator begins as joint project undertaken by the superpowers. Blueprints call for a four-thousand-kilometer-long structure that will orbit the Earth and whose nadir will be reachable by suborbital transport capable of attaining a height of 150 kilometers. Construction time is estimated at four years.

2110: Autumn Rain initiates active operations.

ACKNOWLEDGMENTS

Special thanks to . . .

James Wang, who helped me get this off the ground
Mark Williams, who helped me bring it home
Brian De Groodt, a voice of sanity throughout
Rob Cunningham, who was there when the world was young
Paul Ruskay, for an island on the edge of forever
Jennifer Hunter, for seeing what I couldn't
Peter Watts, for showing me the difference
Jenny Rappaport at L. Perkins, for fishing me from the slush
Juliet Ulman at Bantam Spectra, for working magic and getting this to you

And thanks also to:

Jon Christian Allison, Alyssa Barnum, Michael Briggs, Karen Casey, Erin Cashier, Roz Clarke, Jessica Dawson, Lauren Doran, Tom Doyle, David Louis Edelman, Jerry Ellis, Kelley Eskridge, Faith Flanagan, Larry Giammo, Vicki Giuggio, Neile Graham, Nicola Griffith, Marc Haimes, Patrick Nielsen Hayden, Leslie Howle, Graham Joyce, Simran Khalsa, Nancy Kress, Jay Lake, Shannon McCall, Molly Mulvanity, Josh Pasternak, J. Michael Schur, Russ Selinger, Diana Sherman, Cassandra Stern, Susan Strayer, Rachel Vater, Melissa Vidal, Albert Williams, Sarah Williams, Susan Williams, and the Clarion West Class of 2007.

And to anyone I've forgotten—apologies, it's been a long haul, but will catch ya next time. . . .

ABOUT THE AUTHOR

David J. Williams was born in Hertfordshire, England. He lives in Washington, D.C. *The Mirrored Heavens* is his first novel.

Learn more about the world of the early twenty-second century at www.autumnrain2110.com.